PACER COULEE CHRONICLES

By Wayne Edwards

Pacer Coulee Chronicles by Wayne Edwards.

Published by Get You Visible Publishing www.getyouvisible.com

Book Cover Illustrated by Gina Daws.

ISBN # print version: 978-1-989848-08-1

ISBN # ebook version: 978-1-989848-09-8

ACKNOWLEDGEMENTS

There's only one place to start in thanking the many people who had a hand in seeing this project through to the finish line, and that would be with my lovely wife Lorinda. She reviewed and critiqued every single written, shredded and then rewritten page—and I can assure you that added up to a lot of pages! She provided valuable input into the development of many of the main characters (Edna Coffman, in particular), and was of helpful assistance in developing the sequence and flow of the book. Her insight and constant positive encouragement is appreciated more than she will ever realize.

A big thank you is also due my three daughters—Sara, Kelley and Katie. Each was kind enough to take the time to review my drafts and provide useful feedback in developing the final product. While I'd like to think they encouraged me to write *Pacer Coulee Chronicles* due to my ability to spin a good yarn, in all likelihood the main purpose was to benefit their mother. The truth of the matter was that I overheard the whispering among the three of them shortly before I retired. . . "He is going to drive mom crazy if we don't keep him busy writing a book!" Whatever the true reason, their support was greatly appreciated.

And then there is the "Big Three"—three former English teachers who were of invaluable assistance in getting my nonsense into book form. Linda Hassinger, a longtime English teacher at Denton High School, was most instrumental in the self discovery of my joy of writing. My feeble attempt to stay somewhat on par with her humorous and mostly handwritten letters in the 1990s kept me on my creative writing toes.

And many thanks to my sister Colleen Murphy, the veteran Minneapolis area high school English instructor, who as three years my senior lived the same rural, small school and town experience that is the subject of *Pacer Coulee Chronicles*. Her patient and constructive advice throughout this project was welcomed and appreciated.

I don't have enough words to sufficiently thank the third member of the English teacher team, my old hometown friend and teammate Gordon Chamberlain. Likely unaware of the burdensome time commitment he was about to embark on, Gordon agreed in the very initial stages of the writing process to read and provide feedback on every page and chapter that was written. Since he also grew up sharing the exact same school, sport and community environment as I did, his perception and perspective of the character development and story line was inestimable. Regrettably, Gordon passed away unexpectedly just shortly after this book was completed. However fitting, it is with great sadness that I dedicate 'Pacer Coulee Chronicles' to his memory.

I would be remiss if I didn't credit the late Stanley Gordon West, the author of the 2005 novel, *Blind Your Ponies*. This delightful read about a boys' basketball season in the tiny town of Willow Creek, Montana sparked the dim lightbulb to flicker, initiating my first thoughts of perhaps attempting to create a similar themed writing based on my own unique, small Montana town experiences. Okay, okay. . . so what if it took me an additional 15 years to fully screw in the lightbulb!

And finally, a big thank you to the primary inspiration behind *Pacer Coulee Chronicles*; all of the young men that I had the privilege of coaching over the six years that I was at the helm of the Denton High Trojans 8-man football program. Those were some of the best years of my life, and the relationships that were built with those players, assistant coaches, parents and townsfolk of all of central Montana are ones that I will forever cherish.

EDNA SCHEDULES A MEETING WITH THE ATHLETIC DIRECTOR

Friday, June 1, 1990 was a day that had long been noted in bold red ink on the calendars of the 97 grade K-12 students who attended school in Pacer Coulee, Montana. The significance of that particular Friday was that it marked the last day of the school year and, equally as noteworthy, the commencement of summer vacation. While the duration of the classes of that final day of the year mattered little from a practical standpoint, the rural, central Montana school could only officially record it as a full day in the eyes of the governing Montana Education Association if students weren't dismissed until 1:00 p.m.

Lester Brewster, by title the Superintendent of the K-12 School District, but also wearing the hats of elementary and high school Principal, Athletic Director, and high school girls' basketball and volleyball coach, waited patiently amongst his not so patient students until the bell tolled 1:00 p.m. He could then finally open the flood gates to flush the rambunctious youngsters from the confines of the school building into the vast expanse of central Montana's Judith Basin.

Longtime Pacer Coulee School District Secretary Lois Alton was chatting on the phone when she heard the bell and the almost simultaneous roar of the students as the mass exodus began. "Got to go, Sylvia," she said to her friend, when she noticed the blinking light of an incoming call on the second of the school's three phone lines. "I hate this new-fangled caller ID thing, especially when it tells me Edna is on the other end of the line."

Edna Coffman was the School Board Chairperson of the Pacer Coulee School District. She was a lifelong resident of Pacer Coulee and had served a nearly 50-year stint as the school's English teacher. Furthermore, she owned and directed the operations of her large family farm and was a prominent and influential member of the community. Although Lois had known her for years, the 64-year-old school secretary always got nervous when having to interact with the intimidating taskmaster that was Edna Coffman.

As usual, Lois attempted to initiate a friendly and pleasant opening exchange, only to have Edna brusquely toss the small talk aside and go right to the heart of the matter. "Good afternoon, Lois. Do you have Lester's appointment schedule for next Monday handy?"

"Why yes, yes I do," Lois meekly replied, frantically searching Lester's cluttered desk for his Daily Planner.

"Tell me Lois, does Lester appear to have the 7:30-9:00 a.m. time slot open this coming Monday?" asked Edna.

"Yes, he does appear to be available then," Lois quickly responded, even though she had yet to locate the schedule.

"That's fine then, Lois. Please pencil me in and remind Lester that I expect to see him at 7:30 sharp on Monday. You can inform him that this meeting will be in regards to his position as the Athletic Director, and therefore his role in the sad state of our current football program. There will also be some frank discussion as to his status as the girls' basketball and volleyball coach. Good day, Lois."

Lois knew that this appointment would infuriate Lester. Unlike the teachers, who were free to leave for the entire summer as soon as their rooms were cleared later that day, Lester's administrative contract called for twelve months of work attendance. It wasn't that Lester minded that he was required to work during the summer months, as he in fact rather enjoyed the slower pace of the summer work routine and the minimal distractions as compared to the normal school-in-session chaos. But he always did look forward to at least getting to sleep in those first few days after school let out for summer vacation. But that extra blissful morning snooze had yet to occur since he had accepted the multiple-hats position at Pacer Coulee Schools four years prior.

By the time Lester had dealt with the school dismissal and handled the final questions and issues with the teachers closing out their rooms, he tiredly returned to his office to address any final items that couldn't be put off to the upcoming weeks of summer solitude. Lois had already left for home, and Lester grimaced and uttered, "damn it, go figure," under his breath as he looked at the appointment schedule for the following Monday which Lois had left conspicuously open on the center of his desk. He couldn't help but notice the 7:30-9:00 a.m. time slot that had been boldly highlighted with a red marker:

EDNA/AD REVIEW: FOOTBALL AND GIRLS' BASKETBALL AND VOLLEYBALL

He did have to chuckle at the drawings of a sad face and hands steeped in prayer that his loyal and supportive secretary had added in the margin.

EDNA'S MEETING WITH LESTER

After dreading the upcoming appointment all weekend, Lester entered his office at 7:15 on Monday morning in an attempt to beat Edna Coffman to the meeting, only to find her having already planted her sizable girth on the 1920s style Mahogany wood bench directly in front of his desk. Edna was scrunched up on the far right side of the bench with her ever present 90-something pound bulldog, Otis Othello Coffman, VII, sprawled out and filling up the balance of the available bench space. He had rolled over on his back with legs splayed, his huge head nestled in her lap. Otis half opened one eye to somewhat acknowledge Lester as he politely patted his massive skull and greeted the big lug by using his entire handle, to include the final portion of his surname—"the seventh." Lester knew when meeting with Edna that it was always wise to address Otis with proper pomp and circumstance.

Since Lois wouldn't be in until 9:00, Lester hurriedly threw on a pot of coffee and checked the little fridge on his back counter, hoping that Lois had remembered to put in some fresh half and half. It was well known to Lester, Lois and anyone else who frequented the main school office that Edna demanded half and half over "that Goddamn sissy-fied French Vanilla or Pumpkin Spice kind of crap!" Fortunately, Lois had come through in the clutch again, as a full container of half and half was placed front and center.

"Well Lester," Edna began, "as I trust Lois passed on to you, this is your annual review as it pertains to your position as Athletic Director, and therefore your responsibility for the current state of the football program. And since you, in your role as the AD, recommended that we hire you to be the girls' basketball and volleyball coach last year, we'll need to review the status of those two programs as well.

"But first things first," Edna continued. "Goddammit Lester, we've got a bad situation on our hands with the football program. As you should know, we have a long and storied tradition of football excellence here, going way back to when my uncle Clarence coached the Bulldogs in the '30s. In the '30s we went 6-3 against the Goddamn Catholics, and Clarence always said he had no doubt we would have been 7-3 against St. Francis except the draught was so bad in '33 that no one in central Montana donned a helmet that year. Now I hate to bring this up Lester, but we went 6-2 and made the playoffs in '85, the year before I hired you as Superintendent and AD. Granted, we didn't beat the Goddamn Catholics that year, but we were at least respectful when ol' Dean Dobbs was the head coach here. But then he left, and I gave you a free rein and you hired that worthless S.O.B. Tim Stratt. We went 4-4 in '86 and '87, 3 and Goddamn 5 in '88, and back to 4-4 last year… and one of those wins was only because Marshall had to forfeit to us due to a bad streak of injuries, so in my mind we were a 3-5 team again. So we haven't made the playoffs since '85, and worse yet, we haven't beat the Goddamn Catholics since '80. Let me repeat that again Lester, not since 1980!"

As Lester's natural blond and pale facial features continued to redden with the embarrassment of being Edna's whipping post yet again, he attempted to counter. "Now Edna, I didn't have much choice in hiring Tim. As I hope you remember, I had Kyle Tyler from across the divide over at Charlo all but hired, but he took an assistant job at Whitefish only a week before the season started, leaving us high and dry. Tim was the only other candidate, and since our long time assistant coach T.O. Barker made it once again clear that he had a farm and ranch to run and didn't have the time nor the interest in taking the head coach position, I had no other alternative but to go with Tim on such short notice."

"Okay Lester, I'll admit that you had a tough situation there, but I expressed my disappointment in the hire during and following that first year and every season thereafter. I don't think you tried very damn hard to replace him, and I've sat on my thumbs and watched our proud tradition go down the tube for too long. Make no mistake about it this time Lester—you are to dismiss Mr. Stratt from his football coaching duties immediately, or I swear to the Almighty that I'll fire you, too!" Edna lectured, her voice nearing the shouting stage with a final fist slam on Lester's desk that was forceful enough to bring Otis from a full recline siesta to an alert, seemingly interested seated position on the bench.

But Edna wasn't through. "By God, I won't keep having .500 seasons or worse, and I'm sick and tired of losing to the Goddamn Catholics!" she bellowed. "No sir! I can't deal with having to listen to those pompous St. Francis S.O.B.s every time I go to Ganlan's IGA in Centertown, or down the street at Country Wholesale to buy dog food for Otis. I've had to listen to their arrogant air of superiority now for eight straight years, and I won't have it anymore!" roared Edna, the veins in her neck protruding as though they may burst. "Do I make myself clear, Lester? Is there anything about our discussion that I may have been vague about?"

Oh yeah, Lester thought to himself, as he wiped the sweat off his brow with a handkerchief. *You're about as vague as a sledgehammer to the forehead.* "Yes Edna, I hear you loud and clear. I'll bring Tim in later today and give him the news. Fortunately, Tim works for a local rancher and isn't on our teaching staff, so we don't have to worry about releasing him from teaching duties and all the accompanying sticky tenure issues. And I'll immediately start the ball rolling on getting the position posted with the Montana Educational Association and the Montana High School Association and hopefully we'll get a decent applicant or two. I know you don't want to hear this Edna, but the reality is that there just aren't a lot of qualified folks out there that are willing to move to remote central Montana and coach an 8-man football team for six hundred bucks a year.

"Nonsense Lester, this is a most desirable place to live and coach. And a chance to coach a football team that actually has some tradition. Not recent tradition because of your weak hires, but a longtime proud heritage extending, as I mentioned, way back to Uncle Clarence in the '30s. Maybe we can't match the teaching and coaching pay scale of the Class A and AA schools, but I know there's somebody out there that will take us over Great Falls and Billings any day of the week, and we would fit their bill perfectly. Plus, I was just informed that Patty Ann Entorf is again with child and will be taking next year off, so we do have Jr. High Math, freshman Algebra and sophomore Geometry open. That should make it much easier to recruit a coach with that opening available."

Oh right, Edna, they'll be busting down the doors to land this kind of once in a lifetime opportunity, Lester sarcastically thought to himself. *People from all over the country will be like stampeding buffalo to get themselves a 600 buck coaching stipend and $14,000 a year to teach some Math classes. Heck ya, I'll need to hire extra summer office staff to sift through the thousands of applications.*

"Of course you're right, Edna," Lester agreed. "I'm quite positive we'll get some very good applications with both a coaching and Math position opening up."

After just witnessing Edna's vein-popping, eye-bulging rant, Lester knew it would be better to let things lie, but since in Edna's eyes the whole declining football program situation was entirely of his doing, he thought he would try to negotiate one other point that might make the football head coach job a little more attractive. Lester cleared his throat and began hesitantly. "I know you don't want to hear this Edna, but as I've pointed out to you before, our strict academic eligibility policy that you authored decades ago is, well, a real deterrent to attracting applicants for this job."

Lester could see Edna's carotid artery begin to pulsate again and knew he should stop this line of rebuke but he hurried to make his case by using Tank Hollister, their gargantuan star football player, as an example. "You know Edna, because of your policy, Tank was only eligible to play in four games in each of the last two years. Not uncoincidentally, three of the four games he played in each of those years were victories for the Bulldogs. You know as well as I do that we would have probably won at least three of the other four games if Tank had been playing. So we would have been minimum 5-3, more likely 6-2 and possibly 7-1, and playoff bound in both '88 and last year if it hadn't been for your strict—some would even say severe—policy."

Edna moved back up to the edge of the bench and rested her elbows directly on Lester's desk, so that her head and laser-shooting eyes were only a few feet from him. Her eyes had narrowed to slits, and what little of them he could see pierced right through him. Lester broke the uncomfortable eye contact, glancing downward before returning his gaze to what he knew was likely to be another Edna explosion. But to his surprise, suddenly Edna's glare softened and she sat back on the bench and put her arm around the still sitting upright Otis, gently rubbing and massaging the numerous layers of folds of skin on the sides of his thick chest. She took in a deep breath and quietly began to speak. "Lester, I proudly admit to being old school. I have been associated with Pacer Coulee Schools as either a student, educator or board member for 63 of my 73 years of life. I am passionate about education. I am passionate about sports. I am passionate about our kids, our school, and our community. I am proud of, and loyal to, all these things. As a country, our young people are rapidly turning into a society of expected entitlement. These days it seems it's all about 'poor me, feel sorry for me. I'm a victim, you owe me this, you owe me that.' Furthermore, if anything goes wrong with our little darlings, it's the teacher's fault. What the hell kind of society have we become, Lester, where everyone feels so Goddamn entitled to what they have not even remotely begun to earn? And hell, our rural Montana kids are way, way less spoiled than the city kids."

Otis had now shifted deep into the crook of Edna's shoulder, his head and closed eyes tilted straight upward to the ceiling. As her soft stroking of his thick neck elicited several satisfied grunts, Edna resumed. "In addition to the three Rs, I firmly believe that we as educators have been given an unspoken mandate to teach these students about responsibility, accountability, and good old-fashioned work ethic. Their parents sure as hell aren't doing it, at least not like they did even a decade or so ago. I'm glad you brought up the Terrance example, or Tank, as you and everyone else call him. While I do take into account the scumbag thug of a father he was raised by, all of our kids need to learn early in their existence that life isn't always fair. You know Lester, I've been around Terrance all his school life and I guarantee you that he is no dummy. There is no question he's more than a little rough around the edges, but he's also very capable of at least average performance in the classroom. He is fully capable mentally of meeting our eligibility standards, but he's too damn lazy and irresponsible to do the work. The big oaf is one of the highest rated football recruits in the state, and could punch his ticket to the Cats, Griz, or even Pac 10 or Big 12 level programs for a free education and a chance to play some big-time college football. As you well know, nobody supports athletics any more than I do, but I think it is downright criminal of us as educators to give a kid a free pass for being lazy and ill prepared. What kind of kid would we be passing on to a college if we overlooked all accountability and responsibility and simply pushed him through? Well, we'd be passing on to them a lazy and unprepared knot-head, that's what we'd be doing, Lester. And I won't stand for it. I've heard and fielded every complaint and criticism about my academic eligibility policy that you can imagine. Hell Lester, I've been threatened and cursed by parents and town folk too many times to count, but I can assure you I sleep well at night knowing that I developed a policy that holds capable students accountable for their efforts, or unfortunately more accurately, their lack thereof."

Edna let that sink in for a moment as Lester sat silently and sheepishly, finding it difficult to dispute much of anything she had said. Finally, Edna broke the silence. "I also have had many old students contact me, sometimes years after they attended here. They thanked me for challenging them and holding them to a higher standard. Those moments confirm to me that we are doing the right thing in raising the bar of expectation at Pacer Coulee to a level at least somewhat above the state of your average amoeba."

Edna stood and rousted Otis, who had again slumped on his stomach on the bench with both front and back legs splayed and stretched out. "One more thing Lester, and then I expect to never, ever have to defend my academic eligibility policy to you again. Do you understand me?"

"Yes ma'am, I understand," he said softly, as Edna continued. "I don't know if you have noticed or not, but I do make exceptions to my policy when warranted. Randolph 'Dolph' Russell is a student who is not capable mentally. In fact, I feel bad that we do not have the Special Ed. resources available in our small, rural schools to effectively and appropriately deal with students like Randolph. But make no mistake: our teachers do an amazing job in working within our limited skill set to help students like Randolph. Again, I emphasize that Dolph does not have the native mental capacity to come anywhere close to meeting our policy guidelines. What he does have is a work ethic. He works his butt off, whether it's in the classroom or on the football field. To get a "D-" is one hell of an accomplishment for Dolph. I would never, ever deny Dolph Russell the chance to participate in sports or any extracurricular activity because, through no fault of his own, he is unable to meet the policy standards. So maybe I am not quite the cruel, horrible and mean-spirited dictator that you all seem to think I am."

Lester took a moment and quietly replied, "No Edna, you are not horrible. As a matter of fact, you are an institution... and a respected and treasured one at that."

"I'm suddenly quite tired Lester, and Otis here hasn't had breakfast yet. He gets cranky and irregular if he doesn't eat on schedule. May we resume the basketball and volleyball portion of our discussion at the same time tomorrow morning?"

"Sounds good, Edna," Lester replied. "See you then."

EDNA'S SECOND MEETING WITH LESTER

Lester had a restless night of sleep following his State of the Union football program review meeting with Edna. His wife Sharon's forceful jousting on his shoulder and loud, "Wake up, wake up—you're having a bad dream," brought him out of his vivid nightmare scenario of Otis Othello Coffman VII, with his badly aligned lower dentition bared in full growl, leaping from the wooden guest bench to Lester's throat in one mighty bound per the directive of a red faced, desk-pounding Edna.

He tried to go back to sleep after the 4:00 a.m. frightful episode, but the attempt proved futile. He finally got up at 4:30 and went out to the tiny kitchen of their rent-free Superintendent house and made coffee. He couldn't help but chuckle at himself about the nightmare. Before arriving at Pacer Coulee four years ago, Lester had been a teacher and a basketball coach at various sized schools in his native Nebraska for the first ten years of his career in Education. He started the long process of using the summer months to complete his Administration Endorsement, and landed his first such position as a Jr. High Principal when they moved to Sharon's hometown of Dillon, Montana. Sharon secured a 3rd grade teaching position at the elementary school, and they remained in Dillon for the next decade until he was hired as the Superintendent and Athletic Director, and Sharon as the 4th grade teacher, at Pacer Coulee.

In looking back over his 20 years prior to Pacer Coulee, he had answered to numerous and varied Administrators and school boards, some of whom were difficult and demanding to work for. But never had he seen anyone the likes of Edna. She had an intimidating, overpowering personality, and ran the school and school board with the proverbial iron fist. While he greatly respected her passion and commitment for academics and athletics, he had yet to wrap his arms around the autocracy that was Edna Coffman. He again snickered and shook his head at how he always allowed himself to turn into a mousy, sweaty and bumbling sycophant whenever he had to interact with Edna.

Since it was Lester's usual routine to work out at the school gym at 5:45 a.m. every morning anyway, he filled his 'Pacer Coulee Bulldogs' go-cup and stepped out of the house for the two minute walk across the elementary school playground to the gym. Even now at 46 years old, Lester's 6'5" slender frame was in good form. He was trim and in great shape for a man of his years, and he was determined to stay that way by carefully monitoring not only his food intake, but the nutritional value of that intake as well. While most all the current 1990 nutritional literature appeared to be firmly in the camp that dietary fat was the root of all evil, Lester was torn by some of the recent re-search papers he had read that indicated that carbohydrates, par-ticularly of the refined sugar kind, might actually be the real cul-prit in America's burgeoning obesity and disease-ridden popula-tion. He wasn't totally convinced in the veracity of this new-found research, and couldn't yet bring himself to quit buying the "reduced fat" versions of the plethora of prepared foods that were on the market.

During his morning visits to the school gym, Lester alternated his days between resistance training and aerobic activity. He would do his weight training routine in the tiny weight room located off the gym and down the hall from the boys' locker room. The equipment consisted of one of the old, three-sided multi-station Joe Weider Universal Gyms that was mostly held together with duct tape and multiple welds from Mr. Mark's shop class. The leg press part of the unit was particularly tricky, as the seat adjustment pin had a propensity to slip out of its slot during the course of the press movement, sending the occupant rocketing backwards to a sudden and spine jolting halt when the seat collided with the end stop. One of the two pullup bars at the top of the unit was lying in the corner, having suffered a disconnect from the frame when Tank Hollister, the 320-pound lineman with the strength of an ox, had been swinging wildly from side to side with both hands secured on the single bar. The rest of the cramped weight room consisted of a shop class constructed scrap iron squat rack and an Olympic bar and plates. The athletic department had budgeted for 6 more 45-lb Olympic plates over the last few years in order to keep up with Tanks' need for an ever-increasing squat and bench press load. In the corner of the room opposite the entrance door, the shop class had built a 3' by 4' plywood box, painted in Pacer Coulee Bulldog royal blue and white vertical stripes, that was divided into four equal sized bins and contained balls and other gym and PE class equipment. When Lester was putting the basketballs away on the last day of school, he had noticed that somebody had drawn an oversized penis and testicles on the wall behind the seated leg press. Lester had to chuckle, thinking the crude mural artist was likely Bo Ramsay or Tucker Greyson, and made a mental note to have Howard, the 'Ever Cheerful' janitor, paint over it.

Lester finished up his morning workout by shooting baskets in the gym for another 20 minutes. Although a little short by 1990 standards, Lester was a power forward at Nebraska Southern in the late '60s. He had perfected a wicked jump hook in order to prevent his shots in the key from being rejected by defenders that were four and five inches taller than him. In order to make himself more versatile and indispensable, he had worked hard to develop his perimeter shooting skills. Lester's practice routine hadn't changed all that much since the college days, in that he refused to end his workout before making 7 of 10 jump hooks from 10 feet on both sides of the key, and 6 of 10 from the 3-point range. He was glad he accomplished both objectives in the first attempt, as he wanted to go shower and beat Edna to his office for round two.

Lester's 7:00 arrival at the office did precede that of Edna and Otis, but he had no more than got the coffee brewing on the noisy old Coffee Maker II when he heard the click, click, click of Otis's toenails in the hallway. *Jesus, I'm already sweating,* Lester thought to himself, unable to thwart the rapid advancement of an Edna-induced panic attack. After a curt greeting from Edna, she and Otis took up their usual positions on the bench across from Lester's desk, although it was a delayed process in getting Otis all the way up onto the bench. In bulldog years, the seven-year-old Otis was already in the golden era. Like all bulldogs, Otis had never met a morsel of food he didn't like nor desperately want. Edna never followed her veterinarian's advice of absolutely no table food, restricted-portion dog food only diet regime. As a result, Otis and all of his predecessors had ballooned to ninety plus pounds at a young age. Having to pack all that extra weight across the school parking lot and down the long hallway to the Superintendent's office had severely compromised Otis's ability to breathe, and he immediately slumped to the floor with a heavy sigh as soon as he entered the office. After a few minutes of rest, he stood back up and on his own was able to thrust his top heavy front end high enough to get his front paws up on the bench. Unable to generate the energy necessary to self-propel his back haunches up onto the bench, he turned his head towards Edna with a "come on, give me a hand" look, and she squatted down and cupped her hands under his rump and with considerable effort hoisted the rest of him up onto the bench. "Poor ol' Otis isn't getting around too well these days. His arthritis is acting up again," she said.

"He sure is breathing hard," Lester added. "Are you sure he's okay?"

"Oh yes, he's fine. Just a little tuckered out from walking all the way in from the parking lot. He's starting to get some age on him, you know," Edna replied. Lester let it drop, remembering a scolding that Howard the 'Ever Cheerful' janitor got when he expressed his concern of the bulldog's weight and his limited expected longevity therefrom. When he suggested that Edna get a smaller dog like his Shih Tzu Barney, Edna quickly snapped, "I wouldn't have one of those yapping little bastards anywhere near me, Howard. If I wanted something as small and obnoxious as a cat, then I'd buy a Goddamn cat."

As expected, Edna got right down to business. "Lester, I do think you know your stuff when it comes to basketball. I don't have any doubt about that. But you have a problem, Lester. And it's a problem I don't see you being able to overcome at this stage in the game. You can't handle those daughters of yours. I don't think you have a clue how to deal with them at home, and you sure as hell don't have any idea how to handle them on the basketball court. Take that District Championship game, which by the way, we should have won handily. Sonya and Sandra were in an obvious spat, and anybody could see that they weren't about to pass to each other going down the stretch in the 4th quarter. You should have called a timeout and grabbed those two little snots by their ears and told them to shape up or you'd bench the both of them. But hell no, you just let their childish selfishness cost us the title. Same thing happened in the Divisional semifinals, only this time Sabrina joined the family spat and none of the three would pass to one another. The result of their petulant behavior? We got our butts kicked and didn't even make the title game. We should have won or at least placed second at Divisional, Lester, and we should have finished strong in the State Tourney."

Lester could feel a red wave of blush crawling up his neck and spilling over into his pale cheeks. *Good Christ,* he thought, *I'm sweating like a 4-H hog at the county fair in August,* and he took a swipe across his brow with his handkerchief. Unfortunately, he knew there was more than a little truth in her accusations. While he considered all four of his girls to be overall good kids, these Jr. High and High School years had been fraught with turmoil the likes that Lester and Sharon had never before experienced. Edna was right in that often times he felt he was in over his head with these teenaged girls, trying to deal with all their period-induced anxieties and mood swings. At least he tried to use their periods as an excuse for their poor behavior, but the truth of the matter was they were ornery even when they weren't menstruating. One minute three of them would be getting along seemingly okay, and the fourth one was odd girl out. And then before you could turn around, two of them would now be getting on fine, but were treating the other two horribly. The 'who's in, who's out' order could change in a heartbeat, and as much as both he and Sharon tried to referee and negotiate even a temporary truce, their efforts were usually futile.

Lester and Sharon took all the responsibilities of parenthood seriously, and they were devoted and attentive parents. Even though Lester had a nervous, high energy type of personality, he was a stable, kind and considerate father who didn't care to argue or engage in anything overly controversial. Sharon was likewise a good-hearted and thoughtful person with an easygoing manner, and they were both genuinely well liked by the school and community. Even though they never directly discussed it, they both found it disconcerting that all four of their daughters could transform instantaneously from somewhat normal and rational teenaged girls to those with mean-spirited intent.

Edna continued. "Again, if your girls were not on this team, I would have no problem with a man of your knowledge of the game continuing as our coach. You also seem to interact well with the other girls on the team that don't share your last name. But let's look at the facts, Lester, and I'll list them in order. Firstly, your youngest, Sammi, will be a freshman this coming year, and she may well be the best player of all your girls. That doesn't bode well for your ability to control the petty jealousies of the older three. Secondly, your four girls are by far the best players on the team. That fact in itself creates issues with the other parents and townsfolk. And to be the father as well as the coach of four girls? Not a good combo. And thirdly, your girls are not well liked by the rest of the team. Quite frankly, they are often selfish, nasty, and even downright mean... to each other, to their teammates, and to you. Based on these facts that I've just outlined, I think it is in the best interests of the Pacer Coulee Bulldogs girls' basketball team, school system and community in general, if we have a different coach next year. One that isn't the parent of any player. And finally, Lester, I think a change is in your best interests as a person, coach, and parent."

Otis was now snoring up a storm, so Edna took this rather uncomfortable moment following her assessment and directive of Lester's coaching future to try to readjust the bulky bulldog to a new and hopefully less ear piercing bodily position. The reapportionment seemed to at least temporarily lower the volume of the snores and snorts to a dull roar. Finally, Lester responded. "I can't deny nor dispute any of what you've said, Edna. I'm often times embarrassed by the behavior of my girls, not the least of when they are on the court. They weren't raised to behave that way, and I'm frankly baffled as to why they act in such a manner. As you correctly pointed out, I'm also at a loss as to how to deal with them, either at home or on the court. You know Sharon. She's a loving and caring mother. She's at her wits' end, too. I don't know what to do Edna, I just don't know."

Lester had spoken with his chair turned to the window facing the reception office, so that it seemed like he was talking and commiserating with someone on the other side of the window. He then turned in his chair back towards Edna and met her somewhat softened gaze. "I understand and even agree with everything you said. I'm almost relieved—no, correct that—I am relieved. A coaching change will no doubt be the best for all parties."

Since women's volleyball had just become a Montana High

School Association sanctioned sport at the Class C level (smallest enrollment classification) in 1986, there simply was not the fan interest yet that women's basketball enjoyed. Lester had actually coached volleyball the years that he was in Omaha, as the sport had been sanctioned there for much longer than at the small Class C schools in Montana. "Since the same dynamic exists with you and your daughters in volleyball, I think it would be best if you stepped down there as well," Edna declared. "However, since it's such a new sport, I get it if we don't receive much in the way of applications. If that were to be the case, I would support you coaching volleyball until we can get an acceptable replacement."

"Yes, I think a clean sweep in both sports should be the goal. I will post those positions this afternoon," Lester stated.

"By the way," Edna interjected, "my sister Harriet has decided at age 70 to slow down and give up some History classes. In addition to Mrs. Entorf's Math classes that I mentioned yesterday, we'll have openings for the High School Montana History curriculum, as well as 8th grade Social Studies and possibly some Junior year level American History, although I'm not sure she will give that up. You can post those position openings along with the coaching. That should help in our recruitment."

"Will do," Lester replied. Edna woke Otis up with a poke to his chest, and with a curt nod they were out the door. Lester could hear the '*click, click, click*' of Otis's toenails on the linoleum all the way back down hall, stopping only when he heard the closing thud of the heavy front entrance door.

LUKE CARTER'S INTERVIEW

Luke Carter's Casper, Wyoming to Montana trek was well underway, and he had been heading north on I-25 for what felt like days. Traffic along the seemingly interminable and desolate Wyoming interstate corridor was brisk on the early July day.

Fourth of July traffic, Luke surmised, as he had to brake and go off cruise control for the first time in many miles when a lumbering Home Depot 18-wheeler pulled directly in front of his 1984 GMC Sierra pickup and onto the left of the two lane northbound thoroughfare. As the big truck inched forward to pass a similarly sized Sam's Club truck that appeared to be going approximately one mile per hour slower, Luke realized he might be settling in for a lengthy rear seat view of an achingly slow giant tortoise race. Sure enough, just when Home Depot would start to edge ahead by a fraction, Sam's Club would regain the lost distance when a flat stretch of road transitioned to an incline, even edging slightly ahead when climbing a steeper hill.

Luke was tempted to take down the number just below the 'Safety is our First Priority—Tell us How We're Doing' sign and call to report that their tortoise's inability to pass the other tortoise had traffic backed up from Cheyenne to Buffalo. Finally able to pass both trucks when Home Depot forged enough ahead to return to the right lane, Luke resisted the urge to flip off the driver as he passed by, acknowledging to himself that witnessing the almost humorous debacle actually made the 35-mile trip from Buffalo to Sheridan go by faster.

Luke had only been to Montana once before when his parents took him and his two older sisters one summer to see the magnificent scenery and the geothermal wonders of Yellowstone National Park. Luke was about to enter the fifth grade that fall, and already loved history at that early age. He remembered how his mom and dad encouraged him to keep a ledger to document the wildlife that they saw, as well as the strange, steaming and bubbling thermal pools and erupting geysers that the early-day Indians had described as ghostly, spiritual and sacred. He had supplemented the ledger with Polaroid pictures of bison, black bear, elk, antelope and deer. He also took pictures of the hot pots and smoldering geyser basins, including several shots of the greatest geyser of them all—Old Faithful. He remembered that after a few days of visiting the Park and staying in a rustic cabin near Old Faithful, his father pointed their old station wagon north to Bozeman, negotiating the narrow two-lane road that would serpentine in concert with the tortuous contours of the roaring Gallatin River as it wove its way down the majestic Gallatin Canyon.

Having only the flat or mildly rolling terrain of Nebraska as his point of reference, he recalled the moment when their station wagon was spit from the mouth of the canyon and into the wide expanse of the Gallatin Valley. Even his perpetually bored and annoyed sisters were in awe of the valley on that early summer day, with the knee-deep pasture grass and hayfields swaying as if they were slow dancing. As his mother studied the map of Montana she had unfolded on her lap, she reported the names of the crystal clear, still snow-capped mountain ranges that bordered the lush valley on all sides: the Bridgers to the north, Tobacco Roots to the west, and the Spanish Peaks and Gallatin Range to the south and east.

They had stayed a few days at another rustic cabin in a small little town just outside of the scenic college town of Bozeman— maybe Four Corners? Or Gallatin Gateway? Whichever it was, the Gallatin River was a stone's throw away, and he and his dad caught rainbow or brown trout every time they cast their fly lines into the Blue Ribbon trout stream, or so it seemed according to the recollections of an excited 11-year-old. He thought he might still have the old tattered Polaroid picture of the 12" rainbow trout that he had caught, attached to the other photos in his trip ledger. To complete his history lesson, his father had him include in his ledger entries how the Gallatin River joined the equally revered and trout-laden Madison and Jefferson rivers to form the great Missouri River.

But Yellowstone Park and Bozeman was as far as he had ever ventured into the state, and the little research he had done before beginning his trip north to interview at Pacer Coulee revealed that Montana was the fourth largest state in the union in terms of total square mile area, with only Alaska, Texas and California being larger. Conversely, only a few states had a lesser population than the 800,000 residents that were spread across the mountains of the west and the plains to the east; one such state being Wyoming, which he was currently passing through.

Not long after escaping the tortoises and continuing north from Sheridan on I-90, Luke passed the "Welcome to Montana and Big Sky Country" sign, and estimated he was only a couple of hours out of Billings and the Holiday Inn where he had made reservations. According to the map, he figured he would have to head out of Billings by about 8:00 the next morning to cover the 150-mile trip to Pacer Coulee in time for the 11:00 interview.

Luke rolled down his windows and welcomed the cooler air that flowed through his cab as the sun began its slow and leisurely journey through the summer evening sky. From both the road signs and a look at his combination Montana/Wyoming map, Luke saw that he would be driving through the Crow Indian Reservation for a good part of his remaining trip to Billings.

He passed by Lodge Grass, Crow Agency and Hardin, taken aback by his interstate view of the forlorn and destitute demeanor of the towns; paper thin trailers and prefab homes, with what little paint that remained peeling away as if now receiving the final rebuke from the very siding where it had long resided. Each shack appeared to be surrounded by a saddened, browned and grass-less yard that was home to numerous dilapidated, tire deprived vehicles, an assortment of mostly in disrepair bicycles and motorbikes, and a seasoned inventory of abandoned appliances—refrigerator doors either missing or hanging listlessly from a creaking hinge.

On more than one occasion he noticed a game of hoop going on, playing to a net-less, drooping rim attached to a telephone pole or a backyard shed. He passed signs for turn-offs to the Custer Battlefield, and made a note to himself to refresh his memory of the events of the Battle of the Little Bighorn, the 1876 massacre of General Custer and his troops.

Luke completed the last leg of the day's journey to Billings by driving into the deepening red and yellow hues of the Big Sky Country's western horizon. Fiddling with his radio dial, he found a Billings country western station called Cat Country. He smiled to himself, thinking that it was a good thing he liked country western music, as he had a feeling he was going to get a steady diet of it if he were to take this job in the heart of Montana's farm and ranch beltway. He turned up the volume in order to hear Garth Brooks croon his latest country lullaby 'The Dance' over the sounds of the wind and the interstate traffic noise whipping through the still open windows of his pickup. Garth gave way to Tanya Tucker and her brand new hit 'Walking Shoes,' and Luke sang along to the ironically applicable verse, 'cause all ya do is treat me wrong... so honey, I'll be good and gone.'

"I hear ya, Tanya, God knows I hear ya," Luke said out loud, talking to his pickup radio dial as if the DJ at Cat Country had played the song at Luke's request. Luke wondered how long it would take him to get over Lorie. Good grief, wasn't two years of mourning enough? Why was he having so much trouble getting his life back in order? Was running several states away to take up shop in some remote Montana town really the answer? Could this drastic change of scenery be the salve to finally soften the thick band of scar tissue reminder of her infidelity? Could he heed coach Sweden's harsh advice of "nothing is fair in love and war, son. It's time for you to pull your head out of ass and move forward."

"I know you're right, coach. I know you're right," Luke mumbled out loud, knowing it was easier said than done.

Although his Holiday Inn queen bed was comfortable, Luke slept fitfully the night before his pending interview at Pacer Coulee. He woke up at 5:30 a.m. in a cold sweat to a vision of Lorie and Richard, both naked in his old bed, her straddling the smirking Richard as they moved in unison in the performance of their impassioned act. Their coital positioning was the same as that which he had witnessed that fateful day when he walked unsuspectingly into his master bedroom.

Knowing he wouldn't be able to get back to sleep, he opened his third floor curtains to welcome the light of the sun, just now peeking the top of its head high enough to say good morning to Billings. He quickly dressed in gym shorts and a t-shirt and walked down the exit stairway to the second floor guest exercise room. Glad that he was the only one there at this early hour, he turned on Sports Center and started pumping the few dumbbells they had on the rack. By the time the Boomer Chris Berman started ed singing his familiar "back, back, back....GONE!" tunes to chronicle the home runs that Jose Canseco, Barry Bonds and Mark McGwire had all hit the night before, Luke was lifting with a fervor, as if the strenuous pumping of iron might elevate his blood flow to a sufficient volume to dislodge and sweep away the fretful nightmare that was stubbornly barnacled to his subconscious.

After showering and hitting the Holiday Inn's complimentary Continental Breakfast on his way out to the parking lot, Luke surveyed his map while he fed the Sierra's always hungry and empty fuel tank. It was 8:00 straight up when he hopped back on I-90 and drove the few miles to the exit for Roundup, which he had determined from his map to be the shortest of the two routes he could take to get to Pacer Coulee. He drove through the brisk Monday morning traffic of what the signs indicated as the 'Billings Heights' area of Billings, whose 85,000 census reported residents gave it bragging rights as Montana's largest city.

Eventually he reached the northern edge of the Heights and city, following the highway 87 exit sign that would take him the 48 miles to Roundup. From there, he would stay on route 87 for the next 75 miles until reaching Centertown, the only town of notable size between Billings and Great Falls. Pacer Coulee would then be a 20-mile stone's throw from Centertown.

As he progressed towards Roundup, the countryside reminded him of the long stretches he had just passed through in Wyoming. The terrain was flat and the grasses that were interspersed amid the plentiful clumps of sagebrush were already shedding their springtime green for various shades of gray and brown. As he neared Roundup the countryside sprouted timber, although the scattered Ponderosa Pine trees that remained stood barren and lifeless, still suffering through the indignities of a forest fire assault that had ravaged the Bull Mountain timber stand a few years prior.

He drove into Roundup and cruised by the Busy Bee Cafe, its crowded parking lot announcing it as a popular breakfast destination. Mud-caked bumpers and rear window mounted gun racks adorned the mostly pickup trucks that sporadically lined a weary looking Main Street. Passing through the outskirts of town, several golfers waved to him as they pushed their carts down a fairway adjacent to the roadway. Luke figured he now knew the true meaning of Cowboy Golf, as both of the older gentlemen donned cowboy boots and hats. Luke's anxiousness and excitement to get back in the game, of both football and life, was laced with an equal dose of doubt and guilt. He still heard the whispers from the deep recesses of his soul, scolding him for his dead of night escape, rather than standing tall to face his demons.

But he was slowly acquiescing to his old college football coach Sonny Sweden's sage counsel to return to what he was born to do—teach and coach. Luke thought back to his surprise visit from coach Sweden only a short week prior. Luke had finished his 12 hour shift driving an oil tanker outside of Casper,

Wyoming, and had just settled on a bar stool and nestled up to a Coors Light at his favorite oil rig dive bar when the highly respected and revered Southern Nebraska legend tapped him on the shoulder. Luke had been coach Sweden's 3-year starting quarterback some 15 years prior, and they had remained in close contact ever since. Sweden had been his go-to guy for coaching and Xs and Os advice at all his high school jobs; at least until he had quit the profession two years before, that is.

Luke had taken the oilfield job when he had resigned his teaching and coaching positions at Lincoln High School immediately following his surprise discovery of another man in his wife's life and his bed. He didn't even get the satisfaction of telling her to move out, nor did he have to hear any tearful apologies and declarations of her love and commitment despite the brief and momentary infidelity lapse. Quite the opposite scenario had transpired, in that she had bluntly stated that she was in love with the man she had been having a torrid four-month affair with, and wanted a divorce. Luke couldn't have been more clueless as to what had been going on under his very nose, nor more devastated by her unsuspected behavior. He simply couldn't face the new reality by staying in Lincoln and continuing on with his teaching and coaching, so he fled from everything that he once considered to be his perfect life.

Plunging into a new job up in Wyoming, he hoped that time and a change of professions would aid in the slow process of healing from his emotional wounds. But without even realizing it, he had managed to systematically distance himself from his family and friends, including his reliable mentor coach Sweden. He had frequently scolded himself during the past year for his inability to put his past behind him and move on, but it seemed as though he was hopelessly swimming against a strong and unrelenting tide.

Luke knew he would always remember every word of the one-sided conversation that took place that evening in the East Side Tavern on the outskirts of Casper. After a brief embrace and very little small talk, coach Sweden started to speak in the authoritative, yet calm and reasoned tone that Luke had heard many times over.

"You haven't been returning my calls, Luke. I've been in frequent contact with your folks since you left Lincoln, and they are concerned. Your friends are concerned. I'm concerned. I'm going to be brutally honest with you here, Luke. I'm fortunate in that I've been happily married to my high school sweetheart for 27 years, so it's true that I have never experienced what happened with you and Lorie. I know it must hurt like hell, but I think you have that incident mixed up with something that's truly tragic. Your wife dying of cancer? That's tragic. Your wife dying in a car accident? That's tragic. Your wife contracting a rapidly advancing form of Multiple Sclerosis? That's tragic. Your wife being unfaithful and your marriage ending in divorce? That's unfortunate, Luke. Unfortunate, but not tragic. Happens all the time. Hell, probably a third of your teammates that you graduated from college with have had a similar bad marital experience and are now divorced. And I'm guessing the vast majority of them are not still moping around two years after the defining incident."

Coach Sweden placed two fingers under Luke's sagging chin and lifted his head as he said, "Look at me Luke. This behavior isn't like you. Do you remember the game at Eastern Illinois your senior year?"

Luke nodded his head yes, painfully remembering the last-minute fourth quarter interception he threw that was run back for a touchdown, cementing the win for Eastern. "So did you mope around for months after that, or quit the team? Or did you shake it off, accept it as a learning experience, and jump back into the fray and focus on preparing for the next game?"

"I shook it off and got ready for the next week," Luke softly replied.

"That's right, Luke. You not only shook it off, but you got back in the saddle and played the game of your career the following week. I always admired your resolve and competitiveness—it's what made you a great player, and in turn a most promising young coach. Where has that guy gone Luke? I'm seeing none of it right now. I'm seeing a guy I don't even recognize anymore."

Sweden grabbed Luke by the shoulders and squeezed to the point of it being uncomfortable, and with a firm and strong tone said, "Luke, it's time to pull your head out of your ass and get back in the game. Get back in the game of life. You're 34 years old, for Christ's sake! You're a born teacher and coach, Luke. Get back in the Goddamn game," he roared, slamming his fist on the bar. Then in a quieter tone, he continued, "Now I don't have anything against truck drivers, but is this what you want to do for the rest of your life? And I like having a cold beer after work as much as the next guy, but is Casper's East Side Tavern where you want to spend every evening the rest of your life?"

"No coach," said Luke. "It's not."

"I didn't think so. I can understand how you might be reluctant to go back to Nebraska to coach and teach. I can understand if you'd like a fresh, new start. But you need to get back in the saddle. As it turns out, I have an old college roommate and close friend, Lester Brewster, who is the Superintendent of Pacer Coulee, a small school up in central Montana. They're looking for a head football coach, and have teacher openings in History as well. Handing him a large manila envelope, he added, "In this addressed, return-stamped envelope is the application for both positions. Fill it out and send it in, Luke. I'm going to tell Lester to be expecting it in the mail. Do it, Luke. Start fresh and get on with your life." With that, Sweden and the teary-eyed Luke embraced, and the old coach strode out the door into the darkness of the Wyoming night.

Luke enjoyed the final 15 miles of transition from the low lying, livestock-laden pastures to the gently elevating stairway that led him up the Judith Mountain pass towards Centertown, then, more abruptly than it had risen, declined to drop him into the scenic community. Since he had plenty of time to get to

Pacer Coulee for his appointed interview, he did a quick loop around the quaint little town before re-checking his map and confirming he needed to follow the signs to Malta and highway 191 to complete the final 20-mile jaunt to Pacer Coulee.

As he drove north through the outskirts of town, he passed the holding pens and corrals of the Centertown Livestock Auction on his right, its message board display announcing the weekly auction sale to occur each Tuesday. To his left, he admired the sizable complex that served as the county's fairgrounds, replete with large white and red barns, lengthy livestock sheds and a rodeo arena surrounded on two sides by an impressive, roof-covered grandstand.

As he continued on towards Pacer Coulee in the lush green shadows of the Judith and the Moccasin mountains, he realized he was getting anxious to meet Lester Brewster, the Superintendent and Athletic Director at Pacer Coulee, who was coach Sweden's former college roommate. He thought it ironic that their traditional monthly 'shoot the breeze' telephone chat had led to this unlikely job interview with his college coach's old friend.

Driving between the north and south Moccasins, Luke dropped down and crossed the rapidly flowing waterway that the sign on the bridge identified as Warm Spring Creek. His destination appeared suddenly as he topped the next hill, the narrow blacktop roadway abruptly widening where the sign welcomed all travelers to Pacer Coulee. *Wow*, thought Luke, *coach Sweden wasn't kidding when he said this would be a small town*. He turned at the first street that led to the football field that paralleled the highway, only then realizing that the 8-man game must be played on a smaller field. The field appeared to have been regularly maintained, as its reasonably populated stand of green grass had been freshly mowed. He wondered if that had been done in anticipation of his interview, or if it had been mowed according to a usual summer schedule. Separated by a dirt road, a less well-attended field lay to the south. *Practice field and the likely site of school PE activities*, Luke surmised. The community park, swimming pool and a baseball field bordered the football field to the west, with the school and its grounds laying directly beyond that. Since he had arrived 15 minutes ahead of his appointment, he decided he would have enough time to take a loop around the town. As it turned out, five minutes more than did the trick.

Superintendent and Athletic Director Lester Brewster came out the front glass door to greet Luke, who was standing on the front entrance sidewalk inspecting the sizable mass of metal that had been bent, molded and welded into a surprisingly accurate likeness of a snarling bulldog. Directly behind and above the iron bulldog was a plywood billboard that announced, in bold and freshly painted blue and white letters, that those who dare approach would be entering "BULLDOG COUNTRY."

The tall and lean Administrator greeted him with a warm smile and handshake, and they traded small talk about his long trip up from Wyoming and their mutual respect and admiration for coach Sweden, the man whose powerful influence on each of them had effectively orchestrated the interview they were about to conduct. As they walked down the hall towards the meeting room, Lester suddenly put a hand to Luke's arm and stopped him in the empty hallway, saying in a lowered voice, "I know what little verbal conversation you've had thus far with our school has been with me. I just feel like I should forewarn you about who is going to conduct the lion's share of this interview. Edna Coffman, our School Board Chairperson, is just a few years retired from her 50-year stint of teaching English here. She is quite assuredly going to be unlike any woman you've ever met. I don't want to influence your first impressions, but she's a spitfire, to put it mildly. Make no mistake, she's the judge and jury when it comes to this hire—doesn't really matter what I think. Hell, she just fired me from the girls' basketball job because she doesn't think I can control my four daughters. Sadly, she's probably right on about that. Anyway, suffice it to say that she can be a pretty intimidating lady; just thought I should give you a little heads up."

With that prelude, they continued down the hall to the little classroom by the library where Lester introduced the handsome, well built 6'3" prospective coach to the woman he was now so curious to meet. Chairman Edna Coffman was a broad, large-framed woman who, Lester's preconditioning remarks aside, commanded such a no-nonsense presence in the room that Luke could easily visualize a 'Don't Mess with Me—I Run this Show' tattoo across her weathered forehead. Releasing his hand from her iron grip handshake, her face brightened as she pointed down to a very large bulldog who was sprawled out on the floor and snoring noisily.

"This here is Otis Othello Coffman, VII. As the name would indicate, he is the seventh generation of an Otis that has reigned as the official mascot for the Pacer Coulee Bulldogs. He's getting a little too long in the tooth to lead the teams onto the battlefield anymore, but he's still got plenty of spunk." As Luke eyed the napping bulldog who appeared to be in the throes of either a seizure or extremely labored breathing, he found it hard to imagine that the word 'spunk' could be used as anything other than an oxymoron in describing the enormous bulldog.

"Let's show you around the school before we get down to business, shall we?" said Edna, as she led Luke and Lester back out into the hallway. Although somewhat familiar with small, rural towns from his upbringing in Nebraska, Luke had never actually lived the small town and small school experience. His high school, college and coaching years were all completed at the larger cities and schools in eastern Nebraska: North Platte, Grand Island and Lincoln, respectively. As a result, he was somewhat taken aback with how small the town and school actually were.

Edna explained that the school building housed the 97 students that comprised the entire K-12 population, of which only 43 were in grades 9-12. It appeared to Luke that the original structure was still in the heart and center of the school, with several later wing additions of classrooms branching off like freshly regenerated limbs. One small, stand-alone structure sat 50 yards off to one side of the main building, looking like the misplaced mistake of parents that didn't expect to have any more children. Edna explained that it used to be the music room, but was so expensive to heat in the winter that they had converted it to storage. The most recent add-ons were to the other side of the original centerpiece; most prominently an attached, late '60s gymnasium with a 700 seat capacity. This replaced the old, 1916 era architecture of three wooden bench spectator rows surrounding the tiny court on two sides, and a band/theater stage set behind one of the baskets. Secondly, a stand-alone steel building, also erected in the late 1960s, housed a roomy classroom and a large, well-equipped shop that was home to the school's purported exceptional Vo-Ag program.

It appeared to Luke that when the new gymnasium complex was built 22 years ago, the vast majority of the funding pie was swallowed up in the construction of the gym itself. The rest of the project—the locker rooms, coaches' room, and training and storage areas all looked like an afterthought, as if the contractor had been told they only had enough budget dollars remaining to build half of the square footage that was called for in the original plan. The confining boys' and girls' locker rooms were separated by a tiny coaches' office, and all three rooms had an entrance to what appeared to be an overcrowded central training room and storage area. A small, cinder block structure protruded like a growth-stunted appendage off the training room, which Edna explained was initially used as another storage area that had been only recently converted to what was generously described as a weight room.

After Luke explained that he had already taken a self tour of the football field on his way into town, they returned to the classroom. Edna informed them that she was expecting T.O. Barker, the long-time assistant football coach for Pacer Coulee, to stop by at any minute to give Luke an overview of the kids that would be on the team that coming fall. "No sense getting started on the interview, only to get interrupted," declared Edna.

With that, Lester started asking questions about their common Nebraska upbringing, especially the status of the South Nebraska University football and basketball programs; the sports that they had each respectively participated in. They hadn't gotten far when T.O. knocked on the opened door.

"Sorry folks!" the barrel-chested rancher exclaimed after the introduction had been made. "I've been out on the swather trying to get some alfalfa knocked down before the showers hit. Damn, it's hot and humid and I don't have any air conditioning in my old John Deere, so I'm sweaty and stinky."

"Thanks for coming in, T.O.," said Edna. "Carl's trying to bale the hay we have down on my place before those thunder-showers hit, too. I know you need to get back out there, so we'll try not to take up too much of your time."

"No worries, the wife took over for me," explained T.O., chuckling as he continued. "She's got a helluva lead foot on the highway, so as long as she goes a little lighter on the swather throttle she shouldn't break down for at least an hour or two."

"Okay then," Edna began, engaging in eye contact with Luke. "As I've already briefly alluded to, T.O. grew up here on his family ranch. He was a damn good three-year starter for the Bulldogs at offensive guard and defensive tackle. Beat the Goddamn Catholics in both '57 and '58, right T.O.?" As T.O. nodded his head in agreement, Lester said in a humorous, yet hint of an apologetic tone, "Hope you're not Catholic, Luke. As you may have already gathered, Edna is not horribly fond of our St. Francis rivals over there in Centertown." Edna threw a pointed glare in Lester's direction before continuing. "As I was saying… T.O. then played college ball for the Lights up in Havre before returning to the ranch. He was suckered into assisting here in '63, I believe, and has been the assistant coach every year since. Mentored under his old coach Del Freid, who successfully coached here for 21 years. Then Dean Dobbs took the reins, and we had decent teams up until he retired in '85… we haven't had a coach that was worth a damn since, and I'm referring specifically to that dimwit Tim Stratt that I regrettably allowed Lester to hire in '86.'"

Luke couldn't help but note the effect that Edna's zinger had on Lester, as his face quickly changed to that of a fourth grader just caught peeking at a classmate's answers to the weekly math quiz. Fortunately for everyone, Edna switched gears. "Anyway, I wanted T.O. to be here to give you the accurate low-down on what kind of team you'd be looking at if you're fortunate enough to be the candidate that is offered this highly sought after job. So T.O., why don't you go ahead and bring him up to speed."

T.O. cleared his throat, wiped the sticky July perspiration off his brow, and began. "Well Luke, Edna and Lester have probably already filled you in, but we're a pretty damn small school in the scope of the enrollment range that is Class C 8-man football. I don't know what your classification system is in Nebraska, but here in Montana it goes AA, A, B and C, with AA being the highest enrollment, and C being the lowest. We only got, like, 45 students in all of high school, and we're lucky in that we usually get almost all of the boys to come out. I figure we're gonna have 17 or 18 boys out this fall, four of which will be freshmen... and only one of them has an athletic bone in his body. So you're really not going to have enough capable bodies to go 8 on 8 in a scrimmage or other drills. With these kind of numbers, it's kind of a challenge to compete against schools like St. Francis, Belt, Ennis, Chester, or Scobey, which are just a few that have over 100 kids and 50 or more boys in high school to build a team from."

T.O. shifted in his chair in response to Otis's grunts, as the big boy struggled to a standing position, moving in small circles in apparent search of a cooler square of linoleum to again collapse upon. "But enough of the sob story. It isn't like our cupboard is bare. Do you have any experience in the 8-man game, Luke?"

"No, no I don't. Never played or coached 8-man," Luke replied. "I grew up in North Platte and played high school at a big school. We had about 2,500 students, so we were in the largest division or classification of Nebraska schools. I guess that would be like your AA schools here. But 8-man football is pretty big in Nebraska and there's lots of small schools like Pacer Coulee in rural, western Nebraska. But sorry to say I am not at all familiar with the game."

"Okay," continued T.O., "well, as coach Freid used to say, there's lots of potential combinations where you can have some success in 8-man football, and if at the end of the day you only have to hide two, maybe three guys max… well, you should win enough games to make the playoffs. So, whether you have one stud and four or five solid guys, or four solid guys and one or two decent players—whatever the math, and you're only hiding a couple of weak players, you have a chance. In our case, we have what I would call one super stud in coming senior Tank Hollister. Tank's a 320-something pound lineman, and he ain't fat neither—just massive. He's got damn good quicks for a guy that size too, and has the demeanor, pardon my French Edna, of a mean-ass bulldog. If he's not the number one recruit in the state, he's in the top two. He's getting interest from the Pac 10 and other major 1A division conferences as well… he's that good."

With a 'now for the bad news' glance towards Edna and Lester, T.O. resumed his analysis. "The downside to Tank is that he's unfortunately ineligible for what seems to be about half the time."

"Does he have some kind of disability that causes him to have a problem staying up with his grades?" Luke asked.

"There's nothing wrong with Terrance's mind," Edna sharply interrupted. "He's too damn lazy, that's the main problem. I would be the first to recognize he's had more than a rough go of it on the home front. His mom passed away when he was in early grade school, and his dad is a vicious drunk— meaner than the proverbial junkyard dog. But tough home life aside, he's capable of at least above average work in the classroom. Call me obstinate and unreasonable; hell, most people around here do at one time or another, but I refuse to cut him any slack. You might as well know this upfront, Luke: I have implemented the toughest eligibility requirement policy in the state. And don't accuse me of being anti-athletics. Just ask Lester, nobody loves sports and views them as critical in the overall development and maturation of our students more than I do. But I've been an educator my entire life and believe our number one responsibility is to ensure that our kids get the education they deserve." Her delivery quickening and her volume rising, she launched into one of her favorite speeches that Lester had heard many times before.

"I was an English teacher in this school for nigh on to 50 years Luke, and I made a pledge to myself and my students from the first day on the job that I'd be Goddamned if I was going to let one of my students head off to college and have to be assigned to a bonehead English college prep class as a result of my incompetent instruction. Now, I've had more than my fair share of knot-heads and uninterested students that wouldn't digest the subject matter if you were feeding it through an IV tube, but I'm dead serious about properly preparing those who are at least somewhat willing to make an effort."

Realizing she had strayed a little too far off first base, Edna cleared her throat and returned to the discussion on Tank. "Back to Terrance and the eligibility policy. These kids need to learn that life, as the kids would say, SUCKS sometimes, and we as teachers, administrators and coaches can't cave into that 'woe is me' mentality that's becoming so popular with parents and folks in general these days. He needs to buck up like everybody else and get the job done."

Wow, thought Luke, *I hope coach Sweden didn't give Lester and Edna my full story, as she wouldn't have much sympathy for the two-year funk that I've been in. Damn, this is one formidable woman.*

"So bottom line," resumed T.O., "we have a big-time stud in Tank, if we can keep him eligible. We have an excellent junior tailback and defensive end in Stefan Tillerman, a 6'0", 180-pound kid that has good speed and elusiveness. We have a real solid fullback and linebacker in senior Aaron Coslet. He's a great leader too, and the kids respect his work ethic and rely on him. We have a solid receiver in Bret Cassidy. He's a 6'2ish", buck-ninety junior kid that won't run by you with his speed, but runs a sweet route and catches everything in sight. He can play D-line too, but doesn't really have much of a defensive mentality... too damn nice of a kid. We also have a pretty solid center in junior Tucker Greyson. He's not the quickest cat in the world and is undersized at only 150 pounds, but he's a gamer— tougher than barbed wire and very football savvy. He's not fast enough to play linebacker, but sticks his nose in it as a D-lineman.

"So, going back to coach Freid's theory, we have a super-stud in Tank, two studs in Tillerman and Coslet, and solid guys in Greyson and Cassidy. And then I need to tell you about a couple of other guys. Let's start with Dolph Russell. Dolph's a bowling ball senior at 5'9ish" and 'bout 220. Other than Tank, he's the strongest kid we got. He's a bull on both sides of the line. Problem is, Dolph's real slow mentally. I'm not sure what's wrong with him—Edna and Lester could answer that question better than me. Anyway, Dolph's not able to comprehend plays or have any idea of who he's supposed to block. He can't remember a snap count either. When at D-tackle, he wouldn't be able to understand anything but just busting straight ahead. Wouldn't ever be able to comprehend if, say, you were trying to run a line stunt, stemming or anything like that. What we've basically had to do is set him next to Tank on both offense and defense, and have Tank tell him what to do as they get to the line of scrimmage, like who to block and such. He relies totally on Tank. If Tank's not in the game, he's lost. He won't listen to anybody else, and you're better off just taking him out 'cause he gets really confused and flustered... jumpin' offside and shit like that. But when Tank's in there with him and can tell him what to do, well, he does a pretty damn good job."

T.O. let that sink in for a moment, and then continued. "We have two other seniors in Tuf Sturm and Danny Schrader. Tuf is a 6'1" beanpole and goes about a buck 40. He doesn't have much going for him in terms of athletic ability, but he's aptly named 'cause he's a tough as leather rodeo kid—team-ropes and rides bulls. We've played him at safety, but he's not a cover guy 'cause he don't have much for wheels, but for such a skinny little shit he can play the run. He'll come downhill hard and knock a running back on his ass, that's for sure. We've sometimes had to play him on the O-line, but he's just so damn light…. Anyway, he's got plenty of try and heart and will play wherever you ask him to and give it all he's got. And Schrader, he's just a scrawny little shit too. 5'10ish" and also 'bout a buck 40. He's started at safety for us the last few years and is a pretty good cover guy 'cause he runs fairly well. Like Tuf, Danny can come up and lay the wood on run support. We can use him as a back-up at running back or receiver, but he is best on defense."

Luke had actually been taking notes on a program roster from last year that Lester had given him, carefully absorbing all the player info that T.O. had been laying out. Edna and Lester had exchanged an unspoken '*he must be interested if he's taking notes*' moment, taking his obvious attentiveness as a positive sign.

"I haven't heard you mention anything about a quarterback," Luke interjected. "How are you sitting there?"

"I was getting to that," T.O. replied. "I'm afraid quarterback is one spot we have to hide. We're really weak there. We have a senior, Virgil Cottingham, who started there last year due to lack of any other options. He's flat out the only kid in our school that can complete a 5-yard out or an 8-yard curl, but even that ain't no guarantee. I think Lester has at least two daughters that can throw a football better than Virgil. We've racked our brain trying to figure out if it would be better to move one of our other better athletes there, but shit, Tillerman, Coslet, Cassidy, Schrader—none of them could throw a spiral if their life depended on it. Maybe an ex big-time quarterback like yourself can coach up a kid on how to throw, but anything other than how to slug it out in the trenches is above my pay grade.

"Couple other kids I'll mention before we wrap this up," said T.O. "We have a senior that's never played football before that I think we've got a chance of getting out this fall. At least Tank and Aaron have been working him hard. Bo Ramsay's a tall, lanky drink of water that has some athletic ability. He placed in State in both the 200 and 400-meter runs this past spring, so he can damn sure run. Hard to say if a guy coming out his last year of high school is gonna be able contribute or not, but at least we'd add an athlete to the mix if he does. Another kid is Kimball Robbins. He'll be a sophomore. Another skinny little shit at 5'10ish" and a buck 40. Great wheels, for sure. He placed fifth at State as a frosh in the 100 meters. Has some damn good hands, too. Has the speed to obviously be a cover guy on defense, but definitely not a physical kid, and he'd rather take a bull whip whuppin' than step in front of anybody. Also not a tough kid at all, and seems to always be hurt. My point is that he could be a helluva weapon at wide receiver, a position where we're mighty thin. Maybe he'll mature from just being another year older, but I wouldn't bet the farm that he'll be able to stay healthy for more than a game or two."

"Well," Luke commented, "doesn't sound like we have anybody that can throw it to him anyway."

"Yeah, there's that," laughed T.O., adding, "so in a nutshell, we've got some players, but we're mighty short on any kind of depth. 'Course that's almost always the case for a school our size. Well Luke, that's pretty much the scoop on the guys. You have any questions I can maybe try to answer or help you with?"

"Do you guys video your games? I sure wouldn't mind looking at a little game tape, long as I'm here," Luke asked. Edna and Lester stole another quick *'This is good, this is good. He wants to look at game tape!'* glance.

"Yup, we just started doing that a few years back, but if you've been down to the field you can see we don't have a crow's nest or anything like that. The only school in our conference that has a good crow's nest is St. Francis, but hell, everything St. Francis has is twice as good as the rest of us. So, most away games are just filmed at field level. For our home games, Aaron Coslet's dad lets us park his grain truck in the end zone and we have a kid video it from the truck box. It ain't very good, especially when play is on the opposite end of the field. Let's just say it damn sure won't remind you of watching Steve Sabol and NFL films."

"I can grab a few tapes and set you up to watch some film as soon as we're done here," offered Lester.

"Okay, thanks. One other thing, Edna and Lester just showed me your weight room. Do you guys have an established in-season weight training program, or any kind of a formal off-season and summer regimen?" Luke inquired.

"No, not really. And I know we should be doing a better job with that, but our last coach didn't really push it much," T.O. stated, as Edna shot Lester a dagger glare at the mere mention of his disastrous hire of the previous coach. "What I know about modern lifting theories, which is damn little, well… even if I did know what I was doing I just don't have the time, especially in the summer, to try to get something like that going. Plus, you saw our little match box of a weight room. Hell, you couldn't get more than three or four guys at a time in there. Tank and Aaron do quite a bit of lifting on their own, but not many of the other guys do at this point," T.O. admitted. "Any other questions?"

"What about access to medical care—Doctors, Orthopedics, Physical Therapy, Athletic Trainers and the such? And who is responsible for taking care of the football field? Mowing, irrigation, maintenance, that kind of thing?"

"If you drove up main street you might have noticed we ain't exactly overrun with doctors, lawyers, accountants and such," T.O. explained, not without a trace of sarcasm to his voice. "If we ain't talkin' busted bones, then Dr. Hockhalter in Centertown sees a lot of the area kids for the run of the mill strains and sprains. He's a Chiropractor. If it's broken bones or busted up shoulders and knees, then it's off to Billings or Great

Falls to see an Orthopod, or wait until the Billings guy comes the few days a month to the hospital in Centertown. There's some pretty good regular docs in Centertown for the flu, bad colds and shit like that. Anyway, the poor man's physician, the athletic trainer, the physical therapist, the head lawn mower, the main irrigator and general field maintenance guy? Well, if you end up with this job, then that'd be you," T.O. stated, pointing his finger directly at Luke.

"Well, if there isn't anything else I can help you with, I'd better get back to the swather before Cindy does a NASCAR on my hayfield," said T.O. with a wry grin.

"Thanks for taking the time to come in T.O.," said Edna, as everyone except Otis stood up for the departing pleasantries.

"Thanks much T.O.," said Luke, as he shook his hand. "It would sure be a big plus for the person who takes this job to have an experienced, readymade assistant like yourself on board. I sure appreciate the info on the boys."

"No worries," replied T.O. "Hope you're the guy runnin' the show when we start camp in six weeks or so."

After T.O. had departed from the room, Edna again took command of the conversation. "Before we get into what your teaching responsibilities would be and Lester sets you up to watch some film, are there any other specific questions that we might be able to answer for you?"

"Yes, yes there is," said Luke, with an engaged, pensive look on his face. "Could you fill me in as to what schools are in your conference, and tell me a little bit about each of them? And maybe give me an idea of the broader picture of 8-man teams statewide? Like who the perennial powers are… stuff like that."

"You bet," replied Edna, as both she and Lester nodded their heads in agreement. "It's about time for Otis here to take a potty break. He's as regular as Kellie Cassidy's mail delivery, except when the school kids—and I'm including Shanty along with Bo and Terrance as the main culprits in this group—don't slip him a polish dog or a slice of all meat pizza. He does a little better if it's just a cheese pizza, but even that will make him gassy. Lester, why don't you go through the schools in the conference while I go tend to Otis; all except for St. Francis. Leave the Goddamn Catholics for me."

"Sure… yes," stammered Lester, resuming after regaining his footing. "Well, there are nine teams in the 7C conference. Besides us, there's Deeden, Stanton, Wyngate, Hodgeman, Marshall, Range View, Heberton and St. Francis. Let's start with Deeden. The Trojans are just 20 miles to the west of us across the Judith River and over on Wolf Creek. Being as close as we are, we are pretty big rivals. They have a fairly solid sports history, especially in football and track. They are about the same size of school, so they deal with the same problems we do in terms of being a small school already and then having to face an ever-decreasing enrollment situation. Heck, all of us in this conference are pretty darn small, except Heberton and most certainly St. Francis," said Lester with a nervous glance towards Edna as she and Otis were going out the door, not wanting to exact her wrath for an out of turn mention of St. Francis. "As you could probably ascertain driving into the Judith Basin, Luke, all the schools in our conference, again with the exception of St. Francis in Centertown, are almost exclusively dependent upon agriculture. And what few businesses these little towns have are agriculturally related. So basically, farm and ranch kids make up 95% of our enrollments. Anyway, Deeden is a solid school and we always seem to have very competitive football games with them. They'll be tough this year, too."

As Edna was steering her bulldog to the deeper native grasses that bordered the mowed and well maintained elementary playground area, she couldn't help but be excited about the prospect of lassoing a coach with the qualifications that Luke brought to the table. And beyond that, he seemed like a nice young man. His past demons notwithstanding, she thought he would be as perfect a candidate as they could hope for.

As Otis circled around in the deep grass and eventually located the ideal spot to lay his deposit, Edna grinned to herself and said out loud, "Well hell, he's the only candidate, but no reason for him to know that!"

Just as they were about to re-enter the school, Edna saw Susan Coslet driving by. The school board chairman began to wildly wave her down as an idea suddenly came to her. Upon on seeing her frantic windmill gestures, Susan flipped a U-turn in the middle of the otherwise empty street and drove up to Edna, lowering her window. "What's up?" asked Susan.

"Hey, is Aaron anywhere close by?"

"Our round baler broke down this morning and Larry sent him to Centertown to pick up parts, but he should be back in just a few minutes. I was just on my way to the Calfe' to meet him for lunch. Do you need him to do something?"

"Yes, I sure do," confirmed Edna. "We're interviewing a prospective football coach and History teacher today, and I'd sure like him to meet Aaron. Let's see, it's 12:30 now. Could you tell Aaron to go grab Terrance? He's working on Kellie Cassidy's corral fence today, and I'm sure she won't mind if he takes a break. Have Aaron and Terrance meet me and Lester and the prospective coach at the Calfe' say, 1:15. Could you have him do that?"

"Sure thing Edna, I'll relay the message. So this guy is a pretty strong candidate, ya think?"

"Very strong. We just need to get him to sign on the dotted line. I figure if I hit him with Aaron's charm and Terrance's bulk, how the hell can he say no?"

"Well, if you can find an inkling of charm rattling around somewhere in that son of mine, then all the more power to you," chuckled Susan. "I'll go find him and tell him."

Back in the little library classroom, Lester continued with his descriptions of the other conference schools. "Heading another 30 miles to the southwest from Deeden is Stanton. They are the county seat of Judith Basin county, so they have a few more state and county-related agencies there. You know, like a courthouse, a Fish and Game office, and stuff like that. They also have a good sports history, usually being pretty darn solid in all sports. Next to St. Francis, I expect them to be right up there in the top of the conference this season. From Stanton, you jump on highway 87 and head back east to Hodgeman and Marshall. The Hodgeman Tigers are about 25 miles from Stanton, and Marshall is just seven miles to the east of them. Then it's only about another 15 miles going east until you hit Centertown. Like all of our schools, again except for St. Francis who always seems to be perpetually loaded with great athletes, Hodgeman has its ups and downs. They've been kind of on a down cycle recently, and I wouldn't anticipate them to have much of a football team this fall. Kind of the same thing with the Marshall Titans. They've had some really good years, especially in basketball, but I think they'll join Hodgeman at the bottom of the conference in football this coming season.

"Then just before you hit Marshall, you turn south at Eddie's Corner to get to Heberton. It's about 40 miles from there, and you pass through what's called the Judith Gap, a relatively narrow passageway that lies between the Little Belts and Big Snowy mountains. Heberton sits down on the Musselshell River and used to be a big railroad town in the early days, hence the nickname of Engineers. But they're mostly just ranch kids now. They're the county seat in Meagher county, so kind of the same thing as Stanton in that regard, although they have a stronger enrollment than the rest of us, again excluding St. Francis. They had not been very good at anything for a number of years and had just plain developed the reputation of having an undisciplined, troublesome group of kids. Then a couple of years ago they hired a father/son team, the Zakrzewski boys. Both named John. They call them Old John and Young John over in Heberton in order to keep them straight. Old John was the Principal and football coach for a number of years back at Stanton and had some damn good teams, to include the ones young John played on. Old John was renowned as a top rodeo guy in Montana in his younger years, not only because he was a damn good dogger, bronc and bull rider, but even moreso for his reputation as being the toughest barroom brawler of them all. He reportedly plied his trade in the cowboy saloons across Montana, Idaho and Wyoming. And rumor has it he was never bested, and although he's getting up there in years now, he still has," said Lester, lowering his voice and looking towards the door to make sure Edna and Otis weren't yet returning, "still has that *don't even think about fucking with me* look about him. Young John was a darn good athlete who played football and ran track at one of the North Dakota colleges, and he's a chip off the old block in terms of being a tough son-of-a-gun.

"Anyway, Old John took the Superintendent job over there, and is young John's assistant football and track coach. They have done a remarkable job of cleaning things up and changing the whole climate over there in just a few short years. They're getting a bunch of boys out for football again, and they have some darn good athletes, too. They will be right up there in the upper echelon of the conference this fall."

Lester held up, as they could hear Otis's toenails clicking on the linoleum as he clod-hopped down the hallway. Lowering his voice again, Lester quickly said, "Another warning, Luke—hope you don't have anywhere to be this afternoon, because when Edna gets started on St. Francis you're usually in for a pretty lengthy rant."

As they entered the room and Edna sat back down in her chair, Otis turned a few circles in search of the ever-elusive cool square of linoleum, and upon finding one flopped to the floor with a heavy sigh. It didn't appear to Luke that Otis had any more spunk than when they had first met a few hours earlier.

"We're down to Range View and Wyngate," explained Lester, continuing after Edna gave him the nod. "You went by Range View on your drive from Billings, Luke. It's 30 miles east of Centertown. I'm telling you that is real cowboy country over in that neck of the woods. I mean, those boys are real hands—no urban cowboys over there. They're known more for their basketball. Not to the degree that Wyngate is, but they usually have darn good basketball teams, both boys' and girls'. They've had some pretty good football teams over the years, but they aren't very good right now. I think I can say with pretty good certainty that the Rangers won't be competitive in the league this year.

"And then north of us about 30 miles is Wyngate. If you would have stayed on highway 191 going north instead of turning west to come here this morning, you would have been heading towards Wyngate. Wyngate is a unique town, kind of up there in no-man's land in the Judith and Missouri River break country. Their town has some unique characters, to say the very least. Both the Bud and Coors distributors say they deliver more beer to little Wyngate than to the 20-times-bigger Centertown. This is a statistic the Wyngate folks take great pride in. Our townsfolk, especially the kids, get along well with them. Maybe it's because we're usually better than the other in different sports. We're usually best in football, and they almost always top us in both boys' and girls' basketball. In fact, the Red Raiders have an impressive resume in basketball, with many district, divisional and even a few state titles. I don't expect them to be among the top teams in the conference this fall, although they do have some good athletes. So that leaves us with St. Francis, and Edna can take it from here. Oh, before I turn it over to Edna, you asked about the top teams in the state. Naturally, St. Francis is year in and year out at the top of the list. I think they've won something like seven or eight out of the last ten State Championships."

"Eight," spat Edna angrily. "The Goddamn Catholics have won eight of the last ten."

"Okay… right, eight it is then," stammered Lester.

"Furthermore," Edna added, "their last loss was to Stanton in the season opener in '85, and they've reeled off 59 straight wins since."

"Uhh, right—59 straight," Lester repeated. Receiving a nod from Edna to proceed, Lester resumed his discussion regarding the other top teams. "As you might expect, the other schools that are consistently up there are big enrollment schools. Scobey, from up in the far Northeast corner; Absarokee, down by Red Lodge in the south; Chester, up north of us; Ennis from the southwest—down on the Madison. Wibaux over in the far east. Seems like those guys are always around deep into the playoffs. Oh, every now and then some smaller school will have a good group of kids and advance pretty far in the playoffs, like a Deeden or a Stanton, Power, Twin Bridges, or a Terry. But you can usually hang your hat on one or more from the group I first mentioned. The obvious favorite would again be St. Francis, with Scobey, Wibaux and Ennis next in line. They grow 'em big out on the eastern plains, and they're just tough, hard nosed kids. They have to be stout to live out in that godforsaken country, although some say the plains have their own brand of beauty. Alright Edna, on to St. Francis."

"St. Francis, as I'm sure you have gathered by now, is located in Centertown," began Edna. "You drove through it this morning on your way from Billings. It's a decent sized town of about 6,000 people and is the main hub for our area of central Montana. All of the little towns in our conference connect to Centertown, like 50 or 60-mile radius bicycle spokes extending from a central hub. Centertown has two schools—Centertown High School, often times referred to as Fergus County High, or just plain Fergus. It's a Class A sized public school with a 9-12 grade enrollment of something over 400. And then you have the private Catholic school in St. Francis. They have a large enrollment of well over 100 students; twice, and in some cases triple, the enrollment of the rest of us. They always manage to keep their numbers just a tad under the maximum of what would mandate them to move up to the next classification level. I guess the Priests and Nuns can add and subtract, because they're pretty damn good at doing the math when their numbers add up to more than the maximum. They also have a plethora of well to do residents and alumni that support the school in a big way. They always have the best of everything… better weight rooms, better facilities, better access to athletic trainers, better equipment, newer uniforms, on and on. They're like the rich kid in fifth grade whose mommy takes him school shopping and they come home with five pairs of jeans, ten fancy shirts and a pair of alligator skin boots, while the rest of the kids get a few worn out hand-me-downs from their siblings.

When Edna finally took a pause to take a deep breath and unclench her teeth, Lester stole a look at Luke, telling him by his expression that there was more of this lecture to come. "While Fergus has had some very good teams in all sports over the years, they haven't had anywhere near the success at the Class A level that their private school counterpart has had in Class C. And much like the private Catholic schools in Billings and Butte, St. Francis is a master in the art of recruiting. They have always been able to snag good athletes out of Fergus, and need I say that the reason is not because the recruit adheres to the principles of Catholicism. The parents and townsfolk are arrogant and condescending. They love to look down their snooty noses at all us little towns, like some Goddamn king peering down from his Ivory Tower at the heathens roaming the countryside outside his protected fortress. And here's what really, really irks me," barked Edna, leaning forward in her chair towards Luke with a now crimson face and neck muscles as taut as a lariat rope. "They think that their private, Catholic school is far superior to the rest of us public school folks. They think those stuffy old nuns that blindly follow the directives of the church's all male hierarchy of Priests, Bishops, Popes, and whatever the hell else there is in between, are the greatest educators of all. Well, I'll tell you one thing for certain," snapped Edna, "it will be a cold day in their proverbial Catholic hell when one of those nuns could even carry my book bag when it comes to teaching English. In sports terms, I'd whip her 70-0 every damn time!"

Whew, thought Luke, his upper torso tensely pressed against the back of his chair as if a more spunky version of Otis was going for his throat. Thankfully, Edna seemed to take the moment to retreat somewhat from the fervor of which she delivered her prior diatribe and forged ahead in a somewhat calmer tone.

"They've been our main rival for years, going back to the days when my Uncle Clarence coached football for the Bulldogs in the '30s. Some people say I go a little overboard on the rivalry thing," she commented, inspiring a hidden eye roll and a '*ya think*?' thought from Lester.

"But what the hell is sport without rivalries? Billings Central/Laurel; Butte/Butte Central; Great Falls High/CMR; Billings Senior/Billings West; Montana Tech/Carroll; Montana Tech/Western; and of course, the granddaddy of them all— Cat/Griz. Anyway, suffice it to say I am quite passionate about our rivalry games against St. Francis. And by the way, we haven't beat them in football since '80. You could be the one to turn that around, Luke, if you're up to the challenge."

Suddenly shifting gears with a further softening of demeanor, Edna moved into the teaching part of the position. Looking down at Luke's resume and her red-inked notes in the margin, she said, "I see you have certifications in History and Health and Human Development. As it turns out, my sister Harriet, who has been around in the History department for damn near as long as I was in English, wants to cut back on her schedule a bit starting this fall. Now, I don't really have a full time position available in History, but all of Harriet's Montana History classes are open. So, you would do the eighth grade Montana History class, and then we offer a high school Montana History class that the students are required to take at some point over the four years in order to graduate. We also offer an advanced Montana History class as an elective, and we usually get three or four seniors wanting to enroll in that. I think I can talk Harriet into giving up Jr. High Social Studies, as well. I doubt she'll budge on American History, as that's her baby. But you might be able to observe her Advanced Placement History class. She has excellent pass rates on her Advanced Placement tests, as did I for many years with my AP English—beat the socks off the old, stuffy St. Francis nun pass rates, I can tell you that for sure!"

"So," Luke interjected, "does your State require some kind of certification or endorsement in order to teach Montana History?"

"Good question Luke. No, you do not need a specific endorsement to teach it, as it's not a state mandated core class that is required to graduate. The requirement that you must complete a full year of Montana History in order to graduate from Pacer Coulee is a self imposed one, not a state one. Being a Nebraska boy, I doubt you would have much knowledge of Montana History other than the well known US History event of the massacre at the Battle of the Little Bighorn in 1876. You know, when the idiot General Custer arrogantly led his troops to slaughter. But I will certainly have some requirements for you in order to teach the class. I can't tell you for certain right now what those would be, but it will likely involve some heavy duty boning up on the subject from yet to be determined sources from now until school starts, and will probably involve some ongoing Continuing Ed from there."

"Okay, that part sounds doable," replied Luke with a contemplative look on his face. "But frankly, I wouldn't even be able to consider taking a position that was anything less than full time. The salary range you posted for the full time position here is way below what I made two years ago at Lincoln. A possible solution to this dilemma could be this; I'm not sure of the terminology used here in Montana, but perhaps we could put my Health and Human Development endorsement, or Phys Ed as you might call it here, to good use in order to arrive at a full time position. I'm not sure what your Phys Ed situation is here at the school, but T.O. told me that you've really never had a consistent weightlifting program for any of your sports, and certainly not a formal off season program. As you may have noticed from my resume at Lincoln, I taught three periods of weightlifting a day for my last two years there, and I set up and supervised the summer weight training program. So that is an area where I have some knowledge and interest. Weight training in all sports is becoming a big deal—the standard, really, as far as getting athletes to perform at their maximum level. What I can tell you with a high degree of certainty is this; if you don't jump on the bus and get up to speed, you will quickly get left in the dust. It makes that much of a difference. And obviously, I can enhance the exercise and recreational experience for the non-athlete student as well."

"I'm sure we can work something out in that regard, Luke," Edna emphatically stated. "There's no doubt that we can get you to a full time position." Glancing down at her watch, Edna announced with a nod to both Luke and Lester, "Luke, before we turn you loose to watch some game film, let's head down to the Calfe' and grab a bite of lunch. I want you to meet a couple of young fellas that are going to join us there. Why don't you take him down in your rig, Lester, and Otis and I will meet you down there."

"Well Luke, what do you think of our school board chairman?" asked Lester, as they walked across the elementary playground to Lester's house to get his car.

"You're right about one thing," Luke said emphatically. "She's definitely a spitfire! Holy cow, I don't think I've ever met a lady as intense as she is. But you know what? I kind of like her. I know I just met her and you may have a very different point of view, especially after she fired you, but you can't help but be impressed by her passion for both education and sports. Seems like you generally have people that are impassioned about one or the other, but rarely both."

"That's true," agreed Lester, as they climbed in his Chevy Station Wagon and headed for the Calfe'. "And don't get me wrong—I respect and admire her enthusiasm for all things Pacer Coulee. Let me buzz you through town real quick. I think the population is around 300 residents, depending on how many elderly widows have moved on to greener pastures on a given day. Pacer Coulee basically has three streets, with Main Street widening out between the city limit signs from the narrow main highway that runs east to west," explained Lester as they passed by one of the two blocks that Luke figured as the business district.

It only took one glance to each side of the street to view the businesses. In block one, the Farmers Merchant State Bank, Walker's Food Store, O.K. Corral Bar and Grill and the Pacer Coulee Post Office lined the north side, while Cole Lumber and Hardware, the Calfe' and a corner lot park and playground lay on the south side. It took Luke a moment to catch the clever, livestock country humor associated with the spelling of the name of the little diner. The second business district block's north side consisted of a large steel building that was the Community Center and City Library. Next to it was Snook's Fuel, a two pump gas and diesel station whose sign indicated they also delivered bulk fuel and heating oil to the rural areas of central Montana. The rest of that side of the block was filled with the whitewashed block building and lot of Osbournson's Case IH and Massey Ferguson Implement dealership. Numerous new and used combines, tractors, swathers, balers, plows, cultivators, seeders and back-hoes were neatly arranged on the sizable acreage.

The south side of block two consisted of two large steel buildings sitting side by side, the one on the corner being the home of Lehman's Service and Repair, and Zenizek's Fertilizer and Chemicals the other. The opposite corner was occupied by an empty and sagging wood framed structure that Luke thought was likely built during the early years of Pacer Coulee's existence. Although if you looked close enough you could make out a faded 'Wick's Drug Store' on the store front, Lester said it most recently housed the town's only other bar. But the dwindling population of the small rural communities across the country was turning them all, with the one notable exception being Wyngate, into one bar towns.

Lester continued to drive to the west edge of town and pointed out the three towering grain elevators and the store and offices of the Farmers Co-op. Adjacent to that were the offices and engine repair facilities of the Central Montana Railroad. Completing that end of the town was a well maintained set of livestock holding pens and loading chutes that Lester explained were busy in the fall when the ranchers were shipping their calves to market.

As Lester swung back to town and drove through the small, three street residential section, he said, "As you can see, this no-traffic-light little berg is a pretty well kept town. Most of the homes are older, but folks here take pride in maintaining their homes and yards. It's one of the nicer little towns I've been in, and I've been at a few over the years. The school district owns the little Superintendent's house that I live in, so all I pay for is utilities."

"What's rent like, and is there much available for teachers?" asked Luke.

"As it turns out, most of the elementary teachers are married to local farmers and ranchers, so they live out of town. There's two little homes on this street that I'll point out to you in a sec that Edna has owned for a number of years and rents out exclusively to teachers. There's a few others as well, so you shouldn't have too much trouble finding a place to rent. Oh, and as far as rent goes, these little rural towns are really cheap. A couple hundred bucks would go a long way to knocking out the rent bill."

As Lester completed the short tour of Pacer Coulee and parked in front of the Calfe', he said to Luke, "I'm not sure who Edna has lined up for you to meet. I expect it might be a couple of the football boys. By the way, you should know that we have very few discipline problems here. These farm and ranch kids are mostly damn good kids. Pretty tough and hard-nosed for the most part, and come from parents that don't put up with too much nonsense. As such, they usually are used to working. Not saying we don't have some challenges from time to time, but overall we have significantly fewer problems than you run into in the larger cities and bigger schools."

At the 1:30 p.m. hour, most of the regular lunch crowd had already dissipated. As Lester and Luke entered the door, they saw Tank Hollister and Aaron Coslet waving at them from a larger table in the back of the diner. "Boys, I'd like you to meet Luke Carter. Luke, this little fella here is Tank Hollister, and this is Aaron Coslet. These are two of our top football guys. Luke is here looking at the football coaching position," explained Lester.

From what T.O. had said, Luke was expecting Tank Hollister to be big, but this kid was huge. Luke had large hands, but when Tank latched on for the handshake, Luke's right paw disappeared like an unsuspecting jellyfish being funneled through the gaping jaws of a great white. *Good Lord*, thought Luke, *this kid is massive*. Not tall—maybe only a tad over six feet, but thicker than a locomotive and wider than a dairy barn door. Most of the linemen that Luke had on his own Southern Nebraska college teams, as well as on the other teams they played against, had some body fat and varying degrees of a pot belly protruding over the belt. But big Tank had a snug, sleeveless t-shirt on, and Luke could see nary a sign of a pot belly or a love handle.

Glad to get his hand back with no nerve damage or loss of circulation, Luke exchanged greetings with the boys. Tank muttered, "Yo... nice to meecha." The handsome and solidly built Aaron gave Luke a firm handshake, and with a warm smile and full eye contact said, "Pleased to meet you, Mr. Carter. Welcome to Pacer Coulee. I understand you came up from Nebraska?"

"Pleased to meet you too Aaron, and thanks. Yes, I've spent pretty much all my life in Nebraska," Luke replied, immediately liking the well spoken youngster who also addressed Lester with a handshake and a, "Hello Mr. Brewster, how is your summer going so far?" Luke smiled to himself as Aaron's polished and affable manner elicited a vision of the popular old *Leave it to Beaver* television show from his youth. The silky smooth and obsequious Eddie Haskins would greet the Beav's mother with a syrupy polite, "Good evening Mrs. Cleaver. How was your day,

Mrs. Cleaver? You sure look lovely in that pretty blue dress, Mrs. Cleaver."

Sitting at the table next to the large picture window that afforded a full view of Main Street, Lester, Luke and the boys watched Edna pull her Pacer Coulee Bulldogs blue and gray colored 1988 King cab Pickup into the space next to Lester's car. Everyone chuckled looking at Otis, the 'Tank' version of local canines, who sat turned at such an angle in the front passenger seat that he could rest his elephantine head on the ledge of the rolled down window sill.

"Watch this," said Tank, pointing out the window as Edna came around and opened the passenger door to extract the bulldog from his front seat perch. "Watch this," he repeated with a big grin spreading across his face. "Big ol' Otis is getting too old to jump out of the pickup hisself. Watch Miz E's squat form when she lowers him to the ground. 'Course if she didn't bend at the knees she would bust her back getting that big lard-ass on the ground, for sure!"

Just as Tank predicted, Edna moved up close to the seat, and with one arm wrapped around his chest and the other under his rear end, she hoisted him up and out away from the door. *Tank was correct*, Luke thought, in that Edna kept her back straight and bent deeply in the knees to lower him to the ground; *perfect form.*

Luke saw the first sign of spunk he had seen from Otis when he perked up at the sight of Tank. He almost broke into a semblance of a gait that would be considered faster than a waddle—a totter trot or a waddle jog—when Tank leaned over in his chair and clapped his hands together. "Come to Tank, big boy." Edna sank into a chair as the enormous dog and even more gargantuan boy made a fuss over each other.

"You know Terrance, he only likes you because you give him all the food that's bad for his weight, not to mention his digestive tract," Edna stated, admonishing further with, "and don't you dare give him any of that Puckered Pig BBQ pork sandwich you always order, either. You're not so big that I can't grab you by the ear and haul you out behind the woodshed and put the hickory stick to your very wide behind if you don't mind me!"

"I know Miz E, I know," replied Tank, with a wry smile. "But I think you're bein' pretty hard on ol' Otis. A guy's gotta have a little treat now and again, don't ya think Miz E?"

Edna ignored him, turning to Luke. "So, I take it you've formally met these two knot-heads? I don't suppose you would want to coach anybody as scrawny as Terrance, or his lousy running back/linebacker sidekick Aaron?"

Well I'll be damned, thought Luke. *Could it be she has a morsel of a sense of humor?* "Nah, I've never coached a scarecrow like Tank before," laughed Luke. "I might as well not waste my time in watching any of their game film."

"I'll apologize in advance about the quality of the game film, Mr. Carter," Aaron interjected. "We had an eighth grade girl doing the filming last year, and she misses about half of the game because she's too busy flirting. Or even if she is paying attention, she hasn't figured out that there's a two second delay from when you press the camcorder on-switch until it actually starts recording. So the play is usually half over by the time film starts."

"I'll keep that in mind as I review a few game tapes after lunch," said Luke. With that, they ordered lunch and Luke had an enjoyable visit with the boys about school, football and their summer ranch jobs. Aaron did most of the talking, with Tank becoming more active when the discussion turned to weight training.

"I best be getting back and set some posts in Kellie's corral," said Tank, and Luke followed the boys out of the Calfe' to say their goodbyes and see them off.

"Damn, I think the boys really hit it off with Luke, don't you?" whispered Edna, as she and Lester watched them all shake hands in front of Tank's old, beat up Chevy pickup.

"Yeah, I think they did," Lester whispered back. "That was smart of you to have the boys come down and meet him. What do you want to do from here?"

"Okay, you take him back to the school and set him up in library to watch some film. And for God's sake, don't give him the St. Francis or Stanton tapes from last year. If he watches either of those whippings we'll lose him for sure. Then meet me down in your office. We need to talk."

"If I could watch two game films, that would be great," said Luke, as he and Lester approached the school. "And if you would, I would like one of those tapes to be the St. Francis game. That way I can get a look at the top team in the state. That'll give me an idea of the talent and performance level of the upper echelon 8-man teams in the state."

Shit! Edna's gonna kill me, thought Lester. But he didn't see how he could get around a direct request. He rummaged through the cardboard box that contained all the VHS tapes since the just-fired Tim Stratt started the practice of filming two years ago, and unfortunately came across the dreaded film lurking at the top of the pile. He half expected the 'SF-66 PC-18/1989' label that identified the contents of the tape to start flashing like a neon sign, cruelly mocking the Pacer Coulee faithful. He wanted to make sure that the second tape he pulled was also a game that Tank had been eligible to play in, so he pulled the past year's 32-12 win over Wyngate. *At least that choice should please Edna*, he thought.

Luke watched the Wyngate tape first, shaking his head in amusement at the poor quality of the tape. He realized he was spoiled, as the condition of the film he had been accustomed to at Lincoln High was as professional as you could expect at the high school level. Although taped in color, the film was grainy and dark. The grain truck that masqueraded as a crow's nest had been parked directly behind the goal posts, placing the eighth grade camcorder operator at such a height that the goal post crossbar blocked a portion of the view of any play that was run from midfield to the opposite end zone.

To make matters worse, Aaron wasn't exaggerating when he

said the young gal didn't press the record button on time. Every play was well underway by the time the camera actually started to record, making it difficult to impossible to determine what offensive or defensive formation the teams were in before the ball was snapped. Luke quickly fast forwarded it to the parts of the game that were being played on the end of the field closest to the camera, but even the view that didn't have crossbar interference was pretty much useless in gathering any kind of meaningful footage to evaluate the execution of a play or the individual performance of a player. Poor quality film aside, there was one thing that was crystal clear; Tank Hollister was a beast.

The St. Francis game was also played at Pacer Coulee, and obviously filmed from the same grain truck box by the same camera operator. Despite the similarly poor quality of the film as the Wyngate tape, Tank was again impressive, even though it was obvious he was going against far superior competition. T.O. was correct in describing him as being super mobile for such a large young man, as he was quick and powerful off the ball. St. Francis double and triple teamed him on every one of their offensive plays. Luke was also impressed with the running back and linebacker play of Aaron Coslet and Stefan Tillerman. Tillerman was a shifty runner with breakaway speed, and Coslet appeared to be fundamentally sound. He was a straightforward north/south guy, running with good body lean and power. From the few plays where the tape was started in time to see him block, Luke again liked his effort and technique. He was also a solid linebacker who seemed to read and react quickly, and was a sure tackler.

But Luke was blown away with the Trojans of St. Francis. From the parts of the film where their sideline was included in the view screen, he could see they had more than double the 15 or 16 that were dressed out for the Bulldogs. Unlike either Pacer Coulee or from what he could tell from the tape of Wyngate, the Trojans had so many players that they were able to platoon to keep players fresh. Poor film quality aside, he could identify at least four players on defense that weren't back out there on offense. It also looked like they had four or five different running backs that they rotated in and out without much drop off in yardage production, although they did have one back that was decidedly their top runner. And while they didn't have anyone of Tank's mass, it appeared they had excellent size on both sides of the line. After removing the tape and slipping it back inside its cover, Luke knew one thing was for sure; Pacer Coulee had a long, long way to go if they were ever going to satisfy Edna's lofty expectation of a win over St. Francis.

"So Lester, give me your candid opinion and impression of Mr. Carter being our next football coach here at Pacer Coulee," Edna demanded. Always nervous that he would say the wrong thing around Edna, he was comforted by the fact that he was 99.9% sure that she was convinced that Luke was the perfect choice, albeit the only choice that they currently had.

"Well, it's hard not to be impressed by his background and credentials. He obviously played the game at a high level in both high school and college, and being a Nebraskan myself, I know the level of play at that high school and the conference that Lincoln is in, and it's pretty darn high. Obviously, having coach Sweden as one of his Letters of Reference is impressive. And I like him as a person, and thought he interviewed very well. I was also pleasantly surprised with how easily and comfortably he interacted with Tank and Aaron. I guess the only potential negative is the possibility of a repeat of the event that caused him to take a two year break from his coaching position in Lincoln. I did quiz coach Sweden about the incident that led to that hiatus, and he said it was because Luke was blindsided by an unfaithful wife who wanted a divorce. Of course, it's impossible to predict those type of things."

"Not only am I impressed with this kid," Edna began, either not hearing or simply choosing to ignore Lester's closing comment about Luke's hiatus from coaching and teaching, "but we've got to have him! Whatever it takes, we've got to get him signed on the bottom line. When he's done looking at film, I'm going to offer him a contract. We need a done deal by the time he leaves here this afternoon."

"I hope that isn't a bad omen," suggested Lester, nodding towards the window where they could see the gray and black thunder clouds building up and rolling in from the west. "I did show him the 4-plex and your two little teacher houses."

"Good, good. Well, that settles it. I'll offer him the position as soon as he gets back," declared Edna. Lester wanted to ask whether she had consulted with, or been given authorization from the other school board members to offer such a contract. He laughed inwardly at even the presumption that it would occur to Edna to seek approval from the rest of the elected officials that were tasked with collectively governing the school.

"One other thing," said Lester sheepishly, "he specifically asked to see the St. Francis tape."

"Damn it. If I was the type to use the F word, which I'm not, this would be a good spot to throw it into the mix. Damn it!" she said again, this time with a stronger emphasis. Lester had to admit that Edna was a selective swearer. She could drop the *Christ*s, *Goddamn*s, *damn*s and *hell*s around like a drunken sailor. Some had even suggested she swore with a dash of class and elegance. But he'd never heard her utter the lower status curse words that lingered in or near the murky confines of the bottom half of the gutter. "Well, let's hope that tape doesn't come back to haunt us," sighed a grim-faced Edna.

Luke had no sooner put the St. Francis tape back in its cover when Edna and Lester re-entered the little classroom. "I hope the videos were useful," Lester offered.

"Frankly, they're of such poor quality that it's pretty hard to glean much useful information from them," replied Luke truthfully.

Ignoring Luke's pointed film deficiency remark, Edna jumped right in to the heart of the matter. "I'll cut to the chase, Luke. Of all the candidates that we have interviewed thus far, you're at the top of the list. Even though we have several more interviews scheduled over the next few days, I've consulted with the other members of our board and am prepared to offer you a contract to be the next football coach to add to the legacy of our long and storied history of football excellence here at Pacer Coulee High. The board has also authorized me to combine your History and Physical Education endorsements into a full time position. We have plenty of time to work out those details between now and when school starts. I also twisted a few arms and got you an $800 per year coaching stipend, as compared to $600 in the past. So what do you say to signing on the dotted line and getting this deal all wrapped up?" asked Edna, with all the bravado of a confident car salesman.

Lester almost had to turn around to keep a *'What the Fuck, Edna?'* look from spreading across his face. For a lady with a reputation as a no-nonsense straight shooter, her nose should have been growing exponentially before their very eyes from the monumental yarns she had just woven. Of all the candidates we have interviewed? *Really?* And additional applicants scheduled to interview in the next few days? *Please!* And the board gave you authorization to submit a contract offer? *Are you kidding me?*

"Well, I would appreciate it if you could extend me the courtesy of being able to think this over—just overnight, that's all I'd need. I need to make sure I've asked all the pertinent questions and thoroughly considered the positives and negatives of taking this position. Would you be able to give me the night to think this through?" Luke inquired.

"Why yes, we can do that. Don't you think we can accommodate Luke on that request, Lester?"

"Well, I wouldn't see any problem with an overnight extension Edna, but I suspect you'd need to get this accommodation, insignificant as it is, authorized by the board, wouldn't you? You know how they get when they aren't consulted in regard to matters such as this, always going by the book the way those guys do," said Lester, instantly regretting tugging on the tail of the already aggravated mountain lion that was casting a stony glare in his direction.

"Then I think I'll head back to Centertown for the night, if that would be alright. Would it be possible to meet out here again at, say, 8:00 or 9:00 in the morning?"

Before Edna could answer, Lester couldn't help himself and interjected. "Don't we have that one candidate coming in for his interview at 10:00, Edna? Or maybe you want to defer him and all the other applicant interviews until we have Luke's decision?" Deflecting another honed arrowhead-sharp glance from Edna, he moved forward. "But if you could get here at 8:00, that should give us enough time should you decide to conduct the 10:00 candidate interview, don't you think Edna?"

"Ah, yes… yes, 8:00 would work fine."

"Great, I'll see you at 8:00 then. What would you suggest for a motel in Centertown? I noticed a Sapphire Inn that looked pretty nice when I was driving through."

"That would be your best bet," said Edna quickly, not giving Lester a chance to continue mocking the fibs she had been telling. "And they have a lounge and restaurant in the motel, too."

Since it was only 3:00 p.m., Luke took out his map again and decided to drive the loop to see at least most of the towns that were in the conference. A nice long drive might be just the ticket to clear his mind and come to a decision. He decided to head west to Deeden and Stanton, and then swing back towards Centertown, catching Hodgeman and Marshall along the way. He decided Heberton was too far off the beaten path, but depending on the time and how he felt upon getting back to Centertown, he might take the 40 mile jaunt out to Wyngate.

The first few miles out of Pacer Coulee was slow going, as betwixt the angry lightning strikes and bellowing rolls of thunder, the black clouds released a battalion of torrential rainfall, switching tactics intermittently to fire marble-sized hail instead, as if the rain had called in for heavy artillery reinforcement. But by the time he dropped down from the hill that overlooked the bridge that crossed the Judith River, the storm had dissipated and the sun shone brightly. Luke rolled down his windows and tuned in to the country western station KMON out of Great Falls, the only radio station that came in clearly. The pleasant scent of the freshly cut alfalfa that lay on both sides of the road swirled about his nostrils, and he felt himself relax.

As he topped the hill on the opposite side of the river, Luke was so taken aback by the expanse of country that opened before him that he pulled off the main highway onto a graveled approach to a pasture gate. From his map, he gathered he was viewing the heart of the Judith Basin, an immense swath of a valley bordered on all sides by distant mountain ranges. Under the now clear skies, he could look back to the east and see the just passed North and South Moccasins, and the Judith Mountains further to the east. To the south was the wide and flat-topped Big Snowy range; the Little Belts to the southwest; the Highwoods directly to the west, accompanied by two lonely, but substantial outcroppings— one round and the other square, extending from the basin floor like they had been second thought volcanic burps. He studied the map closely, and determined the vertically protruding intruders were appropriately named 'Round Butte' and 'Square Butte.' An additional search of the map identified the mountain range to the north as the Bears Paw, appearing to be far enough north to be the gateway to Alberta, Canada.

With the geography of the beautiful land that lay before him now identified by name, Luke continued his trek towards Deeden. Settling into the somewhat comfortable lap of his Sierra, he relived his impressions of the day, starting with Lester. One would be hard pressed to not like the friendly and affable Nebraskan, not to mention that he was a close friend to coach Sweden. From all outward appearances, Lester seemed to enjoy his Superintendent and AD positions at the school, as well as living in the Pacer Coulee community. Luke surmised he would be easy to work with as his boss in both the classroom and on the athletic field. However, the probable reality that Edna was the real boss was not lost on him.

He laughed out loud when he thought of Edna. Never in all of his 34 years had he ever met a woman like Edna. Smart, determined, strong, demanding, unyielding, opinionated, decisive, and unforgiving came to mind. Yet he sensed a softer, more understanding side lived hidden from view in the narrow alleys of her psyche. Something about the interaction between her and Tank threw off a flash; a fleeting glimpse of an unlikely connection between the two. Perhaps a kindred spirit link that those on the outside were unable to see or grasp. He had a sneaking suspicion that there was a dark side to Tank. Edna had referred to a troubled home life, and it seemed likely to Luke that Edna shared a disturbing event or secret from Tank's past that no one else was privy to.

He entered the little town of Deeden, realizing it was probably only a couple of teetering widows away from having the exact same 300-resident population as Pacer Coulee. Their football field lay adjacent to the highway as he entered the east edge of town, and typical of small town rural America, a set of bleachers 15 rear ends wide and five rows high bordered the home town sideline—plenty of room to seat the entire elementary and secondary student body to cheer their team on to victory. An older, smaller rust-laden bleacher rested across the way on the visitors' side, giving the appearance of a destitute and down-on-his-luck relative.

The field looked to be in fairly decent shape, with numerous lengths of irrigation pipe stored on the little six lane cinder track that looped around the 80-yard field. Presumably the pipe would be placed and the irrigation activated when the early summer rains of June were put to bed in favor of increased temperatures and drying winds. Other than a discernible sag of the turf at the east end of the field, the field itself looked well attended to. Luke noted the business district consisted of the same two block radius as Pacer Coulee, although Deeden had a higher concentration of boarded up store fronts, slumping sadly as if yearning for the bustling activity of years past.

As he reached a table top flat bench that was planted in what he presumed was wheat for as far as the eye could see, he realized he was closing in on the magnificent hunk of geology that was Square Butte, the very same outcropping that he had identified from the top of the divide some 25 miles back. As he drove towards it, he admired the wonder of its creation, its sides rising straight up from the ground and the top lying as prone as a sniper in shooting position. His thoughts wandered to how abrupt the change would be if he accepted this job. He would be going from a high school of 2,500 students to 97 in the entire K-12 grades. He would be going from the familiar 11-man football game that he had always played and coached to an 8-man game he knew little about. He would be going from having all the amenities offered by the large schools—top facilities, top training tools, top weight rooms, top technology, top auxiliary staff… and so on, to conditions that would be substandard in comparison in every way. He also knew that with the reputation he had built as being one of the brightest young high school offensive minds in Nebraska, he could practically name the school where he wanted to be the offensive co-coordinator, and even Head Coach, back in his home state.

So what the hell are you doing, he asked himself, *even considering such a huge step backwards? Because you're still running from your ex-wife and all the painful memories of her that you have allowed to seep into your Nebraska experience subconscious, that's why! At least I'm admitting my inability to go back and face my old familiar coaching and teaching life,* Luke reasoned.

His forays into Stanton, Hodgeman and Marshall revealed the same small town and school layouts as those of Deeden and Pacer Coulee, with Stanton boasting a few more buildings due to their county seat status. He laughed out loud that he now had firsthand knowledge of the old adage about driving through small town rural America—don't blink on your way through or you'll miss it.

After returning to the main road from the short detour into Marshall and heading on to Centertown, he realized he was pleasantly surprised at how comfortable he felt at the Pacer

Coulee interview. Lester was easy to talk to and a delight to be around, and while certainly formidable, he found himself liking Edna. The idea of a new start in a distant state was truly becoming an appealing concept. Even the challenge of a small school, so totally opposite of all prior experience, was starting to look entreating. Of course, it didn't hurt that he had met Tank. He fully realized he could be coaching a kid that appeared to have size and physical attributes that could possibly land him on the Cornhusker recruiting list.

He spent the last few miles into Centertown convincing himself to take the job. And since he had a pretty strong feeling that Edna may have been exaggerating more than a little about the supposed bevy of candidates lining up to interview for the position, he decided to use a little leverage in the morning meeting to bargain for some additional considerations that might help level the playing field with, as Edna would say, the Goddamn Catholics.

Luke was up early and took his morning run through the historic Main Street business district and on up the steep hill that led to the west end of town. At the top of the hill he veered over two blocks and ran by the spacious and modern looking campus of the Central Montana Hospital. From there he ran downhill on Boulevard Street, passing the Newt Dean Chevrolet and Cadillac Dealerships, surprised at the plentiful units on display for a town that size. Where the hill dissipated into a level surface, he came upon the St. Francis school, tucked comfortably behind the beautiful sandstone constructed St. Francis Cathedral. He ran around the entire several blocks that housed the Catholic school, noting the well maintained rock and stone edifices. Unlike Pacer Coulee, the Grade School, Jr. High and High School were all in separate, detached buildings. He burst into laughter when he was suddenly hit with a vision of Edna perched high above the school entrance on an extension ladder in the dark of night, spray painting 'Goddamn Catholics' over the existing 'St. Francis High School' lettering.

Luke ran back to the Sapphire Inn and showered, grabbing a
quick breakfast at the motel's Bull's Pen restaurant and headed
back to Pacer Coulee. It was the third of July, and he drove into
a clear and beautiful morning that was all decked out in bright
and bold shades of Big Sky blue. He used the 20-minute drive to
rehearse the conditions he would request to consummate the
contract that would send him 1,000 miles across the country to
coach a game he knew nothing about, and teach a subject of
which he had no knowledge. "Helluva plan, Luke, that's one
helluva plan," he said out loud. But he took it to be a good omen
when Dave Wilson, KMON's melodic, country drawling DJ
took a break from the agricultural futures report to spin a Ricky
Van Shelton song that seemed to have been chosen with Luke
specifically in mind:

'That I've cried my last tear for you
Wasted my last year on you
There's no trace of the heartache I knew
It's been raining pain since you walked out...'

"I get it Ricky, I really do," he said to the radio dial. "God
knows I've wasted too much time already."

Only Edna's pickup and two other cars occupied the school
parking lot when Luke pulled in at 7:52 a.m. Edna, Otis and
Lester were already in place, with a freshly brewed pot of coffee
and Calfe'-made maple bars and cinnamon rolls on the table in
front of them. "Help yourself to coffee and donuts, Luke," said
Edna. "Jeannie down at the Calfe' bakes a beauty of a cinnamon
roll." Otis sat on his haunches in front of the table, mesmerized
by the delicious smells emanating from the baked goods that sat
just agonizingly out of his reach. His sad, droopy eyes seemed to
indicate that he longed for the younger and less arthritic years of
his youth, when he could launch his front end upon the table and
devour the entire donut population in a few short gulps.

"Oh for Christ's sake, Otis!" said Edna. "Since Tank didn't

rain havoc on your digestive tract with a pork sandwich yesterday, I guess you can have ONE maple bar—but no more begging, you hear me? Don't even think about a cinnamon roll! That will give you gas so bad that I'll have to keep you outside for a week!" She dropped a maple bar to his mouth before she lost a hand to his snapping jaw.

Lester had had a fitful night's sleep, concerned that his insouciant sarcasm directed at the Pinocchio-esque fibs that Edna had told Luke the day before would elicit a firm scolding from the school board chairman. To his surprise and relief, she hadn't mentioned the subject.

After exchanging pleasantries and discussing the merits of ordering the breakfast bar buffet at the Bull's Pen, Edna got right to the point. "I hope you had a good drive yesterday afternoon and were able to sort out and contemplate all the aspects of this exceptional challenge and opportunity. So, what concerns or questions can we answer for you before we sign on our respective lines and get this show on the road?"

Luke fought off the intimidation factor emanating from Edna's imposing presence and began his rehearsed speech. "Well, first of all I would like to thank you for giving me the opportunity to interview for this position. And I did think long and hard as I drove across central Montana yesterday afternoon and evening. There are a couple of things I would like to request that would be helpful in my decision as to whether or not to accept this offer."

"Very well," replied Edna. "What kind of requests do you have in mind"?

"You must understand that I come from coaching in a large high school," Luke began. "And while I do realize that schools like where I was at in Nebraska have far more resources at their disposal in terms of facilities, equipment, technology and so on, your school has some glaring deficiencies that would need to be addressed in order for me to accept this position." Luke paused for a moment and looked for any change in Edna's facial expression that would indicate he might be treading on thin ice with his bold approach. Seeing no sign of an impending thundercloud boiling from behind her piercing green eyes, he continued confidently.

"My number one concern is getting this program into the modern world when it comes to weight training. As I mentioned yesterday, you're going to fall behind the 8-ball in a hurry if you don't get up to speed. What you loosely refer to as a weight room is not only located in too small of a space, but the equipment is horribly outdated and insufficient to properly train young athletes. And I'm not talking just football. At Lincoln, all of our athletes, boys and girls, weight train for their respective sports. And beyond that, we have excellent techniques and programs in today's training world that can enhance speed, quickness, agility and flexibility as well.

The bottom line is this; if I'm going to be expected to develop a team that is going to be capable of competing with the St. Francises of the world, then I need at least the basic tools at my disposal to get that done. So I'd need a commitment written into the contract, at minimum, to substantially upgrade the exercise and weightlifting equipment according to my specifications. I guess I could live for a while with that cramped weight room if I had the equipment upgrade, but making that kind of expenditure without a decent place to put it just doesn't make much sense, at least in my view. I would hope that you would consider knocking out that exterior wall on the east end of the room and making it at least triple the size that it is now."

He was pleased to see that he had Edna and Lester's undivided attention. Both leaned forward in their chairs, listening intently with earnest expressions on their faces. "Okay," replied Edna thoughtfully, "go on."

"Again, I come from a large school that has all the tools on hand to be successful in the sports arena, but after inspecting the football equipment I truly think you have significant safety concerns in that area. There are only a few helmets that appear to be somewhat recently purchased. The rest of them look like they were bought the year after leather helmets went out of vogue. I couldn't find any documentation that any of these helmets have ever been reconditioned, which by the way, is not just a state law kind of a thing, it's nationally mandated for safety. So basically, I view your helmet situation as a concussion waiting to happen, not to mention the legal liability side of things. And there's only a handful of shoulder pads that have been purchased any time close to recently. That's not as dire as the helmet situation, but in the last five years or so there has been significant improvement in the design and materials used in shoulder pads. These newer pads are much more protective than the old ones, creating yet another safety issue."

Luke shifted his position on the chair, and seeing that he still had looks of engrossment from his audience, he continued. "So, the contract would have to include confirmation that you will address these serious equipment safety issues to my satisfaction. Seriously, if you don't address this, you will be exposing the coach, the AD, the School Board, and even your School District to significant liability risk. And thirdly, there is no way I can deliver you a winning product when we have some ditsy eighth grader running an outdated camcorder from the box of a grain truck. Your film quality is so poor that it's not one bit useful in being able to grade out our own players' performances, let alone be able to utilize it as the critical coaching tool I've become accustomed to using it for. Anyway, my next condition would be a clause confirming an update of the video equipment. Additionally, I'd have to have a crow's nest built down at the field. It doesn't need to be any kind of expensive or elaborate thing, basically just four telephone-sized poles with a roofed platform at the top. But it is a must for me to have the film shot from a high enough angle to get both teams and most of the field in the view screen on the film. Otherwise, you might as well not even waste your time trying to film, as it's useless for evaluation purposes."

Luke took a lengthy pause to again test Edna's water temperature after hearing his demands. In seeing no boiling water at the surface, he forged ahead.

"And finally, I would need you to utilize my exercise and weight training background by filling up my non-History class periods with weight and exercise training. And I don't mean just for the football guys. As I said, schools that are successful in all sports have sport specific programs available to the kids, for both boys and girls. In today's world, going out and playing Frisbee golf or dodge ball during PE class just doesn't cut the mustard anymore. Even for your non-athletes, some form of weight and agility training simply improves their overall health and conditioning. So again, I would need to see a History and Phys Ed class schedule that utilizes the strengths I can bring to your table before I could sign a contract. It would also be nice if you could firm up the plan on what we discussed yesterday in regards to what I would be expected to do to in terms of preparation to teach the Montana History classes. If I take this job, I need to get going on educating myself so I can enter the classroom this fall without sounding like the village idiot."

Wow, thought Lester. *This guy has some large kahunas to come in here and make such significant demands on the school, not to mention Edna.* But he was very impressed with Luke's presentation. He had obviously done his homework, and his requests were well thought out. His comments regarding the safety issues of the football equipment had especially hit home, and he could see it had impacted Edna as well. Everything he proposed made sense, and he could already envision his talented daughters improving their volleyball and basketball skills under Luke's implementation of the latest training methods. What he couldn't envision was the school board being able to come up with the sizable funding necessary to meet Luke's demands. *Look out Bill Koch*, Lester thought to himself, *you're gonna get hit up big-time*! Edna had told him in the past, under a Boy Scout's promise level of secrecy, that the local banker Bill Koch was the mystery donor who always came to the rescue in funding the needs of the school or the community.

Edna must have been pretty sure of Mr. Koch's compliance

in picking up the tab, as she leaned further in her chair towards Luke and said, "Luke, I appreciate your concerns and your conditions of acceptance. None of your requests are unreasonable, and in fact are long overdue. If you have some time and are agreeable, let's spend the rest of the day going over your requests in detail and see if you can help me arrive at a ballpark dollar figure to get it done. Then I'll have you and Lester huddle up and work out a class schedule that works for us both. In the meantime, I will consult with my board and get a contract finalized for you to sign by 5:00 this afternoon. Does that work for you?"

"That works for me," said Luke with a grin.

Lester wanted to bait Edna again by reminding her of the fictitious 10:00 interview she had told Luke was scheduled with another amazingly qualified candidate, and that two of her board members happened to be in Bozeman for meetings with the Montana State Agricultural Experiment Station, but he figured he'd pushed his luck to the limit the day before.

"Edna, I do have a meeting here shortly with Greg Bolstad about replacing those windows in the old bus barn, but I'm free the rest of the day to help you and Luke out in any way I can," said Lester.

"That sounds good, Lester. I can fill Luke in on what's expected of him on the Montana History matter while you're doing that. When you're done with Greg, send him over. He can get us our ballpark figures on the crow's nest and expanding the weight room in pretty short order."

Greg Bolstad was the local handyman and contractor, and he did a thriving business in Pacer Coulee putting up steel grain bins and shop and machinery shed buildings for the farmers and ranchers, as well as being in demand for remodels and general contracting. "Whatcha got going, Edna?" quizzed Greg a short time later, after being introduced to Luke.

"Two things I need your immediate help with, Greg. We need a quick and dirty ballpark-only estimate for building a crow's nest down at the field so that Luke can get a decent game film angle. Secondly, I need you to look at the little cinder block room that's off the east end of locker rooms; the one we use for a weight room. Give us an idea of what it would cost to blow out a wall or two and add a double or triple sized extension, if you would."

They spent the next hour giving Greg enough input for him to sketch out a poor man's set of blueprints on a yellow legal pad for both the crow's nest and the weight room addition. Greg went home to price the materials and said he'd return in a couple hours with some figures. Edna set Luke up in the secretary's office to put together a comprehensive list of all the new equipment needs: football helmets and pads, weight and exercise equipment for an expanded weight room area, and video recording equipment. Lester had opened his Rolodex to Universal Athletics, the Bozeman-headquartered company they used for all their sport related equipment and uniform needs, so that he could call and get pricing for his equipment requests. He also left Luke a few numbers for places in Centertown and Billings that would likely carry the video equipment that he wanted.

They all met back in the little classroom off the library at 4:00 p.m., and Greg presented his information first. "Well, starting with the weight room, I think the best way to do it would be to blow out all three cinder block exterior walls and build the addition with a steel structure similar to what I do with shops and sheds. It's cheaper than using traditional construction materials, and it goes up in a hurry. Okay, I've got a ballpark figure for you—so the basics, standard cement floor, steel frame, block in insulation and sheet rocked, wired for electricity; let's see, you're looking at being able to do that for about $20 a foot. If you're gonna do this, you might as well make it big enough. You have the room to go out to 30 feet to the east, and about the same on the width. So Luke and I figured 30 by 30, or 900 square feet. That would be a nice sized room," he said, adding with a laugh, "Better than the 200 feet you got now, right Luke?"

"No kidding," replied Luke. "That would be awesome."

"So," continued Greg, "at 20 bucks a foot that's around 18 grand. Now remember, I'm not including anything in here about a floor covering—like if you want to tile it, or whatever. I'm also not figuring anything for heat, as I'd have to take a look at the capacity of your current old boiler to heat the additional 700 feet. I'm also not including the cost of knocking down the old walls and disposing of the materials. So again, ballpark of 18 Gs for the basic structure.

Now for the crow's nest—it's not really as simple as throwing up some telephone poles and putting a ladder up to the platform. I did some checking and that wouldn't meet State Code, so you'd have to tin the exterior and have a lockable door to gain entry to the interior. The ladder up to the platform would have to be on the inside. Anyway, to purchase four telephone poles of 24-foot lengths would be 300 bucks a pole, or $1200 total. You'd obviously have to frame and brace it to put on the tin, so all that, including the platform and the tinned roof is going run you about another four grand. Burying 24-foot telephone poles isn't your standard post setting either, so we'll need to bring in the same kind of big auger to dig them that Montana Power uses in setting their poles. Not counting that, let's see... minimum five Gs for the crow's nest," Greg concluded.

"But," the affable builder said with a smile, "this is small town America, right? So I'm gonna give you all the materials at cost—no mark-up from my end at all. And we'll use the Booster Club and the Lion's Club for some free labor, which means there won't be any expense for the demolition of the old weight room. And I've already approached our in-town Montana Power guy, Gary Pemberton, and he's pretty sure Montana Power will donate the poles. We'll probably have to pay an hourly rental fee for the use of their auger, but Gary can run it at no charge. I'll also have plenty of volunteer help in framing and putting the tin on the crow's nest, so that'll knock the hell out of my labor costs. When taking all the volunteer help into consideration, I think to be on the safe side you should figure on the crow's nest running about four grand, and another 18 for the basics of the steel building. It should come in less than that, but better to plan for the unexpected… you know how these things go sometimes."

"Okay, Okay," said Edna. "Thanks a million, Greg, for putting all this together on such short notice. We'll let you get back to something you're actually getting paid for," said Edna with a smile.

As soon as Greg departed, Edna turned to Luke and asked, "Do you have the figures on the cost of the football gear and weight room equipment?"

"Yes, the guy from Universal Athletics was really helpful. I'm afraid the football helmet and equipment expense is pretty high. We'll need about $3,500 to get up to speed," reported Luke, noting the raised eyebrows of both Edna and Lester. "And the weight equipment doesn't get any prettier. About $6,500 to buy the weight sets and an upgraded Universal Gym. But that figure also includes some mats we will need to put down on the floor, regardless of whether we tile over the cement or not. We need the mats to do certain exercises, including some of the speed and agility aids that I was telling you about. So pretty much ten grand to cover it all."

"Alright," sighed Edna, as she tallied up the expense of Luke's demands. "We're looking at four plus 18 plus ten…so $32,000. Let me see what you guys came up with for a class schedule." She took a few minutes to review the schedule they had prepared.

"Well, that looks fine to me. And Luke, are you clear on what you'll have to do over the rest of the summer to meet our requirements to teach Montana History?"

"Yes, I understand now what I need to do."

"It's 4:40 right now. I had Lester's secretary, Lois, come down and revise the contract to include the conditions you requested, Luke. I further commit to you that we will come up with the money to satisfy the dollar amount it will take to complete the addition, crow's nest and all your equipment requests. I will honestly tell you that the funding will have to be a collaborative effort between the school and private sources. I ask that you trust me when I say that I can and will get this done. I ask that you sign this contract based on my word that I'll get all of this funded."

Upon an affirmative nod from Lester, his expression telling Luke that he had no doubt that Edna would deliver, Luke replied, "I trust that you will be true to your word, Edna."

With that, Edna got up from her chair and stepped over a snoring Otis to slam the revised contract and a pen in front of Luke. While desperately trying to hide a growing smile, she emphatically barked, "Then sign this Goddamn contract before you dream up something else we need to provide for you!"

MADISON DANIELSEN'S INTERVIEW

It had been exactly one week since he and Edna had interviewed and stamped Luke's signature on the football and History openings. Now Lester had to sit next to Edna and interview Madison Danielsen, the only qualified candidate they had for the girls' basketball, volleyball and Math positions. There was actually one other applicant for the girls' basketball job, a twenty-something housewife from Deeden who had most recently coached their Jr. High girls' team. When Lester called Deeden's Athletic Director to get some background information on her, he had laughed and said they would be happy to pass her off to Pacer Coulee. He said that being an obnoxious screamer who was despised by kids, parents and fans alike were her good points, and that she was mad as a hatter at him for not renewing her coaching position. Laughing even louder, he had remarked that the inhabitants of Deeden would have him pistol whipped at high noon in front of the Deeden Pub and Grill if he would have hired her back.

The irony of sitting in on an interview of a candidate to fill the coaching positions he had just been fired from was not lost on Lester. But if that same irony registered with Edna, you wouldn't know it. It was as if he was already a distant memory, long since buried away in some forgotten cemetery alongside countless other nameless and discarded coaches. Despite the initial embarrassment and sting of being let go from the job, Lester was surprised at how relieved he actually felt to not be coaching his daughters. Coaching one of your kids was not an uncommon circumstance but coaching three of them as he did the prior year, and all four if he were to continue, would be a recipe for disaster. He hated to admit it, but Edna was right. It was better for him, his girls and the team for him to step away.

Because of the involvement of all four of his girls in basketball, not to mention his own passion for the sport, Lester was anxiously awaiting the upcoming interview. He had thoroughly vetted the young woman, had called every reference, and followed up on every concern and question that came up along the way. Although she didn't cause quite the 'OVERQUALIFIED' red light to flash to the same degree as Luke, she was certainly capable of leading the Bulldog girls' program.

Madison Danielsen had grown up in Whitewater, a tiny town in northeastern Montana. Much like Wyngate, Whitewater was noted for almost always producing top basketball teams. Lester's research indicated that she had been a star player for the Penguins all four of her high school years, and was a solid performer for Rocky Mountain College in Billings, where she earned a Math and Education Degree and graduated with Honors. For the next eight years she bounced around the Billings area, serving as the Junior Varsity coach and varsity assistant for three years at each Class B Shepherd and Class A Laurel. She then moved on as the head coach in both basketball and volleyball for two years at Class C Fromberg, taking her basketball team to the State Tournament in her second year.

But oddly, after her successful two year tenure at Fromberg, she abruptly left the teaching and coaching profession in favor of a position as the Executive Secretary to the CEO of a large petroleum corporation in Billings; the job she still currently held.

Lester thought it fortuitous that he knew two of Madison's references quite well. The first one was James Drew, now the Athletic Director at Bozeman High School, but a Principal and AD at Laurel when Madison was there. He had nothing but good things to say about her as a teacher, coach and person. If he knew anything as to why she left teaching and coaching these past two years, he didn't disclose it. The second reference was Marcella Connor, the longtime women's basketball coach at Rocky Mountain College. She had coached Madison all four of her years there, and since she was currently recruiting Lester's oldest daughter Sonya, she promptly returned Lester's call.

"What's up, Lester?" asked Marcella. "I hope you're calling to inform me that Sonya wants to commit right now."

Lester laughed and replied, "Well, I know you're right up there at the top of the list, but I'm actually calling you regarding Madison Danielsen. As you probably know, she has applied for the girls' job here and has listed you as one of her references."

Coach Connor went on to strongly recommend her former player, raving about her character and work ethic. Marcella had also closely followed her coaching career and dubbed her as a natural who not only understood the Xs and Os, but was a good communicator and even better role model for her players. Lester thanked her for her honest assessment of Madison as a candidate. But there was one more thing that he needed to ask. "To be truthful Marcella, there is one thing that we are curious about. Do you know the reason why she took a two year hiatus from teaching and coaching, and furthermore, why she has now decided to come back to it?"

After a bit of a pause, Marcella replied. "I'm not 100% sure of the details, but I do know she had a rough stretch in her marriage. As you probably know, she has a daughter. She would be ten or 11 now, I think. When her husband left them she felt like she needed to take a higher paying job to provide more security for her and the daughter. I spoke with her shortly after the divorce decree was finalized three or four months ago, which clarified the degree of child support that the ex would have to pay. She told me then that, despite the better pay from her new job, she missed teaching and coaching terribly and felt like she could go back to it now that she knew where she stood financially post-divorce. I'll be frank with you, Lester—she would have likely gotten either the Shepherd or Laurel head job if she had applied, but she decided she wanted to start anew outside of the Billings area. Pacer Coulee fit that bill, plus it puts her closer to her parents up in Whitewater. Of course, I put in a pitch for you guys by telling her she would be coaching some mighty fine talent in the four Brewster girls."

It didn't take more than a few minutes of interviewing Madison for both Edna and Lester to be impressed with their only candidate for the Math and girls' basketball and volleyball positions. Madison was an attractive 5'11", 33-year-old woman with shoulder length, light brown hair. She presented with a pleasant and outgoing demeanor, her face brightened frequently by a warm and engaging smile.

"Such a handsome boy!" exclaimed Madison when Otis struggled to his feet and waddled over to greet her. "Is he your mascot?"

"Sure is," replied Edna proudly. "Meet Otis Othello Coffman, VII. The seventh of a long line of Sherman Tank English Bulldog lineage descendants to lead the Pacer Coulee Bulldogs into battle. He doesn't take to just anybody he meets, like he has you. You don't happen to have experience with a bulldog, do you?"

"No I don't. We always had cattle dogs when I was growing up. Blue Heelers, to be specific. Like most ranch kids, I was raised around animals. I grew up on a horse and did the whole County Fair 4-H thing, starting with show pigs and graduating to steers and heifers," explained Madison. Her face lighting up in a big smile, she leaned forward and said with a feigned air of importance and braggadocio, "I'll have you know, I was back-to-back Phillips County Fair Swine Showmanship Champion in third and fourth grades!"

Even Edna burst out in laughter at that declaration, and they flowed easily into further discussion about her rural, small town upbringing. Madison and Lester then spoke at length about her playing days at Rocky Mountain College for coach Connor. After discussing her coaching experience at Shepherd, Laurel and Fromberg, Madison's expression turned serious as she changed to a different subject.

"I'm sure you are wondering, as you should be, why I suddenly up and left the teaching and coaching profession for these past two years. Let's just say I made a poor choice in a marriage partner. And if you could, I'd prefer to leave it at that. I hope you will understand and respect my wishes to keep the unsavory details of my failed marriage private. That being said, you do deserve to know that the main reason I changed careers was purely financial. Again, I don't care to go into much detail here, but suffice it to say that my ex refused to contribute financially to the expense of raising our child during the divorce process. Without knowing to what degree of child support, if any, the court would mandate from him in the final decree, I felt compelled to take a higher paying job to ensure that I could support my daughter in the event the ruling went against me. Fortunately, the divorce decree demanded that he step up to the plate and pay his fair share. And that fair share was in an amount sufficient for me to go back to the job that I love, and that is teaching and coaching at the high school level."

"We totally understand your concerns for privacy Madison," said Lester, glancing at Edna in a hopeful search for any sign of agreement with his statement. "Providing for our families is obviously our main priority."

"Yes, that is understandable, indeed," confirmed Edna. "But I do think it is fair game for us to ask this: are there ongoing issues related to your divorce that could negatively impact your focus and ability to perform your duties as a teacher and a coach at the high level we demand here at Pacer Coulee?"

Lester grimaced in his mind's eye, thinking, *Yes Madison, it is because of these lofty standards and high expectations that you were the only person besides that nut-job over at Deeden to have enough courage to actually apply for this position.*

"Yes, that is a fair question, Ms. Coffman. I will be very forthright on this with you. Yes, there are ongoing issues with my ex-husband as it pertains to our daughter. Again, I would prefer to not get into those details, but I can tell you that those issues will not deter me from carrying out my teaching and coaching responsibilities to the best of my ability."

"That's what I needed to know, and thank you for your honesty," replied Edna. "One other question, Madison. At the risk of making Lester uncomfortable, the fact is that his daughters, all four of them, essentially represent the entire talent pool of this team. Sorry to have to say this Lester," Edna said, with a quick wave of her hand towards Lester, "but the Brewster sister rivalry and pettiness was the downfall of our team last year. I would like to hear if you have any experience in dealing with sibling rivalry, and if so, how you would intend to deal with the Brewster sister situation."

As the hues of embarrassed red spread from his neck to his face, Lester thought to himself, *'Don't be silly Edna. Why on earth would you think slamming me and my daughters in front of my coaching replacement could possibly make me uncomfortable? No need to be sorry for such a minor slight. Why, I was hoping you'd finish out this interview by properly scorning and admonishing me for my grievous parental and coaching sins by stripping me naked and taking the bull whip to me in front of my successor.'*

Casting a surprised and sympathetic glance towards Lester, Madison said, "Well Ms. Coffman, let me first take my hat off to Lester for even attempting to coach three, rather long four, of his own daughters. You're either a saint or a fool for attempting such a thing," she said with a laugh.

"Let me further say that girls, siblings or not, present a special challenge to a coach. Not to say that guys don't have their jealousies and spats, but such disagreements usually come to head rather quickly. They either work it out or duke it out, and then it's over and done with and everybody moves on. Girls? Not so much. They can and will carry on their petty jealousies and spats for weeks—even months. They are also capable of holding a grudge pretty much into perpetuity," declared Madison, again lighting up the room with her engaging smile and laugh.

"Have I had any experience with sibling rivalry? Yes, yes I have. Whitewater is a very small town—smaller than even Pacer Coulee—and for many years both our boys' and girls' basketball teams were primarily made up by just a handful of families. In my era, there were four Hamlin brothers that farmed in our county. The family sizes were six, seven, and two of them had eight. They were roughly divided equally between boys and girls, so it seemed like there were always either sisters or brothers on the same team, and most certainly a conglomerate of cousins.

In many instances, there would be five Hamlins on the floor at the same time. At tournaments, the radio announcer would just go by first names, "Bob passes to Frank, Frank passes to Art, Art passes to Carl, Carl passes to Jim... Jim shoots and scores!" For the most part during my 18 years there, the female siblings and cousins got along well and were generally supportive of one another. However, there were also a few situations where the sibling rivalry was not healthy, and deep jealousies and divisions were apparent and it negatively affected our team. Try as he might, I think our high school coach literally tore his hair out in trying to figure it out. In his defense, I don't think that even Pat Summitt herself could have smoothed over that particular sibling mess.

"Then I played with two sets of sisters during my college years at Rocky. One set was great. Their play complemented each of their skill sets, and they were supportive of one another and their teammates. The other one was a nightmare. Coach Connor, who has way more coaching knowledge and strategies on how to deal with players than I'll ever have, finally cut one of the sisters from the team to solve the problem. Easier to do at the college level, and practically impossible to do in high school— especially at a small Class C school. So, to truthfully answer your question as to how I would handle the Brewster sister situation? With all due respect Ms. Coffman, I would not approach this with any kind of bias or preconceived notion, whether it be from you or anyone else. To be fair to everyone involved, especially to the girls, I would need to take the time to independently observe and evaluate the interactions and dynamics of the entire team, not just the Brewster girls. If and when the melding of personalities turned such that it elicited untoward behaviors, which invariably happens with any team at some point or another, I would address it promptly in my own way. I am a very positive person by nature, and that is my coaching style. I am not a screamer. I don't rant and rave. I strongly believe in positive reinforcement, and I believe my ability to communicate with these young ladies is a major strength of mine. That's not to say I can't be firm and demanding when circumstances require, and there will be no doubt in the girls' minds who runs the show."

Good for you Madison, thought Lester. He was becoming more enthralled with the idea of her coaching his recalcitrant daughters by the minute, and standing up to Edna and essentially stating that she would formulate her own opinions about his girls without influence almost caused him to leap to his feet and cheer. As far as Lester was concerned, they couldn't get Madison's signature on the dotted line fast enough.

Although you couldn't tell from Edna's facial expressions or body language whether she approved or disapproved of Madison's answers to her interrogation, she apparently had heard enough that she was ready to bring the interview to a close. "Well Madison, we appreciate you coming down today and interviewing for this position. Since we covered the Math position opening and your qualifications quite thoroughly in our initial telephone discussion, I don't think we need to spend further time on that subject," stated Edna as she leaned forward to earnestly summarize the status of the job opening process.

"Here's the situation. We are getting down to the finalists for this position. Rest assured that you are in the top tier of remaining viable candidates, but we still have three, maybe four more to interview over the next few days. Then, of course, Lester and I will take our recommendation to the school board for final selection and approval. Let's see... today is Wednesday, so I can say with a good degree of certainty that I'll be able to get back to you by Monday of next week with our decision. Will that work for you?"

OH.MY.GOD. Although Lester rarely used the 'F' word, he

silently mouthed to himself, '*UN-FUCKING-BELIEVABLE!*'
She's really going to play the 'we are besieged with a boat full of
highly qualified candidates' *card again*? Lester thought it an
appropriate summary to Edna's nonsense when Otis awoke with a
snort and noisily passed wind.

With all in the room pretending to not notice the lingering
foul odor, Edna and Otis bid their goodbyes to Madison. Lester
then escorted her from the building and out to her car. "Quite the
interesting boss you have there, Lester," she said with a big smile.

"Yeah, and unfortunately her bite is as bad as her bark," said
Lester with a laugh. "But as frustrated as I get with her
sometimes, she has been a legend in this school and town for over
50 years, and she's been solid as a rock in her unwavering pride
and commitment to the students and this community."

"No wonder there's so many applicants for every position that
opens up," said Madison with a wry grin that belied her belief of
Edna's claim that she had three or four more promising
candidates left to interview. "Hey, I'm not that naive. You have to
remember I come from Whitewater and have coached in
Fromberg, so I'm not unaware of how hard it is to get qualified
applicants for a small town position."

Without commenting on Edna's fibs, Lester gave her an
acknowledging look and said, "If I have anything to say about it,
which of course is very little, you will be hearing from us soon."

As Lester walked back to his office, he sincerely hoped that
Edna hadn't run Madison off with her brusque ways. He chuckled
that he was finding himself acting like his wife with his thoughts
of matchmaking Madison and Luke together. In fact, he couldn't
wait to tell Luke that the new basketball coach, or at least
hopefully the new basketball coach, was an attractive young lady
with an endearing personality. He found it sad that Edna seemed
incapable of looking beyond the business aspect of teaching and
coaching to recognize such things as personal relationships.
Perhaps that was a reason why she had never married.

When Lester entered his office, he was surprised to see Edna and Otis sitting on the visitor bench. "Well, I think we set the hook when I told her we still had additional applicants to interview. I assume you agree that we should hire her?"

"Well, I think we should wait until we interview all those highly qualified candidates that are lined up out there in the hallway before we make a final decision, don't you?" asked Lester, unable to resist throwing in a jab of his own.

Ignoring his tongue in cheek comment, she continued. "I'll wait until Friday, and then I'll call her and tell her the board has selected her and has authorized me to offer her a contract."

As she and Otis started out the door, she stopped and looked back over her shoulder and said, "Otis sure likes her. He doesn't seem that enamored with Luke, and I must say that concerns me a bit. Speaking of Luke, don't you think those two would be the perfect match? I can just see the news in Sylvia's Pacer Coulee Chronicles now, 'Handsome young Pacer Coulee coaches find love and success at Pacer Coulee High.'"

"Well I'll be damned," said Lester out loud when Edna was out of ear shot. "Will wonders never cease?"

LUKE MOVES TO PACER COULEE

Life had been more than a little bit hectic for Luke ever since he put his signature on the Pacer Coulee teaching and coaching contract. He had headed back to North Platte immediately after signing on the dotted line in front of his new bosses, arriving at his parents' home on the fifth of July. He spent a few days wrapping up some loose ends, and it hadn't taken him long to load up his belongings from the basement of his Nebraska childhood home and into the box of his pickup and the U-Haul trailer that was hitched behind it.

"I still don't know why you left Lincoln without taking at least a few pieces of furniture. That woman shouldn't have gotten anything other than the clothes on her back after what she did to you," observed Luke's mother, deflecting a *'Jesus Christ Eileen, let's not start that now'* look from her husband. It was true that he had hurriedly thrown his clothes and personal items into the back of his pickup and left within 20 minutes of walking into the scene of his ex-wife's infidelity. He had returned only once to the rented Lincoln home he had shared with his now ex-wife Lorie to gather his school and coaching materials from the spare room that had served as their office. He didn't want to be reminded of Lorie by keeping any of the furniture or household items that they had purchased together, so he retrieved only his bats, balls and golf clubs in a final pass through the house and garage before quickly exiting the premises.

After strapping down the tarp on the pickup bed and promising his parents that he would stay in frequent touch, Luke began the long trek back to central Montana. He smiled as he pulled out of the familiar driveway, admitting to himself he was feeling a similar excitement and anticipation towards his future as what he had experienced when heading off to college some 15 years prior. He turned on the radio and found a country western station. "Might as well get used to it, Luke," he said aloud, with a smile, "'cause I think you're gonna hear a bunch of it in the days ahead."

FARMERS MERCHANT BANK HAS A BOARD MEETING

70-year-old Bill Koch pulled up in front of the Farmers Merchant State Bank of Pacer Coulee at his normal 7:30 a.m. workday hour. The bank President parked his old red and white striped 1972 Ford pickup in the alley on the side of the building, where all four of the bank employees were expected to park. This left the few Main Street angle parking stalls at the front of the bank available for the customers. Since both Bonnie Cottingham and Lennis Stone, who had shared the duties of Teller and Office Operations at Farmers Merchant for 32 and 29 years, respectively, usually walked to work from their in-town homes, the limited parking space availability in the alley was not generally an issue. As usual, Bill was the first employee to arrive, and he unlocked the door and hustled to the back of the bank to enter the code to deactivate the alarm. He went back and relocked the front door, as the bank did not officially open until 8:00 a.m.

At 16 years old and in the year of 1905, Bill's father, Matthew Blaze "M.B." Koch, left Pennsylvania for the hope and promise of the reported opportunity that lay to the far west of his boyhood roots. He left home on horseback with little more than the clothes on his back, and slowly worked his way to Montana. His journey was interrupted several times by lengthy work stops, as he hired on as a cowhand at several ranches in North Dakota and eastern Montana whenever he needed to replenish his depleted canvas money sack that he kept hidden in his saddle bags. He ended up in Centertown, Montana in 1908 only by happenstance, as he was just passing through the little berg on his way to explore what he had heard to be a good business opportunity in Great Falls, the growing city that bordered the bends of Missouri River some 100 miles to the west. But Centertown, the bustling community of 2,500 residents that was comfortably nestled in the scenic valley between the Judith and Big Snowy mountains, proved too attractive to M.B. to simply pass on through. So it was Centertown where he set down his anchor and began his lifelong stay in the encompassing womb of the Judith Basin.

M.B. was an industrious young man with dreams of being a businessman, and though he only had the measly wages from his last ranch job to his name, he was able to convince the local Big Snowy National Bank to loan him enough for the down payment to purchase the Judith Mercantile. M.B. quickly proved to have business acumen beyond his years, and his reputation as a trustworthy young entrepreneur developed to the point over the next several years that C.A. Mathis, the President of the Big Snowy Bank, lent him the funds to buy the lot next to the Mercantile and expand into the lumber business.

When the 20-mile-to-the-northwest town of Pacer Coulee sprung to life in 1914 along the newly laid Milwaukee Railroad track, C.A. called M.B. into his office and suggested that he consider opening a bank in the new town. After much discussion of the value of the rich and fertile grazing and crop ground surrounding the Pacer Coulee location, and thus the excellent opportunity for a bank in the town to prosper, M.B. decided to take his advice and sold his Centertown businesses for a handsome profit and used those funds to provide what C.A. had determined as an adequate capital contribution for his *de novo* banking venture.

With a loan from C.A. and the Big Snowy National Bank, M.B. bought a well-positioned main street lot and in the spring of 1914 built his sturdy, fortress-like bank out of brick and stone. All of Centertown and the emerging towns in the Judith Basin benefited greatly in the construction arena because of the significant Croatian population that had settled in or near

Centertown. The immigrant Croats were renowned for their masonry skills, and they used sandstone and brick to erect many beautiful churches, city and county government structures, main street buildings, and a good number of residences in Centertown and throughout the Judith Basin. M.B. was able to hire Ivan Curkovic Construction (of the same extended family of master stone masons that had just recently completed the new St. Francis Catholic Church in Centertown) to build the smallish, yet aesthetically pleasing stone and brick structure. And so began the now 76-year reign of the Koch family owning and operating the Farmers Merchant State Bank.

M.B. and his wife Marcella had one child, a son born in 1920 whom they named William Frederik. Young Bill grew up in a Curkovic-constructed two story house that M.B. had built in 1916. The home sat on a hill above a gentle curve of Warm Spring Creek, an energetic stream that originated in the Snowy Mountains south of Centertown and completed its sojourn when spilling its contents into the Judith River ten miles downstream from the 80-acre Koch property.

After attending grades one through 12 in the Pacer Coulee School system, Bill graduated in 1938 and was dispatched by M.B. to a two year banking school in Chillocothe, Missouri. Bill returned in the spring of 1940 and went right to work at the bank with his father. His young banking career was abruptly interrupted less than two years later when he enlisted in the Army to join the fray that was WWII. Upon his discharge from the service when the war ended in August of 1945, Bill immediately went back to work with his father at the Farmers Merchant. Bill proved to be a worthy understudy of the shrewd and capable M.B., and by 1952 he had been elevated to Assistant Vice President and Sr. Loan Officer. He was fortunately more than prepared to take over the reins of the bank when his father died suddenly of a heart attack at his President's office desk in 1956.

Bill was a quiet and kind man, who over his 46-year stint at the Pacer Coulee bank, 34 as its President and sole owner, had more than earned the reputation that he enjoyed as a respected pillar of the community. Much as his father did, he took the responsibility that came with being a small town banker very seriously. As M.B. used to tell him when he was a young loan officer, "Being the only bank in a small town is like being the only sheepherder tending to a large flock of sheep. They need to be able to count on you to protect them from the wolves and coyotes. Oh, you will inevitably lose some of the strays and stragglers along the way, but the flock needs to know you are in it with them for the long haul. Unlike the big banks that jump in and out of agricultural lending in accordance with the prevailing wind, the small town independent and locally owned bank should stand as the cornerstone of the community. In other words, son, the flock needs to know that you will stand with them, and they expect your guidance to be well-directed."

The monthly bank board meetings were scheduled for 9:00 a.m. on the third Thursday of the month. There were three directors on the Farmers Merchant State Bank Board: Bill, Joseph Patrick "Shanty" Sweeney, and Edna Coffman. The truth of the matter was that only one vote really counted, and that was Bill Koch's. When it came to the management and operation of the Farmers Merchant, much the same as it had been under his father, he was the sheriff, prosecutor, judge and the jury. Although he respected, and in fact carefully considered the opinions and the advice of both Shanty and Edna regarding loans, loan customers and other issues pertaining to the operation of the bank, the buck definitely stopped at his desk.

Shanty had been on the board for what seemed like forever, as M.B. had first asked him to serve in 1939. M.B. had also always had a board of three, so upon the death of director Charles Osburnsen in 1948, he appointed Wendell Reed to join him and Shanty to round out the count. When Wendell passed away in 1961, Bill raised the eyebrows of some of the prominent area farmers and ranchers when he appointed a woman, Edna Coffman, as Wendell's replacement.

Shanty announced his 15-minute early arrival with his usual, 'top of the mornin' to ya' greeting, and promptly occupied one of the two teller windows located within the original Mahogany teller cage to chat with Bonnie and Lennis. Edna and Otis entered the bank at precisely 9:00, and much to Edna's chagrin, Otis immediately waddled over to greet the little Irishman. Shanty dropped down to one knee to meet him, enjoying Edna's obvious irritation that the big dog was so excited to see him.

Bill held the board meeting in the small room at the rear of the bank. The room was stark, the walls adorned only with the Charlie Russell 'A Quiet Day in Utica' and 'Charles M. Russell and His Friends' prints, both framed in wide pine trim where early day Judith Basin cattlemen's brands had been burnt into the wood. There was only enough space in the room to have an old oak table that could seat a crowded six occupants. Bill took great pleasure in dispatching the bank examiners to this cramped space during their regulatory examinations in the winter, as the under capacity heating duct to the single register in the back corner of the room was an afterthought when the heater was converted from coal to fuel oil in 1969. The two windows in the room were a far cry from being hermetically sealed and insulated, and when it was -10 degrees with a not uncommon 30-knot wind swirling across Spring Creek and through town, a full Carhartt insulated pair of bib overalls, heavy gloves and a stocking cap was the fashion choice of the day if you were to survive a stay of any length in the board room.

Only the three antique oak chairs that had been fairly recently re-upholstered were at the table. As usual Bill took his seat on one side of table with Edna and Shanty on the other. Again to Edna's dismay, Otis collapsed nearer to Shanty's chair than her own. The other three chairs in the room were uncomfortable metal folding chairs, and they were neatly in the folded position and stacked against the wall, not to again be stretched out and utilized until the next crew of examiners arrived.

Bill had a standard agenda for the board meeting that contained the minimum information that the examiners expected to see in the minutes in order to determine that the board was properly informed and provided sufficient oversight of bank operations and management. Bill was Chairman of the Board, Chief Executive Officer, President, Chief Loan Officer, Chief Financial Officer, Chief Compliance Officer, HR Director, Chief-Chief-Chief ad nauseum. Such was the nature of small, independent banks, as due to their small asset size they had to run lean to make a respectable profit. But that fact didn't stop the bank examiners from criticizing the concentration of power. Since it was simply illogical, impractical and fiscally impossible to expect small banks to have the widespread employee numbers to effect proper audit and control, Bill had learned that keeping minutes that demonstrated robust director involvement and oversight was vital to offsetting their concerns about the concentration of power that lay in his hands.

Bill greatly enjoyed and looked forward to each and every board meeting. It was a welcomed break in his usual routine to spend a couple of hours watching the traveling circus show that was Edna and Shanty. There was a pattern to the meeting, and it never deviated. The initial stages of the meeting were always pleasant enough, with all three directors engaging in the conversation that was focused on all things affecting agriculture. Weather was always a priority item of discussion, as were local and national commodity prices.

But inevitably, the congenial discussion about weather and general agricultural conditions would turn less agreeable. Like two heavyweight boxing contenders at the weigh-in before a title fight, either Edna or Shanty would invariably jut out their chest and crowd the other, turning the previously civil press conference into a pushing and shoving match. It was as if Bill had assumed the role of the wild haired boxing promoter Don King, sandwiched between two behemoth pugilists, futilely trying to separate them as the scuttle escalated.

Although Bill's political views leaned heavily in Edna's conservative direction, he never interjected his personal opinions one way or the other, nor did he participate in the ofttimes heated frays. He would simply lean back in his chair with a slightly amused 'let the games begin' expression on his face and enjoy the sparring match. His head would bob to the right, then to the left, and back and forth he would go as though he was watching a Connors/McEnroe tennis match volley.

Any independent observer of a nasty Edna/Shanty verbal exchange would think the two hated each other, but nothing could have been further from the truth. While both were fiery and opinionated individuals who weren't shy about expressing their points of view, they truly considered the other as a dear friend, each holding their arguing partner in high personal regard.

On this particular day, Shanty threw the first punch. "Well Edna, I suppose you big, rich ranchers aren't going to like it very much if George H.W. breaks his promise to the fat cat Republicans and goes along with the tax hikes in the proposed Budget Reconciliation bill, huh?"

"That's what I love about you Democrats, JoePat," replied Edna, with a 'here we go again' kind of bite to her tone. Edna frequently referred to a person by both first and middle names when making a point in a serious conversation, and Shanty always graduated from 'Shanty' in the non-controversial portion of the meeting to 'JoePat' when things got heated. Bill presumed that Edna found using the full 'Joseph Patrick' handle to be tedious and time consuming when engaging in verbal warfare with the old Irishman, and had modified it to the shorter JoePat as a matter of expediency.

"You always love to raise everybody's taxes in order to pay

for all your pet social programs and otherwise reckless government spending. But one thing I've noticed about you and your liberal friends, JoePat, is that you are only in favor of tax increases when they apply to those in the tax bracket just above yours. You Dems need to change your motto of 'Spread the Wealth' to 'Spread Everyone Else's Wealth Except Mine.'"

It didn't take much to raise the ire of the little Irishman, and his face had already taken on a bright red hue as he stammered and stuttered to formulate his response. "Well... well... by damn, here's what's wrong with you Republicans. You cave into the lobbyists for the rich and corrupt big corporations and insurance companies that run roughshod over us little people— those of us in the middle and lower class. Thank God we have the organized Unions to protect the little guy from the greedy big corporations!" spat Shanty.

"Ha, that's a good one, JoePat," Edna fired back. "Speaking of greedy and corrupt, the Unions rule the roost of all that is greedy and corrupt, and they steal your eggs from the hen house right under your Goddamn Democrat nose! The worst day in my long career in education was when the damn State mandated that we had to join the Teachers' Union. Talk about running roughshod over the little people, JoePat; forcing millions of unwilling employees to join any kind of organization is downright un-American in my view. And what did the Union ever do for me other than take 75 bucks out of every damn one of my measly paychecks? Their claim to fame is that they guaranteed tenure for the teachers. What does that mean? I'll tell you what it means. It means that, unlike the rest of business world, JoePat, where one actually has to perform a job at some kind of competent level to ensure continued employment, in the Teachers' Union world you are pretty much guaranteed a job once you reach tenured status, regardless of performance. That's right, if your tenured High School Math teacher's students can't come up with the answer to two plus two before they graduate, what happens to them? Nothing! That's what happens. They can't fire you. I've got a couple of teachers at the school right now that should be fired on the spot. We're doing a huge disservice to our students, school and community by continuing to ignore their incompetence, but the school board can't touch them because of your Union protections. What the hell kind of incentive does such allowed ineptitude provide to the many serious teachers that take pride in their work and perform at a high level? About as much incentive as it gives a small businessman like Bill or myself to increase their level of productivity when you damn Democrats raise taxes and take all their hard earned profit away from them anyway."

"That's just not true about the Unions!" shouted Shanty, crouched on the edge of his chair like a Missouri River breaks mountain lion in final launch position to take down an unsuspecting white tail deer. "What would have happened to the poor miners in Butte when the greedy Anaconda Company forced them to work long hours in unsafe conditions? Do you think they would have ever got a fair wage and improved working conditions without the unions? Hell no, they wouldn't have!" roared Shanty, now all the way off his chair with the few strands of white hair that he had on his glowing red scalp standing straight up on end. "And those dirty Anaconda Company bastards had their goons gruesomely murder Frank Little in 1917 for trying to organize the miners so that they had a say in their wages and safety. Murdered him, they did… the dirty bastards!"

Bill smiled to himself at the reference to Butte. Shanty was a widely cherished school and community relic and was long since retired from his 40-year stint as the Station Agent on Pacer Coulee's Old Milwaukee line. Most all of the little towns in central Montana had sprung up in the 1912-15 era as a result of the rail line that was being constructed across the central and eastern plains of Montana to create a rail transportation corridor connecting the country's middle section to the Pacific Ocean. The practice of having Station Agents located at 30 to 40 mile intervals in the small, rural towns of the Dakotas and Montana was maintained until the late '60s and early '70s, when passenger trains became specialized into large, government subsidized carriers like Amtrak. Improved efficiencies of transporting cargo and more cost effective methods of having fewer and more centralized track maintenance locations eliminated the need for the multitude of small town Station Agents.

At 20 years widowed, Shanty had kept himself busy and his mind active by throwing himself into the school and community. He had driven a regular school bus route ever since retiring from the railroad, and despite being a lousy driver, he was the students' top pick to escort them to out of town sporting and other school-related events.

But somehow all conversations with Shanty were eventually funneled back into the lap of the historical and cultural melting pot that was his hometown of Butte, America. Shanty was the seventh of nine children born to miner Kevin Patrick and Mary Katherine Sweeney, and was raised in Butte's rough and tumble Irish borough of Dublin Gulch. Butte was born as a mining camp in the 1860s, as the Silver Bow Creek valley location sitting high against the Great Continental Divide of the Rocky Mountains held more than just the promise of vast silver and gold deposits. The discovery of Butte's massive inventory of copper, buried deep in the belly of its hillsides, quickly grew the town exponentially due to the demand for copper for its critical use in the newest technology of the day—electrical power. The influx of immigrant miners to extract the vast deposits of ore was astounding. Butte soon became a gigantic pot of cultural stew, with the recipe calling for the mixed and varied ingredients of the Irish, Italians, Germans, Serbs, Croats, Austrians, Finns, Celts and Chinese, to name a few. For each ethnic group of notable presence was their own neighborhood.

For the Irish it was Dublin Gulch or Cork-Town; Centerville for the Cornish; Meaderville for the Italians and Chinatown for the Chinese. Kevin Sweeney began work in the mines in 1891 at age 16, and experienced much of the rich history of the development of Butte, to include being part of the labor force that by 1910 had made the Montana Continental Divide city the largest copper producer in North America, and second only to South Africa in world production of metals; hence its earned nickname as the 'Richest Hill on Earth.'

He also lived in the time period when the bursting-at-the-seams ore mining activity fueled Butte's staggering growth to where it became the largest city between Chicago and San Francisco. Shanty's father also bore witness to the commencement of the labor union movements that were organized to address the dangerous safety and working conditions of the miner workforce. Butte was pegged the 'Gilbraltar of Unionism' due to its exerting union activity.

Kevin and two of his miner brothers were at the forefront of the labor union activism, working tirelessly to improve working conditions and wages for them and their fellow miners. He was a member of the late 1800s Butte Miners Union, and then part and parcel of the internal union strife that led to the 1914 riots. The Sweeney brothers were also witness to the 1917 Granite Mountain Mine fire that cost 168 miners their lives. Shanty was nine years old at the time of that tragedy, and the event had been indelibly branded deep in the lobes of his young brain.

Shanty also vividly recalled the aftermath of the mine fire disaster, and the front row position his father and uncles took in the protests and strikes that were sparked from the incident, to include the newly formed Metal Mines Workers' Union. The Frank Little incident that Shanty always referred to in his rants with Edna was in reference to when Little came to Butte to promote the affiliation of the Metal Mines Workers' Union with the larger and more revolutionary Industrial Workers of the World. It was widely recognized in historical accounts that the Anaconda Copper Company had directed their henchmen in the killing of Little, where he was tied to an automobile and dragged for more than three miles before being hanged from a Milwaukee Road trestle on Centennial Street, all to make a statement to the miners and their union.

"Goddammit JoePat, you always go back to this! Even when it doesn't have a thing to do with what we're talking about. You know damn well I am fully aware of the mining history in Butte, and although I didn't live it like you and your family did, I certainly recognize that the Anaconda Company was corrupt and greedy, and that the organization of a labor union was absolutely essential to force the large corporation to improve working conditions and pay a fair wage. You try to make it sound like I would have sided with the Anaconda Company back then, and Goddammit, I wouldn't have," she shouted at Shanty. "What you can't seem to get through your thick skull is that those events, while again recognizing how these historical events impacted you as a youngster, happened 73 years ago. It's a different time now, JoePat... different time and a different place."

"Well, we best get to the bank business," Bill interjected before the fiery Irishman could retaliate, deciding it was time to ring the bell and send the two heavyweights to their respective corners and take off the gloves until the next meeting. Bill was also cognizant of the Sweeney family curse—some kind of genetic heart defect that took lives before their time with regularity within the extended family. As such, Bill was always careful to steer the discussion in another direction when Shanty appeared to be getting too worked up or stressed.

It didn't take long to go through the bank agenda, as Bill led them through the previous month-end Financial and Income Statements and then gave a brief summary of the loans that were made during that month. Bill didn't spend much time on explaining the bank's efforts to stay in compliance with the ever increasing regulatory compliance burden, rightly figuring that as long as the bank was well run, profitable and able to serve the Pacer Coulee community's needs, Edna and Shanty would consider their Board Director oversight to be adequate.

And take care of the community needs Bill Koch did. Edna knew Bill better than anyone in central Montana, save for his wife Marge. Edna had returned to Pacer Coulee at age 20, with her Teacher's Certificate from the Normal College of Great Falls proudly in her possession. She began her lengthy career as the English instructor at Pacer Coulee Schools, but two years later her father Claude died suddenly from a heart attack. With her younger sister, Harriet, still finishing the teaching program at the same Great Falls college, Edna was suddenly saddled with the responsibility of managing the sizable farm and ranch that Claude had slowly and meticulously built from the ground up, starting with his first 160-acre homestead property.

Although he was two years behind her in school, Edna knew Bill from the Pacer Coulee school days. Fresh from banking school, Bill had just returned to work for his father at the bank, and since M.B. seemed very intimidating to the young 22 year old, Edna was more than relieved when the elder banker brought in son Bill to their first meeting regarding the handling of her father's estate.

"Young lady, I've been your dad's banker for many years now, and a finer and wiser man I've never had the pleasure of knowing," said M.B. "I'm very sorry for your loss. Now you of course know my son Bill, and like you, he's a young whippersnapper who's not yet dry behind the ears when it comes to banking or the business world. Both of you have a lot to learn here. You need to figure out how to best manage a large agricultural operation, and Bill needs to learn how to be your adviser and loan officer.

"Make no mistake that I'm going to oversee every detail down to the proverbial gnat's ass in the game plan we're going to develop for you, as I owe it to my friend Claude to make damn sure you don't drop the ball on everything it took him years to build. But Bill here is going to be your loan officer, and you two are going to work together to develop a plan for the administration of your dad's estate and the management of its assets," M.B. concluded with a very stern, knowledgeable and matter-of-fact look on his face. "I look at this as a great learning opportunity for the both of you, and I'll walk you through it step by step. How does that sound?"

"Thank you, sir," said Edna, with visible relief showing on her face and in her voice. "I'll need all the help I can get, and I look forward to working with both of you in order to continue my father's legacy at the ranch. I won't let him down, and I won't let you down, sir, lest I die trying."

And so began the 50-year business relationship and developing friendship between Edna and Bill. With M.B.'s careful and sage guidance, the two youngsters crafted a plan for Edna to lease the 4,500 farm ground acres to her Uncle Clarence, and employ another local born and bred rancher and former classmate to tend to the feeding, calving, haying, fencing and all other matters relating to the 350-head cattle operation. With the exception of Bill's four year hiatus from the bank during WWII, he was her trusted adviser and lender. The respect between the two of them was mutual, as Bill admired the work ethic and business acumen it took to not only be a top rate educator, but to oversee and manage such a large agricultural enterprise. Edna was surprised and extremely honored when Bill asked her to sit on his bank board in 1961 when longtime M.B. era descendant board member Wendell Reed passed away. It was almost unheard of in that era for a woman to sit on any board in any small, rural agricultural town, and though his selection of Edna was unintended as a statement or promotion of women's rights or advancement, it caught the eye of the heretofore male dominated leadership and governance of town businesses and organizations. Her appointment to this critical town business opened the doors to the idea that women were more than capable and worthy of consideration to effectively contribute to any business or community organization from their boardroom. By 1970, Edna had been asked to sit on the Pacer Coulee Farmers Elevator Co-op board, as well as co-chairing with Kellie Cassidy on the Pacer Coulee Volunteer Fire and Ambulance department. Upon Bill's recommendation in 1980, she was asked to represent the Pacer Coulee area on the Central Montana Medical Facility board. This 40-bed Centertown located facility was the only hospital between Billings and Great

Falls, and was critical to the care and convenience of all of Central Montana.

Other than Marge, Edna and Shanty were the only ones who knew Bill's impactful financial commitment to the Pacer Coulee school system and community. If a farmer or rancher was honest and hard working, Bill would go more than the extra mile to stick with him through the inevitable tumultuous swings in the agricultural economy. Whether it be devastating weather events or wild fluctuations of commodity prices, Bill was there for the long run. He seldom had a failed agricultural credit, and over his many years at the bank you could count on one hand the times he had to initiate a foreclosure or collateral sale.

Bill also took great care of the non-agricultural townsfolk in Pacer Coulee. Like his father before him, he was the steward for all the elderly widows in town. He did their tax preparation, oversaw and guided them through any trusts or leases that might need administered to, advised them on all matters insurance or financial—all for free, refusing to take any compensation for his time other than gratefully accepting the homemade pies that frequently came his way after rendering a service. He considered it a bank obligation to serve the community's needs for consumer loans—the car loans, washer and dryer loans, short term 'catch up with my bills until the tax refund gets here' kind of loans. Much as he would do in the agricultural loan arena, if a customer was honest and hard working, Bill would quietly make a delinquent monthly loan payment or two for them to help out folks that might have run into temporary hard times. "Don't tell anybody what I'm doing," he'd say to the fortunate customer, "because I can't afford to be doing this for everybody." And if a person simply didn't qualify for a bank loan but was of the character that Bill considered to be trustworthy, he'd make the loan to them personally. Edna was also aware of several situations where Bill would anonymously cover for grocery store purchases or meals at the local cafe. She knew for a fact that the old widow Hazel Folke didn't have enough money to pay her utility and grocery bills, and Bill took care of both. The owner of the grocery store, in a hushed, secretive tone, had told Edna on several occasions about Bill paying the grocery bill for needy townsfolk. "Don't you dare tell anybody! Bill made it very clear I was not to tell anybody where the money came from," she would say. Edna also knew that Tank ate three meals a week at the Calfe' that were paid for in advance by Bill, and that he also gave a monthly stipend to Kellie Cassidy to feed him supper the other four days. All were told to keep his donations under wrap, as he never wanted anyone to know who the benefactor was. Edna always marveled at his unwavering support for the school and community. Being a director, she knew how much the bank had donated each year, and to say it was substantial would have been a gross understatement. She had no idea how much he did personally, but assumed it was more than generous. She also found it amusing that Bill was so naive as to think his philanthropy could remain anonymous. As a lifelong Pacer Coulee resident, he of all people should have known that the lid could never stay secure atop the secret bin in a small town.

After the bank business portion of the meeting was concluded, the final subject addressed at every board meeting was always the same: an update from Edna on the state of the Pacer Coulee school system. Typically the conversation would lead to the performance of the Bulldogs in the current season sports events.

"So I hear you hired a new football coach?" asked Bill, as he lit up another Camel cigarette.

"We did, but you won't live to see him coach his first game if you keep sucking on those damn things. Don't you know that there is an emerging uprising on the horizon, and count me as among the most arduous proponents, to get our State Legislature to pass a no smoking ordinance that would apply to all public buildings—like bars and restaurants—and yes Bill, that would include banks."

"I get daily smoking lectures from the Sheriff, so I don't need you adding your two bits," Bill said, using his stock reply to Edna's monthly board meeting admonishment of his smoking habit. Shanty just sat back and grinned, always tickled when Edna was brandishing her irons at someone other than him. He also had a chuckle every time Bill referred to his wife Marge as 'the Sheriff.' Shanty was very fond of Marge, as she and Shanty's wife Jeri had been best friends for many years. Marge was Shanty and Jeri's Rock of Gibraltar during Jeri's long-suffering death journey from cancer more than twenty years ago, and he still gratefully accepted the long standing invite to join her and Bill at their house for a homemade breakfast immediately following the every-other-Sunday 8:00 a.m. mass at Pacer Coulee's St. Anthony's parish.

"So again, before I was so rudely interrupted, who is the new coach and where is he from?" asked Bill.

"His name is Luke Carter, and he comes to us from Nebraska. He is 34 years old and grew up in North Platte, NE, where he was an All-State quarterback for a school that would be comparable in size to one of our largest Class AA schools. He played collegiately for Nebraska Southern in Grand Island, which is a member of the Missouri Valley Conference and in the same division as our Bobcats and Grizzlies. He played for Sonny Sweden, the legendary Nebraska Southern All-American offensive lineman who was also an All-Pro left tackle for the Steelers for six seasons until injuries to both knees forced his retirement."

Bill was always amazed at Edna's grasp of all matters sports. It didn't matter if it was football, basketball or baseball, or if it was high school, college or professional. She was a walking sports trivia encyclopedia. The only person in town or at school that could maybe even be visible in her sports knowledge rear view mirror would be upcoming freshman Earl Wonderwald, and the two of them would converse at length in a spirited attempt to claim one-up-manship on the other.

"Anyway," Edna continued, "Luke played for Sonny and

was an All-Conference quarterback his Junior and Senior years at Nebraska Southern. After a couple of years serving under coach Sweden as a Grad Assistant, he was hired onto the Lincoln High School staff as a History teacher and the quarterbacks' and receivers' coach. He stayed in that capacity for three years, and was then promoted to the Offensive Coordinator. In doing a little research, I found that Lincoln High has consistently been one of the top football programs among the big high schools in Nebraska. Furthermore, under Luke as the Offensive Coordinator, Lincoln led their conference in total offense every year he was the coordinator, and a good number of his offensive kids went on to play college ball, including one of his quarterbacks and a wide receiver that signed with the Cornhuskers."

"Jesus Edna, what the hell does a kid with these kind of accomplishments have lurking in his past that he's applying for a Class C 8-man coaching position in the middle of nowhere Montana?" asked Bill, incredulous over the young coach's credentials.

"Well hell, Bill! Who wouldn't want to come to a tradition-rich school like Pacer Coulee?" interjected Shanty, making fun of Edna's unwavering stance that coaching the Bulldog football team would be coveted by coaches nationwide. "I heard that Tom Landry hisself was thinking of coming out of retirement when he heard that the Pacer Coulee position was open—and rumor has it that this is the only job that could entice Dennis Erickson to leave the University of Miami Hurricaines."

"Oh, keep your smart alec remarks to yourself, Shanty!" Edna snapped, but with a grin tugging on her lips. "Okay, okay, there is more to this story. In a nutshell, Luke had some major personal problems with his wife, or now his ex-wife as I understand it. He quit his teaching and coaching job at Lincoln High after whatever it was that happened between them. Sounds like he just needed to get out of town and try and get his head straight, so he's spent the last few years up in Casper driving an oil tanker. As it turns out, our very own Superintendent Lester

Brewster was coach Sweden's roommate at Nebraska Southern. They still keep in regular touch, and when they were chatting last month Lester was lamenting over the lackluster response to our football coach posting, and apparently coach Sweden suggested that taking an out of state job in a small town might be just what the doctor ordered in giving Luke a fresh start and a renewed purpose in life. Anyway, the word is that Sweden tracked Luke down and convinced him he was wasting his life away working in the oil fields and needed to return to his love of teaching and coaching. Next thing we knew, he'd applied for the job."

"So Edna, you must have had hundreds of applicants. How many did you end up actually interviewing?" asked Shanty, already knowing from attending the last school board meeting that there was only one other person that had applied, and his credentials were so weak that for all intent and purpose, Luke was the only true candidate for the position.

"Oh hush up JoePat, you are such a pain in my you know what," barked Edna, perturbed enough to revert back into 'JoePat' mode. "We did have one other applicant that we interviewed—some guy from Culbertson. Let's just say he didn't meet our high standards here at Pacer Coulee Schools, either as a teacher or as a coach."

Ever the level-headed and pragmatic one, Bill asked, "Okay, so we've got a guy who has football qualifications up the yin-yang, but that doesn't much matter if he has personal issues to the degree that he's running from his old life and all that it stood for. What was your overall impression of his stability from an emotional standpoint?"

"My general impression is that he's a good kid that temporarily lost his way due to a personal tragedy. Not a tragedy in the 'oh my God, his parents, wife and three children were brutally murdered' sense, but his perception of whatever happened between him and his 'love of my life' wife put him over the edge for a couple of years," replied Edna. "I admit that this may be a stretch. Who knows, he may bail after the first week he's here. But I do take a lot of stock in Lester's relationship with coach Sweden, and his recommendation of Luke as a football-savvy guy that just needs a little direction in his life."

"Well Edna, I trust your judgment and hope this all works out." Bill said, as he lit yet another cigarette.

"Before Otis and I die of Goddamn lung cancer from second-hand smoke, I should tell you that we also hired a new girls' basketball and volleyball coach," stated Edna.

"What about me? Aren't you worried I'm gonna die from lung cancer from Bill's smoke, too?" asked Shanty.

"Hell no, you old coot! I'm not worried a bit. You're too damn ancient and ornery to die from a little second-hand smoke. Back to my news before I was so rudely interrupted... the new coach's name is Madison Danielsen. She's a Whitewater native, and played on all those good Whitewater teams that used to compete with the great Wyngate teams back in the late '70s for Divisional and State titles. She then played hoops at Rocky Mountain College. She's been an assistant coach at Shepherd and Laurel, and then spent two years as the head b-ball and volleyball coach at Fromberg. She really interviewed well. Plus, she has an 11-year-old daughter, so we'll add another kid to the school system."

"What the hell happened to Lester as the girls' hoop and volleyball coach?" interjected Shanty. "I thought he did a damn good job."

"Couldn't control those daughters of his," snapped Edna. "We should have gone to State in both basketball and volleyball, but his three little snots couldn't get along or play together. I agree that Lester knows his stuff, but Xs and Os don't mean much when you can't control your players. I felt like we had to make a change."

"What's this 'we' stuff? As you might recall, I'm at every board meeting. I mainly go just to see my friend Otis, here," said Shanty as he leaned over and patted the big fella just hard enough to change a snore into a snort. "Anyway, I didn't see any evidence of any other school board member wanting to give Lester the boot. So just face up to it Edna, there ain't no 'we,' only 'I' when it comes to you making sports decisions... or any decision at that school, far as that goes."

"Does this Danielsen girl have a husband?" Bill quickly asked in an attempt to defuse another flare up between his two directors.

"No, she's divorced," replied Edna, and in anticipation of Shanty's sure to be forthcoming Catholic view of divorce admonishment said, "Yes Shanty, we know divorce goes against the Pope's views on marriage. Please spare us the lecture for now, if you would."

Hurrying on before the stammering Shanty could find his retaliatory footing, Edna continued. "I'm sorry to come to you yet again, Bill, but after Luke inspected our facilities, grossly under-equipped weight room and the outdated football gear, I told him we would find a way to pay for those improvements. In fact, I basically had that promise written into the contract."

Before Bill had a chance to reply, Shanty jumped in full throttle. "Isn't that just like you, Edna! Making false promises that the school can't deliver on, and then come running to Bill and expect him to bail you out, time and again. Shame on you!"

"Well don't you worry JoePat," Edna slammed back, "I won't be asking you for a damn dime."

"Let's settle down, both of you," said Bill, not wanting to open the door to allow the start of another verbal brawl. "How much do you think you'll need to get this done, Edna?"

"Well, roughly we'll need a little over 30 grand to add on to the weight room, build a crow's nest at the field, and upgrade the football and weight room equipment. But we'll have some savings off that, as Greg is doing his part at cost, and we'll have lots of volunteer labor in building the crow's nest. I'm afraid to say that we can only cough up about four or five thousand from the athletic budget."

Shanty had calmed down a little, and inquired in a more agreeable tone, "What about the Bulldog Booster Club? Don't you have enough in that account to help out at least little bit?"

"No, unfortunately we don't," said Edna, who was also President of the Booster Club. "Even though we made a couple grand at the annual Booster function and auction last fall, we've already spent our budget for this year helping out with new uniforms for both men's and women's basketball, as well as new volleyball standards and nets. We could probably designate the proceeds from this coming fall Booster function, though."

"Well, go ahead and do what you need to do, and just let me know how much you need to cover it," said Bill. "Between a hefty bank donation and maybe a small loan to the Booster Club, we'll make it work. Happy to help."

"As always, thank you so much, Bill. I don't know what this school and community would do without you," answered Edna, then quickly added, "And don't worry Bill-if anybody asks, we'll say the funds came from that anonymous donor."

"Heck yeah, Bill, nobody in town has any inkling that all these anonymous gifts over the years came from you," said Shanty sarcastically.

"Well, one thing the whole town does know for sure is that it didn't come from any tight wad Irishman!" Edna fired back.

"Thanks Edna, I'd appreciate that," said Bill, ignoring both Shanty and Edna's previous comments. He was firm in his belief that no one would ever connect him to the donor ghost that rode the wind down the slopes of the North Moccasins, discretely dropping off its anonymous gifts with the stealth of Santa Claus before hitching a ride on a Warm Spring Creek ripple and escaping into the central Montana darkness.

EDNA HIRES LUKE TO READY THE RENTALS

Luke had been moved into the smaller of Edna Coffman's little side by side rental houses on Lehman Street for just over a week, making good use of his early, mid-July arrival by accepting Edna's proposal to do some painting and minor repair work on the two properties in exchange for two months of free rent. Edna had told him that the slightly larger, two bedroom house next door was going to be rented to the new Math teacher and girls' basketball coach, and that he needed to have the work done on that house before starting on his own, as they were moving in by end of the following week. Lester had dropped by several times to give him a hand in shoring up and re-hanging the doors on the old single stall, dirt floor garages that bordered the backyard alley of both rentals.

"I heard you the first time, Lester," assured Luke, when Lester just happened to mention for the second time that the new basketball coach was not only a very nice lady, but a quite attractive one as well. "With the collapse of my marriage and the ugly divorce process I've just gone through, jumping into any kind of new relationship is definitely not on my bucket list at the moment, but thanks for thinking of me," Luke had said.

"Okay, okay… just saying," Lester had replied, "but coach Sweden thinks you need to get jump-started in the female relationship side of your life."

Ignoring the comment that came from his old coach, Luke quickly changed the subject. "Thanks for hooking me up with Shanty down at the football field. I'm glad he likes to run that old riding lawn mower. Gives me the time to concentrate on trying to get the irrigation system down at the field up to speed. Since I don't know beans about irrigation, I sure was happy when Larry and Aaron Coslet stopped by and showed me how to get that pump fired up and how everything worked. And Larry said he'd bring a few lines of some of his old pipes down for us to get at least a little water on the practice field. With all this heat and wind we've had, it's about as hard as the asphalt parking lot at the school. Aaron said he'd grab Tank and some of the football guys to help me move the pipe, so I'm happy with the way that's going."

"Good to hear," said Lester. "At least we know we have other skills to eke out a living when Edna fires the both of us if we don't beat the Goddamn Catholics this fall."

"Yep," laughed Luke. "Maybe Sylvia will let us put our 'Irrigation and Handyman Specialists' business cards up on the bulletin board down at the Post Office."

MADISON AND ROSE MOVE IN

Luke was putting the final coat of trim paint on the A-frame eave of the front porch of his new neighbor's house when he saw a pickup pulling a huge horse trailer drive up in front of the house. He panicked for a minute, as he was sure Edna had told him that the new tenants weren't to move in until the following day. A large man wearing a John Deere baseball cap and a pleasant looking lady whom Luke assumed to be the wife stepped out of the vehicle and came up the sidewalk.

"Good afternoon. I'm Carol Danielsen, and this here is my husband Arnold," the woman said with a friendly smile as Luke came down from his step ladder. "We are Madison's parents—Madison being the new teacher and basketball and volleyball coach who's moving in here. She and our granddaughter Rose should be along any minute now."

"Hi there," said Luke, shaking her hand and then taking on the rough-scaled hand of her husband. Arnold's years-of-working-outdoors-in-the-elements weathered face slowly softened into a smile as Luke said, "Hello, hello. I'm Luke Carter, and I'm the new football coach and History teacher. I just moved into Miss Coffman's other rental house next door, and Edna asked me to do some painting and repairs on both houses. I wasn't expecting you until tomorrow, so sorry about not being done with this trim. I'll get out of your way and finish this little dab that I have left at a more convenient time. Let me know if you need an extra hand in moving anything in."

"I might just take ya up on that when we get to the heavier furniture in the back of the trailer there, Luke," said the big man. "Madison's brother was gonna come help us, but movin' some hay bales took priority today. And go ahead and finish up with this trim. Hell, you'll be over to the side and out of the way by the time we get ready to start moving stuff anyway."

Luke took Arnold's advice and was just finishing his painting as Madison and Rose pulled up to the curb. Once the introductions were made, Luke again reminded Arnold that he would continue painting in his backyard. "Just have Rose come and fetch me when you're ready to bring the furniture in. I'd be happy to help."

He scolded himself over his immediate attraction to the new basketball coach from Whitewater, trying hard to refocus on his pledge to never enter another relationship that could potentially cause a painful repeat of the past one with Lorie. Try as he might to concentrate on the painting task, the trim around his back porch door kept transforming into the image of the pretty and smiling face of his new neighbor.

EDNA TAKES LUKE TO THE HOLLISTER RANCH

Luke was sitting in the one of only two chairs in the tiny coaches' office that could be loosely labeled as an office chair. It looked as if the janitor had failed in an attempt to resuscitate the cracked and disintegrating vinyl seat by applying copious strips of Bulldog blue duct tape, finally declaring a time of death and covering the entire chair with a couple of faded yellow shower towels. Luke chuckled to himself that he should have added office furniture to his list of demands at his interview. He tried to find room for his football books and instruction videos on the shelves above the desk, but since the little office was home to not only the football coaches, but the basketball, volleyball and track coaches as well, there wasn't a spare slot to be found. He made a note to ask Lester if it would be alright if he installed another shelf above the three-hook coat rack that hung by the door.

He was interrupted by a "are you in there, Luke?" shout from outside the door, and after telling the intruder to enter was surprised to see that it was Edna. "Don't complain to me," she said, as if anticipating Luke to make a retroactive demand for a bigger coaches' office. "I was just a lowly teacher when they built this, or I would have suggested they make the coaches' room bigger than a broom closet." Luke laughed. "I just made a note to ask Lester if I could put up another shelf in here... there's just not the space to store all my stuff."

"Well, since there's nowhere to put your stuff, would you have time to take a jaunt out to see Terrance?" asked Edna. "Sure," said Luke hesitantly, curious as to why she thought he needed to see Tank. As they walked towards Edna's pickup in the empty parking lot, Luke could see that Otis was firmly implanted in his usual spot in the front bucket passenger seat, so he squeezed his 6'3" frame into the back seat of Edna's extended cab pickup. When they drove through town and received a friendly wave from every car and pedestrian they passed, Luke commented that it would take some time for him to get used to how friendly everyone was. "Yes, it's just the nature of small towns, I guess. Everybody knows everybody, and that can be positive or negative, depending upon circumstance," Edna explained. "For example, I wish to hell I didn't know Terrance Hollister, Sr., as he is the main reason I'm taking you out to see young Terrance this morning. Actually, my intent in regards to this visit is twofold; I want you to get a firsthand feel for the type of life this young man has had to this point, and to secondly give you some perspective as to what we as teachers, coaches and townsfolk are trying to do, or at least what we should be trying to do, to get this young man a better hand than what he's been dealt thus far.

"Otis doesn't really like the air conditioning blowing in his face," Edna offered, as if Luke needed to know why the big bulldog had shifted positions and now leaned across the center console to rest his head against Edna's shoulder. As far as Luke could tell, Otis had yet to acknowledge his presence in the back seat. "He likes to be scratched behind his ears," Edna suggested. Mindful of how quickly that maple bar had disappeared into his snapping jaw at his interview, Luke hesitantly reached for his huge head, thankful when the only reaction to his ear scratching was something between a deep sigh and a grunt.

"As I think was mentioned during your interview, Terrance senior is a drunk—and a drunk of the worst kind. He's a mean SOB, and quite frankly a pitiful excuse for a human being. He was physically abusive to both Terrance's mom and to him," said Edna with obvious disdain.

"Can I ask you a question before we go on? Why do you call him Terrance when everyone else seems to call him Tank?" inquired Luke.

"Because officially his name would be Terrance Jr., and he's embarrassed by that. He doesn't want to be associated in any way with his old man, and while I certainly understand that, I keep telling him he needs to show the world that Terrance Jr. is a very different man than Terrance Sr. I keep encouraging him to prove to everyone that the name Terrance can be one of honor and respect."

"Okay, I understand your reasoning there. Do I remember correctly in someone saying Tank's mother died when he was fairly young?" Luke asked.

"Yes, I think he was in the third grade when she passed. And that miserable SOB husband of hers killed her, sure as I'm living and breathing. Oh, he didn't kill her in the standard sense, as in a single incident shooting or stabbing. No, nothing like that. He killed her over time, slowly choking the life out of her one day at a time. He abused her physically, mentally, and emotionally. The dirty SOB learned where to hit her and where not to. In her last years you wouldn't see the bruising on her face that you did earlier. No, he delivered the marks of his brutality to the areas hidden by long pants and long sleeved turtlenecks. That's why he was never charged with her murder, even though most folks in the county knew that he had methodically killed her over time."

"And he physically abused Tank as well?" asked Luke.

"Oh my God, yes," Edna immediately replied, turning off the main highway and parking the pickup on the side of the gravel road leading to a set of buildings about a quarter mile away that she identified as the Hollister place. "The old man was very cautious about where he beat on Terrance too, but the kids in gym class and the gym teacher would say that he always had bruises on his shoulders, back, chest and upper arms—always where it was hidden by his clothes. When questioned he would lie, saying he got butted by a cow or a calf in the corral, or some other plausible ranch accident excuse."

Edna gently pushed Otis back into the passenger seat and turned so that she could look at him directly. "I'll never forget this. He came into my first period class one winter day when he was an eighth grader, looking like his face had been smashed in by a big rock. I couldn't believe how bad he looked, both eyes black and blue and nose and lips all cut and swollen. When asked about what had happened, he said he was driving up to the barn too fast for the icy conditions and slid into the barn door with enough impact that his head was slammed into the steering wheel. I knew it was B.S., so I had him stay after class and told him so... that I knew what was going on and that I was going to call in the sheriff. What he said next just broke my heart. He spilled his guts, telling me how his dad used to beat up his mother, and how he'd go charging at him to try and protect his mom by kicking him and hitting him with his little second grade legs and fists, only to get slapped, punched and slammed into the wall. He told me he got his recent badly bruised face from a knock-down, drag-out fight with his dad the night before. He said his dad had come home drunk as usual, and started hitting him," Edna explained, then interjecting: "You have to remember, Tank was already over 250 lbs as an eighth grader. Now, his dad is also a huge man, and had always been able to manhandle Terrance, but not that night. For the first time ever, he got the best of his dad in a fight. Not only did he beat him, but in his words, 'I kicked the livin' shit out of him, Miz E. I beat him to a pulp. You think I look bad, you oughta see him. I wanted to kill him for what he did to my mom, but I didn't. He'll still be a mean drunk, but I whupped him so bad I don't think he'll ever try to fight me again. So please don't call the sheriff. I'll just lie if you do... I'll go smash the pickup into the barn, so it will look just like I said.'

"So I told him I'd back off for now, but if it happened again I would definitely go to the authorities. I asked him why he wouldn't want the sheriff to come and put his dad in jail so that he couldn't hurt him anymore. It's hard to associate the word 'cute' when you're talking about Terrance, but if it wasn't so sad it would have been cute when he told me 'You know, Miz E, I watch TV, and I know that if they take my dad to jail they will take me away too. I'll end up in a foster home, probably in Gt. Falls or Billings, and I don't want to go there. Especially now that my dad can't beat me up anymore. So that's why I'd lie and tell the sheriff that he never hit me,'" explained Edna, with an air of caring and concern that Luke found a little surprising coming from the imposing woman.

"So here's what has happened since then. The old man, at least to my knowledge, has never tried to physically fight or abuse him since. But he's become even a meaner and more worthless drunk. When we drive the rest of the way up the lane, you'll be able to see that he does nothing on his place. He only has a half section of ground, and he's let his place literally go to the weeds. He has about 25 head of cattle, but he doesn't do anything to take care of them... doesn't put up any hay, doesn't feed or calve them. The only thing he does manage to do is to have one of his drinking buddies load up his calves in the fall and take them into the Centertown auction. But pay day on 25 calves doesn't go very far to keep him in booze and food for two.

"For Terrance's sake, any and all work that gets done tending to those 25 cows comes from me and my crew. Trust me, I make sure Terrance does most of the actual labor, but I supervise it. When his ornery old man is passed out or off drinking somewhere, I have my guys come over and swath what little decent hay there is in that field over there behind the barn. Then Kellie Cassidy brings out her little tractor and small square baler for Terrance to use to bale the hay. Terrance and Bret Cassidy clear the bales from the field on a flatbed trailer, the only still-functioning piece of machinery that old man Hollister has. The boys haul the bales and stack them by the barn. Hell, Terrance Sr. doesn't even know the stack is there. Or if he did see it, he wouldn't know how it got there. Again under the loose supervision of my crew, young Terrance feeds those cows during the winter, and calves them too, although I have my guys give him a hand with that."

Edna edged back out on the gravel and slowly started down

the lane leading to the Hollister place. "When Terrance was a freshman, our local banker Bill Koch—whom, by the way, is a man that you need to meet, as he paid for most all of the new construction and weight and football equipment that you requested... You're not supposed to know that, as he prefers that his generous support of school and community remain anonymous. Anyway, back to Bill Koch. He called Kellie Cassidy and me into the bank one day and told us that he wanted us to join him in a project to help Terrance. To make a long story short, he paid me market price to buy 15 of my older cows for Terrance. We can't run them on the Hollister place because the old man would just sell them for himself and spend it on booze, so I keep them at my place. To do my part, I have my crew feed and tend to them at no cost. When I sell the calves in the fall, I bring the proceeds to Bill and he puts it in an account he has set up for Terrance. Bill said he doubted, and Kellie and I fully agreed, that Terrance could ever get much in terms of a decent meal out at his place, so he asked Kellie if she would feed Terrance three or four nights a week if he paid for the extra mouth to feed. Well, with Terrance it's more like three mouths to feed. Anyway, Bill said he had made arrangements at the Calfe' to take care of the rest of his weekly meals. I don't think Bill uses much of the calf money to pay for all that, as I'm guessing he's saving most of it to give Terrance a little head start on things when he gets through high school. Anyway, that's the story on Terrance. I thought you should know. And I'll make sure you meet Kellie Cassidy soon. She's a remarkable lady, and she's Otis's vet."

"She's a veterinarian?" asked Luke.

"No," replied Edna with smile, "barely a high school education, and yet she's the best damn vet in the county. But that's another story for another day."

"So how is old man Hollister going to receive our visit?" Luke inquired as they drove slowly down the lane towards the Hollister buildings.

"We shouldn't have to deal with him," Edna said. "I avoid him like the plague, and only come out when I'm sure that he's not here. His pickup is gone, which means he is too. He probably crashed at some drinking buddy's place in Centertown." As they neared the yard, Luke could see that she wasn't exaggerating in the deteriorated condition of the place. The house was a small, A-framed rectangle, the weathered and rotting wood siding long since devoid of any paint. The barn was in even worse disrepair, and with the exception of a few faded red paint chips that still clung stubbornly to the wood, the siding was every bit as gray and forsaken as the house. The barn door hung canted from back to front, as if the tilted side had finally succumbed to the relentless forces of gravity. The only other structure was an open on one side lean-to that served as the garage, housing Tank's battered old pickup, a flatbed trailer and an open space that was apparently reserved for the elder Hollister vehicle.

As Edna and Luke exited the pickup and approached the house, Tank opened the mostly detached front screen door and stepped out on the warped and sagging 2x10 planks that served as the front porch floor. "Good morning Terrance," said Edna in a business-like tone. "You remember coach Carter from the Calfe' a few weeks back?" Tank engulfed Luke's extended hand with a slight nod of his head and said, "Hello Miz E." Looking past them both upon hearing a deep throated 'whoof' from Edna's pickup, he inquired, "Care if I get him down Miz E?"

"Might as well. He'll just make a fuss until you do." Tank opened the door and the two roughhoused for a bit before Tank extracted the stocky dog from the seat with one arm as if he was grabbing an empty lunch pail. Otis circled around Tank a few times with about as much enthusiasm as one could expect from an arthritic, seven-year-old bulldog before finding the front porch step and lifting his leg to leave his mark.

"As long as your dad isn't going to be here, I thought I'd have Carl come over this afternoon and swath that grass hay," said Edna as she pointed to a weary and weedy field behind the barn. "It's a pretty thin stand, and as warm and windy as it's been it should dry out in a hurry. It'll be ready to bale tomorrow afternoon as long as we don't get a shower in the meantime. I'll have Kellie or Bret drop off the tractor and baler by tomorrow noon."

"That should work," said Tank. "I don't know if the old man will be around or not. Must be on a pretty good bender—ain't seen him for a couple days… oh shit, here he comes now!"

Staring down the lane at the slowly approaching pickup with a startled and frightened look on her face, Edna asked Tank, "We should get out of here, right?"

"Naw, he'll just run ya off the road if you try to leave. Better to just sit tight," said Tank, as he quickly moved to where Otis was napping in the shade and picked him up and put him back in Edna's pickup. Returning to Edna and Luke's side to await the confrontation, he calmly said. "Best let me do the talking."

The old and dented pickup slowly chugged into the yard, and although there was plenty of room in the entry yard to park elsewhere, Terrance Sr. parked directly behind Edna's pickup, lurching forward to within inches of her bumper. Luke almost audibly gasped when he stepped out of the truck. He thought Tank was huge, but his dad was gargantuan. 6'5"ish, somewhere well north of 400 lbs, Luke thought, with the same wide, thick trunk and redwood tree-sized legs as his son. But there were two glaring differences between father and son; the first was that old man Terrance sported a belly of monumental proportions, his once white Caterpillar t-shirt now filthy with yellow stained underarm rings. His gut spilled over his Carhartt jeans like runaway dough overflowing the edge of a bread pan. A pair of strained and tired looking suspender straps extended over each shoulder and down either side of his enormous belly, disappearing to somewhere deep beneath his circumferential fat roll to presumably attach to the tent-like pants. The second distinction between the two was in the face. While probably not considered handsome, Tank's looks were not unpleasant. Terrance, on the other hand, could be a top candidate for a role in a horror movie. His cold, deep set eyes were rimmed in red, and his full-face beard appeared to be the storage site of the remains of a just-eaten breakfast special at the Empire Cafe in Centertown.

Luke could sense the fear and anger emanating from Edna, who stood between Luke and Tank, body tensed and fists clenched. Terrance wobbled a little closer to them, the putrid odor of evaporating alcohol and weeks-old sweat washing over them. After taking a moment to focus through blurry eyes to identify the intruders, he pointed at Luke and said with a voice that sounded like it was coming from the hidden recesses of a deep cave, "Who's this fuckin' asshole?"

Before Tank could respond, he turned his attention to Edna, and with a face reddening enough to match the hue of his eyes, he shouted, "Is that the Coffman bitch? Takes a lot of nerve to show your face around here, bitch. Get the fuck off my property!" Tank stepped protectively in between Edna and Terrance, and said firmly, "Shut the fuck up, old man. They were just leaving."

Terrance glared at his son and turned and stumbled back to his pickup. *Sweet Jesus, what the hell am I getting myself into*, thought Luke when he saw that Terrance was extracting a rifle from the gun rack in his truck. He felt somewhat better when Tank whispered at them through the side of his mouth, "Don't worry, it ain't loaded… let me handle this."

"I shoulda shot ya years ago, ya thievin' fuckin' bitch," Terrance spat, staggering back and forth trying to get around Tank so as to get a direct purchase aim on Edna. "Put that gun down, you old fool. Put it down right now, or I'll grab it and shove it up your ass. You know goddamn well I can do it, too."

Holy shit, thought Luke, *I'm watching the standoff between Wyatt Earp and Ike Clanton at the OK Corral!* After several more attempts of trying to get around Tank to get a clear shot at Edna, Tank threw out an arm and grabbed the gun and jerked it from his grasp. "Goddamn ya, Tank—dirty son of a bitch!" Eyes full of hatred, Terrance stumbled up the porch steps like a petulant child whose parents had just taken away his favorite toy, hollering back as he passed through the screen door, "Get off my land, you fucking Coffman whore!"

As he disappeared into the house and Luke and Edna breathed a sigh of relief, Tank shook his head in disgust and said, "Sorry you had to see that. Miz E, probably better not have anybody come over and swath. He'll most likely sleep this off for a couple of hours and then head back to Centertown. I'll call you when he leaves."

"Okay Terrance, that makes good sense. Watch your backside with that maniac, will you?" replied Edna.

"Sure thing, Miz E. He still tries to talk a big game, but he knows better than to mess with me. He knows I'll kick his ass and not think twice about it," said Tank as he closed her pickup door and nodded a curt goodbye to Luke and watched them drive out of the yard.

"Well, I didn't expect for you to have to see that," said Edna.

"Holy cow, that is one frightening man," confirmed Luke. "I was sure glad when Tank said that gun wasn't loaded. And him calling you a thief and all those other nasty things? What was that all about?"

"Old Henry Hollister, Terrance Sr.'s dad, once owned three sections of land, or 1,920 acres that directly bordered my father's place... now my place. You might as well get a quick lesson on land math since you're living in agriculture country now. There are 640 acres to a section of ground. A square containing 36 contiguous sections makes a Township. That's how they identify land from a legal description standpoint—a numbered township, range and section. Anyway, Henry was about as worthless of a drunk as his son Terrance is, and through abject neglect of his farm and ranch the bank had to initiate a foreclosure on the property. What ended up happening is that Henry had to sell off 2 ½ sections of his land in order to satisfy his bank debt, leaving him with this half section, or 320 acres. The 2 ½ sections went up for auction and my father bought it as the highest bidder. He didn't steal anything, just took advantage of a piece of ground that came up for sale and paid full dollar for it. Well, old Henry had to find somebody to blame other than himself for losing most of his ground, so he always bad-mouthed both the bank and my dad. Terrance Sr. simply inherited the same 'it's the bank and the Coffmans' fault that we lost our land' approach. Of course, Bill Koch won't lend him any money, so he has a big-time hatred for both me and Bill. That's why we only come over and help Tank when the miserable drunk is away from the place."

Edna pulled up to the school gym to drop Luke off, put her pickup in park and turned in her seat so that she could look directly at Luke. With a very determined and stern look on her face, she said, "Luke, I'm actually glad you ran into Terrance Sr. You should now have a better understanding about what young Terrance has had to experience in these few, short years of his young life. I fully expect you to be a positive role model for him. He doesn't have a relationship with an adult male. T.O. is probably the closest, but Tank's shortcomings in staying eligible has prevented a good association between those two. I believe he somewhat trusts me, and maybe Kellie Cassidy, but that's about it. Since I'm retired from teaching, I've made Terrance one of my main missions in life. We don't want another Hollister apple to fall so close to the tree again. This goes far beyond football, although football could be the ideal ticket for him to punch his way to a better life—a life away from the abuse and emotional pain that's all he's known thus far. I want to do everything I can, and I ask you to do the same. I expect you to make every effort to mentor him into becoming a decent man… a proud and productive citizen. And the way to do that is by lending him a tough love hand. He doesn't need to be coddled. No—no, I won't stand for that. We need to set the expectations bar high and not allow him to settle for less. As I've told him many times before, 'you've been handed a pretty raw deal, but don't fall into that trap of feeling sorry yourself. Buck up and get the job done in spite of the hand you've been dealt.'"

With that, Edna turned back around in her seat, giving Luke the not so subtle hint that it was time for him to get out. "Okay Edna, I understand. I'll do my best, I promise," he said, as he unwound his lanky frame from the back seat of the extended cab.

What in the good name of Christ have I gotten myself into, thought Luke, as he watched Edna and her co-pilot pull away from the parking lot. Nothing like having a not so jolly red faced giant waving a gun in your face to make you question your sanity in accepting the Pacer Coulee employment offer.

LUKE AND MADISON HAVE SUMMER CAMPS

Luke was used to the 60 or 70 kids that would show for the summer football camp back in his days at Lincoln. "Well, Lincoln High summer football camp it ain't," he muttered to himself after sending the ten boys, four of whom were Jr. High age, to the school shop after the first day of summer camp. He had organized the summer session in conjunction with Madison's girls' basketball camp for the first three days of the fourth week of July, hoping to get a jump start on meeting the kids, evaluating the talent level, and getting them accustomed to the in-season weight training program that he would be implementing.

While Lester had conducted annual summer basketball camps for the girls, no one could remember when the last football one was held. "It's just like I explained at your interview," Luke's new assistant coach T.O. Barker had said. "This is farm and ranch country, and these kids have to work in the summer. Late July and all of August is a very busy time of year with haying, field work and harvest, so it's a crap shoot to get much of a turnout when official practice begins in August, never mind trying to get anybody to show up for a camp in July. And sorry Luke, but I'm slammed with my own operation too. I'll try to stop by for a few minutes here and there when I can, but shit, I'm trying to get my combine ready for harvest."

Luke was happy that at least the core group of his team showed up for the first day. Tank, Aaron Coslet, Bret Cassidy, Dolph Russell and Stefan Tillerman were all there, and he was pleased with the level of athleticism and conditioning they displayed. Since Greg Bolstad had already started the demolition of the old weight room, Lester had approached the school's

Shop and Vo-Ag teacher, Lyle Marks, to see if he would let them put the weight equipment in one corner of the expansive automotive floor. The weight equipment that Luke had ordered was supposed to arrive by August 15th, and Greg was hopeful he would have new the addition completed and ready to go by then.

With the exception of Tank and Aaron, it was obvious that the knowledge of weight training was as foreign as deciphering an essay written in Russian. Luke knew he had a ton of work to do to get the boys up to speed, but he was happy to see their interest and enthusiasm. After the first weightlifting session was completed, one thing was for certain: Tank Hollister was stronger than a prize central Montana Angus Bull.

"OH. MY. GOD. Coach Carter is SOOO HOT!" whispered Anna Rimby to Betty Ann Drury when Madison introduced Luke to her campers. "Coach Carter comes to us from Lincoln, Nebraska, where he was at a high school that would be larger than Great Falls High or Billings West. In addition to coaching football, Mr. Carter ran both the summer and school year weight training programs for boys' football and basketball, as well as girls' basketball and volleyball. He also coordinated those workouts to include sport-specific speed, agility and flexibility," explained Madison. "Now as I understand it, coach Carter will be incorporating those specific training modalities into our Phys Ed curriculum offerings this upcoming school year, but in the meantime has graciously offered to start working with you girls during this camp.

"He can work with me any old time he wants to," giggled Betty Ann.

"Shhh, let's pay attention girls. Mr. Carter will help us further when the new weight training addition is completed and furnished with all new equipment. We expect that to occur sometime during the week after we start official basketball practice, which is scheduled for Friday, August 10th. So with that, let's please welcome coach Carter with a round of applause."

Ignoring the muted giggles and the, "who would have ever thought I'd love weightlifting so much" whispers from the girls, Luke gave them a brief introduction to some of the statistics that supported the efficacy and benefits of improving strength, speed, flexibility and agility to any sport training regime, and Madison had the girls finish the camp session by running through some agility drills that were demonstrated by Luke.

Madison reddened that her thoughts had wandered to Anna's blurted out assessment of coach Carter, and sheepishly admitted to herself that she couldn't agree more. She quickly admonished herself for even thinking like that, as the last thing she was looking for was a new boyfriend. She simply wasn't ready to risk the possibility of another disastrous relationship like she had just experienced with her now ex-husband... not only for her, but more importantly she couldn't bear to see her daughter Rose go through that kind of disappointment ever again.

ELVIS AND CLARE

"Good morning, Edna," said Bill Koch, answering the phone in his office at the bank. "What can I do for you?"

"Sorry for the short notice, but could we have an impromptu board meeting sometime this afternoon? I've already contacted Shanty, and he's available anytime."

"Okay," said Bill hesitantly. "What's up that requires an emergency bank board meeting? Somebody going to default on a big loan that I don't know about?"

"No, nothing like that—not even bank-related. But it is very important that I talk to you and Shanty about this critical matter."

"Fine, let's have a meeting. 1:00 work for you?"

"For Christ's sake Bill, don't you have an extra fan somewhere in the bank that we can aim directly at Otis before he dies of Goddamn heat stroke?" snapped Edna, wiping the sweat off her brow with one hand while fanning the panting bulldog with the other. "Does it have to hit 110 before you bring out the extra fans?"

Summer month meetings held in the cinder block addition to the main bank building could be as brutally hot as winter month meetings were frigidly cold. According to the old and weathered thermometer that was mounted at the outside entrance of the bank, it was 99 degrees. "And why don't you break down and replace that 50-year-old thermometer you have out front? You do know that it's faulty? It runs about two degrees above the more modern and accurate one that Sylvia has at the Post Office just across the street," declared Edna.

"Haven't you heard yet that we have global warming over here on the north side of the street?" questioned Bill with a grin. "Personally, I think the higher temps over here are due to all the hot air being exchanged between you and Shanty. And if we happen to catch Otis on a day when he's passing a lot of gas... well, that just adds to the problem. The good news is this: the hotter it is in here, the less energy you and Shanty have to pick a fight with each other. But I can see that poor ol' Otis is overheating, so let me go grab another fan out of the basement."

Bill came back with a fan and bucket of ice water, and Edna and Shanty wiped the big bulldog down with cool rags as Bill searched for a long enough extension cord to set the fan in the optimal cooling location. Once everyone was comfortable that Otis appeared to be on the road to body temperature recovery, Bill said, "So Edna, what is this non bank-related news bombshell that we urgently needed to discuss?"

"Okay, hold on to your hats, boys. I got a call first thing this morning from an old friend of mine up at Hays Lodgepole. Jannine Good Strike is a full-blood Assiniboine who was raised on the Fort Belnap reservation. She retired after 30 years as the Superintendent up there, and is now the Tribal Council Chairperson. There isn't a lady in this state that I have more respect for, as she went to college fresh out of high school and earned a degree at a time when you seldom saw someone from the reservation attempt a secondary education, much less a woman. And then to go back and make a demonstrable difference in the lives of her people is just remarkable," said Edna. Leaning forward in her chair with the excited expression of a coffee shop regular dangling a juicy and tantalizing gossip bone, she continued. "Anyway, she called to give me a heads up on two kids from the Fort Belnap reservation. I'm sure you two have heard of Elvis His Own Horse?"

"He'd be the basketball star?" asked Bill, as Shanty nodded his head in recognition of the name.

"Yes, that's him. He put up some amazing numbers for the Hays Lodgepole team last year as a freshman. Well, Jannine is a cousin to the grandmother of Elvis and his one-year younger sister, Clare Comes at Night. Unfortunately, this story is a pretty familiar one on the reservation. Neither Elvis's nor Clare's fathers were ever in the picture—gone before either of them was ever born. Their mother was an alcoholic and died from a drug overdose when the kids were just toddlers. So their grandma, Laura Jo Crazy Bear, took them both in and raised them until she died of cancer when the kids were just eight and seven.

"As Jannine reminded me, there isn't a homeless population on the reservation because the Natives take care of their own. Someone always takes in a stray when need be. In this case, Elvis and Clare's great grandmother, Carmen Crow Fly High, moved the kids in with her upon Crazy Bear's death. Jannine thought very highly of Carmen, and thought she was a wonderful guardian for the kids, providing them the stability and positive encouragement that is woefully in short supply on the reservation. Sadly, Carmen passed away suddenly last week at the age of 70."

"I guess I was figuring the great grandmother would be in her 90s," mused Shanty.

"You would think, but often times the Native Americans are like you Irish in that they start young and have many," said Edna.

Bill, surprised that not only didn't Shanty take immediate offense to the comment, he actually broke out in a grin, then asked Edna, "So what's all this have to do with us?"

"Hold your horses. I'm getting to that. As I mentioned, Jannine is a relative and has kept a close watch on the kids since they were born. She thinks that with the death of Carmen these kids would now be taken in by a sister of their mother and sees that scenario as a horrible wreck. She says they are really good kids, and that Elvis, in addition to being one hell of a basketball player, is especially bright and does well in school. She feels if she can get Elvis off the reservation and into a small school and living with a responsible guardian there will be an opportunity for him that has eluded 99.9% of the plethora of great Native American basketball players over the years; a college scholarship and a college degree."

"You mention kids as plural, but I'm only hearing Elvis

from you. So what's the deal with what's her name, Clare, is it?" inquired Shanty.

"Yes, it's Clare. She'll be a freshman this fall. From what I gathered from Jannine, she's a damn good player in her own right, but doesn't have near the interest in school that Elvis does. But Jannine says they're very close, so it would be a package deal."

"Okay," said Bill, "I think I have an idea where this is headed, so why don't you cut to the chase and fill us in."

"Yeah, please do," echoed Shanty, pointing to the snoozing and panting bulldog at his feet. "The suspense is killing both me and Otis."

"Okay you two smart alecs, here's the deal. The Goddamn Catholics have caught wind of Elvis and Clare's potential move off the reservation, and the St. Francis recruiting machine is already in full court press. Dr. Bertal, the St. Francis grad and Orthopedist for St. Vincent's in Billings who comes to Centertown to see patients a couple of days a month, is a huge donor to St. Francis. He has led their sneaky, illegal and behind the scenes recruiting blitzkrieg for years. Jannine doesn't like or trust him, plus she worries that Elvis and Clare wouldn't fare well under the polar opposite environment of a strict, disciplined Catholic school like St. Francis. She'd much rather direct them towards me, us, here at Pacer Coulee. She knows they'd have a far better chance for success at a town and school such as ours."

Edna paused long enough to redirect the air stream from the fan to Otis's slightly changed position, rolled over on his back, and continued. "Naturally, the main roadblock we have in preventing St. Francis from securing yet another prize recruit is in locating housing here in Pacer Coulee for Elvis and Clare. The first person to come to my mind was Kellie Cassidy, so I approached her about the idea. But with four kids already under her roof she just doesn't have the room to take on two more," stated Edna. She then turned toward Shanty and with an earnest, expectant expression said, "And then it occurred to me that this might be the perfect opportunity for you, Shanty, to do something really meaningful for your town and school. Even more importantly, think of the personal satisfaction you could enjoy by providing a home for Elvis and Clare."

"Me?" exclaimed Shanty. "I'm about to be 83 years old, Edna. I've already raised five kids of my own! Why in the good Lord's name would I want to take on two high school aged kids? And Indian kids at that, coming from a whole different culture? And how on earth could I afford to feed and clothe them on my measly pension?"

"Oh for Christ's sake JoePat," Edna fired back. "I guess I've been mistaken for all these years thinking that it was the Scots that were cheap. Obviously, I stand corrected—it's the Irish that are the ultimate penny pinchers. You've probably squirreled away more of that fat union railroad pension than the Vatican has pilfered from you parishioners, and God knows they have extorted enough funds from their faithful to pay off the national debt."

"Dammit Edna, I barely make enough off my retirement pension and social security to get by on. Unlike you, I don't have any hefty wheat and cattle checks to cash, nor do I have any of those government farm assistance welfare checks waiting in my mailbox like all you whiny farmers do. And about the Vatican, that's just not true. The Vatican and its benevolent Catholic charities donate millions for the benefit of poor people worldwide."

"Well, they sure manage to keep enough gold on hand to plate the pillars and altars in all their cathedrals around the world too, especially at the Vatican, don't they JoePat? Seems to me they should, as you Democrats always say, spread more of their wealth towards the needy than fleecing the flock's hard earned money to erect statues in their opulent churches and pay their fat cat attorneys to sweep all of the church's scandals under the rug."

Bill leaned forward and adjusted one of the fans so that he could better catch the cooling air flow as he settled back in his chair to witness the next round between his two angry and red-faced directors. The continuing skirmish on the topic of religion was one that Edna and Shanty had stood toe-to-toe and slugged out at many a board meeting in the past. Bill suspected that Edna's frequent 'Goddamn Catholics' phrase was more directed at the competitive sports rivalry with St. Francis than with any particular vendetta against the Catholic church. He further surmised that getting under Shanty's skin was the primary motivation of her vitriolic affronts. Whatever the case, Bill always found the religion exchange to be one of the most entertaining of their varied subject matter scuffles.

"So as long as we're talking about the Goddamn Catholics, maybe you could enlighten me on a few things. What's the deal with you Catholics that you blindly follow the orders of this Pope of yours? To begin with, why do those Cardinals, or whatever you call that layer of hierarchy just below the Pope… you know, the ones that wear the pointy hats, always select a guy that's about 108 years old to be the next Pope? Is it a Vatican rule that you have to be over 100 to be considered for Popedom? Good grief! How can you expect some old ex-Cardinal that has one foot in the grave and the other on a banana peel to lead your church? I just don't understand it, I surely don't. Thank God we Methodists don't feel the need to carry on with such nonsense."

"That just goes to show how much you don't know what you're talking about," snapped Shanty. "I'll have you know that our current Pope, John Paul II, was only 58 years old when he was appointed by the second Papal Conclave in 1978, so he was a far cry from being an old man. And at only 70 now, he's still a relatively young man."

"Well, I'll freely admit to having no Goddamn idea whatsoever as to who the second Papal Conclave is or was, but it seems to me you've always got some decrepit old guy in the Vatican who's lost touch with the issues of the day."

"Such blasphemy! How dare you talk about the Holy Father that way!" shouted Shanty.

"And how about the way they treat women in your church? A woman can't be a priest. In the Catholic church's eye, my only rightful or allowed position would be that of nun. Just think, I could be like Sister Anne Marie and all those other stuffy old battle-axes at St. Francis, blindly obeying orders from that old drunk Father Coughlan."

"There you go again!" cried Shanty, "Blaspheming a man of God when you have no idea what you're taking about. And do we really have to hear all your women's lib crap again? There's nothing wrong in staying with the tried and true traditions of the Catholic church that's worked for centuries. And it's not like the church discriminates against women. The nuns have a very important role in our church."

"Just goes to show how far you've all been brainwashed. To begin with, everyone in the whole damn county except you Catholics knows that Father Coughlan is a boozer. I know for a fact a certain county sheriff stopped him at Brooks a couple of Sundays ago when he was coming back from saying Mass out at Pacer Coulee. Drunk as a skunk, he was, and the sheriff should have given him a DUI, but as a practicing Catholic himself he chose to look the other way. And furthermore, don't give me that crap that women play an important role in the Catholic church. How many women do you suppose are wearing those pointy hats and hobnobbing with the Cardinals when they're all huddled up and about to elect a Pope? Zero, that's how many, JoePat. That old 'women play a vital role in Catholic church' vessel just doesn't hold water, and you know it!"

"Okay, we're getting a little off track here folks," Bill interjected, worried that Shanty was approaching the stress level stage of initiating some kind of cardiac event. "Let's go back to the beginning of this conversation. Edna, I do think that asking an 83-year-old to take on two kids is a bit unreasonable, especially when you consider that Shanty would be 87 by the time the youngest of the two graduates."

"Thank God at least one other person in this room has a

brain," snapped Shanty, shooting a glare of disgust in Edna's direction.

"Well, how about you Bill? You and Marge live all alone in that big old three story house. You might as well put all that extra space to good use," Edna reasoned.

"That's the last straw!" shouted Shanty, again leaping up from his chair quicker than any almost 83-year-old should be able to do. "Isn't that just like you? My God woman, have you no shame? For all that Bill does for this town and the school, and you have the nerve to expect him and Marge to take in a bunch of kids? I declare, you have some nerve!"

"Settle down, Shanty, settle down," Bill said calmly, waiting to further speak until Shanty had eased back into his chair. "Edna, as you well know, Marge and I never had children of our own. And frankly, at our age of 70, we would have no desire to take on a readymade family. Thanks for thinking of us, but this is one request I won't be able to accommodate."

"Speaking of big houses, Edna, maybe it's time you step down from your high horse and stop bossing everybody else around. If you're so worried about these reservation kids falling into the hands of St. Francis, then maybe it's time you pick up the shovel and clean out your own horse stall for once instead of expecting everyone else to do it," barked Shanty.

"Well... well," sputtered Edna, "I've obviously never had a family, and you know how shy and private my sister Harriet is. I'm sure she wouldn't approve of me taking anyone else into our house."

"Hogwash!" exclaimed Shanty. "When did she ever have any say in your household? Just like at the school or this town, you carry the biggest stick and everybody except me follows your commands like obedient little puppy dogs. Besides, it would give her something to do around that big old house of yours. I hear she's a good cook, so it might even make her feel useful with a couple more mouths to feed."

"Well," huffed Edna, "since neither of you seems to have any concern about these kids ending up in the dangerous and incapable hands of Father Coughlan, Sister Anne Marie and the rest of the Goddamn Catholics, then I guess I'll just have to take them in," snapped Edna. "Of course, if they did go to St. Francis, they'd probably escape back to the reservation in no time just to avoid having to go to church so much. Do you know that there at St. Francis they expect their students to go to Mass every damn day? Good Lord, Shanty, how do you Catholics find the time to sin as much as you do when you spend the majority of your sorrowful lives in church?"

Bill threw his head back in laughter at that final jab and noted that even Shanty was fighting the smile that was twitching at the corners of his mouth.

LUKE AND MADISON DISCOVER THE PACER COULEE CHRONICLES

Luke didn't know if it was good or bad that he had rented the smallest of Edna's two rental houses in Pacer Coulee. His 1920s-something built one bed, one bath pad on Lehman Street suited his needs just fine, but he wasn't sure he needed the distraction of being next door neighbors with one Madison Danielsen. It wasn't that he didn't like her; in fact, quite the opposite. He had liked her immediately upon their initial introduction when she and Rose pulled in front of their rental while he was painting their trim. What wasn't to like? She was warm and outgoing, with a friendly smile that could light up the room. She had one of those engaging personalities, quick to both laugh and quip. And oh yeah, there was that little thing of how very attractive she was.

Luke knew that it was time for him to emerge from the protective cocoon that he had woven around his wounded and battered self. He knew he had brooded over his ex for too long and that it was time to throw caution to the wind—throw the deep ball, go for it on 4th down. But he had spun the cocoon tight, and whenever he was tempted to reenter the relationship world his risk aversive gene seemed to raise its domineering head. Furthermore, he had heard from Lester that Madison was also trying to recover from a bad marriage and nasty divorce, so it would stand to reason that she may have no interest in even considering a new relationship with anyone at this point in time. Plus, there was the matter of Rose, her 11-year-old daughter. Developing a relationship between two single adults was one thing. Throwing a child into the mix was quite another. Thankfully, both Luke and Madison had been so busy with practices and getting settled in that they hadn't seen enough of each other to get acquainted.

It was the 19th of August, and Luke was sitting at the small, weathered picnic table that the last renter had left behind to furnish the slab of concrete that served as his patio in his small backyard. The late afternoon Sunday sun was shimmering through the branches of the sleepy Elm tree that sat just on his side of the chain link fence that was the property boundary between him and the Danielsens. There was just enough room on the patio to accommodate the table and the well-used three burner BBQ Grill that coach Barker had brought him a couple of weeks before as a housewarming gift. T.O. had explained that he wasn't prone to giving gifts to anyone other than those that were required and expected by his wife and kids, but the brand new four-burner Webber his family gave him for Father's Day had made his old one expendable. To ease the slight of gifting Luke a worn out BBQ, T.O. had included a cold pack of Bud Light under the lid with a "don't say I never gave ya anything" over the shoulder retort as he was walking out the gate.

Luke looked back over his first few weeks of practice with an equal mix of satisfaction and trepidation. As forewarned by T.O., the coaches had conducted single, early morning practices to accommodate the high percentage of farm kids on the team who were required to work the harvest fields during the day. While Luke was used to the standard two-a-day sessions of his high school, college and coaching days in Nebraska, he took the 'it is what is' approach and tried to utilize his two hour, once a day practice to the maximum. For the most part, he had the majority of the 17 players that had come out at each session.

When the time came to put the pads on after the first three days of shorts and jerseys, Luke and T.O. had drawn up a contact plan that allowed sufficient work on the basic fundamentals of blocking and tackling, yet limiting any unnecessary hitting and pounding to preserve the razor thin number of players. With only 17 bodies, and seven of them being not yet ready for Prime Time Freshman or Sophomores, injuries to any of the upper class-men would be devastating.

He was pleasantly surprised with the players, as they were

down to earth kids with good attitudes. It was obvious, with just a few exceptions, that their parents had instilled strong work ethic into their characters. As expected, the boys that T.O. had told him about at his interview were as advertised. Tank Hollister was the most complete lineman he had ever been around, either as a coach or a player. His raw size, strength, quickness, and sense of the game were simply unmatched. Aaron Coslet and Stefan Tillerman were very good players, and Bret Cassidy, Tucker Greyson and Dolph Russell were solid. Luke felt he had two wild cards in Kimball Robbins and senior rookie Bo Ramsay. Both had athleticism and speed, but Kimball's desire to play was questionable at best, and who could guess how quickly Bo would develop and pick up on the game. Despite the skimpy depth chart, Luke was reasonably pleased with his group, less one exception—quarterback. Any semblance of an acceptable quarterback he did not have.

Luke had thrown a burger and a couple of hot dogs on the grill and had just started reading the few pages of the Centertown News Argus after finishing the much thicker Great Falls Tribune, the more popular of the two larger city newspapers among the Pacer Coulee residents. The Billings Gazette was in favor by enough of his customers that Kip Jordan, the owner of both the Calfe' and the O.K. Corral Bar and Grill, carried both. As far as Luke could tell, the general consensus was that the Tribune had superior sports coverage of central and north central Montana, whereas the Gazette catered more to the eastern side of the state.

The third newspaper that Kip carried at his establishments was the Centertown News Argus. Luke had never seen anything quite like the family owned, two editions per week publication. The News Argus was a true small town local paper, and according to Lester there was never any national news reported. Lester had joked that he doubted they would cover WWIII if it were to break out. State news was occasionally noted, but only when it directly affected Centertown or central Montana. Local politics was thoroughly examined at the city and county level, whereas State politics was only reported when related to matters concerning elected central Montana State Senators and Representatives.

Luke had learned that the 68-year-old publisher of the little family run newspaper was a sports enthusiast. Ward Fluegel was a three sport standout graduate of Centertown High School and was committed to full sports coverage of Centertown High, St. Francis, and all of the surrounding Class C schools. Although there were an isolated few from the outlying smaller schools who accused him of biased reporting in favor of St. Francis, the vast majority of all of central Montana appreciated his dedicated efforts to include all the schools in their coverage, especially since he operated with a bare bones staff. Randy Mason, Fluegel's only other staff reporter, and a part timer at that, had come to Pacer Coulee the day before to take team pictures and interview both Luke and Madison for inclusion in the annual 'Preseason Central Montana Football and Girls' Basketball Edition'. Veteran Sports Editor George Geisel and his Great Falls Tribune sports staff also put together a fine preseason fall sports edition on all Class AA, A, B, 8 and 6-man C conferences in the greater Great Falls area, but Luke was more than taken aback with the efforts of the little Centertown newspaper to provide such a comprehensive look at the entire 7C conference in both football and basketball.

Luke started reading the prior Wednesday's edition, and couldn't help but laugh out loud when he came to the section labeled as the Local Community Page. Once a month, each small, outlying town had an appointed correspondent that would send in a report of the newsworthy events of their respective communities. Each local area had their own label headline. There was the Wyngate Whispers, Marshall Meanderings, Stanton Statistics, Hodgeman Happenings, Range View Rustlings, Deeden Recorder and last but not least, the Pacer Coulee Chronicles.

Luke had met Sylvia Graham, the local Post Mistress who

served as the Pacer Coulee Chronicles correspondent, and he began to read her column.

PACER COULEE CHRONICLES
Sylvia Graham, Correspondent

Another summer has come and gone, and the start of the Pacer Coulee School year is just around the corner. Congratulations and a big thank you is in order to Harriet Coffman, who is slowing down after 47 years of teaching History at our fine school. She's not retiring completely, as she will continue to teach junior, senior and Advanced Placement U.S. History. So give Harriet a shout out for a job well done next time you see her. We also say goodbye and good luck to Math teacher Emil Gladson, who has decided to go back and teach in his stomping grounds in western Washington. While sad to see these folks move on, it is also an opportunity for us to welcome our new History teacher and Football coach, Luke Carter. Luke hails from Nebraska, and according to School Board Chairman Edna Coffman, comes to us with high accolades from the big high schools in Nebraska where he has been coaching. We also get to welcome new Math teacher and Girls' Basketball coach Madison Danielsen. She comes to us from the Billings area, where she has taught and coached at Shepherd, Laurel and Fromberg. Since she grew up in Whitewater, she's no stranger to small towns. So make sure to welcome our young new teachers and coaches if you run into them when you are out and about.

In other Pacer Coulee news, harvest is getting pretty well wrapped up. Most of the area farmers report average to below average winter wheat yields due to the draught conditions we have had for most of the summer. Butch Cassidy reports that the Brown Wheat Mite was active in some of his fields out north, and thinks it reduced his yield by about 10-15 bushels an acre. Both spring wheat and barley were hurt by the dry conditions, and most of the farmers say the yields are off from a normal year. If there is any good news out there it's that the wheat protein levels are pretty high. I can't write in this column the words Butch used to describe the current price of wheat! Let's just say that it's barely above $2 a bushel and no one, especially Butch, is very happy about it. Speaking of harvest, Bones Bolstad wants to remind everyone to be vigilant in the fields due to this hot, dry weather we're having. He thinks a spark from the muffler of his grain truck was the culprit in starting a fire in his wheat field. Fortunately, they were able to confine the fire mostly to the area of the field that had already been cut. Bones shouts out a thanks to the Pacer Coulee, Plum Creek and Wyngate fire departments for their prompt response, and to all the good neighbor folk who left their own harvest fields to help keep the fire at bay until the fire departments could get there.

In other news, Viola Kottas traveled to the Mayo Clinic in Rochester to be by her sister Dorothy's side during her kidney transplant surgery. Elena Cowger was Johnny on the spot in getting the prayer chain going, so we're all sending our thoughts and prayers in Vi and Dorothy's direction. Also on the medical front, Myles Ullery nearly lost his arm in a grain auger accident, but according to his wife Phyllis he is recovering quite well from the emergency surgery on his arm. Phyllis says he's not as young as he used to be, so he's healing slowly. Myles has also been a recipient of this month's active prayer chain.

Emmy Laughlin and Gail Loos are having a joint yard sale on August 25th and 26th. Several other locals, including Yours Truly, have added some items (if anybody needs Mason jars for canning, I'm putting six of them in the sale) to the mix. Make sure and stop by, as there should be something of interest to just about everybody.

Here's hoping everybody has a wonderful Labor Day weekend. If you are traveling, be extra careful, as there will be a lot of crazies out on the roads! As they used to say on my favorite TV show, Hill Street

Blues-Be Careful Out There, ya hear? See you next month, and call me at 536-2645 if you have any news to report.

Luke was still chuckling over the Pacer Coulee Chronicles column as he approached his BBQ to flip his hamburger and turn the hot dogs. He was finally getting acquainted with the nuances of T.O.'s old grill, to include his discovery that the middle burner ran ragingly hot regardless of where its temperature control knob was positioned. He had quickly learned to grill over the two end burners only, and decided to limit the use of the flame-shooting middle one to a time when torching the nearby Elm tree would be the primary objective.

Luke's train of thought was interrupted when Rose called at him from the Danielsen side of the fence. "Hi Mr. Carter. Whatcha cooking?"

"Well hi there, Rose. I'm burning some burgers and hot dogs. What are you doing?"

"Me and my mom went to the Calfe' for supper. I had the Cheesehead Delight. That's a grilled cheese sandwich, you know. Oh yeah, and a root beer float. My mom said she should just have a salad, but then she thought and thought about whether to have the Bodacious Bovine or the Contented Cow hamburger, but ended up having the Puckered Pig instead—that's a BBQ'd pork sandwich."

"Well, all that sounds better than this little old burger, that's for sure," exclaimed Luke. He was already enjoying having the chatty and all legs fifth grader as a neighbor. One thing was for sure—he was a lot less apprehensive around Rose than when with her mother.

"I had the Puckered Pig the other night and it was really good," Luke continued. "I haven't tried the Contented Cow yet, but I did have the Hearty Hereford. That's the double cheeseburger that has both a fried egg and bacon on top, so you have to be really hungry to order it. It's Tank's favorite, for sure. Have you met Tank yet?"

"No, but I've seen him. He's like really, really, really big!"

"So are you ready for school to start tomorrow, Rose?" asked Luke.

"I guess. I'm kinda nervous. I mean, a new school and everything."

"Hey, I get it. I'm kind of nervous too. But that's normal, starting at a new school and not knowing a lot of people, don't you think? Your mom's probably nervous too."

"She says she isn't, but I think she's just saying that to make me feel better about it."

"Yeah, moms are like that sometimes. They're not above telling a little fib if they think it will make it better for us. You've met a few of the kids around town already though, haven't you?"

"I've met Abby Herman. She's in my class, and Shannon. She's a sixth grader. Oh yeah, and Shane. He's in my class and thinks he is SOOOO COOOOL.... NOT! But I go to all of mom's practices, so I know all the girls on the team. I've even shot around with all the Brewster girls at practice. They're pretty tall. Sonya and Sandra are even taller than my mom."

"Yes, I've seen you in the gym with the girls at practice. I think you are going to be as tall as them when you're in high school. Looks like to me you're a dang good shooter too."

"Yeah, I'm a pretty good shot, but I don't dribble so good with my left hand. Hey, you want me to mow your lawn? I have a mowing business, you know. Grandpa gave me and my mom a hardly used Toro, so it cuts real good. And I'm really careful about mowing in a straight line. Grandpa is very strict about straight lines when he summer-fallows his fields. Especially the ones next to the county road where people can see whether the lines are straight or crooked. Anyway, I'm doing Mrs. Grove's lawn across the street. She's really, really old, but she's cool. Anyway, when we were in the Calfe' today, Mr. Shanty said I could help him in his yard 'cause it's really big and he's pretty busy mowing the football field for you."

Luke suddenly noticed that Madison was standing well back in the yard watching and listening to their conversation with a bemused look on her face. He wondered how much of their chat she had heard.

"Well now Rose, how much do you charge to mow a lawn my size?"

"Mrs. Grove pays me $8 every time I do hers, but her yard is bigger than yours, and like I said, she is really old."

"I see. So you charge younger people like me more than you would an older person?"

"Yes, that's how it works. Like Robbie Hatten that lives over by Shanty? He's like 28 or something, and mom said to charge him like $12 because it wouldn't hurt him one bit to get off his big butt and mow his own yard."

"Rose! I didn't say it that way!" interjected Madison as she rushed over to the fence to stand next to her daughter.

"Yeah, I guess not. I think you said fat ass instead of big butt."

"Rose!"

"Well, you did."

"So Rose," said Luke with as straight a face as he could muster, "is my behind so big that you would charge me $12 to do my lawn?"

"Nah, I could do yours for $8."

"Deal. When could you start? As you can see, it needs mowing."

"Well then, why don't you go get the Toro gassed up and get to work," suggested Madison to Rose. Luke and Madison grinned at each other as they watched her race off to get her mower ready to take on the new neighbor customer.

"Thanks for visiting with Rose. I sheepishly admit to being the fly on the wall for your whole conversation. It was nice of you to ask her about school and help put her at ease that it's okay to be nervous on the first day. Thank you."

"Oh my gosh, she's delightful. I look forward to many backyard fence visits in the future. I have a feeling I'll have the inside track on all the elementary school drama and gossip," chuckled Luke, as his apprehension of being alone with Madison began to evaporate.

"You look to be at least one chair short in your patio furniture inventory, so why don't you grab your burger and hot dogs and two of those Bud Light beers and hop the fence. I have a bag of chips we can add to your BBQ masterpiece while we supervise the 'Rose Danielsen Lawn and Garden Service' in action from this side of the fence," offered Madison.

"Speaking of gossip, I couldn't help but notice you were reading the News Argus over there," said Madison as Luke entered her backyard with the food and drink. "First time you've read it?"

"Holy cow, I've never seen a small town newspaper before. There's some pretty amazing stuff in there. Did you see where we made the news in Sylvia's Pacer Coulee Chronicles column?"

"Yes, I did. I'm surprised she didn't report that the Puckered Pig is my favorite meal down at the Calfe'!"

"I think I'll alert Sylvia about that so we can get that important piece of news in next month's Chronicles. I think I should also reveal the information that Rose let out of the bag... you know, your quandary over whether to go with the Bodacious Bovine or Contented Cow burger. These are the sort of things the public wants to know about their new girls' basketball coach."

"Hey, I guess that's the price of fame when you reach the big-time, huh?" laughed Madison with an exaggerated shrug of her shoulders.

"So did you have the same kind of little local newspaper at the small town you grew up in?" inquired Luke.

"My little town of Whitewater was as close to Canada as it was to Malta, which at 32 miles away was the nearest thing we had to a larger town. It's a Class B school, so not as big as Centertown. They did have a local paper, but I honestly don't remember much about it. It certainly didn't have anything as exciting and newsworthy as the Pacer Coulee Chronicles, Marshall Meanderings or the Wyngate Whispers, I can tell you that!" said Madison, her engaging smile and endearing laugh making her more irresistible than he was willing to admit.

"Okay honey, go put on your shin guards before you use the weed eater to trim around the fence," Madison reminded Rose.

"That's pretty cool, the work ethic you seem to have already instilled in her. Not many 11-year-olds where I come from are out hustling summer jobs. Especially girls."

"With lazy and fat ass Robbie Hatten being the exception, one of the many great things about growing up in small town agricultural country is that the majority of the people are down to earth and hard working. And they raise their kids to be the same. But I admit to being especially blessed with a great kid. Despite the lousy example set by her father, she's turning out pretty darn good," Madison said, her voice and demeanor turning sour when she referenced her ex. "Oh shit, I'm so sorry—no reason for me to spoil our enjoyable chat by bringing my ex into the picture. Sorry, sorry."

"No worries, Madison. As you may have heard, I have a God's plenty of ex baggage myself. Assuming we don't read about the sordid details of our failed marriages in Pacer Coulee Chronicles first, perhaps we can commiserate when we have more time," joked Luke.

"Perhaps we can," said Madison hesitantly. "Perhaps we can."

"That'll be eight bucks Mr. Carter," declared Rose when she had finished the job.

"Hold on there, Miss Rose," said Madison with a stern tone. "You need to ask Mr. Carter if you have completed the job to his satisfaction."

"Oh yeah, sorry mom. Mr. Carter, is there anything else you would like me to do? Did I complete the job to your... like, you know, are you happy with the job I did?"

"Did I do the job to your satisfaction?" interjected Madison before Luke could answer.

"Oh yeah, that's right. Mr. Carter, did I do the job to your satisfaction?"

"You did just perfect Rose," Luke replied. "Best haircut this lawn has ever had, I'd be willing to bet. Would you accept a $2 tip and make it an even $10?"

After receiving a nod of approval from Madison, Rose cheerfully accepted the $10 bill and they bid their goodbyes. Even though he was giving himself the steely 'be careful, don't read anything into this' lecture on the way back through his yard, he couldn't seem to clear Madison's alluring smile and enchanting presence from his thoughts.

WINSTON BLACKBURN'S SCHOOL BOARD REQUEST

Edna cringed when she saw that Winston Blackburn was on the school board meeting agenda under the 'Public Comments/Concerns' section. She wondered what Winston felt he needed to address the board about, but suspected it had something to do with his son Alden. The frail young boy had come out for football to supposedly become the field goal and extra point kicker, but if his performance during the first week and a half of practice was any indication, coach Carter would be either punting or going for it on 4th down, and definitely going for two on extra points. Maybe Winston hadn't seen his son kick it into the backside of one of the offensive linemen every time he attempted a kick in practice. Maybe he envisioned Alden miraculously transitioning into Montana State and NFL Hall of Fame kicker Jan Stenerud, nailing every kick inside of 59 yards. Whatever the reason the annoying beanpole of a man was there, Edna knew she wasn't going to like it.

Winston was already present when Edna called the meeting to order. He was seated at a desk in the public guest section in the small classroom that adjoined the library and served as a study hall during school hours. The room was a popular spot for either after hours school or community meetings when a small, more intimate quarters gathering was called for. The classroom had long been officially booked on the third Tuesday of every month for the regular meetings of the school board. There was a long table in the front of the room where the five school board members sat, their backs to the chalkboard and facing out towards the rest of the classroom. Even though the board meetings were open to the public, it was rare that there were ever more than a few community members besides Shanty present at the meetings. Edna often wondered if Shanty's attendance was due to actual interest in the mostly mundane issues the board commonly dealt with, or whether he appeared for the primary purpose of aggravating her; she strongly suspected the latter. Second only to Edna's distaste of Shanty's political views, Edna was irritated to no end that Otis would waddle behind her into each and every school board meeting and promptly seek out Shanty and collapse at his feet. While Otis was always friendly and welcomed the pets and hugs from the young and old alike, when the greetings were concluded he would always end up at the feet or in the lap of Edna—except when Shanty was in the room. Only if Shanty left the meeting before it was adjourned would Otis make the extreme effort to lurch his 95 pound bulk to a standing position and lumber his way back to Edna's side. And it was the smug delight that Shanty took in the big dog's fondness for him that irritated Edna the most.

As the meeting got underway, only Howard the 'Ever Cheerful' janitor, the moniker that school comedian Bo Ramsay had tagged on the grouchy custodian, joined Shanty and Winston in the public comment/concern section. Howard was there only because he was giving a status report on the condition of the school's antiquated coal fired boiler, and Edna had him scheduled early on in the agenda order so that she wouldn't have to look at his sour countenance for an entire meeting. With his face scrunched into his usual scowl mode, Howard gruffly informed the board that the old, coal dust belching beast was on its last legs. He also pointed out that the only reason it was still functioning at all was due to his capable mechanical skills. *Blah, blah, blah*, thought Edna, but she knew the old boiler wouldn't last much longer and assigned board members Bert Clayton and Art Herbert to do some research and report back to the board within 60 days as to the most reasonable replacement options.

Board member Bert Clayton then delivered the monthly transportation report to the board. He haughtily pointed out that the school was guaranteed to go over budget in the fuel and bus maintenance category should the school board authorize the extra 14 miles per day to accommodate Wesley Cederholm's family transfer to Pacer Coulee. The Cederholms were a long-time Wyngate family, living only ten miles west of the rival community. Wesley had become irate at the Wyngate school the past year when his then sophomore son failed to see the floor for the Red Raiders during district basketball tournaments. Wesley spent the rest of the school year and the following summer stewing and seething over the injustice, and approached Edna in the first part of August to discuss their desire to transfer his son Travis and their three younger, school-aged children to Pacer Coulee, an 18-mile distance from their ranch. Wesley had only one condition to ensure the transfer, and that was for the Pacer Coulee School District to extend their bus route an additional seven miles to pick up and drop off the children at their ranch. Edna had added the proposed change in the bus route as an agenda item, not imagining there would be any opposition to the concept of the school picking up four additional new students.

But Bert, who had been chairing the board Transportation Committee since he was voted in for his second term the year before, came out firing in opposition to the Cederholm proposal. He based his disapproval on the additional fuel costs to be incurred by extending the bus route, not to mention the wear and tear on the already taxed and limping bus fleet. When Edna saw the rest of the board nodding their heads in agreement, she quickly intervened and said, "Before you get all bent out of shape over the fuel bill increase and bus maintenance consequence of accommodating this request, let's look at the big picture. As you all should recall, the State of Montana provides us our educational funding based on our school enrollment. In other words, we get 'X' number of dollars per student per year from the State. I can't tell you what the exact per-student dollar amount for this year is off the top of my head, but you can be sure that whatever it is, multiplied by four, far exceeds the extra fuel and maintenance expense involved in going an extra 14 miles a day to deliver the kids." Upon elucidation of the State funding concept, all of the board members except Bert voted to grant the Cederholm request. In casting the lone dissenting vote, Bert explained his position to the other board members. "Gosh darn it, I just can't in good faith vote for this. I mean, aren't we opening a big can of worms here? Who's next to come in and demand this kind of transportation ransom in order get a bus route extended to pick up their kids? We could be setting a precedent here that tells folks that this school will just throw a bunch of fuel money around and beat the heck out of our bus fleet in order to get more kids so that we can get more State money. I'm sorry, I just can't support this."

With a roll of her eyes in annoyance, Edna directed board secretary Lois to note Bert's objection and dissenting vote in the minutes. *Good Lord*, she thought to herself, *does Bert think we'll end up sending our buses to North Dakota next? Hell, maybe we'll branch into Alberta and Saskatchewan too, and double or triple our enrollment in search of the almighty State funding dollar. For Christ's sake Bert, get a grip.*

Edna was able to move the board through the rest of the regular agenda without much discussion or controversy. The meeting had taken about two hours at this point, and only Winston remained as the final agenda item. "Okay Winston, you're up," she brusquely said. "What can we do for you?"

Winston awkwardly stood from his desk and nervously intertwined his fingers and began to noticeably squeeze and release his bony digits at about two second intervals as he began to speak with his pronounced British accent. "Well Edna, ah, Ms. Coffman, I mean... and board members. As I think you all know, I came here from the Sacramento area. I'm an Agronomist, and I worked for Con Agra down there. My specialty field is fertilizer and chemical applications. Anyway, I wanted to move to a more rural area to raise our children, so I took a job with the Farmers Co-op Elevator here a few months back."

His pause became uncomfortably noticeable, accompanied by the continued wringing of his hands and the now visible and expanding sweat beads, bubbling like surface of a kettle of water just beginning to boil, across his narrow forehead. "Please go on, Winston," said Edna, impatience evident in her tone.

"Yes, ah, very well. As you might know, I have a freshman son, Alden, and a seventh grade daughter, Emily. When we were in California, both kids were on Futbol clubs. I was actually born in, and spent my elementary years in Cheshunt, England, before moving to the States. I played a bit of Futbol myself, mostly as a goalie or defender. Was quite a fan of Tottenham, I surely was, as we lived close by."

Edna was giving Winston her famous 'get to the Goddamn point' stare, and he wisely pressed forward. "Anyway, I've noticed that we only play American football here in central Montana and, by the way, my son Alden is using his Futbol skills to help out as a kicker on the football team. At any rate, I think it would be just splendid if the school board could authorize a state sanctioned soccer club or team, right here in Pacer Coulee, for the lads and lasses to participate in. Yes, that would be splendid, indeed."

His plea for soccer completed, Winston wiped his sweaty brow and collapsed back into his chair. Both Bert and Arthur were tempted to say something to break the awkward silence, but they were well aware of the pecking order and waited for Edna to initiate the response.

"Well Winston, let's get a couple of things straight right off the bat here, shall we? First of all, this is America, and Goddamn central Montana, America at that. We play real American football here. F-O-O-T-B-A-L-L, not F-U-T-B-O-L. You can call it whatever the hell you want in England, Europe, Mexico, South America, and what have you, but here in central Montana what you are talking about is soccer. S-O-C-C-E-R. Do we have that straight Winston?" asked Edna.

"Yes, Ms. Coffman—of course, Ms. Coffman" replied Winston, his brow suddenly boiling over again.

"I'm afraid you will find, Winston, that nobody around here gives a fat you-know-what about soccer. Nobody around here even understands how 11 or 12 people, or however many players a soccer team has to field, can run about for three hours like chickens with their heads cut off to end up in a Goddamn 0-0 tie. Makes no sense to me. Absolutely none. And if you were to go down to the O.K. Corral Bar and Grill and join the Butch Cassidy Hole in the Wall Coffee gang and ask if anyone knew who or what Tottenham was, they'd probably tell you," Edna continued, changing her voice and speech pattern to mimic one of the good ol' morning coffee boys, "Tottenham, ain't he the Duke of Lancaster, or sumpthin' like that?"

Moving back into her own stern tone, she continued. "You also might have noticed that we only have 43 total kids in grades nine to 12. We have a hell of a time some years in fielding enough kids for the sports that we do have, rather long trying to find 11 or 12 more to play soccer."

Otis's regular snoring pattern was interrupted with a loud snort, and he rolled over for Shanty to give him a rub with his foot as Edna continued. "If you want your kids to play soccer, then I suggest you apply for a fertilizer job near Bozeman or Missoula. All sorts of wealthy east and west coast liberals are moving there—mostly Trust Fund babies, if you will. They want to play cowboy and cowgirl, wear leather vests and fancy, colorful boots with their shiny new Wranglers tucked into them. And they all have spoiled little brats for kids that played soccer back in Connecticut or San Francisco. So Bozeman or Missoula is the place for you to be, Winston, if you want to get your children into a soccer club. It's not going to happen here, at least not in your lifetime.

"And one last thing, Winston," Edna lectured. "I've been watching football practice, and I suggest you concentrate on refining Alden's soccer skills to the point that it can translate to actually kicking the football above and beyond Tank's backside. Now I'm the first to admit that Tank has a posterior the width of Arkansas, and I can understand how it's hard to miss something that wide. But, it isn't all that tall. Alden needs to work on trying to kick the football with enough elevation to clear Tank's backside, then above the crossbar and between the goal posts. I think it would be splendid if we could accomplish that at some point. Now, will there be anything else you'd like to bring to the board's attention, Winston?"

"No, no, nothing else, Ms. Coffman," replied Winston, who was already hurriedly passing through the exit door.

MADISON'S POST-BBQ THOUGHTS

Madison attempted to concentrate on preparing for her scrimmage the following day, but the handsome face of her next door neighbor kept crowding into her thoughts. But it wasn't just the well-built ex quarterback's good looks that were getting to her. It was also that kind, friendly and easygoing demeanor about him that he wore like a designer suit. Lester had told her of his impressive playing and coaching resume, and from what little she had seen of his interaction with the players, she could already tell that they had strongly gravitated to him. His coaching disposition was much like hers—not a screamer, but rather calmly and confidently teaching the players the points he wanted to get across, following up with much positive reinforcement. And once her players got over the giddiness of being instructed by the, 'Oh My God, he's such a hunk' in the girls' basketball specific weight and agility training program that Luke had introduced, they clearly took to his knowledgeable and effective coaching style. And then there was Rose. She seemed so at ease with him, and him with her. Luke simply had a way that came to him naturally; not in the least bit contrived or forced.

"Enough!" she whispered to her herself as she shook her head vigorously, as if bouncing her brain off the skull a few times would bring renewed focus. "Okay Madison, get back to the work of how to divide the teams for the scrimmage!"

The disparity between her top five players and the rest of the team was stark; the four Brewster sisters and Clare Comes at Night being light years ahead of the reserves. At 6'1", senior Sonya Brewster was a slender and talented post player who was being recruited by most all of the Frontier Conference colleges in Montana. The Brewster twins were juniors, and while looking alike facially they couldn't have been more different in body

162

structure. At 6'0", Sandra was stocky and slow-footed, whereas the 5'11" Sabrina had the usual Brewster slim build and was agile enough to play on the perimeter. At 5'9", freshman Sammi was already skilled enough to play any position on the court, and the 5'2" Clare Comes at Night was more than a pleasant surprise to round out the starting five. While rarely speaking to anyone, the skinny Native American girl let her play do her talking. She was lightning quick and could handle the ball as well as or better than anyone Madison had ever played with or against—in either high school or college. Compared to Sammi's classic shooting form that Lester had ingrained into her since second grade, Clare's low-to-the-floor shooting launch and odd wrist angle release was anything but conventional technique. But based on her years of playing and coaching against Indian schools, Madison had made no attempt to alter her shooting mechanics, as many current and former Native players could score with alarming accuracy regardless of unique and uncustomary shooting deliveries.

Despite the Brewster twins, particularly Sandra, being considerably less skilled than the older Sonya and younger Sammi, Madison couldn't have been more pleased with the starting five she could put on the floor. They were collectively more talented than any of the fine teams they had when she was an assistant coach at Class A Laurel. But the bottom dropped out of the floor when it came to the five reserves. Five foot six senior Betty Ann Drury and the two juniors, 5'5" Dee Cassidy and Bev Rood, had nary an athletic bone among the three of them. Sophomores Anna Rimby and Cindy Cottingham were two smallish guards that could at least somewhat handle the ball and occasionally make an uncontested layup. After only one practice, Madison quickly agreed with 5'2" freshman Chelsea Ployhar's assessment that she was better suited as the team manager.

Madison's thoughts drifted back to Luke and how she had made him laugh when she stated the starting five would be reversed if the game being played was 'Make-up and Hair Styling' instead of basketball.

"I've got to be careful here," she quietly said out loud to herself. The last thing she needed at this stage was to enter another relationship... not for herself, and certainly not for Rose. Rose was having a hard time with the divorce, especially since her dad had disappointed her time and again by not showing up when he had promised to. He had already moved on to a new marriage that included a newborn child, and he seemed to have little time for Rose.

Madison's thoughts floated to Luke. *Although I like and am attracted to my neighbor and fellow coach, I must keep my distance. As much as a big part of me wants to dive right in, I just can't go there.*

MADISON ASKS LESTER TO HELP AT PRACTICE

Madison only had to use half of her prep period to prepare for her last two classes of the afternoon, so she took the opportunity of a rare free 20 minutes to run down to Superintendent Brewster's office. Secretary Lois was on the phone at the front desk, but she motioned Madison to go on through to Lester's office.

"Hey Lester, you have a minute?" asked Madison as she poked her head around the door.

"Sure, what's up?"

"I think we have a chance to be a really good team. Your girls are awesome, but they need to be challenged by playing against somebody besides each other. I don't think I'm telling you anything you don't already know when I say things can get pretty nasty when I have Sonya and Sandra matched up against each another. And considering the minimal height and skill level we have on this team other than your girls, it's really the only effective match-up I can create in drills and 5 on 5 stuff. As you also know, it's not much better when I throw Sabrina in the mix, especially if she has to go against Sonya."

"I know, I know," said Lester, shaking his head with a dejected look on his face. "I wish they weren't so darn competitive with each other and hard to coach. Of course, they're all too stubborn to listen to me. They don't think I know the difference between a basketball and a baseball. I just don't know what to tell you, I really don't."

"No, no, don't get me wrong here, Lester. I'm not here to complain or suggest that they are difficult to coach, because so far they haven't been. To the contrary, I'm really enjoying working with them. What I'm talking about here is finding a way to challenge them and improve their game without pitting them against each other. I can still play a little, so I can go against Sandra or Sabrina and make them work, but I'm just one person. What I want to do is bring some guys in to scrimmage against them on Wednesday nights when we have the late practice. I was watching a program on TV the other night about Pat Summitt at Tennessee, and she has a group of guys come in to scrimmage against her girls on a regular basis," said Madison excitedly. "That's what I'd like to do; bring in some guys, and I'd like you to be one of them. Don't worry, I've already talked to your girls, and if I'm using you to do individual work with them, like post moves, post defense, or playing man in drills or a scrimmage, then you would go against either Sandra or Sabrina. I've also talked to our boys' coach, Glenn Goettel, and he said he would come in and help out. I know he played some college ball at Tech, and at 6'3" and only 28 years old, he can go against Sonya. And Elvis said he would come. Can't hurt having one of the top players in the state working with us, could it?"

"Oh my gosh, no," replied Lester. "I can't wait to see him play. And yeah, Glenn would be great. But Madison, I'm 46 and have an arthritic knee. Not sure I'm the guy you want, even if you did find one or two of my girls that wouldn't mind if I played."

"Nonsense," said Madison, "I've seen you work out and shoot around, and you'd put most of the 30s crowd around here to shame."

"Well, if you really want me to suit up, then I'd be happy to help. Hey, what about Luke? He's what, 6'3" or 6'4"? I know he was a really good hoops player in high school," said Lester, continuing with a smile, "and I'm sure the girls wouldn't mind having the school's new heartthrob on the court with them either. I know my girls more than look forward to his weightlifting sessions."

"I'd hate to ask him," stated Madison with a bit of red creeping up her neck from Lester's heartthrob reference. "I mean, he's got his hands full with his own football practice."

"You did say you wanted this scrimmage against some guys to happen at your late Wednesday evening practice, right? So that practice starts at 6:30 and Luke will be done by then."

"Yes, I suppose so, but I still don't feel right about asking him."

"Just let me handle that part of it. Wow, the girls should have a helluva workout going against you and three or four guys that are at least 6'3". We'll see you next Wednesday at 6:30," declared Lester, obviously excited at the prospect of getting back in the gym. He thought to himself that at age 46 he should be over his gym loving days, but he felt like he was 26 again and the old saying 'once a gym rat, always a gym rat' was still ringing true.

DOLPH AND EARL HAVE QUESTIONS FOR LUKE

On the Tuesday before the first game of the season with Range View, Luke was in the coaches' room during his prep period watching the tape of last year's Range View game. He had been hopeful that he could glean at least a morsel of information from the film, but it had turned out to be an exercise of futility. The young eighth grade camcorder operator must have been exceedingly distracted that day, as literally every play was almost over by the time she hit the record switch. His frustration was fortunately interrupted when Dolph barged through the door.

"Coach, coach... I was just wondering, coach, if... you know, grades have come out yet, and, you know, if I'm on the bad list. You know what I mean, coach, that very bad list of the guys that can't play in this week's game 'cause they didn't get good enough grades?" Dolph inquired as he wrung his hands nervously.

Luke had to laugh inwardly, as since school had only started on Thursday of the prior week, the football and girls' basketball teams had a free pass from the dreaded eligibility list for the first weekend of games. This was a well known and treasured circumstance that all the kids were happily aware of, with Dolph being the apparent exception. Edna and Lester had previously explained to Luke that Dolph was exempt from eligibility requirements due to his mental limitations, but per Edna's instructions, Dolph wasn't to be informed of that fact so that he would continue to work hard in the classroom. As a result, Dolph worried and stressed incessantly each week as to whether or not he was on the 'very bad list.'

"Good news, Dolph," replied Luke. "There isn't a list this first week, so you're good to go." Dolph's face lit up like a

Christmas tree, and he shouted back over his shoulder as he raced out the door. "Best of news, coach! That's the best of news!"

Dolph had no sooner departed when Earl Wonderwald knocked on the door. "What can I do for you, Earl?" asked Luke. Earl stammered and stuttered for more than a few awkward moments until finally spitting out, "Well coach, I just came from Mr. Brewster's office and Sally was printing off our roster to send to Range View, and I was just wonderin'... uhh, was just kinda wonderin'... see, I'm listed as 5'4" and 97 pounds and, uhh...."

After another awkward pause, Luke said. "Yes, that's right Earl. That was your official height and weight when we measured and weighed everybody last Friday. So what's the problem?"

"Well coach, I know that, but I was wonderin' if we could, like, maybe adjust that a little. You know, just for program roster purposes."

"I see," said Luke thoughtfully. "And what kind of adjustment do you have in mind?"

Earl shuffled in place nervously, and tentatively began to advance his proposed roster alterations. "Coach, I kinda feel like I'm growin' pretty darn fast, and I think by the end of the season I'll be up there around 5'5" for sure. And my mom's been shoveling the chow to me. She's a good cook, and with me eating more and all the weightlifting that you have us doing and everything, I'm thinkin' I'll be, like, like 104 by the time football is over. So I was just kinda wonderin' if you could go ahead and make that change to the roster now. Like, say to 5'5" and 104... do ya think maybe we could do that?"

"Well Earl, that sounds reasonable," said Luke, summoning all of his willpower to keep a serious visage on his face. "But I'm actually thinking you will probably be taller and heavier than that by the end of the season. What would you think if we went 5'5 ½" and 106?"

With a thick coat of relief washing over his now smiling face, Earl confidently replied. "Yes sir, yes coach! I think you're right.

Why, I'm thinkin' 5'6" and 108 by the end of the season ain't out of the question, but 5'5 ½" and 106 will work real good for now, you betcha. Thanks a million, coach!"

Luke waited until Earl was out the door before bursting out laughing. If only he could now figure out a way to get the pale, frail freshman in a game for a few plays without getting him killed.

LUKE AND MADISON DISCUSS THEIR TEAMS

"Mr. Carter," Rose hollered to Luke from across the backyard fence. "Okay if I come over and mow?"

"You bet Rose, have at it," replied Luke.

He had just gotten home from a short Thursday practice in preparation for the season opener at Range View and was throwing a couple of pork chops on the grill. He nonchalantly glanced next door in hopes of catching a glimpse of Madison, but only Rose was visible as she pushed her lawn mower through the gate that connected them at the alley end of their yards. Even though he had seen and briefly chatted with Rose in the cafeteria at school during this first week of classes, he asked, "So Rose, how did the first week of school go?"

"It was good. I like my teacher, Mrs. Hunter, a lot," she said enthusiastically. "She's like really, really cool, and we're going to do a lot of fun stuff this year. And the kids in my class are nice, except for Shane Pierce. He's such a jerk, but Abby says he's like that to everybody, so to just ignore him and not worry about it. Mrs. Hunter has chewed him out, like, a million times already. He even had to stay in the room when everybody else went out to recess today, so he kind of shaped up after that."

"Okay Rose, you'd better quit blabbing and get to work before it gets dark," interrupted Madison from her back porch. Luke walked over to the fence to greet her, and actually surprised himself when he blurted out an awkward invitation for Rose and her to come over for pork chops. Before she had time to respond, he recovered and quickly added, with a wave of the hand and a humorous imparted air of importance, "As you can see, I've made some big-time, very expensive patio furniture upgrades. I'll have you know that I attended Emmy and Gail's yard sale last weekend and picked up those two high dollar lawn chairs. Now, they were priced at $5 a piece, but being the skilled negotiator that I am, I took them both off the show yard for the grand total of eight bucks. I'll also have you know that a fine, leather recliner adorns my showcase living room. Granted, it's a relic and possibly the first recliner ever made, but the footrest still pops up if you have Tank-like strength to push on the lever hard enough. Got her for another bargain—ten bucks!"

"My, my, Mr. Carter, you did get them for a steal, didn't you? I can see it's going to be hard to keep up with the Joneses living next door to the likes of you! Well, if you don't mind having the riff raff neighbors from the wrong side of the fence over for dinner, I have half a tub of potato salad and some of Mrs. Groves' rhubarb pie I can bring."

"So how's practice going? Are you ready for tomorrow night?" asked Luke as they settled into the two yard sale lawn chairs.

"Good, good. Like most coaches, I always feel like I need more time, but yet I'm anxious to get the show on the road."

"Yeah, I feel the same way with my guys. So, are the Brewster girls behaving? From what I've gathered from Edna and what Kip reports as the gossip gospel that's being preached by the Hole in the Wall Coffee gang, they're tough to coach. Heck, even Lester himself told me that."

"Well, let me first say that I take my hat off to Lester. I'd rather be tied to the lamp post and flogged than try to coach a team that consisted of three or four of my own daughters. That's just a recipe for disaster. However, I haven't had any real problems so far. I mean, Sonya is just kind of a difficult one to begin with. She's very quiet, private. You could easily add sullen and moody to the list as well. But at least so far, she hasn't been overly hard to deal with. She works really hard in practice, so that's good. The twins, Sandra and Sabrina, haven't caused me any heartburn either, although it's clear they're not as skilled as Sonya—or Sammi, for that matter. So I can see where it has the potential to get nasty at some point during the season. Plus, none of the younger three get on well with Sonya. I think it's more than just a sibling competition thing, but I haven't been able to put my finger on it just yet. I guess we'll see what develops once we start playing games."

"From just stealing a look or two at your practices, it appears to me that the freshman Sammi is going to be a helluva player."

"Oh yeah, she's very talented, and again, I'm not yet sure how the three older sisters are going to deal with that. We'll see what happens when Sammi outplays and outscores all of the other sisters in a real game. I've seen sisterly love dissipate pretty quickly when the youngest whippersnapper outshines the older veterans. But I'll tell you one thing for sure; I've been around some pretty darn good Class A and Class B programs these past years, and none have had the talent my starting five has. And I haven't even mentioned Clare Comes at Night. For such a skinny little thing, she is highly skilled. I'm telling you, she's quick as a cat and can really handle the ball. She's used to the fast paced, up and down the court in a hurry style of play that most all of the Indian schools employ, which doesn't really mesh with the controlled half court offense that better fits the Brewster girls' skill set. So that's my coaching challenge: how to integrate the speed and quickness of Clare's game with that of the Brewster girls and not handcuff either of their strengths. Don't get me wrong, it's a nice dilemma to have. My main mission is to not get any of my starters in foul trouble, because I go from the top of the mountain down to the deepest valley when it comes to my reserves. Anyway, with the talent of the first five, suffice it to say the Hole in the Wall Coffee gang would have every right to tar and feather me if I can't get these kids to State."

"Well, I hope I can help provide some competition for the Brewster girls when us guys come in to scrimmage your team on Wednesday nights," Luke stated. "Just don't make me guard Clare. I don't really need to blow a hammy trying to stay in front of her."

"Oh my God, did Lester ask you to come play? I'm so sorry. I told him you had way too much going on with your own practices to expect you to take the time to help us out. Besides, you are already spending time on my program by implementing the strength and agility routines, which by the way, I greatly appreciate—especially since I know so little about the new age methods."

"No worries, Madison. I'll be done with practice by the time your session on Wednesday starts. It'll do me good to work up a sweat, plus I love basketball. Do you do therapy for wounded egos? I might need counseling if the Brewster girls take me to school!"

"Yes, I'm a skilled counselor, but it'll cost you," said Madison with that captivating smile that was becoming harder for Luke to ignore. "And no crying. Remember, there's no crying in basketball."

"Well, I can't guarantee that I won't have at least a minor emotional outburst if Sonya dunks on me. Speaking of crying, there is crying in football. At least at my practices there is. Big Brundage Spragg spews a stream of tears every practice that would rival a flooding Spring Creek. I'm talking some serious meltdowns! It's hysterical when T.O. barks at him to dry it up."

"No way! You've got be kidding me! He's like 250 pounds!" exclaimed Madison.

"More like 270, and no, I'm not kidding. I'd like to suggest that he just go home to his mommy, but his daddy thinks he's going to be the next Tank."

"Speaking of Tank, how do you feel about him and the rest of your team as you go into your first game?"

"We'd be pretty good if we had a quarterback. Tank's a freaking beast, as you might imagine. And Aaron, Stefan, Bret and Tucker are all good players. Even my skinny little shits Tuf and Danny are tougher than nails. But we're pretty one-sided. No, let me take that back. We're totally one-sided. All we can do is run the ball, so teams will just stack up against the run and make it difficult for us. But even at that, I think we'll win our fair share of games. But with no passing game, I'm not sure I can deliver on Edna's desperate desire to put one on the 'Goddamn Catholics.'

"Yes, thank God the St. Francis girls aren't all that good. I'd hate to have Edna breathing down my neck about the 'Goddamn Catholics' like she will with you. But she has already made it clear that she expects me to win against the three teams that have whipped us like badly behaving dogs and dominated the Northern Division in recent years; that being Wyngate, Chester and Big Sandy."

"Yeah, I'm thinking we'd both better produce to Edna's expectations or we might get loaded on the proverbial train to nowhere," Luke suggested.

"You've got that right," laughed Madison, who then took on a more serious look as if she was undecided if she should share her thought with Luke. "I might be speaking out of bounds here, but since I grew up in and have coached in a small town, could I make a suggestion to a guy that grew up in and has always coached in big high schools?"

"Of course, I could use all the suggestions and tips that you can give me," said Luke sincerely.

"Well, one of the really cool things that you see at most small schools is that the kids really come out and support each other in all sports. Obviously, during the fall the only two sports in most little schools are football and girls' basketball. The kids will usually go to each other's games without being told to, but just so you know, I've made a pretty big deal with my girls about how important it is to support each other. I've told them I expect them to be at all football games when we don't have a schedule conflict with our own games. I don't know, I just think it promotes a real positive school spirit and pride if you can get the kids used to supporting and cheering for each other. Again, I don't mean to come across as bossy or sticking my nose in your football program's business, but thought I'd let you know my thoughts on the subject."

"Hell no, I ain't going to any of your games, and neither is anybody on our football team," exclaimed Luke, feigning an expression of disgust at the very thought. "Seriously Madison, I'm really glad you brought that up, as you are right in that you don't always see that kind of reciprocal support at the big schools. I mean, I was planning to go to all your games where we don't have a conflict anyway, as I've really enjoyed getting to know your girls a little bit through my weight training and agility sessions, and want to watch them on the floor. Plus, I'm a big basketball fan. But I'll make a point of stressing it to our guys too; you are right on in that it is an important school unity and pride kind of thing."

Luke didn't feel the need to mention that the main reason he intended to go to all the girls' games was that it was good excuse to see her.

GAME WEEK—RANGE VIEW

As Shanty Sweeney leaned over and grabbed the handle to close the bi-fold doors of Pacer Coulee's largest and most recently acquired yellow school bus, Luke welcomed back the familiar first game nerves and jitters that had been on pause for the past two years. "Let 'er rip, Shanty!" somebody yelled out from the back, and the just-turned-83-years-young bus driver gave a thumbs up as he pulled away from the curb.

"Say Shanty, how long ye think til we get to Dublin? Me sis and her late husband Kevin O'Malley, God rest his drunken soul, own O'Malley's Irish Pub and Grill down on Kilkenny Street, and we lads was hopin' ye could stop there for a few pints before and after the game," shouted Bo Ramsay, clearly in his full Irish character mode. Everyone laughed as their beloved chauffeur countered the team clown's remark with a big smile and wave of dismissal.

Having Bo in class and with him coming out for football for the first time this his senior year, Luke was just beginning to appreciate his storied linguistic talents. Aaron Coslet, his often times theatrical sidekick, jokingly described Bo as "a deeply deranged humanoid afflicted with Multiple Split Personality Syndrome, a condition where those so stricken hear and speak the voices of the many and varied inhabitants that occupy their wretched souls."

"Seriously coach," Aaron had explained, "Richard Little has nothing on this guy as an impressionist. He can do all the old actors perfectly: John Wayne, Jimmy Stewart, Clint Eastwood, Marlon Brando, George C. Scott. You name it, he can imitate it. And he can go into just about any dialect—Irish, Italian mafia, British, Norwegian, Native American speak, black ghetto speak, red-neck southern speak, Texas drawl speak, back-woods Blue Ridge Mountain speak, Cajun speak… he can do it all."

It was 11:00 a.m. on the warm and windy Friday morning when Shanty turned to the east for the hour and a half journey to Range View, the game scheduled for a 1:30 start. This first game of the year against the Rangers, and the last one of the season against St. Francis, were the only two games that would be played on a Friday. As the spry old Irishman pointed the bus down the hill and across Warm Spring Creek, Luke reflected on the whirlwind of the past few weeks. They were able to get through the first three weeks of practice relatively healthy, with only two players that Luke had already determined could dress for the game, but not play. The first was Kimball Robbins, who was nursing a sore hamstring.

"Always some damn thing with him," T.O. had said. "Next week it'll be a sprained ankle, then a sore knee. Then he'll get the flu and God only knows what will be next." His questionable game status would have been a much higher concern to Luke if they actually had a quarterback that could get him the ball down field. That not being the case, Luke supposed it didn't really matter that there probably wasn't anybody in the league that could cover the fleet young receiver. But if and when they ever got him healthy, Luke would find a way to get him the ball in open space out of the backfield on pitches and reverses; easy tosses that even Virgil should be able to make. The other injury casualty was Earl Wonderwald, the only Pacer Coulee player listed on the roster in the game program with height and weight-inflated stats. While Luke was careful to have him paired with the smallest guys for drills, at Wednesday afternoon's practice he had barreled into the 150-lb Ernie Rimby in a tackling drill and had bruised his shoulder. Luke was actually grateful that he had an injury so as to have an excuse to not risk putting the undersized boy in the game and getting him seriously hurt.

Luke reviewed the set of formations and plays that he had printed out and placed within a plastic folder that would protect it from any potential weather elements. He couldn't help but smile at the huge departure from the offense he ran in the 11-man game, where he employed multiple formations... Twins,

Trips, 5 wide-outs, 1 tight end, 2 tight ends, 1 back, 2 backs, pre-snap shifts, I-back motion, tight end motion, H-back motion, slot receiver motion, wide receiver motion, and everything in between. Just the simple fact of having only eight players, five of whom had to be on the line of scrimmage, reduced the formation options that could be employed. Upon evaluation of his available talent after the first few practices of the season, Luke had quickly come to the conclusion that 'the simpler the better' would be the preferred approach to the design of the offensive playbook. The fact that the only pass his quarterback could make with any degree of consistency was at Chelsey Ployhar in his Montana History class had narrowed the playbook down to a run-only game plan.

He had learned many valuable lessons about the game of football from the legendary coach Sonny Sweden, both as his player and as his grad assistant coach. Sonny had a way of simplifying a very complex game down to a few common sense principles. Luke would never forget the advice coach had given him when he got his first offensive coordinator job at Lincoln.

"Remember Luke, you can't make cherry pie out of horse shit," he had said. "In other words, especially in high school where you can't recruit players with a specific offense or defense in mind, you need to build your offense and defense around the talent that you have to work with. In your case as the OC, it doesn't make much sense to install all kinds of multiple formations of 4 and 5 wide-outs and throw it 50 times a game if you don't have the QB and wide receivers to execute it. So evaluate your talent and build your offensive around that, not the other way around." Another one of coach Sweden's euphemisms that Luke always kept in mind was the old adage that defense wins championships. "The math tells us that if we hold our opponents scoreless, the worst we can do is tie," his old mentor used to frequently say.

It hadn't taken more than the first ten minutes of the first practice to verify T.O.'s opinion of Virgil Cottingham's throwing abilities, or rather the lack thereof. Luke had even made everybody pair off and stand 12 yards apart and play catch, hoping to see someone that had a semblance of a natural throwing motion. Sadly, he found none. "Jesus Christ," he had said to T.O. after the first practice, "I can't believe we don't have one kid, not one in 17 that can throw better than my grandma. How in the hell can that be?"

"I know, I know," replied T.O. "And what's even worse is that both Danny Schrader and Ernie Rimby are pretty damn good pitchers. They both play Legion ball in Centertown in the summer, and I've seen them both pitch. Beats the hell outa me how you can accurately throw a small round ball into a mitt from 90 feet away, but can't throw an oblong one through a barn door from five feet."

So, run the ball it would be, Luke had quickly concluded. He had scrapped the popular and widely used 8-man 'Balanced Tight' formation, in which there was a closely aligned guard and end on either side of the center, for two reasons: firstly, he was used to the unbalanced formations of the 11-man game. Secondly, and probably most importantly, was the need to have Tank and Dolph line up side by side in order for Tank to give Dolph instructions on who to block. In a balanced formation the center would be in between them, and that didn't work near as well as having them next to each other as guard and tackle in the unbalanced formation.

Other than the acquisition of the highly touted Tank Hollister, assistant coach T.O. Barker was proving to be the next most noteworthy gift of Luke's Bulldog coaching position inheritance. The bulky 51-year-old rancher was not only born and raised in Pacer Coulee, but he had continuously been its assistant football coach for the past 25 years. As such, he had vast and thorough knowledge of the 8-man game and of all the coaches and teams in their conference, not to mention the entire state. "I'll tell ya right up front Luke, I'm just an ol' offensive and defensive lineman," T.O. had informed Luke the day that fall practice began. "I don't pretend to be any kind of overall offensive or defensive strategist, so don't expect much help from me in that regard, as that's above my pay grade. But I damn sure know how to teach and coach line play fundamentals and technique. You should also know that I'm old school, and I'm generally cranky and in a foul mood. I don't coddle these little darlings, so any of this new age shit that these kids need to be showered with hugs and kisses? Well, that's gonna have to come from you, 'cause I got no time for it. I'll also tell you that I cuss, swear and holler at these little bastards with regularity, and I'm hard as hell on 'em. I only give out 'atta-boys' when earned and well deserved. Just telling you up front how I do things, and I'm too fucking old to change."

In the three weeks that had passed from the start of practice, Luke had concluded that he and T.O.'s coaching styles were a perfect meld. Luke was cerebral in his approach, and the Xs and Os and in-game strategies and adjustments came easy to him. He was first and foremost a teacher, and his calm, patient and positive approach was a perfect offset to T.O.'s more traditional coaching style. And since Luke had but one assistant coach, the two quickly came to the conclusion that the most expedient use of their respective coaching resources would be for T.O. to take the O and D-lines for drills and individual position coaching sessions, and for Luke to work with the quarterbacks, running backs, receivers, linebackers and defensive backs. Luke would take primary responsibility for all matters concerning overall strategy and game planning, with T.O. providing input on the defensive side of the ball where he felt more knowledgeable and comfortable.

Looking back to an earlier practice when Luke was first installing his offense, he laughed at an incident that initiated the fondness of the relationship that was developing between him and T.O. Luke had awoken in the middle of the night with the idea of installing a pass play to Bo Ramsay, his weak side guard in his unbalanced formation. Since he wasn't covered by a receiver to his outside, Bo was considered an eligible receiver. Much like the weak side tackle in the 11-man game, the 8-man weak side guard was primarily thought of as a blocker and would rarely be utilized as receiver. Luke's midnight revelation was to design a play in the Twins formation where the two outside receivers would run routes to the opposite side of the field, thereby creating a defender-less gap on that side of the field for the weak side guard to enter after a short delay to block the defensive end. After a play fake to the single back, the quarterback would wait for the weak side guard to run a shallow drag across the middle, resulting in a short and relatively easy pass to the wide-open receiver guard.

The unfortunate downside to the concept of the Luke named 'Bo Weak Side Guard Drag' was that Bo Ramsay had the worst hands on the team. "Jesus Christ, Luke," T.O. had said. "I heard you were supposed to be some kind of an offensive genius, but there's two problems with this brainchild play of yours; first, we don't have a quarterback who can throw it through an open machine shed door if he was standing in it, and secondly you're asking a kid that couldn't catch the clap to be at the receiving end... don't sound too fuckin' genius to me."

Luke had laughed like crazy at his new assistant coach's assessment of his new play, but had responded with, "Well, call me silly, but Bo and Virgil are gonna stay after practice every night and run this play five times. He's eventually going to learn how to catch it and we'll unveil this play down the road at some point at a critical juncture of a big game, and Bo will take it to the house to win the game. Be a Doubting Debbie if you must, but you'll see... it'll happen.

As Shanty brought the bus to a stuttering stop at a railroad crossing at the edge of Centertown, Luke's train of thought was interrupted by uproarious laughter from the back of the bus. He and T.O. turned and looked back to see what all the commotion was about. Bo was standing in the center aisle above a red-faced, but laughing Alden Blackburn, the appointed by his father soccer style kicker for the Bulldogs. Luke felt sorry for the dreadfully thin youngster who was clearly out of his league as a football kicker. Luke had had some excellent soccer style kickers at Lincoln and was knowledgeable about the technique, but try as he might for the past three weeks, he was unsuccessful in getting Alden to elevate a kick more than about three feet off the ground. To make matters even worse, his kicks always squirted off to the right. When they actually set up in a field goal formation, Tucker Greyson was the long snapper and Tank was the first man to his right. At the conclusion of each practice, Luke would call for the field goal team to line up at the 3-yard line and they would try four or five extra point attempts. Usually the first couple were harmless grounders to the right that simply dribbled through the lineman's legs. The one or two kicks that he was actually able to get somewhat airborne spurted off to the right, usually ending with an abrupt collision with Tank's backside. Luke would conclude kicking practice for the day when Tank would grab the football and rifle it back at Alden with an angry retort: "Hit me in the ass one more time and I'll ring your fucking neck like a pheasant!"

Bo was now in his British personality and dialect mode as he talked to the kicker whose father had come to the States from England. "I've noticed that when you blokes are kicking that round ball, yes, the one that has those splendid black and white polka dots on it, yes, kicking that ball up and down a pasture that is big enough to graze 500 of the Queen's favorite bovines for a year—splendid, splendid, but a rather large pasture, don't you think? Anyway, in watching you blokes try to get that polka dot ball into that cage you have on either end of the pasture, I noticed that some of the lads hit the bloody ball with their head! Imagine that, with their bloody head!" cried Bo, popping his head forward from the neck in an exaggerated demonstration of the heading technique. "And why one would want to thrust one's head into the path of a ball traveling at the speed of a bloody missile? Well, I surely don't know, I surely don't. At any rate, the blokes seem to be able to hit it off their noggins towards the bloody cage with alarming accuracy.

"Now Alden, at risk of seeming blunt or unkind, I must say your attempts to strike our American oblong shaped ball through the goal post, well, frankly Alden, your efforts are quite sub-standard. In fact, the way you always strike that bloody ball straight away into Tank's ample arse is quite disturbing, I must say. In fact, I rather think the sight of it would bring Prince Charles, Prince Phillip, and perhaps even the Queen herself to their knees in tears. They might be so upset and distraught with your wayward attempts at finding the lonesome space that resides between goal posts that it might ruin their afternoon cup of tea. Think of it! Yes indeed, ruin their spot of tea!"

By now the talented Bo had everyone's full attention with his mesmerizing British-speak. Luke noticed that even Shanty was watching Bo's performance through his mirror. Not wanting to miss the show, Shanty seemed to be paying more attention to his mirror than the roadway. Still standing in the aisle next to Alden, who seemed to be enjoying the performance as much as anyone, Bo called for Aaron to grab a football and to lean over in his seat and place the ball down in the aisle as if he were the holder for a field goal attempt. "I've a grand plan for you, Alden, that might very well solve the elevation and accuracy problems you are currently experiencing. Now, here's what you do. You approach the bloody ball from straight on like this," Bo demonstrated, bending over and cocking his head as he stepped towards the ball, "and on the last step you launch yourself, head first, towards the ball. Now make sure your bloody head is fully cocked and at the last second," said Bo, as he repeated the exaggerated motion of snapping the head forward like a chicken pecking out for a kernel of corn, "at the last second, right before you auger your head into the ground, you SNAP your head... you SNAP your head into the back of the bloody football, and I'd bet Princess Di's peacock feathered hat that you'll launch that bloody sucker up, up and away! Way up over Tank's humongous arse, over the crossbar and through the uprights! That's right Alden, the bloody ball will pass through that sacred space between the goal posts that one of your foot-launched balls has yet to violate. Excellent, splendid, indeed!"

With his performance completed to a round of laughter and applause, none more enthusiastic than that of Alden, everyone settled back down for the last half hour of the trip. Luke was relieved to see Shanty refocus on the task of keeping the yellow bus on the right side of the center line. As they were completing their descent down the eastern slopes of the Judith Mountain pass and about to spill out to the vast open plains of east central Montana, he saw a road sign for Gilt Edge and Ft. Maginnis pointing back towards the Judiths. *'So that's where it is,'* Luke thought to himself, as he had become somewhat familiar in his Montana History crash course with the days of yore of the 1880 military outpost. It was one of five forts established across the Territory during the Indian Wars following the defeat of Custer at the Battle of Little Bighorn. Although he recalled that Gilt Edge was now a ghost town and that little remained of the fort, he made a mental note to someday drive to the site and check it out.

"Okay guys, it's time to go 1-0," said Luke, beginning his pregame message to the team in the locker room before taking the field. "We've had a good first three weeks of practice, and I like the way things are shaping up for this team. I won't bullshit you. This is a game we should win handedly. They are no match for us up front on either side of the ball. Tank, you need to set the stage from the very first play. Tank, Dolph, Tucker, Bret and Bo... you guys need to collectively dominate the line of scrimmage when we're on offense. Stefan and Aaron, just read your blocks and do your thing. Remember, the main stat that I focus on for our running backs is yards after initial contact. If this wind keeps up like this, we won't attempt to pass. Defensively, we know they like to throw it 50 times a game. Their quarterback Olson is a good one if given time to throw, and he scrambles well and can throw on the run. We know that they have a good receiver in Bratsman. Again, they are small up front, and they'll try to double and triple team Tank. They still won't be able to stop him, but I expect Dolph, Tucker and Bo to have a hay day. If we can, we will make them go into the wind in the first quarter. No way can they throw or punt into this wind, so we should get them into bad field position from the get-go.

"First game jitters? Yep, we're feeling it, me included. But channel that nervous energy into a focus on what each one of you needs to do individually and collectively to contribute to this team. In watching NFL and college games on TV, you've heard all the old adages that we've been preaching to you: defense wins championships; the team that best executes their offense will win; games are won up front; the team with the fewest turnovers will win; don't beat yourself with stupid penalties, etcetera. Well, all of those things are true at any level of football. Especially in the first game of the year, we need to just settle in and not get so hyped that we do some or all of those things to beat ourselves.

"And guys, here's a news alert—you are going to make a mistake or two. Just make sure you're going balls out when you screw up. Use good technique; we don't work on that every day just for the hell of it. Don't get beat on pass rush because you don't use good technique. Don't get stymied on the run block due to poor get-off and bad pad level. Don't get blocked because you don't use good technique in getting off the ball, hand strike positioning and shedding. Don't get beat by a receiver on the pass because you don't use good footwork technique. How you apply that technique is what coach Barker and I are going to be looking for.

"Offensively, we are going about as basic as it gets. We're only running out of a couple of different formations, and we'll run power, counter, sweep and some fullback give off the option look, but only do true reads on speed option. If the wind stays this strong, we won't run speed option and risk a pitch. Up front, let's give Aaron and Stefan some room to run. Give them a seam and trust me, good things will happen. If the wind lets up enough to allow it, we'll throw it a little bit out of play action just to keep them from stacking the line of scrimmage with all eight guys. Again, if the wind stays at this level of severity, we won't throw it at all.

"Defensively… if you hold 'em scoreless, the worst you can do is tie. Which means we'll win, because we'll definitely get a score on the board, right? Nobody is going to be able to keep us out of the end zone. Concentrate on your reads and let's fly to the ball. I want to see everybody rallying to the football until the whistle blows. Let's hit 'em like a freight train.

"And guys, bottom line is this," Luke continued. "Play hard, play with great effort, and play for each other. Remember when you used to play football at fifth grade recess on the dirt patch next to the playground? Play with the same enthusiasm and joy that you played with then. You know how annoyed you guys always get when your parents tell you that these high school years should be the best of your life? Well, it's true, and nothing is greater than high school football—this very moment—that knot you have in the pit of your stomach right now. Go out there and play your asses off for yourselves and your teammates, and most importantly, have some fun!

"Everybody come in," Luke said, as 17 pumped up and excited boys leaped from the bench seats and gathered around Luke and T.O. in the middle of the locker room. "Does anybody have anything they would like to say before we hit the field?" With what Luke would later find to be the final words spoken in each weekly locker room sendoff, Tank moved in front of the team where he could look them all in the eye and roared, "Let's go knock their dicks in the dirt!" "Yeah," hollered Dolph, as he stuck to Tank's side like a mirror image as the team raced from the locker room. "Let's go knock their dicks in the dirt!"

With that, the team enthusiastically charged out of the little locker room and took to the field. Lagging behind and letting them clear the room first, Luke and T.O. exchanged grins as T.O. said, "I forgot to tell you about Tank's one sentence final pregame speech. It's a tradition; and by the way, Dolph gets upset if Tank doesn't say it before every game. I think he just likes to repeat it."

"Sounds like a good tradition," laughed Luke. "Well T.O., we better go see if we are good enough to knock anybody's dicks in the dirt."

As he and T.O. walked down to the field, Luke was not sure he had ever seen so many pickups and horse trailers as had gathered to fully occupy the entire circumference of the Range View field. He was also sure that he hadn't seen this many cowboy hats since he attended the Cheyenne Frontier Days Rodeo in Wyoming a few years back. It was apparent that the Range View field didn't command the same care and attention as did the freshly polished and unusual linoleum-type floor in the gymnasium. Irrigation efforts were obviously prioritized to the outlying alfalfa fields, as what little water that might have been applied to the fields was insufficient to spur growth of the sparse and coarse stand of grass. Even the more plentiful weed population seemed to be left gasping for air in the cracks of the cement-hard turf. With a wry smile to himself, Luke did note that at least some attempt had been made to smooth out the gopher mounds and fill up their holes.

Luke was surprised at how many Pacer Coulee folks had made the trek to the game. He spotted what appeared to be the entire Hole in the Wall gang, and smiled when he saw Edna and Otis, Kellie Cassidy, and Bill and Marge Koch lean into the wind as they made their way to the visitor side bleachers.

Similar to his college playing days, Luke went with a limited pregame warm-up session. As coach Sweden always used to say, "Far as I can tell, they don't give out any trophies to those that win the pregame." Over the years, Luke had seen teams at the high school level spend an hour or more performing elaborate and exhaustive pregame exercises, only to be mentally and physically spent before the game even started. He felt the most important thing was to get the team thoroughly stretched and the muscles warmed up before spending no more than 15 minutes on half-speed blocking and tackling drills to get the pads popping, and then running a few plays to get the timing tuned in. Since the wind was bearing down on Ranger Field at a steady 40 knots with even higher hold-on-to-your-hat gusts, Luke again reminded Tank and Aaron to defer and take the wind if they won the coin toss. Tank had said not to worry about the coin toss, as Aaron was the luckiest gambler on the team and would surely win every away game coin toss of the season. True to Tank's word, Aaron won.

The wind continued to strengthen by the moment as two of the three Range View cheerleaders attempted to take the American and Montana flags to midfield for the presentation of the colors. When they unveiled the flags it was apparent they had the wrong girl holding the much larger and longer American flag, as she was as slight as a sparrow and began to stagger about in a gallant attempt to keep the flag in the air. Both T.O. and Luke broke into a smile when Bo joked, "Holy shit, boys. Mary fuckin' Poppins is about to go airborne!" Fortunately the Range View coach sent two of his players out to help her stabilize the flag, while the audio produced from the instruments of the seven students that hammered out the National Anthem was swept away by the westerly wind.

With the wind strength prohibiting the Rangers from throwing anything but a short pitch pass, Luke and T.O. went with tight single man coverage on their wide-outs and stacked the interior for the run. The Ranger line was undersized and horribly outmatched, and try as they might to double team Tank, he threw them around like rag dolls. With Dolph, Aaron, Bo or Stefan providing surefire support, the first three Range View plays resulted in a net loss of eight yards and forced them to kick into an even stronger, swirling wind from their own 7-yard line. Bo blocked the kick and Tuf Sturm corralled it just before it squirted out of the back of the end zone for a touchdown. Stefan ran in the 2-point conversion.

The next two Ranger possessions were met with similar fate, with the punt from the 2-yard line getting airborne but caught in the teeth of the wind and spit back out of the end zone for a safety. The next punt from the goal line was wisely angled to the sideline, and went for a positive two yards out to the Ranger 6-yard line. Stefan ran untouched for the touchdown on the Bulldogs' first play from scrimmage, following the blocks of Tank and Dolph on a strong side power play. Aaron ran in the 2-point conversion, and the Bulldogs jumped to an 18-0 advantage with eight minutes remaining in the first quarter.

On the next possession, the inexperienced Bo Ramsay lost contain on a QB sweep, leading to a 12-yard gain and the Rangers' only first down of the first quarter. But their drive quickly stalled, and Pacer Coulee scored twice more for a 32-0 lead at quarter end. Unfortunately for the Rangers, having the wind at their backs in the second quarter did little to advance their cause other than improve their field position via wind-aided punting distance. While their quarterback was a good athlete who could wing it with some velocity and accuracy, the ever-increasing swirling winds made it virtually impossible to complete a forward pass. Finally, the Range View coach gave up on the pass and ran the ball on every down, also with negligible success.

Even going against the wind in the second quarter, the Bulldogs ran the ball methodically down the field with two clock consuming drives to take a 40-0 advantage with six minutes to go in the half. Trying to avoid ending the game at half via the 45-point mercy rule, Luke emptied the bench as best he could, but with Alden playing only as a kicker and Earl and Kimball sidelined with injury, Luke only had six available players on the bench. Since Kimball served as the team's only back up QB, Virgil had to remain in the game. Not unexpectedly, as Luke was sending out the reserves, Earl began tugging on his sleeve and pleaded, "Coach, my shoulder is feeling a lot better. I think I'm good to go. Let me at them sum-bitches, coach. Lemme at 'em!"

"Sorry Earl, not this time. We just can't afford to risk further injury to that shoulder."

With Travis Cederholm now at center, the center/QB exchange was bungled on the first two plays, but Virgil was able to recover both. Even though Luke had pulled Tank, he wanted to keep Dolph in the game to see if he could be productive without his security blanket being right next to him. Dolph followed the two fumbled snaps with an illegal procedure penalty and looked to be totally lost. Big Brundage Spragg, the soft and clumsy 6'3", 250-pound freshman, played next to Dolph at Tank's position. "Jesus Christ," snapped T.O., to no one in particular. "I've got dead relatives that could get off the Goddamn ball quicker than Spragg. Jesus H. Christ!"

The rest of the second quarter was a comedy of errors, with neither team able to even pick up a first down. As the Bulldogs headed to the bus to get out of the wind with a 40-0 halftime lead, Skip Nelson, the Rangers coach, waved to Luke to meet him at midfield. "Coach Carter, I appreciate you putting in all your young kids and reserves to avoid the 45-point mercy rule ending this game at halftime, but I don't see any benefit to either of us to try to continue to play in these strong winds. If you don't object, why don't you put your starters back in first series of the second half and let them score. And then let's get our kids the hell out of this hurricane." Luke quickly agreed to comply with coach Nelson's sensible request, and when Stefan broke off a 53-yard run over Tank and Dolph on inside power on the second play of the third quarter, the resulting 46-0 score ended the game.

"Great effort, guys," said Luke, as the team gathered in the locker room. "Granted, we out-sized and out-talented this team, but we didn't play down to our opponents' level as superior teams can sometimes do. Even in that horrible wind, we made very few mistakes. Both coach Barker and myself were very pleased with your attention to fundamentals and technique. Feels pretty good to get the win and go 1-0, right?" "Yes!" the team roared, and Luke called them all in to join hands and finalize the victory with a loud and in-unison, "BULLDOGS WIN!"

The hour and a half trip home was a joyous one, with Bo and Aaron entertaining the troops with a few scenes from the old western movie *Rio Bravo*. Bo presented a perfect John Wayne imitation, and Aaron put forward a more than passable performance as Stumpy, the character portrayed by the great old actor, Walter Brennan. *It felt good to be back in the fray*, thought Luke to himself, as he whispered, "I'm getting back in the game, coach Sweden. One small step at a time." He pushed aside the added thought of how much he was looking forward to getting to Centertown in time to watch Madison Danielsen coach the Lady Bulldogs in their preseason opener.

GIRLS' PRE-SEASON TOURNAMENT

"Hi Mr. Carter," squealed Rose as she and her sidekick Abby Herman skipped to greet him as he waited in the concession stand line at the Fergus Fieldhouse. By the time boys showered, dressed and got back to Pacer Coulee, the girls' first preseason tournament game had already started, and it was halftime when Luke got back to Centertown. "I heard you guys won your game at Range View."

"Hi there girls... yes, we got the win. How are the Lady Bulldogs doing?"

"We're ahead, but mom's mad that we had so many turnovers," reported Rose. "She's probably giving them the business in the locker room right now."

"Yeah, way too many turnovers," Abby confirmed.

Luke took his hot dog and soda into the cavernous (compared to Pacer Coulee) gymnasium, and took up residence next to Bill and Marge Koch, Kellie Cassidy, Shanty and Edna in the Bulldog cheering section. "Where's Otis?" asked Luke.

"Won't let him in... discriminate against him, they do. They say since he isn't a service dog he's not allowed in the gym," adding while jokingly jabbing Kellie, "If my veterinarian was worth all that money I pay her she would sign off on Otis being a service dog."

"Hmmm... so how are the girls doing? Rose and Abby just said they had too many first half turnovers to suit coach Danielsen."

"Typical first game jitters," explained Edna. "I think the biggest problem is that Clare can do those no-look passes like nobody's business, and the Brewster twins can't react fast enough. But I think we'll pull away comfortably in the second half."

"Does Lester like to sit alone? I mean, all alone up there in the upper level like that?" asked Luke.

Enda replied, "Yes, he's nervous as a cat—wants to be by himself."

Just as Edna predicted, the girls pulled away from the Centerville Lady Miners in the second half. Sammi and Clare frequently worked the ball inside to Sonya, whose 24 points led both teams in scoring. Sammi added 14 mostly from the perimeter markers, and Luke lost track of how many assists the skilled little ball handler Clare had.

What he didn't lose track of was coach Madison Danielsen, finding it hard keep his attention on what was taking place on the floor.

BUTCH CASSIDY AND THE HOLE IN THE WALL COFFEE GANG

Kip Jordan wasn't entirely sure why he bothered to open his O.K. Corral Bar and Grill at 7:00 a.m. every morning. It certainly wasn't because of the profitability of selling coffee and donuts to Butch Cassidy and the Hole in the Wall gang, the moniker that Kip had branded the morning coffee and card-playing crowd of mostly older farmers and ranchers who waited impatiently for him to unlock the doors each and every morning. Kip also owned the only other eatery in town, the just across the street Calfe', and the majority of the folks yearning for breakfast went there. But since the Hole in the Wall gang played cards after their gossip and bullshit ritual, they needed more table space than the smallish Calfe' could provide. Fortunately for Kip, a few more people other than the Hole in the Wall gang usually came in and ordered breakfast, delivered from the Calfe', partially offsetting the cost, if not the annoyance, of having to open primarily for the benefit of the coffee gang.

"Thought the boys looked pretty damn good over there in Range View last Friday," said Baxter "Butch" Cassidy, the elder statesman and namesake of the coffee club crew. Baxter was called Baxter until Paul Newman and Robert Redford starred in the 1969 hit movie *Butch Cassidy and the Sundance Kid*. After that, he became Butch to everybody except his mother, who steadfastly remained with the Baxter handle she had given him until her demise. Butch, the grandfather of the Bulldog senior basketball player Dee Cassidy and her younger brother Bret, never missed a football or basketball game—home or away. He continued, "It was a windy sum-bitch though, wasn't it?"

"Yeah, kinda hard to tell what kind of team we have under

those conditions. I do know that Tank ain't got any smaller over the summer. Damn, he's a load. Don't see anybody being able to handle him this year, not even them St. Francis guys," added Duke Dickson, who was always first to arrive, despite the 18-mile drive into town from his farmstead being the furthest of any of the coffee gang.

"What's Bret think about the new coach, Butch?" asked Arthur Fenner, a mostly retired south of town farmer who served as the coffee group's historian of all matters Pacer Coulee.

"He seems to really like him so far. Says that old coach we had the last few years didn't know shit from shine-ola, but we already knew that. Says this guy Luke Carter really knows his stuff. Guess he was a helluva high school and college QB down in Nebraska."

"Too bad we can't clone him and actually have a quarterback that can complete a pass," replied Arthur. "I mean, with as good as both Stefan and Aaron looked against the Rangers, we should be able to run the ball against anybody, but damn, it would be nice to be able to mix it up a little bit. We'll have a helluva time getting by St. Francis, not to mention Stanton, Deeden and Heberton, if everybody can just stack the box against the run."

"You got that right," confirmed Carlton 'Bones' Bolstad, an 8-mile north of town rancher. "I wasn't able to get over to Range View for the game, but by the sounds of that wind I guess even Elway would have had a tough time throwing the ball."

"Yeah, that wind was a bitch, for sure," added Wilbur Rimby, whose grandson Ernie was a freshman who showed some promise as a running back. Like Butch, he also had a granddaughter, Anna, who was a sophomore on the girls' basketball team. "I saw that some of you went to the preseason basketball tournament in Centertown, too. I thought the girls looked pretty darn good. I'm telling you, that youngest Brewster gal is a player—maybe already better than her oldest sister Sonya. And I think that little Indian gal is going to solve our problems at point guard, too. Speaking of Indians, our less than stellar boys' basketball team just became an instant contender with the addition of that His Own Horse kid. I saw him play at the Northern Divisional last year, and damn, he's something else."

"Guess he don't play football, huh?" questioned Bones.

"Nah, the Natives are all about hoops. You rarely see a reservation team that's competitive in football," added bachelor Harlan Horrall, whom at 52 was the youngest of the Hole in the Wall gang. "I went to the girls' game on Saturday night, and damn... that new coach we have, Madison Danielsen, I think her name is. Anyway, guess she's a Whitewater gal. Damn, she's a looker now, I'm tellin' ya!"

"Did you even watch the game or were you too busy being an old creeper and ogling our young new coach?" questioned Duke with a grin. "I hear she's divorced, so in the rare event that she's inclined to hang out with fat and broke guys that are 20 years her senior, then you might be in luck."

"Hey, I dropped 30 pounds last summer, so she'll probably find my new svelte build and perpetual good looks to be irresistible. And as soon as I sell that 2500 bushel bin of winter wheat for this five year low price of $2.18 a bushel, I'll be lookin' good to her as a sugar daddy."

"Looks to me like you put that 30 pounds back on and raised it by 20," said Butch. "But if she prefers bullshit to dollars you may very well be her guy."

"It still just blows me away that Edna took those Indian kids in," Wilbur interjected, shaking his head in puzzlement over the School Board Chairperson bringing Elvis His Own Horse and Clare Comes at Night into her home on a permanent basis.

"No shit!" confirmed Harlan, as the entire group nodded in agreement. "I'd love to be a mouse in the corner and watch the goins' on in that household. Can't you just see 'em at the supper table? Edna and Harriet and two Native kids?"

"I can somewhat see Edna interacting okay with them, but no way can I see Harriet being able to communicate," said Kip, who at 37 was 19 years removed from the Pacer Coulee High

English and History classes taught by Edna and Harriet. "I mean, Harriet was a good teacher, but damn, she's an odd duck. When she's not in the classroom she's virtually a hermit. Never see her out and about. Her and Edna are pretty much opposites, that's for sure."

"So what happened with Lester as the girls' coach?" asked Bones. "I mean, without his girls this team wouldn't win a game, and other than gettin' beat out last year at Divisional when we should have made some noise at State, I thought he did a pretty fair job."

"Lester was a good coach, but from what I heard he was having trouble coaching his own girls. I think a couple of 'em have quite the attitude," offered Arthur. "Although very early in the season, from what I can see it looks we landed a couple of pretty damn good new coaches in that Luke Carter and Madison Danielsen."

"Time will tell boys, time will tell. How often do I have to tell you fellas to not count your chickens before they hatch?" added Frank Cervenka, the hands-down chairman of the doom and gloom chapter of the coffee club gang. "Those reservation kids? Hell, we'll be lucky if they stay here another week before they sneak out of Edna's big old house in the middle of night and head back to the Rez. No different from when you pull your best bull off the cow pasture and put him in the pen right next to it. Sure as hell, he'll go right through the fence to get back in with the cows. Ain't no way he's stayin' put."

"Well shit, that was an uplifting commentary on the state of Pacer Coulee sports, wasn't it?" Harlan sarcastically commented as Frank sauntered out the front door. "Hell, we might just as well cancel the rest of the football and basketball seasons."

ELVIS GETS DISCOVERED

It was the Sunday after the Range View game, and per a new policy developed by Lester, Luke and Madison, there was open gym from noon to 4:00 p.m. every Sunday afternoon for not only students of all grades, but the general public as well. And with the grand opening a week prior of the newly constructed weight room and its refurbished arsenal of weights and training equipment, it was included as a part of the open gym access. Luke was in the weight room refining the program he had developed for his team when Bret Cassidy rushed through the door. "Coach, there's something going on out in the gym that you gotta see!"

"Did somebody get hurt?"

"No—no, nothing like that. Okay, Elvis was playing in a half court game with Mr. Brewster, Miss Danielsen and some of the older guys, and I was on the other end tossing around the football with a couple of grade school kids. The football got away from us and bounced onto their side of the court. Anyway, Elvis picked it up and threw it back to me. Coach, you gotta come see this. Perfect spiral, right on the money. It was a pretty short pass, so I made him do it again, except this time from one end of the court to the other. I'm telling you coach, this guy can throw it. You need to come see."

Lester and Madison had their group take a water break and clear the floor while Luke, Elvis and Bret tossed the oblong ball back and forth. "Can we borrow Elvis for a spell?" Luke asked Lester, and upon an approval nod from both Lester and Elvis, the boys headed for the practice field. Once he got Elvis's arm warmed up, Luke had Bret start running patterns; 5, 12 and 18-yard outs, eventually progressing to slants, curls, posts and flags at varying yardages.

"Holy shit," muttered Luke to Lester and Glenn Goettel,

whose curiosity had got the best of them and had now joined Luke to watch the Indian boy throw the football. "He hasn't missed a throw—not a one!"

When Elvis, Luke and Bret retreated to the coaches' room to chat in private, Elvis confirmed he had never played football before. "Nobody ever asked me to play. Not at Hays Lodgepole, and not since I come here," he explained when questioned by Luke. "I guess everybody assumes I'm only a basketball player."

"Well I'm certainly asking you now, Elvis," said Luke emphatically. "You would be a tremendous addition to our football team. Would you consider coming out and playing for us?"

Elvis shrugged and said. "Sure… yeah, I guess. Why not?"

"Good! Super! You bet!" stammered Luke, unable to hide his excitement. "You can start practice tomorrow, even though it's Labor Day and I was going to give the guys a day off. You need to get in ten practices before you can play in a game. Bret, can you get a hold of Kimball, Aaron, Stefan and Ernie and get them here at 3:00 tomorrow to catch some passes from Elvis? If we have five or six guys here, we can count it as an official practice and Elvis will be ready to go for our home opener against Hodgeman. How's that sound to you, Elvis?"

Elvis shrugged again and nodded, then went back out to the gym to rejoin the group in their half court game. Luke and Bret did a high five and reentered the gym with wide smiles plastered across their faces.

LUKE BABYSITS ROSE

Luke scolded himself when his teenager-like excitement meter went through the roof when he heard Madison's voice on the other end of the phone line. "Hey Luke, are you real busy this evening? I have a huge favor to ask."

"Well, let me look at my schedule. Hmm... the patient I just sewed up was my last open heart surgery case of the day. I am on 24-hour a day call, but assuming I don't have to rush to the hospital to do another emergency surgery I should be available. Why, what's up?"

"Whew, I was afraid that I'd be interrupting a busy day, but I feel better now knowing you weren't doing anything important. I wanted to ask if you would keep an eye on Rose for a few hours. It seems that Mrs. Grove, our new 86-year-old mother hen from across the alley who doesn't drive outside the city limits of Pacer Coulee anymore, has a dire need to get to Albertson's in Centertown this evening to pick up supplies for next Sunday's Daughters of the American Revolution potluck."

"I guess I did hear something about you being appointed as the town's official potluck chauffeur," Luke commented.

"Yes, it's quite an honor, and I'd appreciate it if you would see to it that Sylvia reports it in the next issue of the Pacer Coulee Chronicles. Anyway, when I pressed Thelma on why she needs to go today to get supplies a full week ahead of the actual potluck, the real reason came to the surface; Caramel Delight ice cream is on sale for an unbelievable $2.49 a quart, but only until the 11:00 closing tonight. Can you imagine that?"

"Well, I was gonna say no to looking after Rose, but damn, $2.49 a quart, huh? If you'll pick me up a couple of those, I guess I'll do it!"

"Thanks Luke," laughed Madison. "I owe you one. Do you

mind coming over to my place? She has a little homework to finish, and I should be back to wrangle her to bed by 9:00."

"So what do you have for homework, Rose?"

"Spelling and a little math. I'm pretty good in math. My mom's a math teacher, you know."

"Yeah, I heard something about that. Maybe she could help me, since I still think two times two is 12."

"Ha! You better get a tutor! Could you go through my spelling list with me? I think I've got them all down, but we do have a quiz tomorrow."

After completing the homework tasks, they settled back on the couch to watch TV, but the Sunday night programs the two Great Falls network channels that both Luke and Madison received via their flimsy roof-mounted antennas were uninspiring. Luke didn't know what he was in for when he asked for an update on how things were going in Mrs. Hunter's fifth grade class.

"Well, there's lots of homework in the fifth grade. Mrs. Hunter is really nice, but man, she means business. She can get pretty crabby if you get caught fooling around and not paying attention, that's for sure. Did you know that Shane has missed like ten recesses already?"

"I guess he must be a jerk, just like you said. So how many kids are in your class?"

"There's nine of us. Five girls and four boys. Did you know that Abby and Ryan Lincoln are, like, you know, going steady or something like that?"

"I hadn't heard that. Isn't he an older man? Like a sixth grader?"

"Yes, but don't tell Abby's mom or anything, okay?"

"You got it. My lips are sealed."

"And did you know that after mom's practice last week I saw Anna Rimby and Tuf Sturm kissing? They were holding hands in the hall, too. Both Abby and I saw it."

While trying to hold back a smile, Luke thought of how different this small school was compared to where he grew up.

With the entire K-12 grades being housed in the same building, the elementary kids were exposed to the Jr. High and High School kids in the hallways on a regular basis. He wondered if Abby and Ryan weren't trying to copy the high school aged romances. "Maybe they're going steady too, you suppose?" asked Luke.

"That's what me and Abby think. Anyway, they aren't the only ones. We think Danny Schrader and Bev Rood like each other too."

"I'll be darned—didn't know anything about that. Hey, do you have the inside scoop on Bo, Bret, Aaron and Stefan? And what about Tank?"

"Well," said Rose, sliding closer to Luke to deliver the dating information. "Abby and me think Bo likes Dee Cassidy, and you probably already know that Bret and Cindy Cottingham have been going steady for like forever. And Aaron has been dating Mitzi Reilly. You wouldn't know her 'cause she's from Stanton. And Stefan's girlfriend is Sissy Cercle—she's from Hodgeman and goes to the College of Great Falls."

And then leaning in close to Luke as if she was about to share highly classified, top secret government information, she said with a whisper, "And then there's Tank. You have to promise, promise, promise that you didn't hear this from me, okay?"

"Again, this is just between you and me, Rose. My lips are sealed."

"Okay then. Well, we heard this firsthand from Breanna and Carrie. They're seventh graders, you know. Anyway, they said they overheard Anna Rimby and Dee Cassidy in the locker room after basketball practice," Rose confided in an even more hushed tone. "They swear on a stack of bibles that they think Tank is sweet on Clare Comes at Night. And you know what? They think she likes him too! Wouldn't that be a sight? You know, him being like 300 pounds huge, and her being, like, 90 pounds little!"

"Wow, that would be something, wouldn't it? The biggest guy and the smallest girl in high school."

"Abby and I think it would be cool if they really were girlfriend and boyfriend. We think he's kinda, I don't know...

kinda sad. And she's like really, really shy. Don't you think they'd be a good fit, Mr. Carter?"

"I do Rose, I think you and Abby are right on there. Tank and Clare would probably be really good for each other."

By this time, Rose had almost scooted over on his lap, and she moved in even closer to deliver the next dating scene bombshell. "And do you want to hear the biggest boyfriend and girlfriend news of all?"

"I'm on pins and needles here Rose—let's have it!"

"Well," she said, looking around as if there may be dating spies lurking in the shadows, "there's some talk that Elvis and one of the Brewster sisters like each other. We think it could be Sonya."

"Hmm… you and Abby seem to have a pretty darn good grasp of the Pacer Coulee High School dating scene, that's for sure," said Luke as they heard Madison coming up the front porch steps. "You will keep me posted if there's anything I should know about when it concerns the guys on my football team, won't you Rose?"

"Don't worry Mr. Carter, I'll let you know!" she confirmed.

After dispatching Rose to get ready for bed, Madison handed Luke two quarts of ice cream and said, "Caramel Delight and Daughters of the American Revolution baking goods mission accomplished. Do I need to cough up cash in addition to the ice cream to square up on the babysitting duties?"

"Nope, the Caramel Delight will satisfy your indebtedness in full. Besides, I was able to glean from Rose a veritable wealth of Pacer Coulee dating information that I doubt any other adults in the community would be privy to. Thanks to her disclosures, I'm guessing I know more about the love lives of your basketball team than you do."

"Pray tell, Mr. Carter. Please enlighten me!"

"Sorry Ms. Danielsen. My source has sworn me to secrecy. My lips are forever sealed."

ELVIS DRAWS A CROWD AT PRACTICE

Harlan Horrall leaned against the box of his pickup that he had parked parallel to the Bulldog practice field, and after carefully spitting a stream of Copenhagen tobacco juice so that it would flow with rather than against the brisk, westerly breeze, he turned back to join most of the rest of the Butch Cassidy and the Hole in the Wall gang that had gathered to get a first look at Pacer Coulee's new quarterback. "Shit man, this kid can pitch it," observed Butch, as Harlan, Duke Dickson, Bones Bolstad and Wilbur Rimby vigorously nodded their heads in agreement. "And he's got enough oomph on the ball to throw into wind, too," added Wilbur.

Word of Elvis joining the football team had traveled fast in the little community, starting that very morning when the Hole in the Wall gang waited on the doorsteps of the O.K. Corral Bar and Grill. Butch had already spilled the whole story to the group before Kip Jordan, 12 minutes late, had even arrived to unlock the door.

"Jesus Christ," T.O. had muttered to Luke during practice, "there's been years we didn't have this many people show up for an actual game!"

"Well, from what we've seen so far, there's something to be excited about," Luke had replied. In the few short practices since Elvis had joined the team, he had not only demonstrated a strong arm, but seemed to soak up information about the game he had never played like a sponge. He was also more than willing to stay after practice and throw ball after ball to an excited group of running backs and receivers, and was agreeable to spending every spare minute he had watching film and learning the intricacies of the position from the crash course in quarterback play that he was getting from Luke.

Hole in the Wall member Frank Cervenka, who had been observing practice from his solo position in the corner of the practice field, began to saunter towards the coffee club group. "Let me guess," Harlan whispered to the rest of the group, "Frank will find something not to like about Elvis's pass delivery, or some such shit like that."

"Hi Frank, what do ya think about our new quarterback?" asked Butch excitedly.

"Well," Frank said after a lengthy pause, "I'm sure you boys have been over here getting all giggly and gushy over this kid, but let's wait until we see how he responds in an actual game. This ain't like basketball where nobody's gonna hit him as he's shooting. Let's see what happens when one of them Pekovik boys from St. Francis comes at him and hits him like a freight train just as he releases the ball. Then we'll find out how bad he wants to stand there in the pocket and take a hit. And he's got too much of a side arm delivery to suit my taste. No way will that work when he tries to throw over the Pekoviks and that 6'7" defensive end they got... you know, the Stronge kid. Anyway, we'll see if this Luke Carter character really is a quarterback coach, 'cause he's got his hands full in training this green colt, I can tell ya that."

"What'd I tell ya?" said Harlan as they watched him walk away. "Frank's the most negative and depressing asshole in the whole county. Jesus, I think I'll just go home and fuckin' hang myself from the nearest Cottonwood."

"Mark my words, Elway will never complete a pass in the 7C conference," mimicked Butch. "That side arm delivery won't work in these parts."

BO GIVES ELVIS A NICKNAME

The boys were dressing in the locker room after the Thursday practice before the Marshall game. While it had only been Elvis's fourth practice, it was apparent the quarterback position would take a giant step upward when he was able to play. The usual showers and dress banter quieted when Bo approached Elvis. "Mr. His Own Horse," Bo began, "you do appear to be the guy that can transform the Pacer Coulee Bulldogs from their one dimensional, run-only status and reputation. And while I am grateful to you for that, I do have a problem that I need to discuss with you. You see," Bo continued, the team gathering around him and the puzzled looking Elvis, "I don't know if you've heard this about me or not, but in addition to being the most dashingly handsome cattle baron east of the Judith River, I am also a highly sought after entertainer. A gifted impressionist I am, and pardon me if that sounds unlike my usual humble self.

"Here's my problem, Elvis. I'm sorry, but I just can't call you by your given name. Why, you might ask, can I not call you Elvis? Well, as I have previously mentioned, I am an impressionist. I simply cannot call you Elvis because it totally screws up my ability to impersonate the real Elvis, you know—the King. How can I possibly sing 'Blue Suede Shoes' on stage when I envision you as Elvis? See my problem here?" Bo reasoned to an Elvis who was starting to have a smile tug at the corners of his mouth.

"No, I'm gonna have to give you another handle. Now since you are an Indian, I thought I would just call you Redskin, like they do in the old Westerns; the Cowboy and Indian movies," explained Bo. "But I don't like the Redskins even a little bit, 'cause I'm a Dallas Cowboys fan. I'm sure you can see why I can't call you Redskin. Now, why not call you by your last name, you might ask. Well, that's a tough one too. To be honest, I always get it mixed up. I can't remember if it's His Own Horse, Own His Horse, or Horse His Own. I could never keep it straight, so see my dilemma here, Elvis?"

"Yes," Elvis replied, slipping into a Bo-like Indian speak from an old cowboy and Indian western movie. "Me Elvis understand paleface problem. What name paleface Bo call Injun?"

Managing to keep a straight face with the entire team laughing and clapping, Bo transitioned into his Texas southern drawl speak and replied. "Bo is gonna call his Injun friend 'Skin'... not Redskin, just plain ol' Skin. That be okay with you?"

"Injun like paleface name. Smoke peace pipe with Injun?"

"Dang sure will, Skin. Dang sure will. Glad we got that settled," stated Bo, before addressing the rest of the team in his normal voice. "By the way guys, I'm the only one that will call Elvis 'Skin'. I'll sic big Tank on anybody else that tries it. Everybody got that?"

As everyone nodded their heads in acknowledgment, Bo slipped back into the Texas drawl. "So Skin, I noticed you Injuns have some crazy last names. Like Old Bear, Lone Wolf, Two Moons, Good Medicine, Two Bulls, Skunk Creek, just to mention a few. So how do you Injuns come up with those names?"

"I ain't ever seen two moons in the sky before," interjected Earl Wonderwald, to no one in particular.

"When mama Injun has little one wrapped up all safe in papoose, daddy great warrior name little one after what he see when he first open flap of Tepee. Why do you ask, Two Dogs Fucking?"

Except for Dolph and Earl Wonderwald, who both stood with confused expressions on their faces, the whole team howled uproariously and began to slap Elvis on the back for getting a one-up on the likes of Bo. Just as everyone started to settle down, Earl loudly squealed, "I get it! I get it! Haha, Two

Dogs Fucking! The great warrior saw two dogs fucking when he peeked out the tepee!"

"For fuck sakes, Wonderwald," laughed Bo as everyone chortled their way out of the locker room. "Could there be any doubt that you're the undisputed King of Dipshits?"

HOME OPENER AGAINST HODGEMAN

The second week of the season called for an away game with the Marshall Titans, and the contest turned out to be more lopsided than the Range View game. Luke had pulled Tank, Aaron, Dolph and Stefan at the end of the first quarter, as the lead had already grown to 40-0. He had played everyone except Earl and Alden, with Earl still being out with a shoulder injury. Luke had been looking for the one home game on the schedule where he thought he could best meet some objectives he had for his team and a few of his players. He thought that providing a lift for these individuals could lead to improved overall team unity and morale. He realized his mission would be best accomplished against an inferior team, as he wanted a game where they'd be in control from the get-go. The opening home game with the Hodgeman Tigers seemed to fit the bill, as they had lost five senior starters from last year and had struggled to a 0-2 start this season while having to start three freshmen. He also needed the chosen game to be one that Jack Schye was scheduled to officiate, and Jack was on the list for the Hodgeman game.

The first thing he wanted to do was to make Dolph a special captain for this game. When he brought up the idea to his assistant coach, T.O. had said. "Shit Luke, how the hell is that going to work? You know he doesn't have the mental capacity to make a decision on a penalty call."

"Yeah, I realize that," Luke replied, "but I mainly want to do this for him so that he can just walk out there for the coin toss with Tank and Aaron. Can you imagine how pumped and important he's going to feel?"

"Well, I can see that, for sure," said T.O. "I guess we would just have to make sure that if there is a decision to be made on accepting or declining a penalty that the refs know they would have to consult with Tank or Aaron," T.O. said.

"That's why it's important that Jack Schye is one of the refs," Luke stated. "I know that if I give him a heads up, he'll handle it, and do it in a way that won't cause any embarrassment or undue stress on Dolph."

"Ol' Jack might be gettin' too old and crippled to ref the way he used to, but he still knows how to control the flow of the game and handle the kids better than any official I know," agreed T.O.

The second mark that Luke wanted to check off his list in the Hodgeman game was to get Earl in the game. Even though he had been injured and unable to play in the first two games, Earl had been driving him nuts on the sideline all season long with his "Let me in coach... I'm ready coach, let me at them sum-bitches!" With Hodgeman having to start some freshmen, Luke felt much better about getting Earl some playing time without having to worry about him getting killed. He'd also feel better with Earl on the field knowing that Jack was one of the refs out there to keep an eye on things.

Sixty-six-year-old Jack Schye had been an official in central Montana for 35 years. He had grown up on a ranch near Range View and was a very good three sport athlete for the Rangers in the early '50s. Graduating from Range View High School in 1954 he immediately joined his dad and grandpa on the ranch that he still lived on. He started refereeing both football and basketball the very next year, and had worked the Centertown High, St. Francis High and all the local central Montana Class C school games ever since. Jack was a large man who wore a chiseled, heavily leathered and wrinkled face that any western cowboy photographer or artist would love to get on their canvas. The only time this old rancher's shiny bald head wasn't adorned with a wide brimmed Resistol cowboy hat was when he was officiating a football or basketball game. His hardened look and tough demeanor let the kids know that he wasn't about to take guff from any of them. Whining, questioning a call in a disrespectful manner, or any kind of showboat or smart alec behavior was met with an unsportsman like call in football, and a technical foul in basketball. Bad behavior by the coaches was equally rewarded with a penalty. He commanded respect from the kids and the coaches, and he got it. But the kids also knew that he was in their camp, as he was a strong proponent for athletics and for the kids that participated in it. Even though he wasn't getting up and down the court or field as well as he used to due to his advancing years and the 25 or 30 extra pounds around his middle, they knew he had their best interests at heart and that he would always be honest and fair with them. He had been around so long that he knew every kid in every small, central Montana school, as well as most of their parents and the fans. He still truly enjoyed being around the kids. As for most of the parents and the fans?... not so much.

On the Saturday of the Hodgeman game, Jack and the rest of the referee crew showed up about an hour and a half before game time. Per the usual routine, Luke and T.O. cleared out of the small coaches' office that sat between the girls' and boys' locker rooms so that the referees could change into their game gear. As soon as they had donned their officials' wear, the head referee would meet with each head coach separately to discuss any unusual or trick plays that they might be using during the game, as knowing that information beforehand would allow the officials to have a heads up and avoid any confusion regarding the legality of any funky plays or formations. The officials would also use this discussion time to inspect any soft casts or unusual padding that players might be wearing due to a specific injury to ensure compliance with Montana High School Athletic Association (MHSAA) safety regulations and guidelines.

When Jack called Luke back into the coaches' room for their meeting, Luke informed him that he was not anticipating running any out of the ordinary plays or utilizing any weird formations, nor did any of his kids have injuries that required additional padding protection. Then he said, "Jack, I do have several items I need to discuss with you regarding today's game."

"Shoot," said Jack.

"Well, you're familiar with Randolph... Dolph Russell, right?" asked Luke.

"Yes, I know Dolph well, and I understand about his mental capacities. If you're worried about the opposing team giving him a hard time, don't be. There will be none of that shit on my watch, I'll guaran-goddamn-tee it. And every team around here that you play knows that I won't put up with that kind of thing. Besides," he laughed, "Tank usually takes care of anyone giving Dolph a hard time before I have to get involved."

"I know that Jack, and I can't tell you how much we appreciate how you look out for him. But it's not that I'm worried about. As you know, Dolph is a senior, and I'd really like to make him a special captain for today's game. I think it would mean a lot to him. As you just mentioned, his mental shortcomings render him incapable of making a decision on a penalty call if neither of our regular captains, Tank or Aaron, are on the field at the time."

Jack raised his hand up in front of his chest in a 'stop' gesture and said, "Say no more. I think that's a wonderful thing you're doing, making him a captain for this game. And don't you worry, Luke, I've got his back on this one. If something comes up in the penalty department and your other captains aren't on the field, you and I can exchange non verbal signals as to what you want to do, and I'll damn sure see to it that Dolph makes the right decision. I'll talk to him before the game starts too, just to calm him down a bit, as I 'spect he'll be nervous as a cat."

"Thanks Jack, that would be great, and we appreciate your help so much on this. A couple other matters I wanted to mention. You may have heard that the great basketball player from Hays Lodgepole, Elvis His Own Horse, transferred here this fall. He's a sophomore now, and he's never played football before. Well, we talked him into coming out after school started, and he's gotten his required ten practices in and is starting at quarterback today," Luke explained to a now even more attentive and interested Jack. "So sort of along the same lines as Dolph, I'm a little concerned about the Hodgeman kids talking trash to Elvis. I realize a lot of that goes on, but I'm mainly worried about racial slurs and the like."

"Okay Luke, and yeah, I did hear about him transferring here. I had their basketball game at St. Francis last year, and as a freshman he put 38 on the Trojans. I hope for your sake he's half as good in football as he is b-ball. I'll keep an ear open for any such talk and will damn sure put an end to it if I hear anything."

"Thanks Jack, and the last thing I wanted to mention concerns two of our young freshmen. The first one is Earl Wonderwald. Do you know who I'm talking about?"

"Is that the skinny little shit that can't keep a pair of extra small football pants up over his scrawny ass?" Jack asked.

"Yup, that's him. He goes less than a buck, and that's with full pads on. I've been scared to death to play him for fear he'll get himself slaughtered. But I'm thinking that today might be the day to get him a little time if we can get a good lead. Anyway, I just wanted to give you a heads up that we might have our most fragile one out there at some point in the second half."

"No worries," said Jack. "I'll keep an eye out for him, and for Joe's little fellers too. If the game gets to nearing the 45-point rule, I'll encourage Joe to put his youngins out there too. What's the deal with the second freshman you mentioned?"

"Well Jack, I just wanted to warn you to line up somewhere behind the line of scrimmage, because at some point in the game I'm gonna let our freshman, Alden Blackburn, try to kick an extra point," laughed Luke. "He hasn't kicked it backwards yet, but nowhere except above the crossbar and between the goal posts is safe when he's kicking!"

"Thanks for the tip… I'll line up 15 yards behind the line of scrimmage, just to make sure I'm out of the line of fire," replied a chuckling Jack.

After doing their pregame stretches and warm-up in the gym, Luke and T.O. led the team on the 100-yard or so walk to the football field. Unlike the tornado-like winds at Range View and the unseasonably cold rain over at Marshall, Luke welcomed the 70 degree temperature and mild breeze of the September 15th Saturday. Luke had asked T.O. about the good number of cars and pickups that already surrounded the field at Friday night's practice, and he said, "It's just like Sunday church in small towns where every family has their designated pew, and by God there'd be hell to pay if some other sum-bitch sat there. Same thing with the football parking," he had said, pointing to behind the west end goal post and the '69 Pontiac Catalina that was positioned there. "Now that's Ethyl Grove's Catalina, and she has had first dibs on that spot since Clarence Coffman was coaching the Bulldogs. Harlan Horrall faithfully drives it down and parks it in the exact same spot the night before every home game. And there's Duke Dickson's pickup over there at just the right angle—you get the idea. Everybody's got their very own pew at the football field." As they took the field the clock said 18:36 left before game time and the field was already completely surrounded by vehicles, the crowd being three deep from goal line to goal line on the Bulldog side. With Hodgeman only being 43 miles away they had a strong contingency in place on the opposite side, and their students were filling the little set of visitor bleachers to the brim.

Luke waited until just before they took the field for final warm-ups before he pulled Dolph aside to tell him that he would be a captain today alongside Tank and Aaron. Dolph's eyes got big as saucers, and his mouth formed a big 'O', but no sound came out. He started prancing in place, like a two-year-old will do when excited and waiting impatiently for you to get the cookie out of the jar. Finally he was able to get it out, "So coach... coach...does that mean that Jerry will announce me over the loudspeaker? And like, like say that Dolph Russell is a captain?"

"Sure does, Dolph. He'll say that today's captains for the Bulldogs will be Dolph Russell, Tank Hollister and Aaron Coslet. He'll say that over the loudspeaker, and everybody will know that you're a captain today, Dolph."

A pleased expression and big smile settled over Dolph's face as he envisioned himself walking between Tank and Aaron to the center of the field and hearing his name being called over the loudspeaker. But suddenly his large, round face turned pensive, and he asked, "So coach... coach, should I call heads or tails when they do the coin toss?"

"You won't have to do that today, because the visiting team gets to call heads or tails," Luke explained. But Dolph's eyebrows furrowed as he seemed to fall into deeper thought. "So coach... coach... what if Mr. Jack asks me if we want to kick the ball or catch the ball to start the game? What should I tell him?"

"Don't you worry about that, Dolph. Mr. Jack always asks Tank about that one." That seemed to solve the dilemma in Dolph's mind, as he smiled and replied, "Yeah coach, Tank knows about stuff like that. He'll know what to do."

So with that important captain information apparently settled in his mind, Dolph raced back to join his teammates. Luke watched as he went up to Tank and Aaron, talking excitedly and waving his arms. Luke had already told the other two captains what he was going to do for Dolph, and they were both enthusiastically on board with the idea. He smiled when he saw both Tank and Aaron giving him high fives and patting him on the back.

When referee Schye came over to the sideline to get the captains for the midfield coin toss, Dolph was chomping at the bit. He was so excited that he was doing the little prance again. Jack got him settled down, looked down at his captains' card and said. "Okay fellas, the Pacer Coulee captains today are Randolph Russell, Tank Hollister and Aaron Coslet. Do I have that right?" Luke and all three captains nodded their heads yes, none more enthusiastically than Dolph. "Well let's head out to the midfield for the coin toss," Jack said, as one of the other officials started from the visitors' sideline towards the middle on the 40-yard line with their two captains.

As Jack and the captains started their walk to midfield, public address announcer Jerry Akers, from his perch up in the crow's nest, introduced Tank and Aaron as the usual two Bulldog captains. After a long pause he raised the tenor of his voice and said. "And our special captain today......**RAAAAANNNN-DOLLLLPPHH RUSSSSELLLL!** The entire student section and all the Bulldog fans that lined the field cheered wildly. Dolph was visibly pumped, and was strutting on air as he marched towards midfield behind Jack, and in between Tank and Aaron. Suddenly he stopped the other two captains when they were about halfway to midfield and began talking and gesturing wildly while looking back anxiously at Luke. Jack had continued to walk ahead of them, unaware that they weren't following directly behind. Dolph kept up his frantic display until finally Tank threw his hands in the air and waved at Luke to come out and talk to Dolph.

"What's the matter, Dolph?" Luke asked when he reached the breathless and puzzled looking youngster.

"So coach... coach, I've been thinking, if Mr. Jack blows his whistle and there's a penalty, should I say yes or no? I mean, do we want to take the penalty or not?" With great effort to hold back a grin, Luke looked at Dolph with as serious a face as he could muster and replied, "Here's what you do, Dolph. You ask Mr. Jack if you should take the penalty. He'll help you decide whether you want to say yes or no. How does that sound, Dolph?" Relief flowed over Dolph's face as he said, "Okay coach... I'll ask Mr. Jack. I got it coach, I got it!" With that, he turned and sprinted back to join Tank and Aaron, who were at midfield with the two Tiger captains and the officials, all patiently awaiting the arrival of Dolph so that they could get on with the coin toss.

One of the captains for the Tigers was Austin Greeley, about the only good player that Hodgeman had that year. He was a returning All-Conference senior running back and linebacker, with decent size at 5'10" and 170 pounds. He had good speed to boot, but was a loud mouth who was well known for his extracurricular activities on the field, particularly in pile ups, where he was not above a quick rabbit punch to the groin or grabbing an ankle and twisting it before the officials could start sorting out the pile.

As always when winning the coin toss, unless it was such a windy day that you wouldn't want to have to go into the wind in the first quarter, Luke took the ball. If Elvis was nervous in his football debut, he didn't show it. Luke called two inside power plays in a row to tailback Stefan Tillerman to start the game, easily getting first down yardage each carry as he followed Tank's pancake blocks. He then decided to test Elvis's confidence in throwing the ball, so he went to a Twins formation to the field side and fired a 3-step drop dart to slot receiver Aaron Coslet on a five yard out. The ball was there as Aaron came out of his break, and he took it in full stride and turned it up at the sideline for an additional 12 yards before being pushed out of bounds. Three plays into the game, and they were already down to the Tigers' 22-yard line.

Elvis trotted over to Luke, and Luke gave him "I right, 32 naked boot," in which Elvis faked power to his tailback to the wide side of the field, and after a brief hesitation, rolled back to the short side of the field without any of his backfield or pulling linemen leading the way for him, hence the term "naked." Although he bit for the fake initially, Tigers' middle linebacker Austin Greeley recovered quickly enough to take a good angle and tackle Elvis to the ground with a vicious hit for no gain. The linebacker stayed on top of him longer than need be, and as Tank came over to help Elvis up he heard Austin sneer into Elvis's helmet ear hole. "Don't be trying to run that shit on me, prairie nigger... I'll bury your Indian ass in the dirt every time." As he was getting up, Greeley gave Elvis a quick two-handed punch to his shoulders to help propel himself upward.

Jack Schye was the only official close enough to hear what he said or witness the punch. But he didn't throw his flag.

A little shaken, Elvis again trotted over to meet Luke at the far end of the Bulldog bench, where Luke called another Twins formation to the field side, putting Bret in the slot and hoping to hit him in the end zone on a flag route. But when Elvis called the play in the huddle, Tank said, "Fuck that, we're going Twins right, QB sweep right. I'm gonna be pulling, so Elvis, stay parallel to the line of scrimmage for the first five yards, and then turn upfield when I do. Get on my right ass cheek as soon as you can and follow me into the end zone. And NOBODY block Greeley... leave that sum-bitch for me." Since nobody ever questioned Tank in a game, the huddle broke with everyone on the same page that it was Tank's play, not coach's, that was to be run.

On the way to the line of scrimmage, Tank was pleased to see that Greeley was positioned in coverage on the slot to the wide side of the field. He gave his signal to Dolph indicating who he should block, and then lined up at left guard. On the snap, everyone to Tank's right blocked down to the left as he pulled and went around the right end. Bret was in the slot and, following Tank's orders, he left Greeley and blocked down on the defensive end.

For his 320-some pounds, Tank was not only quick and explosive coming out of his stance, but also had surprisingly good straight away speed for a man of his size. His eyes lit up when he turned upfield on his pull and saw that coming at him at full speed was the unblocked Greeley. The linebacker foolishly didn't try to avoid the direct contact as the distance between them rapidly closed, and Tank dipped down and exploded into him, punching with his hands close together just under the shoulder pads. As he completed the jolt punch with his arms, Tank grabbed him by the jersey with both hands and lifted him up off the ground. The collision barely slowed Tank down, but Greeley's change of momentum and direction was sudden and abrupt. Greeley flailed his arms helplessly as Tank took him on a backwards 15-yard trip into the end zone and then pile drove him into the ground as violently as a spike being driven into a fence post. At the exact moment that Greeley was desperately searching to find a molecule of oxygen to suck into his empty lungs, Elvis had complied with Tank's directive to position himself on his right butt cheek and had followed him untouched into the end zone.

This time it was Tank who took his time getting off Greeley.

He snarled into his helmet ear hole loud enough for all the players and the officials to hear. "I'm gonna tell you this just once motherfucker. You ever call my quarterback those kinds of names ever again, I will fuckin' hunt you down, rip off your ugly head and shit down your throat." With that, as he got off of Greeley, he gave the same hard rabbit punch to his chest as Greeley had given to Elvis's back, only twice as hard.

Art Dohr, the back judge, had thrown his flag on Tank's obvious personal foul and/or holding penalty, and everyone was surprised when head referee Jack Schye came in and called off the penalty as an inadvertent flag. Joe DuBois, the Hodgeman coach, went crazy and stomped up and down the sideline screaming at Jack to come over and give him an explanation for such an outrageous overturn of the bevy of blatantly obvious penalties.

"Jesus Christ, Jack," he bellowed. "How can you miss both a holding call AND a personal foul for the body slam?"

Jack took his time sauntering over to him on the sideline, saying when he finally reached him, "Let me tell ya something, Joe. This is how this is gonna work. You have two options here. First, either you accept my considered ruling that there wasn't a holding or unsportsmanlike penalty on that last play, and just quietly let this whole thing drop, or secondly, I will call an unsportsmanlike penalty on Greeley for taunting. Taunting is the call because of some really ugly racial slurs he spouted towards your young Native American opponent on the prior play. And this is when I will eject Greeley from the game. You can look it up in the Montana High School Football Rules handbook, Joe. Racial slurs are grounds for ejection. So… you got approximately three seconds to give me your decision on your options."

Without saying a word, Joe stomped back to his team on the sideline. With a smile, Jack muttered under his breath. "I guess that means he's going with option one."

The first half of the game went exactly as Luke had hoped. After the Tank/Greeley incident, Greeley was ineffectual. He didn't want any part of Tank, and Tank hunted him up at every opportunity to deliver more hits—of the legal kind this time around. The Bulldogs went into the half with a 30-0 lead.

Earl had been tugging on Luke's shirt sleeve ever since Pacer Coulee went up 24-0 late in the second quarter with his usual "Let me in coach, I'm ready coach... let me at them sum-bitches!" Luke had been able to stave him off by saying "Maybe in the second half, Earl." Just before the team went back to warm-up for the second half, Luke pulled both Earl and Alden aside and said, "Alright guys. Alden, next time we score you're on—we'll kick it. And Earl, I'm probably gonna get you in there at safety in the second or third defensive series, so be ready to go." Alden gulped and turned ashen. Earl jumped up and down hollering, "Let me at them sum-bitches, coach... I'm gonna kick me some Tiger asses!"

The Tigers had the ball for the first series of the second half, and Luke kept Tank and the rest of his starters in the game to prevent giving them momentum with an early second half score. They held the Tigers to a three and out and started their first drive on their own 35. Elvis ran for 22 yards on a quarterback keeper, and Stefan scored on a counter on the next play. "Field goal team, you're on," hollered Luke. As Alden approached the huddle he was met by Tank, who said to his trembling kicker, "Remember, the idea is to kick the fucking ball above the crossbar. Kick it into my ass again and I'll string ya up by the balls!"

The threat from Tank made Alden even more nervous as he measured off his steps and angle from which to approach Danny Schrader's hold position at the 10-yard line. There was really no reason for anyone to be hopeful that this inaugural game situation extra point kicking try would be any more successful than the hundreds of failed attempts in practice, thought Luke. But what the hell, maybe another botched attempt in a game situation would help Alden's dad come to grips with the fact that his kid was unlikely to get any full ride college football scholarships as a kicker anytime soon.

Tucker took his verbal cue from Danny that the kicker and

holder were ready and snapped back a perfect spiral. Danny caught it and spun the laces away from where the foot would contact the ball, setting the ball on the ground in perfect position for Alden to launch it between the goal posts. Luke wouldn't even have had to be watching, as the familiar 'thud' of the ball colliding with Tank's posterior told him all he needed to know about the fate of the kick.

With the score at a safe 36-0, Luke cleared what bench he had for the next defensive series, except for Earl, as he wanted to make sure that Hodgeman was also putting in their reserves. He sent in Wade Hoekstra and Virgil Cottingham, his two senior reserves, sophomore Travis Cederholm and freshmen Ernie Rimby and Brundage Spragg. He also used this opportunity to get Elvis a few reps at safety. When Luke could see that Greeley wasn't at RB on the first play and that coach Dubois had put in the rest of his reserves, he turned and called for Earl.

"Yes coach? I'm ready to go, coach! Let me at them sum-bitches!"

"Okay, Earl, go in for Tuf at safety on the next play. Make sure you protect the deep third. Whatever you do, don't get beat deep," said Luke, unable to suppress a smile as he watched Earl race over to the bench to grab his helmet.

Since neither Pacer Coulee or Hodgeman had enough players to field a regular JV team, a game in which a team was either substantially ahead or behind was the only way to get the reserves any meaningful playing time. The first few plays for both teams played like a comedy of errors. An offside call against Wade Cederholm was offset by an illegal procedure call against Hodgeman on the next play. Then the Tiger ball carrier fumbled, but by the time several players from each side seemingly had the recovery, the ball would squirt forward, sideways or backward until the final recovery by a Tiger resulted in a 4-yard gain in their favor.

Luke suddenly realized several plays had transpired since he had told Earl he could go in, and he was nowhere in sight on the field. Luke turned to his sideline and saw that Earl was sitting all by himself on the bench, helmet in his lap and his face wearing a look of shock and despair. Luke called him to come to his side, but Earl wouldn't make eye contact or respond to him.

Luke went over to the bench and bent over so that he was face to face with the eager athlete and said, "Earl, I told you that you could go in. What's the matter?" Finally, Earl looked him in the eye and said, "Coach, I can't go in."

"Why not? Don't you want to play?"

"Yes, I really want to play, coach. I want to play more than anything in the world!"

Luke hollered at T.O. to take over the coaching duties, and turned back to Earl and asked, "Then why are you still sitting here on the bench?"

"Well coach, I can't go in," explained Earl, as big watery tears suddenly filled his eyes and began to flow down his cheeks. "I can't go in 'cause I got so excited when you told me to go in that I... I... well coach, I shit my pants!"

Well, here's a coaching situation I've never run into before, thought Luke as he shuddered to think what Earl's backside looked like in the white game pants. He only took a moment to ponder how best to handle this embarrassing situation for Earl. "Okay Earl, that's okay. Here's what we're gonna do. I'm gonna have one of the managers run up to the equipment room and get us one of those full length parkas. Then you can put that on, and I'll have the managers get on either side of you and walk you up to the locker room, each with a hand under your arm, like you sprained an ankle or something. How about we do that?"

Tears still streaming from his eyes, Earl nodded his head a relieved affirmative to that plan. Luke then called his two eighth grade managers over and sent one to get the parka. When the knee-length coat arrived, Luke went over and stood with the two managers to shield Earl from the stands. They put the coat over his shoulders and had him stand up while they buttoned it from top to bottom. He told the two managers that Earl had sprained an ankle, and had them each take an arm and help him to the locker room. He left further instructions that they were needed back at the field, so they should hustle back immediately after getting Earl safely into the locker room. Earl gave Luke a quick glance of gratitude, and with Earl's heavy limp they began the slow going 100-yard journey to the locker room.

Despite the continuation of a host of penalties and error-ridden chaos, the reserves played the final quarter to a standoff. Each team actually generated a touchdown, resulting in a 42-6 final score. Freshman running back and defensive back Ernie Rimby shone particularly bright for the Bulldogs, as he broke off a 60-yard touchdown gallop and made a host of plays on defense, to include an interception off a Travis Cederholm tipped pass. Luke let the team linger on the field, mingling with the parents, classmates and fans as the warm, autumn sun retreated from the cloudless sky. Luke slipped away from the cheerful confines of Pacer Coulee Field to return to the locker room and check on Earl. The locker room was empty, the only sign of the young freshman being the helmet and shoulder pads that had been tossed in the direction of his locker. He was relieved that Earl must have otherwise disposed of his soiled football pants, as the laundry bin was thankfully empty.

BO RIBS COACH CARTER

As most of the team members milled around the training room getting their ankles wrapped or taped, Luke was taken aback when team comedian Bo Ramsay went into his Texas southern drawl and said to him, "Whaddya all think there 'bout that new neighbor of yurs, coach?"

As a surprised Luke fumbled for a response, Bo continued, "Why, Miz Madison is 'bout as purdy as the sun settin' over the Rio Grande, she for dadgum shur is. Cuter than a puppy dog in a red wagon, she is. So what do ya think, coach?"

What few guys were not in the training room had hurriedly come running, anxious to hear coach Carter's response. "Jesus, Bo," muttered Aaron, shaking his head in wonderment at his teammate's bold question to their coach.

"Well… well," stammered Luke as he tried to fashion a response. "She seems like a nice lady, wouldn't you say?"

"That she do… that she do. But I'm a thinkin' that ya best get to courtin' that flashy filly afore anudder stallion plum beats ya to it."

Luke could feel his face redden as he glanced at the 17 faces awaiting his response, but the best he could come up with before seeking refuge in the coaches' office was, "Well thanks, Bo. I'll take your concerns under advisement."

TERRANCE THREATENS LUKE

Luke had long since fallen into nighttime slumber when he was awakened with a start by someone pounding on his front door. His night-stand alarm clock said 11:56 p.m. as he slipped on a pair of sweat pants and rushed to the front door, hoping the flimsy wood barrier could withstand the forceful battering it was currently enduring until he got there.

Luke wasn't in any way prepared to deal with what was on his porch when he opened the door. It took a moment before his eyes adjusted in the dim porch light to recognize the grizzly bear sized figure that stood before him, but the stench of alcohol and days-old perspiration that slammed his nostrils immediately announced the presence of one Terrance Hollister, Sr. He appeared to be wearing the same suspender coveralls that Luke remembered from his only other face to face encounter several months prior, as well as the familiar tattered baseball cap that made a haphazard attempt to cover the greasy and unruly strands of hair that splayed out at every angle from beneath its brim.

Before Luke could shake the fog of being awakened from a deep sleep long enough to speak, Terrance spat a stream of chewing tobacco to the planks of the porch and snarled at Luke through his Copenhagen-drenched beard. "I'm only going to tell you this one time, you pretty boy fuckin' pussy. You quit puttin' that notion in Terrance Jr.'s big dumb head that he's some kind of hot shit football player that needs to go off and play college ball somewhere. He ain't shit for fuckin' nothin', and neither are you. I need him to stay right here in Pacer Coulee and help me run this ranch and get our land back from that thievin' bitch Edna Coffman," spat the frightening behemoth of a man, splattering Luke's face and chest with equal doses of rancid breath and tobacco spit. "I'm givin' ya fair warning, you hear? You keep it up with this football and college shit and you and that fuckin' Coffman bitch sidekick of yours just might end up in the bottom of some canyon out in the Missouri River breaks country. You two would be the perfect bait for the mountain lions, coyotes and buzzards."

With his horrifying message delivered, the monstrous man staggered off the porch, shouting out a final notice before getting in his pickup: "And don't say you ain't been warned."

LOCKER ROOM TALK ABOUT EDNA

"So what's the deal with Miz Coffman?" asked freshman
Ernie Rimby, to no one in particular, as the team was changing
into their street clothes in the locker room after practice. "I
mean, is she a lesbian, or what?"

"Fuck ya Ernie, she's a Goddamn bull-dyke for sure!" shot
back the ever-irreverent Bo Ramsay in his classic descending,
sarcastic tone. "I'm telling ya Rimby, better keep an eye on your
mother, grandmother and sisters, or you'll find that ol' Edna has
'em tied up in your barn stall and is puttin' the strap-on to 'em!"

"I've kinda wondered that about Miz Coffman, too," offered
fellow freshman Earl Wonderwald, seemingly oblivious to the
fact that he had just stepped onto the track in front of the Bo
Ramsay Express that was about to hurtle towards him at runaway speed. "You know, just like Ernie said, I been wonderin' if
she's, like, a lesbian or sumpthin' like that."

"Do you two dip-shits even know what a lesbian is?" asked
Bo, quickly warming up to vintage Ramsay mockery mode.

"Heck ya, I do," said Ernie. "My mom's cousin Bobbie, she
lives in Minnesota… she's a lesbian for sure, and my mom even
said so! She has, like, whatchamacallit… a partner. They live
together in the same house and everything."

"No shit?" sang Bo, the sarcasm almost visibly dripping
from his chin. "So you've probably watched the cousin put the
big ol' dildo to her girlfriend, huh Ernie?"

"Uhh, no—no… ain't never seen nothin' like that, Bo."

"I should have never gave you that July issue of Penthouse;
the one that had that layout of the two biker chicks goin' at it,"
teased Bo. "Seein' that you've got yourself your very own bull-
dyke in the family, you probably really liked that issue, huh
Ernie? You probably whack off every night to that Penthouse,
don't you? You're just a little fuckin' perv, aren't you Rimby?"

No one had left the locker room, all riveted to the Bo Show and his verbal torture and dismantling of the two unsuspecting freshmen. All of the spectators, especially the underclassmen, were thankful that they weren't the object of Bo's guided, heat-seeking verbal missiles.

"Heck no! I ain't no perv, Bo! I didn't even look at those pictures, I swear," exclaimed a clearly rattled Ernie, glancing around the locker room in a desperate appeal for a sympathetic expression of support.

"Bullshit! You probably showed Earl those pictures, and both you two sick pervs sit around all day looking at those pictures and pounding your little puds!"

"No way!" both Earl and Ernie cried in unison. "That's just not true, Bo. We ain't never done nothin' like that," Earl confirmed.

Fortunately for the two embattled freshmen, senior Aaron Coslet came to their rescue. Always the pragmatic thinker, the team co-captain was the stable voice of reason. Aaron was a good athlete and a top student, and his determined work ethic and quiet and confident approach to all that he did automatically set him up as an admired and respected leader in both school and sport. Oddly, he and Bo had been best friends since they were toddlers, even though their personalities couldn't have been more contrary. But they grew up together, their parents being close friends and the family ranches located directly across the same irrigated Judith River bottom. As disrespectful and foul-mouthed as Bo was, Aaron was conversely articulate and professional in the delivery of the English language.

"This brings up an interesting question boys, and one that requires our collective consideration and contemplation," Aaron began, the whole team now gathered around him and as intent on his words as if it was one of his famed pregame fire-up speeches. "Now, what young Earl and Ernie have advanced here is the notion that our long time English professor and now School Board Chairperson and community leader, Edna

Coffman, respectfully to be referred to hereafter as Miz Coffman, is in fact a lesbian. Make no mistake, gentlemen, that this is quite a serious, if not inflammatory declaration that requires careful deliberation and investigation."

Aaron was now pacing before his court, in total command of his eager listeners. Only Bo and the older players smirked, anxious to see how their teammate was going to spin the web for the two innocent freshmen. "Gentlemen, what this situation calls for is a Columbo-like approach. We need to ask ourselves: what would Peter Faulk do in a situation like this? Clearly, he would start his investigation of the hypothesis that Misters Rimby and Wonderwald have advanced here that Miz Coffman is a lesbian. Yes indeed, Columbo would begin by delineating the true facts of this premise; separate the wheat from the chaff, so to speak. He would search for what is undeniable truth, and conversely, what of the original premise would appear to be unsubstantiated."

Aaron pressed on like a skilled Prosecutor laying out his case. "So, we move forward in determining the facts in this case. Earl and Ernie, do either of you have actual evidence to support the idea that Miz Coffman has a lesbian lover?" With as serious a look on their faces as death row inmates facing imminent execution, both Earl and Ernie vigorously shook their heads no.

"Need I remind you boys that you are under oath, and as such are obligated to tell the truth, the whole truth and nothing but the truth? So once again, for the record, do you Earl, and you Ernie, have any evidence that Miz Coffman has taken a lesbian lover into her home?" Without uttering a word, both freshmen again vigorously shook their heads, indicating that they didn't have any such corroboration.

"Does anyone else in this room have any credible knowledge of said suggested sexual behavior?" No one indicated they possessed any such damning documentation.

"How about you, Elvis? You live under the same roof as Miz Coffman. Have you ever noticed behaviors that would support the Rimby and Wonderwald Hypothesis that Miz Coffman is indeed a lesbian?"

"No, I have not," replied Elvis, trying to stymie the grin that was that threatening to break his stoic expression.

"Okay, at this point in the investigation I believe Columbo would test the heretofore identified Rimby and Wonderwald hypothesis that Miz Coffman is a lesbian. He would perform his testing based on the following premises:

1) Miz Coffman not only has never been married, but has never been known to even date.

2) Miz Coffman dresses more like a man than a woman.

3) Miz Coffman wears her hair short like a man.

Does that about cover it, boys?" asked Aaron, directing his question solely to the two boys who were now hanging their heads in shame. "Yeah, I guess so," Earl said hesitantly.

"Unless further evidence is brought forthwith that supports the declaration in question, what we have here is a hypothesis that can't be substantiated. And while some might find it odd or unusual that Miz Coffman has never married, or that she wears her hair short or dresses in men's Carhartts most of the time, there is certainly no evidence, no credible evidence whatsoever, that Miz Coffman is, in fact, a lesbian."

Since Aaron had noticed that Tank had been unusually reserved throughout his courtroom spectacle, Aaron said, "Tank, we haven't heard from you today on this matter. A penny for your thoughts?"

All eyes turned to their massive teammate as he spoke. "I don't really think it's any of our fucking business if she is or she ain't. Miz E has always been good to me, 'cept for her Goddamn eligibility policy that's cost me about 100 frickin games these past four years. But that's my fault more than hers. I know you guys are just funnin' with this and everything, but I've heard enough. No more of this kinda talk about Miz E. I won't stand for it."

"We was just wondering about it, Tank... didn't mean no harm nor nothin' like that," Ernie said quietly.

Out of the blue, Travis Cederholm suddenly blurted out. "I

wonder if maybe Miz Coffman is like one of those invertebrates that we learned about in Mr. Hertel's science class. You know, the kind that is asexual—kinda like a star fish. Not homosexual or heterosexual, neither one. Maybe that's it. Maybe she's not interested in either gender in a sexual way. Do you think that could be it, Aaron?"

Bo butted in before Aaron could answer, "What the fuck, Cederholm? Where'd you come up with that shit? You're so weird you're scaring me!"

"That's very possible Travis. I think you might be onto something there," said Aaron calmly, ignoring his sidekick Bo's outburst. "But I, for one, would prefer to continue on in life with my head positioned the way it currently is; above my neck and not deeply embedded in my ass. I am therefore going to take Mr. Hollister's rather strongly delivered suggestion that we close this discussion immediately, if not sooner."

With that, Aaron adjourned court, and everybody started to file out of the locker room, but not before Bo's departing shot to Earl and Ernie. "Hey Wonderwald and Rimby," he yelled out at them, "don't be rubbin' on those teeny little nubs of yours to that Penthouse anymore, ya hear?"

If the freshman boys heard his warning, they ignored it, bolting out the door at breakneck speed.

MRS. GROVE AND THE PACER COULEE CHRONICLES

Luke had just picked up his Tuesday mail and was reading the Centertown News Argus account of the Hodgeman game when his phone rang. His heart skipped a beat, as it usually did when hearing Madison's voice on the other end of the line.

"Have you seen Sylvia's Pacer Coulee Chronicles column yet?" asked Madison with an almost accusatory intonation to her voice.

"No, I'm just getting through the articles about our last weekend's games. Why? You sound like it's something bad," said Luke.

"Maybe more like an 'are you kidding me' than anything bad, but call me back after you've read it, okay?"

"Will do," confirmed Luke. "You've definitely got my curiosity up now!"

PACER COULEE CHRONICLES
By Sylvia Graham, Correspondent

Greetings from Pacer Coulee! Boy howdy and boy-oh-boy, lots going on in our world here by the banks of Spring Creek, so I best get to it. Hard to believe we are already through the first three weeks of the football and girls' basketball seasons, and our Bulldog teams couldn't be off to a better start. Under the tutelage of our fine new young coaches Luke Carter and Madison Danielsen, both teams are undefeated at this point in the season. All us Pacer Coulee fans are proud as peacocks of our youngsters, so keep up the good work! Yours Truly also wants to give a shout-out to our new students this year. We are sure glad to welcome the Cederholm family to our school, as they come to us from over the hill in Wyngate country. We call them the four T's-Travis (Soph), Tim (8th grade), Tawnya (6th grade) and Terry (3rd grade). We also are so pleased with the addition of our two Hays Lodgepole transfers, Elvis His Own Horse (Soph) and Clare Comes at Night (freshman). They are brother and sister, and HOLY SMOKES, can these two play basketball! Elvis had never played football before coming here this year, but he played his first game ever against Hodgeman, and HOLY COW can he ever throw a football! Like Butch Cassidy says, this kid can wing it! So make sure to give all these new students a big old Pacer Coulee welcome and a pat on the back when you see them at a game or around town, won't you?

Speaking of our new coaches, Luke and Madison live in Edna Coffman's side by side rentals on Lehman Street, which is right across the alley from Ethyl Grove, our 86-year young famed pie maker. According to Ethyl, these two young coaches are the very best of neighbors and are just as polite and helpful as can be. Ethyl has been especially taken with Madison's 11-year-old daughter Rose, whom she hired to mow her yard and tend to her flowers and garden, especially her rhubarb patch. And Ethyl said that Madison insisted that she drive her in to Albertson's a while back to pick up some baking essentials for the Daughters of the American Revolution potluck. So Ethyl gives a shout-out to her great new neighbors!

Speaking of Ethyl, 5th graders Rose Danielsen and Abby Herman organized a bake sale to raise money for their class to take a field trip weekend to Yellowstone National Park. So who else do you go to other than Ethyl when you need to come up with high quality baked goods? Ethyl arranged a Bake Day down at the Community Center last Sunday, and snagged Pacer Coulee's other top notch bakers Kellie Cassidy, Jeannie Hauf and Hazel Koutensky to bake pies, cakes and cookies for the 5th grade bake sale. All nine of the 5th graders showed up and helped and learned some baking tips from the experts. And even though Yours Truly shouldn't allow any further expansion of her waistline, she couldn't resist purchasing both a cherry and rhubarb pie and a big bag of Oatmeal Raisin cookies at the event! The sale was a roaring success, and there should be enough money in the coffers to send the 5th graders off to the Park.

In other local news, Hank and Mary Spraggins motored over to Square Butte country last Sunday to help Mary's brother Clyde gather cows in preparation for the delivery of calves. When the work was done, Clyde barbecued up the T-bones he had left over from purchasing his nephew's 4-H steer at the Choteau County fair last August.

Reed Simon of the Pacer Coulee Volunteer Ambulance and Fire District reported a pretty darn busy harvest fire season this year. He said their district responded to a total of seven harvest related fires in Fergus County, and assisted on several more in each of Judith Basin and Petroleum counties. He said the worst fire was on the Eugene Pickett place north of Coffee Creek. In addition to losing his newer model 7700 John Deere combine and 1973 International grain truck in the fire, Eugene estimated he lost about 100 acres of unharvested wheat. Eugene shouts out a big thank you to the farming community that showed up with five combines and even more trucks to finish off his 700 acres of wheat that was yet to be harvested. "You'll never know much that meant to me and Andrea," Eugene said, "and it serves as a reminder of how folks here in the Judith Basin take care of their friends and neighbors in time of need. All those fine folk left their own harvest fields to spend a long day helping us get our wheat harvested, and wouldn't accept one penny in return. We're overwhelmed by their generosity, and are forever in debt for their deeds."

Reed asked me to remind everybody to come to the annual first of November Fire and Ambulance dinner and auction fundraiser, as they desperately need to

upgrade the rural fire truck and its water holding
tank capacity.

On the medical front, Yours Truly got the Prayer
Chain in motion when 83 year young Bid Byrne took a
bad tumble off Blaze, his 17 hands tall roping
horse. Of course, the stubborn old Irishman
wouldn't go to the doctor, but did allow our
resident veterinarian Kellie Cassidy to give him
the once over. Kellie said she is pretty sure that
Bid cracked at least a couple of ribs. We all pray
for a speedy recovery, but when Yours Truly
suggested he leave the team roping to the younger
crowd he told me to quit being such a busy-body and
mind my own business! Ha! I guess he must be
feeling better if he's back to his sassy old self
already.

Last but not least, a status report on our
agricultural community. As mentioned in recent
columns, winter wheat yields were average to below
average due to lack of timely moisture. Spring
wheat and barley were below average for the same
reasons. Dryland hay crops were also below average.
As we approach the time of year where our ranchers
ship off their calves to market, most think the
calves might come in a bit on the light side due to
the poorer pasture conditions. The good news is
that calf prices seem to be up about 5 cents from
last year. Unfortunately the same can't be said for
grain and barley prices. But like Butch Cassidy
always says, "this is next year country, so we have
no choice but to take it and trust that the good
Lord will bring us better yields and prices next
year."

As always, Be Careful Out There, ya hear? See
you next month, and be sure and call me at 536-2645
if you have any news to report.

"I swear Madison, I knew you were joking when you said
for me to tell Sylvia about taking Ethyl to Albertson's! I didn't

call Sylvia, I swear!" explained Luke when he called Madison back.

"I know that, Luke. Coming from an even less-populated town than Pacer Coulee, I get the small town newspaper thing. But I sure didn't expect that we'd be so front and center in the Chronicles. I mean, you just have to laugh, don't you?"

"I guess so, but for a guy coming from the city to have his laundry—dirty or otherwise—right out there in the paper for everybody to read is, well, a bit disconcerting to say the least," chuckled Luke. "But if we were to suddenly start losing a bunch of games, either Edna or the Hole in the Wall Coffee gang could very well hire a hit man out of Chicago to bump us off. And when the hired gun asks where to find us, they'll just send him this Pacer Coulee Chronicles article and he'll know our precise location; side by side homes on Lehman Street!"

"I never thought of that," said Madison, feigning a tone of apprehension and fear. "They'll also have to take out Ethyl—she knows too much! And the hit man will know from this article that Ethyl lives just across the alley from us."

"That's the likely scenario, for sure," agreed Luke. "It won't matter much to us and Ethyl because we'll all be dead, but I guess we can take comfort that the hit man will be caught."

"How do you know that?" asked Madison.

"Well, I'm thinking they will be so enthralled with Sylvia's column that they will read the entire article. They won't be able to resist leaving Ethyl's house without sampling her rhubarb pie. They'll get sloppy and leave their fingerprints on the pie plate. That will be the lead that allows Sheriff Couch to track them down."

"You are so right. Who in their right mind would try to eat rhubarb pie with their gloves on?" confirmed Madison. "It will be most comforting to know from our graves that our killers will spend the rest of their lives in prison."

LUKE GETS BAD NEWS ON TANK'S GRADES

"Uhhh… coach, say… uhh coach," stammered Dolph as he popped his head around the door of Luke's empty prep period class on the Thursday before the Stanton game. "Come on in, Dolph. What's on your mind?" Luke inquired, knowing full well that this was the usual Thursday stress-out about whether he would be eligible to play in the upcoming weekend game. Luke had to hold back a smile as Dolph stepped hesitantly into the room, both hands up near the sides of his head as if preparing to quickly cover his ears in the event he was going to get unfavorable news.

"Well coach, I was just wondering… like… you know, if you'd heard anything about the list. You know, that bad, bad list."

"Oh yeah, that darned old list," answered Luke. "Let's see if I can find that list. It's got to be somewhere on my desk," said Luke as he shuffled through several piles of paper before pulling out a folder and inspecting the contents with a serious look on his face. "Let's see, here it is. Is there a Dolph Russell on this list?" asked Luke as he ran his finger down an imaginary accounting of ineligible students on a blank sheet of paper. "Nope, no Dolph Russell on this list. Looks like you're good to go for the Stanton game on Saturday, Dolph."

Dolph raced out of the room hopping and bucking like one of Tuf Sturm's green colts, shouting back over his shoulder, "That's the best of news, coach! Best of news ever!"

Luke had just finished laughing out loud with what had become Dolph's weekly Thursday ritual regarding the eligibility report when he got a second dose of good news from Alden

Blackburn. "Can I have a moment of your time, coach?" asked the scarecrow-thin wannabe kicker.

"I'm all ears, Alden. What can I do for you?" inquired Luke, already sensing that the boy needed to get something heavy off his chest.

"Well coach, you know how my dad sort of made me come out for football? I mean, I know what he sees out there in high school, college and pros. He sees soccer style kickers all over the place. And most really good kickers were soccer players before they ever started kicking footballs, you know?" explained Alden, continuing when Luke nodded his head in agreement. "But just because most kickers were soccer players, it doesn't mean that all soccer players can kick a football, you know what I mean? But my dad doesn't see that. He thinks because I played a little bit of soccer back in California that I should be able to kick a football. Well coach, truth is, I wasn't any good at soccer either. I mean, I could kick a soccer ball better than I can kick a football, but I really wasn't very good at it at all."

"I hear what you're saying, Alden. I understand." said Luke softly when Alden paused and looked at him expectantly, as if he was trying to assess whether he should go on, or turn and leave in a puddle of embarrassment. "Please continue. I'm not going to bite."

"Well coach, here's the thing. I really appreciate you taking the time and trying to teach me how to kick. And I know my dad has been after you and after you to let me try a kick in another real game. And thanks for letting me try that extra point in the Hodgeman game last week, and I know you did that because my dad kept bugging you. But truth is, I don't want to kick in a game… not ever again. It was embarrassing in front of all those people to not even get the ball off the ground."

"I get it, Alden. I really do. But that kick was nothing to be ashamed of. You've worked hard and tried your best, and that's what counts. I'm really proud of you for trying so hard. So it's more than fine if you don't want to play anymore," explained Luke. "I understand."

"But coach, there's one more thing I need to ask you," the dreadfully thin youngster asked sheepishly. "Coach, I really like being on the team. I mean, I like being around the guys and all that stuff, I really do. I hate to ask you this coach, but could we, like, like just let me stay on the team and keep practicing my kicking, but not put me in any more real games? Could we do that, coach? I know if we do it that way my dad will still be bothering you to let me kick, so I understand if you'd rather I just left the team."

"No worries, Alden. Let me worry about dealing with your dad. I'm glad you want to stay on the team, and you can just keep practicing the way we have been. We'll keep the decision to not have you attempt any kicks in a game between the two of us. How does that sound?"

"Thanks, coach. Thank you so much! See you at practice tonight?" inquired a grinning Alden.

"You bet. See you at practice."

Alden had no sooner got out the door when he heard another knock. "Got a sec, Luke?" asked Madison as she stuck her head into the classroom. His stomach performed its usual flip and flutter at the sound of her voice, but her intonation wasn't of the usual Madison cheery flavor.

"Come on in. By the sound of your voice I take it this isn't the best of news?"

"No. No, it's not, sorry to say. Tank bombed his math test yesterday. When I combine that with a couple of low scores on his daily work and a poor result on the usual Monday math quiz, it drops him well below the eligibility standard. He's not going to be able to play against Stanton this weekend," explained Madison sympathetically. "I'm so sorry, Luke. I worked with him during my sixth period study hall that I have on Monday and gave him some extra assignment homework to do before Wednesday's test, but he still failed the test. I should have done more, but I assumed with the extra help and homework that he'd do fine. I should have warned you sooner. I'm so sorry."

"No—no, it's not your fault at all, Madison. Thanks for everything you did to try to help him. Dammit, T.O. was right. It's not a matter of *if* with Tank, it's a matter of *when*. I asked everybody after Tuesday's practice if anybody was in trouble and needed help, and only Earl, Ernie and Brundage responded. Tank sat there on his thumbs like he was acing every class. Goddamn him. I can't wait for the tongue lashing I'm going to get when Edna hears about this."

"Well, I'm guessing it won't be any worse than the one Tank's going to get from her," reasoned Madison. "I'm guessing Edna is going to want to assign him a tutor for my class. Anyway, I feel so bad for you and your team. Do you think you can beat Stanton without him?"

"It'll be a tough row to hoe. The other problem is that Dolph is totally ineffective if Tank's not there beside him, so effectively we lose both our top linemen, and we take about a half of a continent's step backwards with their replacements. To be truthful Madison, I just hope we're within three touchdowns when the final whistle blows."

T.O. RIPS TANK

"Goddamn it, Tank!" roared T.O. to a head-hanging Tank as he hovered in the corner like a potty trained dog who had just reverted to peeing on the carpet. Luke had called Tank into the coaches' office before practice to break the news to T.O. that he wouldn't be eligible to play in the biggest game thus far in the season against the Stanton Wolves. "Goddamn, son-of-a-bitch, I don't know why I put myself through this eligibility shit with you, Tank. Year after fucking year. And you do it just before we play Stanton? Why in the hell didn't you go brain dead on us against Marshall or Hodgeman? NOOOO, you gotta screw up just before Stanton. Can we look forward to you having a brain fart the weeks we play Deeden, Heberton and St. Francis too? And you know what else happens when you pull this shit, don't you Tank? Dolph turns into jello, that's what he does. He's as worthless as tits on a boar when you're not in there. Goddamn, son-of-a-bitch and Jesus H. Christ!" hollered the burly assistant coach while pacing back and forth in the cramped quarters of the little office. "And here's another thing that I can tell you for Goddamn sure. If the good Lord would have given me a tenth of the size and talent that he gave you, I'd be still be playing nose guard in the NFL. And another thing. I would have never, ever been ineligible. Not one Goddamn time, and I wasn't no Rhodes Scholar either. But I wouldn't have let my teammates down like you have, I sure as fuck wouldn't have. Goddamn it… sorry to do this to ya Luke," declared T.O. as he stormed out the door, "but I ain't gonna be at practice tonight. I can't take anymore of this shit today. Just can't do 'er."

"I'm sorry coach, I really am," Tank said quietly. "I shoulda worked harder on that math stuff. Coach Barker is really pissed, ain't he?"

"Yeah, he's pretty upset. Here's another thing, Tank. I'm going to have to call coaches from about ten different colleges tonight, including Montana State, Montana, Nebraska, Washington State and Iowa, to name a few. They were all sending people out to scout and watch you play."

Tank hung his head even further and whispered, "I'm sorry to let you and all those colleges down."

"Well, even more important is that you're letting your teammates down. We need to get this academic thing back on track, Tank. We can't beat the Stantons, Deedens and Hebertons, and most certainly not St. Francis without you. We just can't. I haven't talked to Edna yet, but I think you can count on being assigned a tutor in every class you have. So you better be not only prepared, but accepting of that concept. I know you can do it, Tank. Can I count on you to take the bull by the horns and do the right thing?"

"You can, coach. You damn sure can."

"Then come and help coach the linemen for me tonight, because it sounds like I'm gonna be short a coach."

EDNA APPOINTS ELVIS
AND DEE AS TUTORS

Luke breathed a sigh of relief when he read the Eligibility Report on the Thursday before the home game against Deeden. He had already given the usual 'best of news, coach' report to Dolph when school secretary Lois delivered it to his classroom. Like most weeks so far in the season, reserves Wade Hoekstra and Ernie Rimby dangled perilously close to the murky waters of academic suspension, but only Brundage Spragg had tumbled all of the way in. As he did every day at practice, the big freshman cried when Luke called him in and gave him the news. "Well, if I have to lose a player," Luke muttered to himself after sending the big freshman out the door with some Kleenex to dab his watering eyes. The rest of the team would have to suddenly succumb to the Bubonic Plague before Brundage would get in the game against the always tough Deeden squad anyway.

Luke was more than relieved to see Tank's name in the solidly eligible category, but he was expecting improved results ever since Edna had called for a meeting immediately after Tank's suspension before the Stanton game. Lester, Luke, Edna, Otis, Tank, Dee Cassidy and Elvis all crowded into the Superintendent's office for the one-sided conversation. As usual, Edna didn't beat around bush and launched into an angry tirade directed at Tank that had everyone else, including Otis, sweating bullets. The presence of the two classmates soon became clear, as Elvis had been appointed as Tank's math tutor and Dee for his other classes. Edna had barked at Lois to bring in the weekly tutor session times that she had typed from the board chair's handwritten notes, which included the when, where and to whom the progress updates were to be delivered.

"You better follow this schedule to a T, young man," she

scolded the sheepish Tank. "You will not let down your teammates, your school and your community again this season because of your blatant and inexcusable lack of effort and attention to your studies. As you can see from this reporting schedule, this is going to be a team effort to keep your damn nose to the grindstone. And Dee and Elvis? The minute this big lug starts slacking or is even one minute late for a tutor appointment, you contact me immediately and by God I will get things back on track in a hurry. In the end, your tutors, your coach, your Superintendent, and especially you Tank, will all report to and answer to me."

With all matters Tank clarified, Edna brought the meeting to an abrupt close with, "Come on Otis, let's get the hell out of here before I drag this big lummox by the ear out to the woodshed and give him a whipping he'll never forget."

As the despondent eligibility victim had shuffled out of the room, Luke had realized he had yet to meaningfully engage Tank in regards to the obvious negative effects his suspension had on the rest of the team as they headed into one of the more pivotal games of the season. Once they were clear of the others, Luke stopped Tank in the empty hallway and said, "Well big boy, I think that between T.O. yesterday, and now Edna today, you have probably been brow-beaten enough over your suspension without me chewing on your ass some more. So I'm just going to say this," Luke said calmly, but firmly. "As I mentioned yesterday, our chances of beating Stanton, Deeden, Heberton and St. Francis without you are somewhere between slim and none, and heavily weighted to the 'none' side when talking about Heberton and St. Francis. You do understand that, don't you Tank?"

"Yes sir, I know," replied Tank sheepishly.

"Good, good. Instead of running up the score on the 'you have let down your teammates and your town' sins that you've already been repeatedly spanked for, I need you to answer one thing for me. Can I count on you to finally step up and take responsibility for remaining eligible for the rest of this season? Will you follow Ms. Coffman's schedule and meet with your tutors when you are supposed to? Can I count on you to do that, Tank?"

"You can," replied Tank quietly, looking down at the ground as he spoke.

"That's not good enough; look me in the eye and convince me you intend to do the right thing here, Tank."

"You can count on me coach, you damn sure can," confirmed Tank with full eye contact. "Won't happen again, I swear."

HOLE IN THE WALL GANG
BETTING POOL

"Damn, I was worried about this Stanton game. I mean, I was nervous even before we found out that Tank was ineligible again," said Butch Cassidy to the fully gathered Hole in the Wall gang. All seven regulars of the morning coffee club crew stood on the crowded stoop of the O.K. Corral Bar and Grill entrance awaiting the arrival of Kip Jordan, the once again tardy owner of the establishment, to open the door.

"Well, I told all you boys last Friday that Stanton would get the best of us," lectured Frank Cervenka, as he looked down at his watch that read 7:05 a.m. "Is it just me, or does it seem like Kip is getting later and later in opening this joint up?"

"Can you blame him?" asked Harlan Horrall. "He's probably so depressed after listening to your gloom and doom predictions every week that he just wants to stay in bed all day."

"Hey, I predicted the girls would win both games last weekend, didn't I?" Frank replied, defying his reputation as the doomsday prognosticator king of the Hole in the Wall gang.

"Jesus Christ," muttered Kip, as he worked his way through the group to unlock the door. "You're like a bunch o' damn milk cows lining up at the barn door. Don't any of you old bastards ever sleep in?"

Once Kip got the coffee pots brewing and the donuts laid out, Butch started the traditional Monday morning ritual of determining the outcome of the past week's betting pool. The winner, in addition to winning the $60 betting pot, would also be exempt from having to contribute to the coffee and donut fund for the rest of the week. It was not an uncomplicated calculation, as every Thursday morning of each week during the fall sports season, every Hole in the Wall gang member received a Butch-created betting ballot that always listed the following contests to be played that weekend: 1) Pacer Coulee football game 2) Pacer Coulee girls' basketball game(s) 3) a Butch selected Class B, A, AA football game of the week 4) a Butch selected Frontier Conference football game of the week 5) the University of Montana Grizzly and Montana State Bobcat football games 6) a Butch selected group of 4 NFL contests. If required, the tie breaker would always be the score of the Bulldog football game.

The ballot for the prior week was:

1. Stanton___ @ Pacer Coulee___ FB (write in score for tie breaker)
2. Range View @ Pacer Coulee GBB
3. Pacer Coulee @ Marshall GBB
4. Malta @ Glasgow Class B FB
5. Centertown @ Havre Class A FB
6. Gt. Falls High @ Helena High Class AA FB
7. Carroll College @ Rocky Mountain FB
8. Weber @ UM FB
9. Idaho State @ MSU FB
10. Cowboys @ Eagles
11. Seahawks @ 49ers
12. Chiefs @ Broncos
13. Bears @ Packers

"Well boys, looks like it's coming down to a tie breaker this week," declared Butch. "Frank and Bones tied with ten correct picks each, but Frank wins because he picked Stanton and Bones went with the Bulldogs."

"Go figure," said Harlan Horrall. "Frank's got about five years worth of wheat stored in his grain bins, and he still has so much cash on hand that he don't need to sell any. Would serve you right, Frank, if the mice and the bugs don't render them bins worthless. Anyway, and to think that the rest of us poor suckers have to give up our betting ante to this wealthy land baron, not to mention buy his damn coffee and maple bars for the rest of the week." Frank pantomimed playing a violin while the rest of the coffee crew chuckled over the good-natured banter directed at the winner of the weekly pool.

Still stinging from the loss to Stanton, Wilbur Rimby began the Monday Morning Quarterback review of the game. "You know, we don't just lose Tank hisself when he ain't eligible. My grandson Ernie says that Dolph just falls apart if Tank ain't there to tell him what to do. So when Tank messes up in school, we actually lose our two best linemen on both sides of the ball."

"I wondered about that," said Duke Dickson, thoughtfully. "I noticed that they started Dolph, but after he jumped offside a couple of times they took him out. I don't think he saw the field in the second half."

"Yeah, Ernie says they just have to take him out of the game. It's like Tank is his security blanket. Says Tank tells him who to block and such, and apparently he won't listen to anybody else."

"All I know is that having Wade Hoekstra and Travis Cederholm trying to replace Tank and Dolph is like replacing the O and D-lines of the Packers with the cheerleaders," commented Art Fenner. "I actually thought the His Own Horse kid played pretty damn good for only his second game of football. Without Tank and Dolph to protect him, poor kid was running for his life most of the game. That was a beautiful pass he threw to Kimball Robbins in the first quarter for our only score of the first half."

"Of course Robbins supposedly tweaked his hammy, yet again, on the play. Never did see him in the second half," said Harlan, then adding, "With the Indian kid being able to throw as well as he does, Robbins is going to be the key the rest of the way. If he's hurt as much as he usually is, we'll have a tough time down the stretch. Your grandson is a damn good receiver, Butch, but he's the only one we got if Kimball is out. And Wilbur, Ernie is going to be a good player, but he's only a freshman. Without Kimball, teams can really concentrate on making sure Bret is covered, and that will create problems. Even though both Tillerman and Coslet can catch pretty well coming out of the backfield, having Kimball's speed as a constant deep threat would sure open things up."

"I'll tell ya this much," interjected Bones, "I think coach Carter called a helluva game to bring us back and make it interesting in the end. Without Tank and Dolph, not to mention losing Kimball for the entire second half, them draws, screens and flare passes he called to get the ball in Stefan's hands out in space kept it close."

"You got that right," confirmed Arthur. "Without three of our studs on the field, the game coulda got out of hand in the second half. Coach's strategy kept us in it. Yep, I'm thinkin' the guy knows what the hell he's doing, I surely do."

Harlan jumped back in on the analysis. "Well boys, my new girlfriend Madison didn't have any trouble with the Range View and Marshall gals this past weekend. Of course, she's always asking me for coaching advice. You know, like when she should go zone versus man, or which Brewster girl match-up she should use to post up... stuff like that."

"Oh, your girlfriend Madison, huh?" laughed Duke, as all the other gang members shook their heads in amusement. "I'll say this for you, Harlan—you have some kind of active imagination, that's for sure."

"Well, an old bachelor can dream, can't he?" said Harlan, spreading his arms with a 'give a guy a break' expression on his face.

"That girl's team is damn good, I'm telling ya," said Butch. "She seems to have those Brewster girls playing together about as well as I've ever seen. They'll be tough to stop if they keep playing team ball like that."

Nodding his head in agreement, Bones added, "Man, I think that youngest one, Sammi, is gonna be better than all of them. And that little Indian gal? Damn, ain't she something? No bigger than a minute, but lordy-lordy, she's quicker than the ol' proverbial bolt of lightning!"

Being the only two members of the Hole in the Wall gang that had grandchildren participating in both football and girls' basketball, Butch and Wilbur were expected to deliver to the coffee group any and all insider information that might not otherwise be available to the public in general. "So Wilbur, what's Anna have to say about the team chemistry so far?" asked Duke.

"You mean other than reporting that boyfriend Harlan gives shitty coaching advice to his girlfriend Madison?" inquired Wilbur, to the hee-haws and cat-calls from the rest of the group. "Well, she says there is definitely a bit of sister jealousy towards Sammi, especially from the twins. But everybody loves playing with Clare. 'Course who wouldn't want to play with a point guard that can distribute the ball like that little gal can? Says that they have a hard time getting a word out of her, and that she's pretty darn shy. Says coach Danielsen keeps reminding the other girls to understand that this is a whole new culture for her, and to have patience with her and help her make the transition as smooth as possible."

"Hate to have to break the news to ya, boys," said Frank, "but history tells us that this ain't the only game Tank is gonna be ineligible for. And Tank or no Tank, we ain't in the same universe as St. Francis. So I don't care how good you think this new coach is, we're gonna be lucky to go 4 and 4. You boys need to prepare yourself for upcoming losses to Deeden, Heberton, and of course, St. Francis. And Kip might as well bring a couple Kleenex boxes over to the table right now, 'cause all you little darlings are gonna start shedding tears when I tell you that going 4 and 4 means we'll miss the playoffs. Again.

"And furthermore, as good as your fantasy girlfriend has these girls playing right now, Harlan, there is no way the Brewster girls can get along for an entire season. So when the Brewsters implode, one little freshman Indian gal won't be able to carry this team on her scrawny back. So Kip, you better keep the tissues coming for these little crybabies for more bad news;

the gals ain't gonna make it past divisional. Again. Sorry boys, but them's the facts, like it or not."

"Thank you, Frank, for your never-ending positive and uplifting commentary and predictions," said Butch, sarcastically.

Harlan took it a step further as he pulled a chair directly across from him, and began to speak to its imaginary occupant. "So what ails you enough to bring you to the Doctor's office, George?" Jumping across to the empty chair to play the patient, George says, "Well Doc, I ain't rightly sure… the missus thinks I might be depressed." Hopping back to the doctor's chair, the Doc says, "I see. Have you by any chance been in close proximity to Frank Cervenka in the last 48 hours?"

"Why yes, we ran into each other at the Co-op yesterday afternoon."

"Hmmm… that explains it then. George, you've contracted the Cervenka Virus. I'm sorry to inform you that this virus is the deadly strain that brings about debilitating depression to 100% of those infected. I also regret to report that there is no known cure. You are now destined to a life of being a depressing old and miserly downer that constantly badmouths and bets against all Pacer Coulee sports teams."

While all present in the O.K. Corral Bar and Grill laughed and clapped at Harlan's clever doctor/patient office visit conversation, Frank again pantomimed his classic violin strumming routine as he exited the bar to a chorus of jeers and boos.

TROUBLE FINDS LUKE, TANK, AND DOLPH IN GT. FALLS

Edna barged into Luke's classroom on the Friday before the Stanton game and announced that she had arranged a field day the following Tuesday for his Montana History classes. She informed him that they would be leaving for Great Falls at 7:00 a.m., which would put them at the Lewis and Clark Interpretive Center in time for their 9:00 a.m. pre-scheduled tour of the facility. The tour would conclude at 10:45, at which time they would board the nine students from his combined two Montana History classes on the little 12-seat, Shanty-chauffeured yellow school bus and head to the Charles M. Russell Museum for a 45-minute presentation on one of America's most acclaimed late 1800s and early 1900s western artists. Edna was her usual blunt self when she pointed out to Luke that he, being a non Montana-educated Nebraskan, would likely benefit even more than the students from the informative field trip.

"I'm going to go with the students on the bus, but I'd like you to take your truck to Great Falls. Every year I order, and Bill Koch pays for, a few super jumbo sized t-shirts and short sleeve shirts for Tank from Universal Athletics. We also always get a pair of gym shoes at UA for Dolph, plus a few pair of jeans for him at JC Penney. Oh, and we get the same t-shirts that Tank gets for Dolph—2XL, at UA. Dolph has a fit if we don't get him matching Tank t-shirts. Anyway, when the bus takes me and the other kids back to Pacer Coulee, I want you to take Tank and Dolph with you to the Holiday Village Mall, which is where both Universal Athletics and JC Penney are located. You will need to have Dolph fitted for the gym shoes and the jeans, but everything else is already ordered, paid for and should be there waiting for you to pick up. It shouldn't take you long to finish all that, and then you and the boys can hit the road and be back in plenty of time for practice."

"You got it, boss," said Luke with a salute. "I might have to borrow T.O.'s horse trailer to haul Tank home, as I'm not sure I can stuff the three of us into my cab."

Luke dispatched Tank and Dolph to the mall's spacious game room while he walked the few stores down to Universal Athletics to pick up Tank's special order 5X t-shirts. As he was checking out, he heard the rapidly approaching footsteps of a breathless Tank. "Coach, is Dolph with you?" he asked, obviously anxious to hear an affirmative response.

"No, he's not with me," replied Luke.

"Fuck! I had to piss, so I left him in the game room to go to that bathroom that's right across the hall. There was nobody else in the game room and he was playing pinball, so I figured it would be okay if I slipped out to the pisser for a few secs. I was only away for a few minutes, and he was gone when I got back. I've looked in every store between the game room and here. Where the fuck could he have gone, coach?" pleaded an obviously upset Tank.

"Sorry for eavesdropping, but there is a heavy steel exit door at the end of the hall that runs along side of the game room," offered the young female clerk that had been helping Luke. "There's like a courtyard out there, where mall employees sometimes go on break to smoke and such. Mostly punks and hoods hang out there now, but it might be worth checking to see if he could have wandered out there."

With that information, Luke and Tank raced out of the store and down the corridor, turning down the hallway that bordered the game room. Tank hit the exit door at full speed, with Luke close behind. As the door burst open, they were engulfed by a piercing scream… a guttural howl of torture that instantly reminded Luke of a video he had recently watched of a Yellowstone Park buffalo attempting a full speed escape from a pack of wolves. The wolves used a systematic team approach, whereby the alongside-loping predators would dart in, one at time, to snap their jaws on the buffalo's flank, ripping out chunks of hide and flesh until the buffalo was finally hobbled to a hamstrung standstill. It is then, when the wolves viciously converge on the defenseless beast for the kill, that you hear the chilling wail of terror and impending death.

The courtyard was long and narrow, maybe 15 feet wide and 50 feet long, with a slender opening at the end opposite the door that led out to an employee parking lot. A weathered wood picnic table sat against one wall, its bench seat sagging towards the dirt. Weeds and broken beer bottles served as the floor of the enclosure. Luke momentarily froze as he caught the first glimpse of the scene in front of him. Three men had Dolph pinned against the wall about 20 feet from the door that Luke and Tank had just exited, his pants and underwear down around his ankles. His legs had been coercively spread into a wide stance, his feet pulled back about three feet from the wall. There was a man on either side of him, each securing an upper arm in a two-armed grasp and pressing his upper torso into the wall to the extent that the left side of Dolph's face was mashed against the brick. The third man stood behind Dolph, and was obviously in the act of attempting to forcibly insert a beer bottle into Dolph's rectum.

All three men were dressed similarly in baggy, low-hung jean shorts with chains hanging from their belts, and sleeveless t-shirts exposing a multitude of tattoos from their necks to their ankles. Luke's initial impression was that this crew was not a punky group of teenagers. They were older, maybe mid to late 20s with the definite look of seasoned hoods and criminals.

With Dolph's ominous, terrified bellow still bouncing like ping pong balls off the walls of the courtyard, Tank's "MOTH-ERFUCKERS!" resonated down the confined enclosure as he sprinted towards the offenders. Only the one with the arm grip on the far side of Dolph had the sensible instinct to run, and he hurriedly disappeared through the alleyway opening out to the parking lot. The man with the bottle quickly turned, only having a split second to throw it at Tank's rapidly advancing head. His pitch was fortunately low, and the bottle thudded off of Tank's chest, resulting in another resounding "MOTHERFUCKER!" before the thug was savagely driven into the dirt by a technique-perfect Tank tackle.

Luke's "Look out, he's got a knife" warning as he ran to Dolph's side was fortunately not necessary, as Tank had already leapt up from his momentarily stunned victim and had turned quickly to face the other remaining man who was warily approaching him in a knife waving crouch.

"Bad fucking decision, asshole," snarled Tank, just a moment before he charged directly at the hood. Surprised that anyone would be foolish enough to bull rush a man yielding a knife, the thug only had time to launch a round-house swing with his knife arm. Tank blocked the thrust with his near forearm, the knife dropping harmlessly to the ground. In one smooth motion Tank grabbed the now knife-less arm at the wrist with his opposite hand and forcibly spun his body around. The sound of the shoulder joint dislocation that resulted from the body going one way while the arm was violently being reversed in the opposite direction was loud; almost as loud and disturbing as the pain-ridden screech emanating from the thug as he crumpled into a motionless pile on the ground.

Though he kept a watchful eye on the confrontations behind him, Luke concentrated on trying to calm down a sobbing and hysterical Dolph, while at the same time attempting to ascertain the extent of any injury that the thugs might have inflicted. A quick inspection of Dolph's bare backside, while reddened and already developing welts, thankfully didn't show any signs of bleeding from the anal orifice. Luke kept talking to him in an as soothing and consoling tone as he could muster, and finally was able to settle him down enough to get his underwear and pants back up in place.

Meanwhile, satisfied that the knife-wielding man no longer posed a threat, Tank went back to the first man, who was just starting to get his breath back and attempting to get up on his hands and knees. Tank reached down and jerked him to his feet, spun him around and grabbed him with both hands under the armpits and lifted him off the ground and slammed him into the brick wall. The thug tried to holler, wildly flailing his arms and his suspended in the air legs to no avail.

"Okay motherfucker," Tank spit out, his face inches from the man's face. "So you like to lure in helpless boys and get your rocks off by doin' sick shit like this to them, huh? Well asshole, you just fucked with the wrong guy. Here's what I'm gonna do. I'm gonna give you a healthy dose of your own medicine. When I'm done with you, I'm gonna shove your shriveled up dick, balls and your favorite bottle so far up your fuckin' ass that the doctors are gonna have cut open your throat to find them."

With that, Tank quickly drew back his leg and drove his knee so hard into the man's crotch that the large bolus of air that was forcefully expelled from his lungs sounded like cannon going off.

"Doesn't feel too fuckin' good when it happens to you, does it fuck-face? Let's see if it feels as good the second time," growled Tank, driving his knee violently into the groin again. As before, no sound other than rapidly expelling air came out of the eye-bulging face of Dolph's now listless assaulter.

Still tending to a somewhat settled down Dolph, Luke hollered at Tank. "Tank, that's enough… let him go. We have to get out of here." If Tank heard him, he didn't acknowledge it, and he grabbed the thug by the neck with one hand and started to rapidly punch him with his other hand; back and forth, like a boxer working the speed bag. Luke had no choice but to temporarily leave Dolph, and he raced over and tried to grab Tank by the arm to pull him off the bloodied offender, again shouting. "That's enough Tank—let him go. You're gonna kill him!" Tank backhanded Luke to the shoulder, sending him reeling backwards as if he were a just-swatted fly. One look at Tank's cold eyes made Luke realize his giant player was in a zoned outrage, so for lack of a better idea Luke ran and jumped on his back, loudly shouting in his ear, "Tank, it's coach. You gotta let him go!" Finally, his muscles began to relax as he came out of his trance and he released his grip on the thug, who slumped to a bloodied pile on the ground.

When it came down to the final minutes of a close game, either as a player or a coach, Luke had always demonstrated the rare ability to slow the game down in his mind, to think calmly and rationally, and focus in on the kind of decision making and execution that usually led to victory. But this was a whole different ball game than being down a field goal with a minute to go. He was faced with monumental decisions and had precious little time to make them. He tried to clear his head and prioritize the situation. Of most importance, Dolph didn't seem to be seriously injured, albeit assessed under rushed and cursory circumstance. And though he was still subject to intermittent sobs, the episodes were becoming less frequent and he seemed to be regaining some semblance of emotional control. The second item of concern was whether the injuries that had been explosively inflicted on the two assaulters were life-threatening.

Okay, thought Luke, two minute drill here we come. Was it a no-brainer that that the cops be called to arrest these criminals for, at the very minimum, attempted sexual assault? Wouldn't putting those thugs away be the right thing to do? Not only for Dolph, but for the public at large to prevent these misfits from preying on other helpless subjects? As reasonable and responsible as that approach sounded, there was another very problematic side to the situation that could arise. It wasn't lost on Luke that there was not only a possibility, but in all likelihood a certainty, that the alleged assaulters would play the 'their word against ours' game, and use their far more visible and serious physical injuries as grounds to file assault, or even attempted murder charges against Tank.

Luke weighed the various scenarios for only a moment before taking the bull by the horns and making his decision.

"Tank, take Dolph back through the door where we came out, and get him in that little family bathroom right across from the game room. Lock the door, and don't let anybody in until I can get there. Keep trying to calm Dolph down—can you do that?"

"I can do that. Come on Dolph, let's you and me go clean up a little."

"Okay Tank," replied Dolph, holding on to Tank's arm while they went through the door. As soon as they disappeared Luke turned his attention to the thugs. He bent over the guy that had wielded the knife first and took note that he was still breathing, but it was grossly apparent that his arm was positioned at a very unnatural angle off the shoulder. Luke figured that the rude and sudden detachment of the ball of his humerus from the shoulder socket was resulting in the onset of shock. He quickly moved on to the main assaulter, who was still lying in a fetal position at the base of the wall, his breathing gargled as the passage of air had to circumvent its way through his blood filled nose and mouth. Luke could only speculate as to the condition of his gonads, but thought that Tank's earlier prediction that the hood would find them somewhere near his throat was probably fairly accurate.

Satisfied that neither was facing imminent death, Luke hurried back through the exit door and went directly to the bank of pay phones across the hall from the game room. He dialed 911 and informed the dispatcher that he had heard there had been a fight in the mall courtyard that had resulted in serious injury to one or more of the combatants. He quickly hung up and raced to the bathroom, Tank letting him in immediately upon identification.

It appeared that Tank had done a good job in continuing the calming process, as the episodic sobs seemed to have ceased. "How you doing Dolph?" Luke cautiously asked. "I'm ok coach... better now that I'm away from those mean guys."

"Yeah, you're safe from those guys now, Dolph," assured Luke. "Dolph, that one mean guy was poking at you with that bottle. I need to take a look at your bottom to make sure he didn't hurt you there. Is it okay if I take a look just to be sure he didn't hurt you with that bottle?"

"Sure coach." Luke knelt behind him as Tank helped him undo and lower his pants and underwear. "I'm sorry Dolph, but in order for me to get a good look I need you to spread out your feet and bend over a little bit."

"Kinda like when the doctor was giving us our physicals for football?" Dolph asked.

"Yes, kind of like that, Dolph."

"So coach, do you need me to cough like the doctor wanted me to?"

With a smile that Dolph fortunately couldn't see, Luke replied, "Sure Dolph, go ahead and give me a couple of coughs."

Luke took a more thorough look this time, and breathed a deep sigh of relief that there was no indication that the bottle had penetrated his anus or rectum. The scumbag had definitely jabbed him numerous times in the butt cheeks, as the welts were more angry looking than they had been earlier. Feeling more confident that Dolph hadn't been violated, he gave his keys to Tank and told him to go get the truck and meet him and Dolph at the side entrance next Universal Athletics.

To say it was cramped quarters to stuff two big guys like Luke and Dolph next to a giant was putting it mildly. But they squeezed into the single bench seat pickup and Luke pointed them east down 10th Avenue South and out of town for the two hour trip back to Pacer Coulee. All was quiet until they reached the Interstate on the edge of town and Dolph asked in a matter of fact tone, but with a puzzled expression on his face, "That one mean guy was trying to put that bottle up my bum hole, wasn't he coach? My nuts hurt, too. That guy squeezed them really hard. He pulled on my Johnson too, coach. Really hard. How come those mean guys would do somethin' like that to me?"

"Cause they're a bunch of sick fucks, that's why," Tank blurted out before Luke could respond, "but I'm thinking that fucker's balls are gonna hurt a whole helluva lot worse and for a lot longer than yours will."

"There's some bad people out there Dolph," Luke explained. "I think those bad guys belong to some kind of gang, and they do bad things. It's why we always have to be careful when we are in bigger towns. It's not like being in Pacer Coulee, where everybody knows everybody and people look after each other."

Dolph contemplated that remark for a few moments, and then said. "Coach… coach, do we have to tell my mom and dad? If we tell 'em my mom and dad are gonna be really, really mad at me. I'm never supposed to talk to strangers, that's what my mom and dad tell me all the time. I disobeyed them and talked to those bad guys. My mom and dad are gonna be so danged mad at me!"

Before Luke could respond, Tank interjected. "Not your fault. It's me they should be mad at. I'm supposed to take care of you, and I didn't, so this is all my bad."

"It's nobody's fault but mine," said Luke. "I was in charge of both of you, and I dropped the ball. And to answer your question Dolph, no—we don't have to tell your mom and dad. In fact, I don't think we should ever tell anyone. We need to keep this our little secret, just between the three of us. What would you say to that idea, Tank?"

"Yep. You're right coach. Best if we keep this our secret. Just between coach, me and you, Dolph," Tank confirmed. "That's how we'll do it."

A look of great relief washed over Dolph's expressive face, and placing his fist in front of him with his pinky finger extended he said, "Boy Scout promise?"

"Boy Scout promise," replied Luke and Tank in unison, as the three of them intertwined their pinkies and shook on it.

"I'm really tired now, coach. I'm gonna take a little snooze, is that okay with you coach?"

"You bet Dolph. You go ahead and rest a bit," agreed Luke, tears welling in his eyes as he watched his 320-pound nose guard put his massive arm around Dolph and gently pull him into his chest and shoulder, much like a mother hen gathering a chick under her extended and protective wing.

Luke drove in silence for a few miles before Dolph, his eyes still closed and his head nestled into Tank's chest and neck said, "We're good at keeping secrets, ain't we Tank? Like when you tell me who to block. Nobody knows who I'm gonna block 'cept you and me, right Tank? That's kinda like a secret, ain't it Tank?"

"Yep, that's right little buddy. That's a secret that just you and me know about."

"And we're best-est friends too, ain't we Tank? Kinda like brothers, don't ya think?"

"Yep, we're like brothers, Dolph. We damn sure are."

The truck cab went quiet again for the next few miles, giving Luke his first chance to start the process of trying to get his arms wrapped around the disturbing events that had just transpired. As Luke drove past the sign that indicated a turn to the south would lead to Neihart, Showdown Ski Resort and White Sulphur Springs, he stole a peek at his passengers and found them both asleep, Dolph's head securely nestled into his big friend's shoulder and neck. *What a day*, thought Luke. In a matter of a few seconds, he had witnessed three felonies in an attempted sexual assault and two near homicides. And in less than an hour of elapsed time he had viewed the far distant reaches of each end of Tank's emotional spectrum. From a terrifying violent outburst to a calm and gentle gesture of kindness, both acts carried out to protect someone close to him. Luke understood the violence response, as it was all that Tank had likely ever known in growing up in a home with a violent and abusive father. But where did the soft and compassionate side come from? Perhaps distant memories of feeling safe and loved in his mother's embrace? Luke hoped with everything in him that his big lineman had just such a remembrance, however remote and out of reach it must seem to him now.

Just as Luke made the curve to bypass the tiny hamlet of Geyser, Tank opened his eyes and glanced down to confirm a still soundly sleeping Dolph. "Thanks coach," he whispered, "thanks for keeping today's activities between just us. I know what you did for me, and I appreciate it. Thanks for pulling me off that asshole. I might have killed him and coulda ended up in jail pretty easy, either way."

"No worries, Tank. That's what teammates and coaches do; we look out for each other."

Tank nodded his head in agreement and closed his eyes again as Luke drove in silence until descending the long hill into Stanton. Dolph awoke suddenly, and with his head still in the crook of the sleeping Tank's neck asked Luke with the familiar pensive look on his face, "Coach… coach?"

"Yes Dolph, what is it?"

"So coach, ol' Tank sure knocked them guys' dicks in the dirt, didn't he?"

Trying hard not to smile, Luke confirmed. "Yes Dolph, there's no doubt about it. There were some dicks in the dirt today, that's for sure."

DEEDEN COMES TO TOWN

"After last week, I never thought I'd be so glad to hear Tank actually give his usual pregame speech," commented Luke to T.O. as they sent their team out of the locker room and down to the field to face the Deeden squad.

"No shit," confirmed the growly assistant coach, "We'd probably be headin' for another loss if Tank was on the ineligible list again. Hey, I saw Dolph jawin' in your ear last night after practice—what was that all about?"

"Well, he was nominated to be one of the Homecoming King candidates along with Aaron and Tuf. I think it's a very cool thing that the kids voted to include him in that. Anyway, it was kind of like when we made him captain for the Hodgeman game. You know how he is… gets all pumped and excited when he first hears about it and then starts worrying and stressing about the what ifs.

"'Ahh, geez coach, like, like what should I do?'" said Luke in a much less than Bo quality impersonation of the portly lineman. "'You know, if'n I get to be the King, should I kiss the Queen or what? And what if the Queen is Dee Cassidy? That's Bo's girl, so he'd be pissed at me if I give her a smooch, wouldn't he?'"

"Haha," chuckled T.O. "This is why they pay you the big bucks, coach. So tell me, what was your sage advice as to how to resolve this prickly dilemma?"

"I told him Bo be damned, and to lay a big old smooch on whoever the Homecoming Queen ended up being."

As Luke and T.O. started the trek down to the field, Luke reflected back to the past week's contest against Stanton. Even though he had tried to play him, T.O.'s prediction of how Dolph would play without his big friend by his side was an accurate one, and Luke had pulled him from the game after only three plays. Wade Hoekstra and Travis Cederholm, the only real re-placement options that he had on his depth deprived roster, were significantly overmatched on both sides of the ball. Without Pacer Coulee's two stalwarts dominating the line of scrimmage, the Bearcats methodically ground out a 22-6 halftime lead.

"We just can't run our between-the-tackles stuff against these guys without Tank and Dolph. And now with Kimball out, there goes our speed advantage," Luke had explained to T.O. as they huddled before addressing the team at halftime. "Our only chance to move the ball is to get it to Stefan out in space. Flare passes, screens and the like. Any suggestions for what we can do on defense to do a better job against their run?"

"What would you think if we moved Bret to tackle alongside Tucker, and brought Tuf down to replace him at defensive end? Since throwing the deep ball isn't a strong suit for these guys, I'm thinkin' we could stick Virgil back at Tuf's safety position without risking much. Even though they'd be playing out of position, at least we'd have our best eight on the field."

"Sounds like a plan, let's do it."

The offensive and defensive changes made at halftime were effective, and other than giving up an early third quarter score to increase the Stanton advantage to 28-6, the Bulldogs held them scoreless the rest of the second half. Elvis played well for only his second game and was able to beat the Bearcat pass rush by getting some quick passes to Stefan on the perimeter, two of which he turned into long touchdown runs. With successful 2-point conversions on a Coslet run and an Elvis pass to Bret, Pacer Coulee had pulled to within six and had the ball on their own 12-yard line with just 28 seconds to go. With no timeouts remaining for the Bulldogs, Stanton blitzed everybody but the team manager on the next play and sacked Elvis back on the 5-yard line to seal the victory.

But with Tank being freed from ineligibility prison and Dolph back to his usual self, the Deeden Homecoming game was a vastly different story than the Stanton game. The Bulldogs took control from the opening kickoff, which Stefan took to the house for the first Pacer Coulee score. Then Tank got a hand on the pass that the Deeden quarterback threw on the first play of ensuing possession, and Danny Schrader intercepted it in full stride and raced into the end zone. With the conversion of both extra point attempts and only 20 seconds elapsed in the first quarter, Pacer Coulee had jumped out to a 16-0 lead. Despite having a solid ball club, Deeden could never get back in the game. Still angry from having to miss the Stanton game, Tank was a one man wrecking crew. Whenever Deeden would get a little momentum going, the huge man would blow up a play for a big loss. And with the offense clicking in both the pass and run game, the Bulldogs cruised to a 28-0 first half lead.

The late September afternoon was an uncharacteristically warm 81 degrees, and was accompanied by intermittent blasts of a hot, westerly wind. With the game firmly in hand, Luke's main halftime focus was to make sure the managers provided ample water, Gatorade and buckets of ice and orange slices to the players. From the team's usual intermission location in the west end zone, Luke kept his eye on the Homecoming Royalty ceremony that was being conducted at midfield. He was relieved that Dolph wouldn't have to fret over who to kiss when Jerry Akers announced over the loudspeaker that Aaron Coslet and Dee Cassidy were the newly crowned King and Queen.

With Deeden receiving the second half kickoff, Luke kept his starters in for the first series on defense. But when the Bulldogs forced a three and out and Stefan returned the punt for a touchdown and a 36-0 lead, Luke began to substitute freely. Every reserve except the kicker Alden Blackburn got playing time in the second half, although he held off until the final minutes of the game to relent to Earl Wonderwald's frequent plea of, "Let me at 'em, coach! Let me at them sum-bitches!"

"Shit coach, with a lead like this it might be a good time to practice your brilliantly designed 'Bo Weak Side Guard Drag' play," scoffed T.O. to Luke.

"Go ahead and laugh, go ahead and laugh. Some day you'll be thanking me for it," laughed Luke, "Someday you will."

Deeden scored three second-half touchdowns to make the 36-18 final look a little more respectable when read in the Tribune, Gazette or Centertown Daily News, but Luke meant what he said when the team finished mingling with family and friends on the field and returned to the locker room.

"I think we lived up to our potential today, guys. Total domination on both sides of the ball. And this wasn't Marshall or Hodgeman we were playing, either. Deeden is a good club that will be battling for a playoff spot, so great effort in a big win. Enjoy your evening, and don't forget to go support the girls over in Stanton tonight. I've got two empty seats in my pickup, so let me know if anybody needs a lift."

RECRUITING LETTERS PILE UP

"So what kind of prospect do you have in this Hollister kid?" coach Sonny Sweden asked his ex-quarterback when he came on the phone line.

"Hi coach," said Luke. "Well, there is some good and bad when it comes to Tank, but I can honestly say I never saw a kid on any of the teams I coached or played against at Lincoln High with the pure physical tools that Tank has. My best comparison would be Jaxon Kollar from Central High in Omaha, who as you know played nose guard for the Huskers and was a first round pick of the Chiefs. This kid is just massive. I have him listed at 6'0" and 317 in the program roster, but he's more like 6'2" and 330. He can run a 4.9 forty, and you should see him do the agility drills; explosively quick off the ball, and he can move laterally too. Benches 480 and squats over 700."

"Holy shit," Sonny replied. "That's pretty damn impressive. I assume he's getting a ton of interest?"

"Oh yeah. A bunch. You ought to see the stack of recruiting letters I have piled on my desk. Montana State, University of Montana and of course all of the smaller colleges in Montana, Idaho and the Dakotas. Lots of Pac 10—Washington State, U of Dub, both the Beavers and the Ducks. Getting interest from Big 12 also, to include the Huskers and the Sooners."

"So what do you see as the downside on this kid?" Sonny asked.

"Well, playing 8-man football at a really small school, so the level of competition would be a minus. But we all know of kids that have come from small schools and have done well as walk-ons and such, with Nebraska being proof of that. Frankly, I am more concerned about him adapting to the college atmosphere from the academic and social aspect. He's not dumb, that's not it at all. But he just doesn't have any interest in school. As you know, he had to sit the game two weeks ago because of academic suspension. Granted, we have an old gal that runs this school who has the toughest eligibility policy that I've ever seen, so we have to ride his ass and assign him tutors to keep him eligible. And then there's the question of whether this kid can adapt to living away from home. He's had a rough home life. Abusive father and all of that. Never been farther than a couple hundred miles away from the ranch and the town of Pacer Coulee. I have no doubts about his ability to play, but can he function away from his comfort zone nest of central Montana? Frankly, I don't know the answer to that."

"Thanks for the honest assessment, Luke. Well, I've certainly taken my fair share of kids over the years who have come from tough home environments and were a couple of continents away from being the valedictorian of their graduating class. Some adapted, others didn't. There are similarities to the inner city kid and the rural, isolated country kid in that they come from different worlds than your average recruit. As you know, it can be a crap shoot sometimes with these kind of guys. Can you send us some film on him?"

"Sure will, coach," replied Luke, saying with a laugh, "Just had a crow's nest built at the Pacer Coulee field, so the angle of the film should be better than prior years when it was filmed from the box of a grain truck that was parked under the goal post!"

"Haha, I'll be sure to take note. So how you doing, Luke? Everything going okay?"

"Yes, it's different for sure, but I'm really enjoying it. These small town farm and ranch kids are a joy to work with, both on the field and in the classroom. They're just down to earth kids, and I haven't had any kind of serious discipline problem yet. Seems like I spent half of my time dealing with asshole kids when I was at Lincoln, but fortunately there's damn little of that here. It's taken some time to get used to the small town way. The people are all really friendly, and good Lord do they ever support the community and the school. So that part of it is very refreshing. I had a little trouble getting used to the fact that everybody in a small town knows your personal business before you do, but they generally mean well. And your old roommate Lester is a great guy to work for and with. He's made my transition to coaching and teaching really easy."

"That's great, glad to hear it," said Sonny. "By the way, Lester tells me that the new girls' basketball coach is a pretty great gal. And easy on the eyes, too. Hope you're moving on in that aspect of your life, Luke."

Luke was glad that his old coach couldn't see the red creeping up both sides of neck when he replied, "I'm working on it coach—I'm working on it."

EDNA GETS A VISIT FROM THE SHERIFF

"Clare, would you please go see who's at the door?" asked Edna. "It's probably just Carl wanting to shore up the numbers on the hay we're going to purchase from that irrigated alfalfa grower down in Belgrade." Clare hurriedly swallowed a mouthful of Harriet's scrambled eggs and disappeared from the kitchen in her typical lightning quick fashion.

She opened the door and stood frozen in place upon viewing the sizable bulk and holstered pistol of Fergus County Sheriff Trent Couch. "I didn't do anything bad, Sheriff," Clare said softly as she stared at the shiny badge attached to the left shirt pocket of Fergus County Sheriff Trent Couch's uniform.

"I know you didn't, honey. I'm here to see Edna... err, Ms. Coffman. Could you fetch her for me please?" requested the long time Sheriff who was looking forward to his retirement at year end. The Deeden native began his law enforcement career as a Fergus County Deputy nearly 40 years ago, spending the last 16 as its multi-term, duly elected County Sheriff.

Being the Sheriff of a rural county of only 10,000 residents, most all of whom he knew on a first name basis, had its advantages. But attempting to geographically cover a county that was nearly the size of the state of Connecticut with a minimal deputy staff wasn't one of them. There was so little crime in the county that Trent had to dig deep to come up with much for the daily Sheriff's report that was broadcast on KMON out of Great Falls. For the most part, other than traffic violations and warrants, legal filings and notices that they were required to serve, Fergus county wasn't exactly a hot bed of criminal activity. Most of the calls taken by the dispatcher were of a mundane nature; dogs at large, livestock or wildlife on the highways and back country county roads, and the occasional home safety or security check was about as serious as matters generally got. Oh, there were always some domestic disputes to attend to and the usual weekend late night bar altercations, but serious crime routinely detoured around Fergus county.

There was the occasional break-in and theft of a Centertown residence or business, but such activity was extremely rare in the smaller outlying communities. Most of the rural folk didn't even have locks on their doors. Whether living in town or out in the country, neighbors looked out for one another, and Trent couldn't remember a theft being reported in the rural towns since the Deeden bank's security system was disabled and robbers drilled into the safe and got away with $5,000 back in 1972. Most of the outlying town calls came during hunting season, when out of area and out of state elk, deer and bird hunters forgot to play by the private property owner trespassing rules. The Fish and Game department was the primary contact for such matters, but since they were also understaffed it was Trent's department that was frequently dispatched to handle violations and disputes.

But there wasn't any such season for the purpose of Trent's call on this day. The call he received from his dispatcher before daybreak that morning was the one he dreaded the most—a traffic accident likely resulting in a fatality. A rancher on his way to one of his fields came upon a pickup that had hit one of Spring Creek's bridge abutments and had flipped and landed upside down in the creek. The rancher couldn't get to the truck, but he thought he could see a figure moving with the current as it flowed through the broken windows of the cab. He identified the pickup as one belonging to Terrance Hollister.

Much like the Sheriff's office, the Montana State Highway Patrol assigned minimal coverage for the sparsely populated county, but Joe Stenson, the lone Patrol Officer stationed in Centertown, arrived at 7:00 a.m. at the Spring Creek bridge; the same time as Trent. The sun was just about to peek over the Judith Mountains and several area ranchers and farmers were already gathered along with the Pacer Coulee Fire Truck and Ambulance. Another of the nearby ranchers was idling up on the other side of the creek in a big 4-wheel drive tractor with a front end loader and a winch, as such machinery would most certainly be needed to extract the pickup from the creek. One of the volunteer ambulance attendants and a local rancher were sitting on the bank of the creek, their wet clothes indicating they had both already been in the water to inspect the contents of the cab.

"It's old man Hollister," said the rancher. "I'm thinking he's been dead for some time. Probably was headed home after the Western Tavern closed down, that would be my guess."

Joe was already pacing the tire marks off and inspecting the damaged bridge abutment. "I'm guessing he fell asleep, or knowing Terrance, passed out. I don't see any sign of him braking. These tire marks occurred after he hit the abutment and before it flipped into the creek."

"That's sure what it looks like to me, too," agreed Trent. "You see any reason to not have Clint hook up the winch and pull the truck out on the far bank before we extract the body?"

"Makes perfect sense to me, Trent."

"Clare, you run back inside and get ready for school now," said Edna, waiting to address the Sheriff until the wisp of a girl disappeared from view. "What brings you out this early in the morning, Trent? Likely it's not good news."

"Well, all depends on how you look at it, I guess. Old man Hollister drove into the bridge abutment at the Spring Creek crossing over by Brooks sometime after two this morning and flipped his truck upside down into the creek. Anyway, he's dead. I know there's no kin other than Tank, and that you and Bill Koch look after the big fella, so I thought you should be the first to know. I'm on my way to the Hollister place to give him the news now. I think it would be best if you came along with me—you know, to provide support and be with him."

"Yes, yes of course. Thank you Trent. I'll go tell Harriet to make sure the kids get to school, and I'll follow you right over."

"Just a heads up, Edna. I know what Tank's situation is, living alone and all. I also know that he's under 18. What that means, Edna, is that Social Services won't allow him to stay there on the place alone without a guardian. I know that he's been essentially on his own most of his life, but them's the rules. I know from recent experience with a case over east of the Snowies that Social Services won't budge on that issue. So again, a heads up in that you're gonna have to take the lead and work with the proper folks to handle all this from a legal standpoint. There's some appointments that will have to be made, like a legal guardian and the such. He'll need to reside under the roof of an adult until he turns 18."

"Okay, thanks again Trent. I'll meet with Bill and we'll get in contact with my lawyer, John Stockdale, and we'll get the ball rolling in short order."

EDNA GETS A NEW RESIDENT

"I'm sorry about your dad, Tank," said a somber Shanty, as he, Kellie Cassidy, Luke, Bill Koch and Edna took their seats alongside Tank in the bank boardroom.

"Well I ain't," mumbled Tank, his eyes locked through the window on the old black baldy cow in the pasture across the alley from the bank that was rubbing the fall flies off her hide on the gate post. "I'm glad the asshole's dead."

The sound of silence from the others in attendance confirmed their agreement with Tank's blunt statement of fact. Not one of them held even a sliver of sadness in the passing of the despicable man that was Terrance Hollister, Sr. In fact, all were more than relieved that Tank's 17-year reign of terror had finally ended.

"Terrance," Edna began, with a sweep of her hand to include all those seated at the table, "we're here as the people that care about you, and as the adults that I imagine you know and trust the most. First of all, I need to know if you're okay with me taking the reins here. As I told you yesterday morning after Sheriff Couch left, there's some decisions that have to be made on your behalf as a result of your father's passing. These good people are all going to help me make and implement those decisions, but someone needs to be the captain here. So are you okay with me stepping into that role?"

"Yep, I'm okay with that Miz E," replied Tank, his attention now turned to rubbing the ears of the contented and grunting bulldog, Otis, whom he had lifted off the floor and placed on his lap.

"I know this is unpleasant to think and talk about Terrance, but the first order of business concerns your father's burial. Did he ever mention anything to you whether he had made any plans in that regard?"

"Don't know what you mean, Miz E."

"Well, like whether he wanted to be cremated or not. Or if he had purchased a burial plot next to your mom up at the Pacer Coulee Cemetery, or over in Centertown. Or if he wanted a standard funeral service in a church—those kinds of things. Did he ever talk to you about any of that?"

Tank didn't take long to ponder the question before angrily responding. "I'll beat the livin' shit outa any sum-bitch that tries to bury him next to my mom. He killed her, so I don't want him anywhere near her. And the miserable fucker—'scuse my bad language Miz E and Miz C, but that's what he is... or was. Anyway, he should be cremated. The rotten bastard should burn twice, once on earth and again with the devil in Hell. And he don't deserve no Goddamn funeral service either. He always used to tell me the only thing I was good for was buzzard bait. Well, give me his ashes and I'll spread 'em down on the banks of the Judith for the Goddamn buzzards to peck at. That's the only kind of service the asshole that killed my mom should get."

Tank's comments about the buzzards immediately brought back the memories of Luke's own night of terror when Terrance Hollister, Sr. had threatened him on his own porch in the middle of the night. He still woke up in a cold sweat remembering the exact statement: "You two would be perfect bait for the mountain lions, coyotes and buzzards;" the 'you two' referencing Luke and Edna. *What a helluva life this poor kid has had*, thought Luke, his heart aching for his big lineman.

With tears visibly tumbling from the eyes of Shanty and Kellie Cassidy, a subdued Edna quietly continued with the day's unpleasant task. "Okay Terrance, I'll let the Harrell Funeral Home know of your wishes. Now, let's move on to other matters that we need to tend to today. First of all Terrance, you are considered a minor until you reach age 18. Current state law requires you to have a legal Guardian appointed; you know, sort of a Trustee or Custodian to oversee your care and look out for your best interests," explained Edna.

"Don't need no Guardian. I ain't two years old, for Christ's sake. Been lookin' after myself since I was a kid, so I sure as hell don't need, don't want, no damn Guardian lookin' over my shoulder now," stated Tank emphatically.

The adults in the room all gave each other the 'this isn't going well' look, so Bill decided to take a turn. "I understand that Tank, I really do. We all do. You've been forced to be the grown-up in your household ever since your mom passed away. But there's laws we all have to abide by, whether we like them or not. The good news is that Judge Rauch understands your situation and will likely trust whatever this group recommends in your behalf."

Bill's kind and reasoned grandfatherly tone seemed to at least somewhat penetrate the steely veneer of the protective shield that Tank had placed in front of him, and Edna nodded at Bill to continue. "Let's take a look at the issues son, one by one, that have arisen as a result of your dad's passing: Firstly, it seems that your father did not have a Will. As you probably know, a Will is the usual and standard document whereby a person instructs the distribution of their assets. In other words, their belongings. A Will also names what we call a Personal Representative or an Executor to administer the directives of the estate. Let me try to explain all this in a way that makes sense. For example, let's say the person that died had owned five cows, a horse, a tractor and a house. So in this person's Will, he or she lists who gets what; you know, kid one gets the cows, kid two gets the horse, neighbor John gets the tractor... you get the idea. The Personal Representative makes sure that the instructions as to who gets what are followed to a T."

Edna was pleased that Bill seemed to be getting through to surly boy, and again gave Bill the sign to continue. "In this case, your father didn't leave a Will with instructions as to how to distribute his belongings. So what happens in a no-Will type of situation is that the estate passes to the court. Without getting too technical here, a Judge would normally distribute the assets of the estate equally among the heirs. In this case, you are the only living heir to your father's estate, so you will receive all the assets and associated liabilities of estate. Liabilities mean debt, like if your dad had borrowed money in order to purchase livestock, machinery and the such. The problem here is that under current law you are not yet considered to be of adult age and therefore cannot take possession of your father's estate assets until you reach the legal age of 18, or next June 12th. This set of facts requires, by law, a couple of things to happen. First, the Court will need to appoint a Personal Representative for the estate to manage and tend to the business matters until you reach legal age. Secondly, it will appoint a Guardian to tend to your care until you reach legal age. Please understand that you will not be able to continue living alone out at your ranch. Again, it's the law; nothing you, me, coach Carter, Shanty, Kellie or Edna can do about it."

Despite the presence of an ominous scowl, Bill could see he now had Tank's undivided attention and pressed on. "Now, as I mentioned earlier, Ms. Coffman and I took the liberty of already meeting with Judge Rauch, and he knows we have your best interests at heart. He has indicated he will approve whatever appointments we decide to recommend as a result of this meeting today. Now son, I want to make this perfectly clear. If you ignore this and don't take our advice and help us select the PR and the Guardian, then Judge Rauch will make those two decisions for you. Trust me, you're not going to like who he selects. Why? Because he'll appoint Social Services as your Guardian. And once that happens, none of us in this room can do a thing about what they decide is best for you. It'll be out of our hands. So I'm strongly suggesting that you cooperate with us today Tank, and help us help you make the best decisions we can under the circumstances."

Tank turned his gaze back out the window as he helped the big bulldog reverse his position on Tank's lap, finally speaking after a lengthy pause and a prolonged sigh. "Okay Mr. K, I get it. Don't like it one bit, but I hear what you're saying. So what do you guys think for these appointments that we gotta make?"

"Well Terrance," answered Edna, jumping back into the captain's role, "we are going to recommend that Bill is appointed as the PR for the estate. I don't know how much you know about this, but Bill has been taking care of you financially for quite some time. He's the one that bought the cows for you that I run at my place. He has an account for you at this bank and uses the money we get for the calves to help pay for the meals at the Calfe' and for the suppers that Mrs. Cassidy cooks for you. He's the one that pays for all those 5X pants and shirts that we have to special order for you every six months or so. Anyway, being the banker and the financial adviser to most everybody in town, Bill would be the best one to manage the estate for you until you reach 18."

"I know you done a lot for me already, Mr. K. I'm plum okay with you bein' the whatever... lookin' after the estate and stuff."

"Okay, one issue resolved," said Edna as she moved forward to the next item. "Now, the Guardian matter is actually two-pronged, as in who the actual guardian will be and who you will live with until you are 18. We all think that I should be appointed as your Guardian. That means that I will be in charge of your overall care. I'll work with Bill on making sure the money is available to tend to your basic needs of food, clothing, etcetera. And I'll work with whoever houses you on all things related to your well-being, such as school and other related matters. And I'll continue to help you with running your ranch. My crew and I will do a thorough inspection of your dad's cows. As you are well aware, the only care they ever received came from you and my guys. It's a Heinz 57 bunch of old and mangy cows that need to be heavily culled, and we'll help you with that. I also want you to know that you aren't going to get any free pass because of your dad's passing. If I'm your Guardian, you are going to be expected to do even more of the work now. So, now that you know I'm going to work your very large rear end off, are you okay with me being appointed as your Guardian, Terrance?"

"Yep, that's okay by me, Miz E," said Tank with a grin pulling at the corners of his mouth in reference to Edna's remark about his big backside.

"Now, about where you could live until you turn 18 and can return to the ranch. Mrs. Cassidy says you could live with them. She doesn't have any extra bedroom space, so we'd have to get you a king sized mattress to put out in the living room, but that could work. Both Bill and Shanty have extra bedrooms and have offered to let you live with them until you turn 18. What are your thoughts about those living options, Terrance?"

Tank looked down at the snoring Otis in his lap and pondered the alternatives presented for an uncomfortable length of time before finally speaking. "Don't get me wrong—I 'preciate what y'all in this room have done for me, but there's only one person I will live with."

"Okay," said Edna hesitantly. "And are you going to tell us who that person would be before the sun goes down?"

"Yep. That would be you, Miz E. Ain't gonna live with nobody else."

As Bill, Shanty, Kellie and Luke all exchanged bemused glances, Edna threw up her arms with an exasperated look on her face and said, "Well for Christ's sake! I guess that since I already have half the Assiniboine Nation living under my roof, what the hell is one more mouth to feed? I'm probably going to have to butcher most of my cowherd to have enough food to feed you, you big lug! Who the hell is going to help me pay for that?"

With Kellie having to leave for her mail route and Luke and Tank needing to get back to school, only Bill, Shanty and Edna remained in the boardroom. "Well, I guess that went about as well as we could or should have expected," Bill said. "Edna, do you want me to contact Stocksdale and Judge Rauch and get the appointments confirmed?"

"Yes, I'd appreciate it if you handled that. I'll get in contact with the Funeral Home and tell them to fry the remains of that miserable old cuss Terrance Sr."

Bill and Shanty both chuckled at her choice of words, and Bill commented, "Poor kid, no youngster should have to grow up with the likes of that monster."

"That's for sure," added Shanty. "And Edna, who woulda ever thunk that your family would have grown this fast and you would be vying for the 'Den Mother of the Year' award?"

"Oh, hush yourself, you damned old Irishman!" Edna barked back, turning her head to hide the grin that was spreading across her face.

WHO'S VERNON HIGGINS?

Luke had several matters of importance to occupy his thoughts as he turned onto the gravel road by the Deerfield Hutterite Colony to take the shortcut to Hodgeman for the girls' game.

He couldn't have been more pleased with his team's effort in the just-completed game versus Wyngate at Pacer Coulee Field. Granted, Wyngate was one of the weaker teams in the conference and it was a game that everyone expected the Bulldogs to win, but Luke was always concerned about the tendency to play down to the opponent's talent level. As it turned out, there was no need to worry as his starters were sharp and focused as they raced to a 40-0 first half advantage. Luke pulled them at halftime, as he and the Wyngate coach agreed to utilize the second half as a JV game. Even the enthusiastic "let me at them sum-bitches" Earl Wonderwald saw plenty of playing time, and despite a raggedly played and error-prone performance by both teams, each of them somehow managed to score two touchdowns in the final half.

As he slowly cruised through the tiny berg of Danvers, he took note of a number of sad and sagging wood buildings that were leaning into the dirt street as if finally acquiescing to years of the prevailing westerly wind. He tried to imagine what a couple of the dilapidated structures once housed in their early years, deciding a bar and a mercantile would be the likely best guess. He supposed the crumbling brick pile at the edge of town was once a bank or a post office, and the only edifice that looked as though it was still in use was identified by the weathered and wilting wooden sign as the Danvers Catholic Church.

His thoughts turned to his fellow coach and next door neighbor, Madison Danielsen. It was going on four months since she and Rose drove up in front of Edna's two little rental houses. He had tried at first to fight his immediate attraction but found that his defense mechanisms were disabled in fairly short order. With their common background of failed marriages, he had sensed that she was also reluctant to be in any hurry to enter into another relationship. But it seemed as if their resistance meters went down in direct proportion to the increase in frequency of the over-the-fence chats and shared barbecues. And although they had yet to talk frankly about the prospect of taking the next step into a more serious and romantic relationship, Luke had felt they were on the fast track to do just that. Up until the last few weeks, that is.

He couldn't quite put a finger on the why and when it happened, but he had detected a definite chill in her vibe in recent weeks. While she wasn't exactly avoiding him, she wasn't her usual cheerful and outgoing self either. He wracked his brain in search of something he might have said or done, or didn't say or do, that might have upset her, but came up empty. "Well, go talk to her after the game like you usually do," he said out loud to himself. "Maybe she's just stressed out about something with her team. Or maybe you're just imagining things."

But when the final horn sounded to announce a convincing Pacer Coulee victory, Luke climbed down the bleachers and started to work his way towards where she stood in front of the visitors' bench. But he had to make an abrupt and awkward detour when he spotted a tall, handsome man in a cowboy hat making a beeline towards Madison. Luke tried to push his rapidly deflating ego into his back pocket when he saw the stranger take her hand and not let go, as one would normally do in a standard congratulatory handshake. His last remaining puff of air was expelled from the ego bag when he saw how engaged she was in their continued conversation. Stopping only long enough for a brief chat with Lester and to congratulate Clare and the Brewster sisters on a well-played game, Luke dejectedly left the gym and pointed his truck towards Pacer Coulee.

ELVIS AND SONYA GET CAUGHT

"Are you sure they're all gonna be gone for at least an hour?" Sonya questioned Elvis after hiding her bike behind a storage shed that sat next to the garage.

"I'm sure. Like I said, Edna and Harriet make us all go to church with them at 10:30 every Sunday morning. Everybody 'cept Tank, that is," said Elvis, lowering his voice and doing an almost Bo-like impersonation of his new roommate. "'Fuck that shit. I ain't goin' to any Goddamn church with the rest of you pansy ass bible thumpers.' Anyway, the after church ritual is to go have brunch down at the Calfe', so everybody will be gone for at least a couple of hours."

"So if he's not at church, where is Tank? And how did you get out of going to church?" asked Sonya.

"Tank went out to his place to check on his cows. He spends his Sundays at his ranch, I guess. I told her I wasn't feeling good, and thought I was getting the stomach flu. She bought it, I know that for sure."

"Well, if you're sure we are safe. Where should we do it?"

"Up in me and Tank's room. Don't worry, we have separate beds."

After going upstairs to the room and shutting the door, the two teenagers held hands and sat awkwardly on the edge of Elvis's bed. "Does Otis sleep in here?" asked Sonya, pointing to the thick dog bed that was laying on the floor next to Tank's jumbo-sized mattress.

"Yeah, sometimes. He kinda goes back and forth between Tank and Clare. I think it pisses Edna off that he don't sleep in her room anymore. Otis don't like me much, but he sure loves both Clare and Tank."

Elvis attempted a clumsy kiss to get the ball rolling, but Sonya kept interrupting. "So you've done this before, right?"

"Yeah, I've done this before."

"More than once?"

"Yes, more than once."

"I've never done it... you're the first guy I've even kissed."

"I know."

"So you know how to use a condom, right? The only way I'm doing this is if we use a condom."

"Yes Sonya, I know. And yes, I know how to use a condom."

"You have one with you, right? It seems like every time we play the reservation teams in basketball or volleyball, well, some of their players have babies. Like, people are holding them right there on the bench. So you reservation guys must not wear your condoms all the time, huh?"

"That would be true, Sonya. Condoms aren't always used on the rez. But don't worry, I'll put one on today."

"So are any of those babies I saw behind the Hays Lodgepole bench yours?"

"Not that I know of."

"Okay, that's good, that's good. So, you Native guys have, like, big, well... you know, big dealy-bobs, right?"

"I've never heard a penis called a dealy-bob before," chuckled Elvis, "but I'm afraid you're thinkin' of the black guys. They're the ones that have the big thing-a-ma-jigs... no, what'd you call 'em? Oh yeah, dealy-bobs. They have the big dealy-bobs. Us Natives have normal, white guy sized dealy-bobs." Sonya punched him in the shoulder as she said, "Okay smart ass, I'm not as worldly as you, so I don't know much about this kind of stuff."

"Well, are you sure that you want to do this? We don't have to do anything, you know."

"No, I want to do it. I've been a prude and a goody-two-shoes for way too long. So what do we do next?"

"Let's take our clothes off and then we can start fooling

around. You know, kissing and stuff. You can let me feel you up. Then when we're ready, I'll put the condom on and we'll do it."

"Okay you two," Edna said to Harriet and Clare as they walked out of the Methodist church, "go ahead and walk down to the Calfe' and get us a table. I left my purse in the front entryway at home, so I'm going to go grab that and stop back at the church to give Pastor Smythe our weekly donation and then I'll be back. Save me a seat."

As Edna entered the house, she thought she'd better go check on Elvis. He had said he was feeling poorly when they left for church, and with a big game against Heberton coming up she wanted to make sure they got a head start on treating the flu bug that was making the rounds through the school. She hesitated at his bedroom door when she heard suspicious sounds emanating from within, and then barged in to witness two bare naked teenagers in the throes of an act of passion.

Sonya let loose a horrified scream as she tried to rip the blanket off the bed to cover her exposed skin. Elvis was much calmer, simply pulling the sheet over his crotch as if acquiescing to the death sentence that was surely about to be levied against him.

"Please, please, Miz Coffman—don't tell my dad! Oh my god, don't tell my dad!" wailed Sonya.

"If you don't stop that screaming this very instant, I will tell him for sure," Edna admonished. "Now pull yourself together young lady, and dry up those tears."

When Sonya had settled down to the point where her sobs were only coming in five second intervals, Edna said, "So, what makes you two knot-heads think that you've got the green light to fornicate like a couple of Goddamn rabbits within the confines of my house? You first, Miss Brewster, and knock off that sob routine, and I mean right now!"

"I'm... sorry... Miz Coffman," stuttered Sonya, obviously struggling to smother another round of wailing that was bubbling at the surface like an expectant volcano awaiting eruption. "I… I… don't know… what we were… thinking."

"That's because you weren't thinking. At least not with your upstairs brain." Then with a stern look back and forth to each of them, she asked in a demanding tone, "Were either of you thinking enough to consider using a condom, or are we going to be moving a crib into the Goddamn corner over there in about nine months?

"Stop that incessant bawling Sonya, and answer the question," barked Edna when the crib comment brought back the onslaught of tears from the distraught teenager.

"Yes Miz Coffman, we used a condom," confirmed Elvis.

"Was I talking to you? I don't think so. I'll deal with you later. Right now I want to hear it from you, Sonya. Did you or did you not use a condom before you started rolling around in my house?"

"Yesss," cried Sonya, "we used a condom. Are you… going… to tell my dad?"

"Here's what we're going to do. I'm going to take my sweet time in deciding what to do with the two of you. I'm having a little trouble figuring out right now whether to just scalp your little native friend here, or to cut off his you-know-what. Maybe I'll do both. And I'm going to have to think long and hard—pun intended—as to what I'm going to do with you, young lady. But for the time being, you need to pull those pants up and over that scrawny little butt of yours and get the hell out of my house. I'll let you know later what I decide to do.

KIMBALL'S FAKE INJURY

Luke checked his watch and upon seeing that it was approaching 4:00 p.m., ejected the video he had been reviewing of the prior day's Wyngate game. He went to check the weight room and gym to see if he needed to nudge any stragglers out of open gym and into the cool and breezy late September Sunday afternoon. Seeing no one left in the weight room, he stuck his head in the locker room entrance to the gym door and saw that only Kimball Robbins and his girlfriend Cindy Cottingham remained. Just as he was about to enter and tell the two teenagers that he was going to have to close the gym, Cindy threw Kimball a basketball that sailed wide of the mark and bounced lazily towards the other end of the gym. Kimball, who had been hobbling about school and unable to practice or play in a game since pulling a hamstring in the first quarter of the Stanton game, nimbly spun around and raced after the ball with nary a limp. Luke waited until Kimball had retrieved the ball and was back standing next to Cindy before entering the gym and asking to speak with Kimball back in the coaches' office.

"What's up coach?" asked Kimball, walking lamely in front of Luke to the office.

"Just wondering how the hammy is coming along. I was hoping we could start working you into practice this week. We're sure gonna need you against Heberton."

"I dunno, coach. It's still so sore and tight that I can barely walk. Hopefully it will be healed enough to start practice next week," Kimball said as he winced while rubbing the 'injured' muscle.

Luke motioned for Kimball to take a chair. "Kimball, I was watching from the doorway when you chased that ball down a few minutes ago," he said as he watched the color drain from his wide receiver's face. "You were sprinting, son. No sign of a gimp or hitch in your giddy-up whatsoever. Would you like to tell me what's going on with you?"

The caught-red-handed youngster tried to speak, but nothing came out. He tried again, but could only stammer nonsensically. Luke decided to break the embarrassing impasse and started to calmly and softly speak. "Kimball, look at me. Let me tell you a true story about when I was playing in high school at Grand Island that could very well be closely related to what is going on with you right now. Our best receiver, a classmate and good friend of mine that I will refer to as Tom, was one hell of an athlete. Like you, he had real speed and very good hands. He had a great year at wide receiver as a junior... was All-Conference, and started off our senior year as a house on fire. But we lost the top three guys in our secondary in the second and third games of the season, and our coach needed him to go both ways—to be both our starting receiver and defensive back."

Kimball was keeping consistent eye contact now, and was listening keenly to what Luke was saying. "Well, I'm going to be brutally honest about this, and mind you, this isn't anything that you need to be embarrassed or ashamed about, but Tom was much like you in that he didn't like contact. He didn't like it at all. Now as a receiver on offense, unless catching a pass in traffic or having a defender tackle you immediately after a catch, one can use speed, quickness and elusiveness to minimize the direct hits taken, right? Even speedy, shifty receivers in college and the pros try to limit the direct hits they take. They use the sideline as their friend to get out of bounds, and they know when to go down to prevent taking a huge hit. But when you're playing corner or safety on defense, it's more than just covering the wide receiver and defending against the pass, isn't it? You need to come up on run support and take on the ball carrier. Whether in zone coverage or man, you have to run to the ball and initiate contact. You need to tackle the guy; get the guy on the ground, right?"

When Kimball nodded his head in acknowledgment, Luke

continued on. "Now Tom was just like you in tackling drills, in that no matter how much he and the coach tried to practice proper tackling technique, he just couldn't bring himself to gather and explode through the ball carrier. As he approached the runner, he would hesitate; almost come to a stop, duck his head and take all of the force from the collision. It's the same situation with you, Kimball. Exactly the same."

"I'm sorry coach. I, I just can't help myself. I try really hard to do it right, but... maybe it's like some of the guys say, that I'm just a chicken shit—just a pussy. I should stop pretending I'm hurt and just face up to it and quit the team. Is that what that Tom guy did? Did he quit?" Kimball asked, tears now rolling down his cheeks.

"I learned a lot about being an effective football coach from observing how my old high school coach handled the situation with Tom. And no, Tom didn't quit the team," said Luke, pausing a long time for effect.

"What happened?" Kimball finally asked.

"Well, as I said, I think there are a lot of similarities between you and Tom. Like you, he was a really good receiver that didn't like to play defense. He just didn't care for the inevitable contact that comes with playing D. But more importantly, and like you, he faked injury to avoid having to play defense. Obviously, holding up the perception of injury also kept him off the field for what he really liked to do, which was to play receiver on offense. That pretty much describes you right now, doesn't it Kimball?"

"Yes," said Kimball, breaking eye contact and hanging his head.

"Look at me, Kimball. Again, this isn't anything to be ashamed about. It is what it is, and it doesn't make you any less of a man or an athlete. What isn't okay is to fake injury and avoid playing at all just because you don't want to play defense. Not having you on offense? That hurts your teammates and coaches, and it especially hurts you. Now, answer me honestly Kimball. Do you like playing receiver?"

"Yes, I really like to play receiver," confirmed Kimball enthusiastically, "especially now with Elvis being our quarterback."

"Okay, here's what our coach told me later about how he handled the Tom situation. He said that our job as coaches was to get to know and understand as much as we could about each of our players. He told me that coaching the old school way of treating everyone the same was outdated, and that a good coach handles each kid on an individual basis so that he can best utilize his player's talents in order to maximally benefit the team. It's all about the team, and if you coach each individual with that in mind, then you were coaching effectively," explained Luke. "Here's what coach did about Tom's situation. He told him that he wasn't going to play defense anymore. Even though we were really shorthanded in the secondary, it just didn't make any sense to lose our best receiver on offense in order to make him play defense. So from there on out, he just played offense. It worked out great for the rest of the team, especially for me, as I got my best receiver back."

Luke leaned in and grabbed Kimball on the forearm and squeezed firmly for emphasis. "That's what I want to do here, Kimball. From here on out, you will just play receiver. Bret is a good end, and although he runs a good route and has good hands, we both know he doesn't have much in the speed and quickness department. With a good quarterback like Elvis here now, we can stretch the field with you. Teams have to respect your speed, and they can't just load the box to stop our run game. Make no mistake that this is a team thing we are doing. We are a much, much more effective team when you are on the field for us on offense. How does that plan sound to you?"

Kimball grabbed Luke's hand and shook it vigorously. "Oh man, thank you so much, coach! I don't even know what to say. Thank you, thank you," said Kimball excitedly before his face took on a serious look. "But what do we tell the guys? What do we do about the injury? Are you gonna tell them I was just faking it?"

"Nope, we're not going to tell them about that. You just adjust your limping so that it looks like you are getting better each day. I want you to start some light jogging on Monday, and work into it so that you are pretty much running full speed routes by Thursday's practice so that we can get the timing down with you and Elvis. If anything comes up about you not playing defense, we'll both say that the backpedaling that you have to do in coverage aggravates the hamstring to the point I won't let you play D anymore. You okay with that?"

"That's perfect, thanks again coach," Kimball shouted as he raced out the door.

"Whoa there, Nellie," reminded Luke. "Don't forget that you still have a limp for the next few days."

"Oh yeah, right... right. Thanks coach," replied the receiver as he re-implemented his Hop-along Cassidy shuffle for the walk out of the gym.

ROSE TALKS TO LUKE ABOUT VERNON HIGGINS

Luke had just pulled up in front of his house from monitoring his 12:00-4:00 Sunday open gym session, and couldn't help but notice the nearly new ¾ ton GMC pickup with '36' Judith Basin county plates parked in front of the Danielsen house. He no sooner had entered his house when he looked out his kitchen window and saw Rose hop the backyard fence and run to his back door.

"What's up Rose?" he asked as he opened the door and watched the obviously upset youngster rush past him and spin around in the middle of the kitchen with her hands on her hips and a pained look on her face.

"Vernon Higgins is what's up, Mr. Carter. See that truck out front? That's his. He likes my mom and he's been calling her every night now for like the last few weeks. And here's the other thing: my mom has gone into Centertown like a couple of times lately. She said she had to go a meeting and sent me over to Abby's house until she got back. Well, she wasn't telling me the truth, Mr. Carter, because Chelsey Ployhar's mom saw her and Vernon Higgins eating supper at the Hackamore Club. Abby says I might as well accept that they're going out. I don't know if they're, like, going steady or anything, but I guess Abby must be right. They're definitely going out."

Luke tried to respond, but he couldn't get a word out. He felt like he'd been kicked in the gut by the same mule that had belted him the night before over in Hodgeman. He saw a flash from his old nightmare, inwardly groaning over the return of a vision that until this very moment had been on the brink of extinction. *So Vernon Higgins is the guy's name, huh? Okay, pull yourself together for the sake of Rose*, he told himself, finally gathering his composure to the point of being able to speak. "Well, I'm sure he must be a good guy if your mother likes him," he attempted unconvincingly.

"No he's not!" cried Rose. "He's not a good guy, and I don't like him one bit. We had to go to his ranch today for Sunday dinner and I had to hang with his daughters Haley and Anika. They're like 16 and 14, and they were mean to me. They, like… like, they think they are really hot stuff, and all they can talk about is boys and makeup and stuff like that. And they talk mean about all the other girls at their schools. I know this is a bad word and I shouldn't say this in front of adults, but they're little bitches. Sorry Mr. Carter, but that's what they are. Anyway, Haley goes to Marshall and Anika goes to Fergus. They have like different moms, I guess. Anyway, we've only been home from their place for like an hour, and guess who shows up at our house again a few minutes ago? Vernon, that's who. Like he hasn't been with my mom enough already today."

While jumping up and down with joy on the inside with Rose's declaration of dislike for Vernon and his girls, Luke forced himself to respond on a positive note. "Maybe you just need to give him a chance, Rose. He might be a good guy once you get to know him a little better. And same thing with the girls; maybe they'll be nicer to be around after you get to know them better."

"No it won't," Rose responded angrily, "that won't help. Vernon just bugs me. He tries real hard to act like he's so cool. I don't know how to say it exactly, but it's like, you know, it's like a phony cool. Not like you, Mr. Carter. You are a cool guy, and you don't have to try to fake it because it's, like, natural for you to be cool. Do you know what I mean, Mr. Carter?"

"Well Rose, I don't know about the part of me being cool. But I understand what you are saying, and I get what you are feeling. But I really do think you need to try to give Vernon and the girls a chance for your mom's sake. Can you do that, Rose?" asked Luke, hoping his body language didn't reveal either the total dislike he already held for Vernon Higgins, nor the degree of devastation he felt from Madison's apparent rejection of him in favor of the Hodgeman phony who was trying to sweep his next door neighbor off her feet.

"I guess I can try," replied Rose dejectedly, her lower lip quivering as she stepped into Luke for a hug. "But I don't know if I can ever like any of them, I really don't."

DETECTIVE BESSEL CALLS SHERIFF COUCH

As he delved into the messages that had piled up on his desk while he was dispatched to tend to a tipped over livestock trailer that was blocking the highway near Wyngate, Fergus County Sheriff Trent Couch noted that Detective Marv Bessel of the Great Falls Police Department had requested a call back. Marv was a 30-year veteran of the Department, spending the last decade or so as a plain clothes detective. Great Falls and Cascade County were among less than a handful of cities and counties in Montana that had enough population to support a full time detective that concentrated entirely on solving homicides and major crimes, and both city and the county law enforcement agencies shared his services and salary. Trent had worked with the detective on occasion over the years, and knew him to be a respected and competent investigator.

"So what's up Marv? You got some of Great Falls and Cascade County's unsavory characters holed up over here in my county?" asked Trent in a joking tone.

"Well, maybe something along those lines," Marv responded with a chuckle. "I'll get to the point. As you well know Trent, here in Great Falls we've been battling a small, but persistent population of transient gang thugs that work their way over to Montana from the northwest—Portland, Seattle and Spokane, mostly. Their presence is mainly due to the meth and drug trade that's sweeping across the land these days. Anyway, a few weeks back there was altercation at the Holiday Village Mall that led to a couple of these gang guys getting thumped and ambulance hauled to the hospital in pretty tough shape."

When the detective paused for a moment, Trent interjected.

"So a couple of thugs get the shit kicked out of them. Don't see the problem—what am I missing?"

"Exactly, exactly. Hear what you're saying, Trent. The problem is that one of them got his arm ripped out of the shoulder socket so bad they had to undergo emergency surgery to basically reattach his arm again. To make matters worse, after surgery he got a staph infection and is still in ICU receiving a 24-hour a day antibiotic drip."

"Still don't see what the problem is, Marv. So what if somebody beats a gang guy within an inch of his life. I'm guessing he likely deserved the shit-kicking he got," said Trent.

"Exactly, exactly," the Detective repeated, "but here's the problem. Like your little hospital over there in Centertown, our medical facility here operates as a Not-for-Profit. As you also know, a hospital under that designation cannot turn down a patient due to inability to pay. So here's the deal: with the emergency surgery and two weeks of being tended to in the ICU, the thug is looking at a medical bill that is already in excess of $50,000. The hospital administrator knows that getting anything more in payment other than the packet of meth that was found on him when they wheeled him in is not only unlikely, but ain't gonna happen."

"So let me guess," interrupted Trent. "The administrator called the Cascade County Sheriff and the Great Falls City Police Chief and requested that they open an investigation to find the party responsible for the assault in hopes there might be a deep insurance pocket to cover the fifty grand they're going to have to otherwise eat?"

"Exactly, exactly," confirmed Marv. "And who said you law enforcement guys over in Centertown and Fergus County ain't very bright? So yes, I was called in by my superiors to investigate the assault and determine if a deep pocket might indeed exist."

"Okay," said Trent hesitantly. "And I'm getting this call from you now because?"

"Well, I just got back from interviewing this gangster in his hospital room. And by the way, I'm guessing his life of crime career choice might not be looking too good to him right now," said Marv with a chortle. "He's not saying much. Like you say, he no doubt instigated and deserved the horrific beating he received. What I did get out of him was, and I quote, 'some fuckin' 350-pound giant wearing a blue hat with a bulldog on it viciously attacked me for no fuckin' reason.' The only other detail I could get out of him other than the assaulter was huge and fast was that he was young. Eighteen to 24 is the estimated age range."

"How old is the thug?" asked Trent.

"As you might guess, no identification on him and he's not disclosing a thing. Real imaginative original name he gave us, too... George Smith. I'd say our George Smith is in his late 20s or early 30s."

"Not that I don't enjoy chatting with you Marv, but are you ever gonna get around to telling me why this involves me and my county?"

"Well, like I say, I've been dispatched by those who pay my meager salary to investigate this and find some overloaded fruit tree insurance policy for the hospital to pluck. So I'm investigating, right?" confirmed Marv. Hearing only silence on the other end, he continued. "Okay, so I began my investigation by snooping around a little bit at the mall—you know, the site of the assault. I'm not getting much cooperation there, as none of the mall employees are wild about the fact that their workplace has become a hangout for these gang types. I've been in this game long enough to know when a witness has pertinent information, but won't give it up. I found a few employees that either know or have a good idea what happened but aren't talking because they're sick and tired of these criminals lurking around the mall. Furthermore, they consider the guy that beat these jerks to within an inch of their lives a hero, and aren't about to give up his identity. So, I'm starting with the two things I have to work with: a giant and a blue bulldog hat. Now, there might be sizable number of folks out there wearing a blue bulldog hat. But giants wearing blue bulldog hats? Probably not so many. And late teen or early 20-something giants wearing bulldog hats? Probably even less of those."

Trent was getting a bad feeling about where this was going. "Jesus Christ, Marv. First of all, how in the hell can you think you have a credible witness in a frickin' gang member? And a big guy in a blue hat that the creep thinks might have a bulldog on it? That could be a guy from Florida wearing his old high school hat. Or it could be a rival gang member that stole the hat from somebody in Texas five years ago. For Christ's sake, Marv. Aren't you kinda hunting for the proverbial needle in the haystack here?"

"Exactly, exactly. All solid points Trent. But humor me for a minute here. It's true that there are a lot of high schools and colleges across the nation that have the bulldog as a mascot. For the sake of argument, let's narrow down the high schools and colleges in Montana that have the bulldog designation. Furthermore, let's narrow it down to central and north central Montana. Only college in Montana that has a bulldog as its mascot is Western Montana College in Dillon. As a point of information, their colors are red and white. Let's go to the high schools. There's the Butte High Bulldogs—purple and white are their colors. There's Choteau, up north about 50 miles. Maroon and gold. There's the Brady Bulldogs about 60 miles north of us. Orange and black. Then there's the Townsend Bulldogs about 100 miles south of Great Falls. And guess what? They're blue and white. And then another 100 some miles to the east is the Pacer Coulee Bulldogs. Yep—as you know, also blue and white."

"Still seems like a helluva of a stretch to me to come to any kind of conclusion based on the color and mascot of college and high school hats," Trent emphatically stated.

"Exactly, exactly. But bear with me a bit longer. I've done a little investigating over at Townsend and talked with Broadwater County Sheriff Sam DeBoever just this morning. He thinks the only two guys in his area that are well north of 300 pounds are father/son ranchers down by Toston. The dad is 82 and the son is 63, so not really likely candidates to take down a couple of seasoned gangsters. And the biggest kid Townsend has had in high school over the last decade was about 240 pounds. That's big, but certainly not in the giant category. Now, that brings me to Pacer Coulee. I'm a sports fan, Trent. I follow all of Montana football closely, especially the central Montana area. Any serious Montana sports fan knows about Tank Hollister. Well over 300 pounds. Fast. Quick. Strong. You get the idea."

Trent's heart sank as he listened to the narrative. He knew well of Tank, and had followed him all through his high school career. He also knew of his difficult upbringing, as he had arrested his father on numerous occasions over the years. Along with Edna Coffman, he was the one to bring Tank the news that his scumbag abusive father had died after driving off the Spring Creek bridge in a drunken stupor. He knew Tank would be more than capable of putting a beating on a couple of thugs if he had to.

"I'm sorry to have to ask this, Trent. I don't want to get this kid in trouble anymore than you do, but my hands are pretty well tied here. Before I go sniffing around out there at Pacer Coulee myself, I'm giving you a heads up. I want you to discretely do a little leg work for me and see if Tank was up in Great Falls on the 2nd of October. I hate to say it, Trent, but I'd bet the farm that he was. Let me know what you find out, and if it's bad news, I'll let you know how I'll have to proceed from there."

HEBERTON GAME

"The tale of two halves, that game was," said T.O. to Luke in describing the just played 34-32 loss to the Engineers of Heberton. Even Bo's attempt to lighten the mood with his Irish brogue wit when Shanty took the yellow bus into the Roy's Truck Stop turn a little too fast was met with sullen silence.

Luke knew that the under-the-lights contest at Heberton's well-maintained field would be a battle. The father/son coaching combination of the Zakrzewskis had rebuilt the languishing fortunes of the football program into one that was a force to be reckoned with. The Engineers had enjoyed a successful season, their only loss being a 58-22 drubbing at the hands of St. Francis.

Luke couldn't have scripted a better first half for the Bulldogs. Stefan returned the opening kickoff for a touchdown and tacked on two other first quarter scores on long touchdown runs. Meanwhile, Tank, Stefan and Aaron were all over the field in holding the Engineers offense at bay, and the Bulldogs were further assisted by the inability of Heberton's young quarterback to accurately deliver a pass to the ofttimes wide open Randy Zucker, the Engineers' speedy and talented sophomore running back. With Kimball Robbins back in the fold for the first time in three weeks, Luke had drawn him prominently into the game plan. When Elvis threw him a strike as he crossed the goal line for a 31-yard score, the Bulldogs took a commanding 26-0 lead midway through the second quarter.

But with 1:02 left in the first half and the Bulldogs starting a drive from their own 23 in attempt to add to the 26-point lead, the tide suddenly turned when Stefan was tackled awkwardly on third down as he planted his foot to make a cut. The resulting ankle sprain was severe, and when Luke and Aaron helped the hobbled stalwart off the field the burst of renewed hope and energy from the Heberton sideline and their hometown crowd was more than palpable.

Facing 4th down and not wanting to risk a big punt return from Zucker, Luke had instructed Tucker to kick the ball out of bounds. But in his attempt to guide the direction of the punt, the ball came off the side of his foot and squirted out of bounds at midfield. Coach Zakrezewski took immediate advantage of the rattled Bulldogs by dialing up another deep pass attempt to the fleet Randy Zucker, who took the now accurately thrown pass in stride for a touchdown. The successful 2-point conversion closed the gap to 26-8 as the second quarter came to an end.

Luke and T.O. used the halftime to get their team settled down, and to try and prepare a nervous Ernie Rimby to fill the large shoes of Stefan Tillerman at both the running back and linebacker positions. But the injury bug bit again on the opening second half kickoff when Tuf Sturm incurred a painful hip pointer when he took a helmet to the hip from an Engineer blocker. With the next-man-up Ernie already being forced into duty at linebacker, the only reasonable option remaining was to insert Virgil Cottingham into secondary. And even though Luke had quickly moved the veteran safety Danny Schrader over to defend Randy Zucker in Tuf's absence, it didn't take young John Zakrezewski long to find his most favorable match-ups in exploiting the Bulldogs' weaknesses as a result of the injuries to Stefan and Tuf. Despite the continued stellar play of Tank and Aaron, the Engineers methodically put two scores on the board in the third quarter to narrow the Bulldog margin to a 26-22 advantage.

Although Pacer Coulee was able to mount several promising drives in the fourth quarter, a lost fumble by Ernie and an Elvis interception thwarted their opportunities to put points on the board. When Zucker took a screen pass and broke it loose for a long TD jaunt, Heberton took their first lead of the game at 28-26. Jim Wasser, the Engineers' other fine senior running back, closed out a long and time consuming drive with a short touchdown run to make it 34-26 with only 1:58 remaining in the contest.

Starting at their own 15-yard line, Luke judiciously used two of his three available timeouts to move the ball to the Heberton 26 with 19 seconds remaining. When Aaron took it to the 13 on a draw play, Luke used his last timeout to stop the clock, and the Bulldogs scored on the hastily designed-on-the-clipboard play that Luke had drawn up when Elvis connected with Kimball in the back of the end zone.

Needing a successful 2-point conversion to send the game into overtime, the roar of the opposing sideline and honking of the horns of the surrounding cars aptly illustrated the fate of the Elvis pass that sailed just beyond the outstretched reach of a leaping Bret Cassidy.

To add insult to injury, as Luke made the 11:30 p.m. turn into the Lehman Street street alleyway to park by his garage, he couldn't help but see the just departing white pickup truck with '36' plates pull away from his neighbor's driveway. "Great, just freaking great," muttered Luke to himself. "Quite the roll you're on, Luke—quite the roll."

TANK AND CLARE

Tank was riding Blaze, the stout, 17-plus hands buckskin that 83-year-old Bid Byrne had brought out to Edna's for him. "Been ridin' this big ol' bastard for 12 of his 14 years with nary a hitch, but the sum-bitch flat bucked me on my ass in the middle of a team ropin' run, he did," Bid had explained when he delivered the big gelding a few days earlier. "Damn near broke all my ribs while he was at it. And me and Duke Dickson were a lock to win the over-70 division if we coulda closed out that last throw. Anyway, Bill and Edna mentioned that your nag went lame, so I figured I'd let ya borrow ol' Blaze here till my ribs heal up. Actually, if you'll have him I'll just give him to ya." Then with a chuckle, the hard ridden old cowboy had said, "I figure the two biggest sum-bitches in the whole damn county deserve each other."

Tank glanced over at Clare, who fit like a well-worn glove on the high strung, saddle-less little dun that Tuf Sturm had brought over for her to ride. This was the second Sunday they had spent riding together, their long treks taking them along the scenic contours of Spring Creek, Plum Creek, and even up into the North and South Moccasins. Although there hadn't been more than a handful of words spoken between the two of them since they met on the first day of school six weeks prior, it was as if they were kindred spirits that found comfort and tranquility in each other's muted presence. He assumed they would eventually verbally communicate to a much greater extent, but for now their aura of silence was not at all unpleasant. Rather, it felt relaxed and serene to them both.

As Tank swung off the big gelding to open a barbed wire gate to pass from his ranch into Edna's expansive 6,000 acre property, he pondered just what it was that made him feel so comfortable with his new 14-year-old house mate. He had never had what one would consider a girlfriend in all his school years at Pacer Coulee. He had always felt uncomfortable around girls, even in grade school. He supposed it was partly due to the fact that even in the first or second grade he was twice the size of his male and female classmates. And it didn't help his self-esteem, nor his perception of how he likely presented to the females when his dad constantly reminded him that he was the "ugliest fucking spud in the potato sack" from as long as he could remember. Proportional to his massive body structure, he always assumed his large, square head with wide, deep set eyes framing a broad, flat nose wouldn't be considered in any way handsome or appealing to the ladies.

The closest thing he had to a female friend before Clare arrived on the scene was Dee Cassidy, and he realized that was because she was used to being around him because he ate so many meals at the Cassidy residence. Theirs was never a romantic relationship, but because Dee, like her mother Kellie, was such a warm, caring and outgoing person, he eventually opened up to her and began to trust her as a friend. Even so, he had never allowed himself to reveal any of the horrific details of growing up in the same household as Terrance Hollister, Sr.

Although nothing had been mentioned between Tank and Clare in their limited conversations of their respective histories, Tank could clearly sense that she had her own demons to contend with. And while not yet spoken or explained by either of them, they innately knew that they shared an upbringing fraught with hardship and abuse.

Clare was only truly happy when doing two things: riding horseback and playing basketball. As she watched Tank mount the big buckskin with surprising fluidity and grace for a man of his size, she thought back on the whirlwind of events that had turned her life upside down six weeks past. It wasn't that her life on the reservation was great, as it surely wasn't. She had never met her dad, and remembered precious little of her mom, who died of a drug overdose when she was three. And while she loved both the grandmother and great grandmother who raised her, each had many others to tend to—kids, grandkids, nieces and nephews that needed to be housed and fed under the roofs of their modest trailers or prefab modular homes. They did the best they could for her and Elvis under the circumstances, to include stressing the importance of regular school attendance. Most all of the Montana reservations were noted for dismal attendance rates that ranked far below the average of the non-Native Montana schools. Although Clare was not near as responsible and diligent as Elvis, her grandma and great grandma made sure she didn't skip as many days as most of her friends did.

Clare was very shy by nature, and life at great grandmother Carmen Crow Fly High's home became more difficult when she took in a 27-year-old son of a cousin that had done a stint in the Montana State Prison at Deer Lodge for the armed robbery of a Casino in Havre. Upon his release from prison he immediately began drinking again, even though avoidance of alcohol was a condition of parole. But law enforcement on the reservation was a different animal entirely, and it wasn't long until her cousin was back to his usual drunken and lawless ways. That pattern of behavior included sexual assault, and Clare was twice his unfortunate victim. The first incident occurred when she was but 12 years old, and the second only weeks before she and Elvis moved to Pacer Coulee. Since sexual assault was rarely reported on the reservation, Clare told no one, and buried the traumatic experiences into the deep recesses of her subconscious.

Harriet had prepared sandwiches for their ride, and Tank broke the cool, late October morning's silence by suggesting they rest the horses and take lunch under a stand of Aspens that hugged the inner bank of a long, looping bend of Spring Creek.

"So how do you like living at Miz E's?" asked Tank, getting a no-eye-contact, noncommittal shoulder shrug for an answer. After several minutes of more quietude, Tank tried again. "I'm figurin' it had to be tough on you and Elvis to leave the reservation and come to a plum different place… and, you know, a new school and place to live, and everything like that."

Finally Clare responded. "It's a lot different."

Tank patiently waited, wondering whether she would expound further on his question, or if that would be the end of the discussion. He was okay with it either way. After a long pause and in between bites of her sandwich, she continued. "Elvis and me lived with my grandma until we was like eight and nine. When she died, my great grandma took us in. She was really nice, but there were like eight people living in her little two bedroom, one bath house. When she died a few months back it was… well, not so nice without her to look out for us."

They finished the rest of their sandwiches in silence, and she added. "Reservation life is tough, but it's the only life I've ever known. We don't trust white people, so to all of a sudden to be the only Natives in an all-white school is kinda scary."

"Yeah, I can see that, for sure," answered Tank thoughtfully.

"And it's okay living with Miz Coffman. Speaking of scary… I mean, her way of life is really different for me and Elvis, and it's taken a while to get used to all her rules and stuff," she explained to a now smiling Tank.

"You got that right," confirmed Tank. "She's damn sure a stickler for her rules. But Miz E is okay. She just don't put up with no bullshit. She expects a lot out of you and she don't want to hear no excuses for bad behavior or bad performance. She's been good to me, I'll tell ya that for sure. Always has looked out for me. Nobody better bad mouth Miz E when I'm around. Won't stand for it; won't tolerate it."

"I can tell you two are close. But the other sister, Harriet, what's up with her?" quizzed Clare. "She's pretty weird, don't you think?"

Tank again broke into a wide grin and said, "She's different, for sure. Different in school than at home, too. She keeps to herself, which is good by me. One Coffman woman bossing me around is enough. I sure do like her cookin', though. Next to Kellie Cassidy, she's the best cook around."

"Well, anyone can see that you need to put on some weight," deadpanned Clare.

"Holy cow! Wait until I tell the rest of the white kids that the scrawny Indian mute has a sense o' humor!" exclaimed Tank with a laugh. When that brought a grin to her face, Tank couldn't help but notice how pretty she looked when she smiled.

THE WEEK OF ST. FRANCIS

Luke was grateful when Lester stopped by the coaches' office the Sunday morning following the tough loss at Heberton the night before. "I figured you'd already be watching some film and game planning for St. Francis. Just wanted to let you know that Glenn Goettel and I will handle open gym for you today, so you can continue your preparation for the Monsters of the Midway without interruption."

"Thanks, Lester. Yeah, I'm going to need every spare moment and then some to get ready for these guys. T.O. will be in soon, and we'll start the process of trying to figure out how to do something nobody has done over the past seven or eight years... pull off a win against the 49ers of Class C football."

Throughout the course of the season, T.O. had already given Luke the full history and low down on the perennial 8-man champions from Centertown. There were a number of family names that kept showing up on the Trojan program rosters through the years, none more prevalent than the Pekovics. The four Pekovic brothers were young, Croatian immigrant Stonemasons that settled in early day Centertown, and to say that the proliferation of succeeding generations of Pekovic DNA was robust would be an understatement. And if one was restricted to only one universal phrase to describe the Croatian descendants it would be, 'Large-Bodied and Foul Tempered.' There were three Pekovics on the current roster; 6'4", 240-pound senior Paul and his 6'2", 235-pound junior brother David anchored the Trojan line. A 6'3", 225-pound senior cousin rounded out the interior of both lines. Another familiar St. Francis family name was Stronge. Scott Stronge, the lengthy 6'7", 205-pound senior offensive and defensive end, was additionally an impressive force to be reckoned with. And then there were the Bellini brothers, Will and Wyatt. They were the latest of a long string of athletes produced by the Italian family, and they operated as bookend running backs and linebackers. Brian Bertelson was a four-year starter at quarterback, and the skilled, veteran signal caller led the St. Francis offense with unparalleled precision and efficiency. To make matters worse for their oft over-matched opponents, the Trojans had just this year added sprinter speed receiver Ricky Rae to complement the towering and sure-handed Scott Stronge in their stable of talented receivers.

"Yet another damn Fergus High recruit and transfer," was how T.O. had explained it, adding with a sigh, "do any of those Fergus studs ever transfer out here? Or to Stanton, Deeden or Heberton? Hell no, they don't. Always to St. Francis."

But all discussion of St. Francis dominance started and ended with their legendary coach, Darryl Brunner. With the exception of the nine years that the 60-year-old had coached in his native state of North Dakota, Brunner had spent the past 29 years as the head football and track and field coach of the Trojans. "He's an old school coach, is what he is," T.O. had said. "And everybody, especially his players, hate the miserable prick. Well, everybody except the St. Francis fans, who are happy to overlook that he's such an asshole because he never fucking loses. Think of the brutal fall camp workouts that you used to read about when Bear Bryant and Frank Kush were coaching in the '50s and '60s, because that's who Darryl emulates. If you think I'm rough on our guys sometimes, I'm an absolute sweetheart compared to Brunner. He rides those kids so hard it's unbelievable, and it amazes me that more of them don't just quit. But that's just sour grapes coming from all the rest of us when we bitch about him. Bottom line is we're jealous as hell of his incredible record and success. His teams are well-oiled machines, and while the parts might change somewhat from year to year, the engine always hums along in the same relentlessly efficient way.

One good thing about Brunner is that what you see is what you get. I'll bet he hasn't changed his offensive and defensive formations and schemes since he's been there, which has been forever. He runs a tight, balanced formation with either split or I backfield about 98% of the time. Nothin' fancy… just runs power, counter, sweep and play action pass. Oh, every now and then he'll move one of his backs to a slot or split out an end, but no Twins, Trips or any other of the spread formations that are becoming popular in today's game. In the passing game he loves to send his ends on crossing routes, but you don't see a lot else. Maybe an occasional flare pass or wheel route to a back, that's about it. He likes to say he just beats people up front, and drags 'em way out from shore to see how long they can tread water in the second half. Hard to argue with him, 'cause that's pretty much what he does. And he always runs a standard 4-2 defense except when he's in goal line. Always straight man in coverage, too. Since he gets such good pressure from the hogs up front, he rarely blitzes. Gotta tell ya Luke, I hate 'em… I hate Brunner and I hate St. Francis. Maybe not as much as Edna, but right up there."

"The obvious key to this thing is whether we'll have a healthy Stefan or not," stated Luke. "From what I've seen on film, we'll need a full complement of players to have a chance against these guys. I think it was pretty apparent last night that while little Ernie is a gamer, he isn't quite ready for Prime Time. And we're way over-matched in trying to defend the St. Francis receivers, even when we have our top two safeties playing. If Stefan can't go and we have to bring Danny down to play linebacker and plug his spot at safety with either Virgil or Ernie… well, we're pretty well screwed. I'm thinking we'd better play zone and hope we can get some pass rush, even though they'll double and triple team Tank. But I'm thinking Rae and Stronge will kill us if we go man."

"Hell Luke, they'll kill us either way, but I agree. Even if Stefan plays, I think we should go mostly zone. I've also been thinking about doing some different shit on the D line, but I'm afraid we'll mess Dolph all up if we do anything different than what he's used to."

"I'm all ears—let's hear it," Luke said quickly.

"Well, I'm thinking we should move Tank around on the D line so that they can't just audible at the line and go away from his side. Plus, if we put him at nose and head up on big Paul Pekovic, then he will have a harder time getting off Tank and out to block our linebackers."

"I like it, but as you pointed out, what do we do about Dolph? It's hard enough to get him lined up right when we've been doin' the same thing all season."

"I know, I know. He's like getting a milk cow into a different stall than what she's used to; good luck with that. But if you're okay with it, I'd like to work on it this week in practice and see where it goes," reasoned T.O. "But promise you'll come over and help work with Dolph on this? You have way more patience with him than I do. I'll probably tear out what little hair I got left gettin' him to figure out where he's supposed to be, rather long what he's supposed to do."

"Consider it done," laughed Luke.

"So what's your plan on offense?" T.O. inquired.

"All depends on Stefan. If he can go, I'd like to run some more option. We haven't shown much of it because I didn't want to overload Elvis's learning curve, but I've been working with him after practice every night and he's picking it up well. And by the way, hasn't Elvis been amazing? I mean, I can't believe how he's picked things up. He's smarter than a whip, and is really starting to understand the game. Throws it beautifully, and can run it too."

"Couldn't agree more," said T.O., "couldn't agree more."

"Anyway, back to the offensive game plan. Especially if Stefan isn't playing, we're going to have to throw it more. I think we'll need to go more Slot and Twins and roll our line out right along with Elvis so that he's setting up directly behind Tank. It's the only way we'll have time to throw. With Kimball now back in the fold, we can run some underneath combo routes with him and Bret so that Elvis can get the ball out quickly. And maybe, just maybe we can get them to bite on an out and up and hit Kimball for a few deep ones."

"Goddamn Kimball," muttered T.O. "If he wasn't such a pussy we could play him at safety. That would solve the mismatch that Rae creates."

"I know, I know. We've been over this a thousand times, but I'd rather have him playing one side of the ball than not have him at all."

"Yeah, I get what you did there, but it still pisses me off. I'll guarantee you that if Kimball played for Brunner he would be playing both receiver and safety. It just sticks in my craw, Luke... can't help it."

"I'm gonna start calling you T.O. Bryant or Kush Barker, you old hard-ass," chuckled Luke. "We might just need those two old tyrants to come in and coach if we're ever going to beat Brunner. Fight fire with fire, as the old saying goes."

Luke sent T.O. home at 2:00 p.m. and stayed in the coaches' office to watch more film and game plan until Lester started giving the students and the townspeople the boot at 4:00. Luke's chance meeting of Madison as they passed in the hallway on his way out was awkward, even though they stopped and briefly chatted about their upcoming week and games. *What the hell happened*, Luke asked himself, knowing only that he desperately missed those first months of the enjoyable interaction he had with Madison. "I know she liked it too," he said to himself as he climbed in his pickup. "What in the hell happened?"

TRENT MEETS WITH LUKE

"Hey Luke, Sheriff Couch here. Imagine you're getting ready for the big game against St. Francis, huh?" said the voice on the other end of the line when Luke answered the ringing phone as he walked into his house after the Monday night practice. "Uh, yeah Sheriff," said Luke hesitantly to his unexpected caller. "As you know, biggest game of the year for us."

"Yep, yep. I know I sure look forward to it every year. Say Luke, I've got a matter I need to discuss with you, and I think it's best we meet privately so that we don't have the town buzzin' about the Sheriff being at the school or your house. Don't suppose you could meet me in about half an hour out behind the abandoned grain bins over on the Phillips' place off the Pacer Coulee Cutoff road, could you?"

"Ahh... yes, I suppose I could. What's this about, Sheriff?" asked Luke, his anxiety level meter rapidly rising.

"Best we discuss it there. Just pull in behind the grain bins, cut your lights and hop into my rig. See you in about 30."

"Here's the deal, Luke," began Trent after Luke climbed into the passenger seat of the Sheriff's cruiser. "I got a call today from a Detective Bessel up in Great Falls. Seems there was a fight a few weeks back somewhere around the Holiday Village Mall, and a couple of gang members got pretty roughed up. In fact, one guy got his arm ripped out of the socket and he damn near died. He's still in the hospital on IVs, as I understand it."

Luke tried to swallow, but couldn't get past that lump in his throat that had been growing ever since he answered the phone 30 minutes prior. Unable to speak just yet, he nodded his head to acknowledge the Sheriff's opening remarks, and Trent continued. "To make a really long story short, Detective Bessel's initial investigation has led him to suspect that Tank Hollister was the one that assaulted these guys. You wouldn't happen to know anything about that, would you Luke? Or whether Tank was up in the Great Falls area on the 2nd of October? That was a Tuesday, I believe. Know anything about that Luke?"

"Ahh... ahh," stammered Luke, the lump now growing to what felt like the size of a county fair prize watermelon.

"Okay Luke, here's the thing," said the Sheriff with an almost amused looking expression spreading across his face. "I've been doing this law enforcement gig for a long time now, and I can spot when I'm about to get bullshitted from a mile away. I think you're an honest kind of guy by nature, but I'm thinking from that look on your face that you're about to try the dishonest approach on me. I gotta tell you Luke, going that route just doesn't work for you."

Trent paused, but before Luke could respond he repeated, "Here's the deal. If you know anything about this, you need to tell me now. Detective Bessel is a bulldog, and he is very good at what he does. The guy has a ton of experience, and he just works and works a case until he gets to the bottom of it. The guy has solved a whole bunch of cold case homicides up in Great Falls over the years. So if Tank was in Great Falls on October 2nd and had anything to do with this, trust me, this guy will find out. He's letting me gather the initial information here as a courtesy to me and my county, and he's saving Tank, and probably you, the embarrassment of him walking into your school and interrogating the both of you in the Principal's office. Now I'm not saying I can make this go away if Tank is in fact involved, but with me acting as a go-between there's a better chance of at least getting a fair shake.

Caught redhanded with his paw in the cookie jar, Luke laid out the whole story, to include full details about the catching of the thugs in the middle of an attempted sexual assault on the mentally impaired Dolph. He thoroughly disclosed his thought process at the time that led him to the decision to not call the police and to keep the incident under wraps.

"Well Luke, I can damn sure see why you did what you did," said Trent. "Probably would have done the same thing myself. But I'm not calling the shots on this one, you understand? So I'll plead our case to Detective Bessel to let this thing drop, but like I say, his hands are gonna be pretty well tied. Only thing we can do is wait and see if, and when, the hammer will drop."

EDNA SCOLDS LUKE AND MADISON

Madison was surprised to find that the visitor who had just knocked on the door and entered her empty classroom was none other than Edna Coffman. She knew all too well that the School Board Chairperson was not one to drop in for idle chit chat. She tried to push down her escalating anxiety level as she ran a quick brain search to identify what this unexpected visit could be about, but came up empty. It couldn't be any concerns about her team's performance so far, as they were still undefeated. Furthermore, although the temperature of the Brewster sister kettle was definitely heating up, it had yet to boil over; at least nothing that had been noticeable in a game. She was confident that her teaching skills were more than satisfactory and, at least to her knowledge, her classes were going well and she did not have any out of the ordinary student or parent issues that she was currently contending with.

"Hello Ms. Coffman. Please come in. What can I do for you?"

"Good afternoon, Madison," said Edna as she strode across the room towards Madison, taking up residence on the student desk in front of the teacher's desk while motioning Madison to be seated. "As you likely know by now, I'm not one inclined towards mindless prattle, so I'll get to the point."

No shit, mused Madison. *Who would have ever guessed that about you?*

"I'm also not one to meddle in people's personal lives, but when I see things occurring with my teachers and coaches that in all likelihood will not only negatively impact them, but ultimately the welfare of our students, I can't stand passively by and not attempt to intervene."

"Okay," said Madison hesitantly. "What is it about my personal life that you apparently think has gone awry?"

"Let me begin by saying this," stated Edna, "I'm also not known to have a warm and fuzzy side, but I do need to tell you that as recently as two weeks ago I couldn't have been happier or more pleased with my hire of you and Luke. By all appearances thus far, you are both very competent teachers and coaches. You are positive influences on our young men and women, not to mention a breath of fresh air for the entire community. That being said, if you continue down the current path with Vernon Higgins as your personal choice of a running mate, then I struck out when it came to evaluating your character when I hired you.

"You are headed for train wreck. I know nothing about your ex-husband, but whatever kind of man he was, I can assure you that this one would be a step down. Don't let that slicked back hair, good looks and phony charm of this chameleon fool you. He's nothing more than a womanizer that over the years has tried to bed every woman in central Montana between the ages of 18 and 40. He's got two daughters from different mothers, so that should raise a red flag right there. And despite the big front he puts up, he's a spoiled brat who was handed one of the nicest ranches in all of the Judith Basin on a silver platter, and he's on the fast track to run it into the ground and lose everything his father and grandfather built before him."

A stunned Madison gulped as she pushed further into her chair back, awaiting the further scolding that was sure to come.

"That being said," continued Edna, "any damn fool can see what's going on here. You'd have to be deaf and blind not to see that you and Luke are meant for each other. But since you're coming off a painful divorce, you have all of a sudden contracted a case of cold feet. So what's happening here is that you are trying to mask your true feelings for Luke by hanging out with this Higgins character. What have you done by keeping the ice packs on those feet of yours? Well first of all, you couldn't have hurt Luke more than if you would have run over him with a Goddamn grain truck. Try as he might, he's not in full focus on either the field or in the classroom. With St.

Francis coming up this Friday, we need every ounce of attention to detail and positive energy that he can muster. And don't think your teams don't perceive what's going on here between their two coaches. It's a shame that the childish behavior of our coaches is preventing our students from getting the focus, concentration and effort that they should be able to expect from their leaders; especially with tournaments and playoffs just around the corner."

With Madison still leaning back in her chair, wide eyes and mouth agape in disbelief, Edna stood and, while striding to the door, turned her head and snapped, "There's still time to right this ship. Do the right thing, Madison; for you, for Luke, and especially for these kids of Pacer Coulee."

"Hello Edna," said a surprised Luke as the Chairperson entered the coaches' office after a cursory warning knock on the door. "What brings you to my spacious coaching suite?"

"I won't beat around the bush. We need to have a chat," Edna replied as she sat down on the folding chair that served as the only other seat in the cramped office. "Let me begin by saying that you have been a pleasant surprise as our new teacher and coach. The kids worship you, and other than what I would consider a few questionable calls on 3rd and long in the Heberton game, it is most obvious that you are a very astute and effective coach. That being said, to say that I've been disappointed in your reaction to this Madison incident would be a huge understatement."

"And what Madison incident would you be referring to?" asked Luke, attempting to paint a puzzled expression on his face.

"Oh, don't give me that crap. You know damn well what I mean. I knew about your divorce and the tough time you'd had dealing with it when I hired you, but I thought you had more of a spine than what you've shown me so far. One would have to be deaf and blind not to see that you and Madison have a strong connection. All of the kids see it, all of the teachers see it, even

Lester sees it; hell, the whole damn town of Pacer Coulee sees it. Granted, both of you are coming off the experience of a bad marriage and I can understand why you might be overly cautious about jumping into a new relationship; but good grief Luke, are you so dense in the brain matter that you can't see that the only reason Madison has taken up with this Higgins character is because she got cold feet and was scared to allow her true feelings for you to show through? Are you so naive you can't see that?"

Not allowing Luke enough time to respond, Edna forged ahead. "And to top it off, when slicked-back-haired Higgins stepped on your toes, you just folded your tent; you didn't even throw a punch. And we have the most important game of the year coming up this Friday with Goddamn Catholics! How in the hell do you expect these kids to compete and fight like hell when the chips are down when they've just watched their coach stick his tail between his legs and run at the first sighting of Vernon Higgins? Really? What the hell kind of leadership is that?" barked Edna as she stood up and wagged her finger in Luke's face.

"These boys deserve more from you. Pick that lower lip of yours off the floor and show your team what it's really like to be a competitor and not accept losing as an option. Goddamn it Luke, put all this old relationship baggage behind you and go fight for her. Go get your girl back. Trust me, she's worth the effort and then some."

LUKE CONFRONTS MADISON

Madison had just tucked Rose into bed and was sitting down to grade the last of her Geometry quizzes when the phone rang. She was surprised to hear Luke's voice on the other end of the line. "Is Rose in bed yet?" he asked.

"Ahh, yes, she just went down," Madison confirmed.

"Is your Hodgeman friend there now?"

"Uh... no, no he's not," replied Madison hesitantly. "What's this about, Luke?"

"I need to talk to you. In person... in private. Could you slip over to my house for a few minutes?"

"Okay, I guess I could. Give me a minute to leave a note for Rose in case she wakes up, and I'll be right over."

Luke had spent most every moment since Edna's outright demeaning scolding processing her message. *As if learning that Tank was being investigated for assault and trying to prepare for a team that hasn't been beaten in 69 games isn't enough to worry about this week,* thought Luke. Once he got by the shock of being blindsided by his boss, he went through the angry 'the nerve of her to interfere in my personal life' stage. From there, he had to take enough of a break from dwelling on the disturbing conversation to conduct his Tuesday night practice.

Immediately upon getting home, instead of seething over Edna's verbal spanking yet again, he forced himself to calm down and attempt to objectively evaluate the substance of her message. *Dammit, she's got a point,* thought Luke. *I was so gun-shy of a recurring Lorie-like rejection that I did as Edna claimed; I ran from the situation with my tail between my legs. I didn't even fight for Madison, or for Rose. And Edna is right again that, as a result, I'm not able to give my boys the focus and leadership they deserve from their coach.*

It was then Luke decided it was time to fix his situation. The only way he could deal with the worry of the Tank investigation and apply his full and complete attention to his football team was to approach Madison and plead his case that it was he, not Vernon Higgins, that was the right choice in love and companionship for her and Rose. And one other thing was suddenly clear to him; the conversation with Madison had to happen right now.

Since the old recliner that he had bought at Emma Laughlin's yard sale when he first came to town was still the only piece of furniture to occupy his small living room, Luke motioned Madison to follow him to the kitchen, where they both sat on the edge of the seat of the two folding chairs that were tucked under the card table that served as the kitchen table. Luke wasn't sure where or when he summoned the courage to begin, but after a short and awkward silence he blurted out, "I don't want you to see that Vernon guy from Hodgeman anymore. Okay, let me back up for a second," stammered Luke, more than just a little aware of the sea of red that was climbing up his neck. "When I came here last July, I was a wreck. I was still reeling from my divorce. I mean, being rejected by her in favor of another man she had been having this lengthy secret affair with pretty much took away any and all self-confidence I had left when it came to the female gender. In fact, I had sworn to myself that I would never, ever let myself fall for anyone and risk having to go through the pain of another failed relationship. Not ever again.

"And then I saw you, moving in next door. Even though I tried hard to push away what I was feeling inside that day, I was smitten from that very first moment I laid eyes on you. And I haven't been able to quit thinking about you since. And then later on that very day that you moved in, I met Rose. I think I fell in love with Rose before I ever really let myself confront or explore the feelings I was having about you. And then the evening barbecues started—the visits over the fence in the backyard when Rose was doing the lawns. Man oh man, I was sucked in big-time. It was like being in the path of whirling winds of a hurricane, and I couldn't mount enough resistance to keep from being swept off my feet and pulled into the central eye of the storm," Luke confessed, the words flowing easier now that he had gotten started.

"I was just starting to finally put my failed marriage and all the heartache that went with it behind me. I was slowly but surely getting a little self-confidence back. My nightmares of the infidelity were gradually being replaced with much more pleasant dreams about you. And then that guy from Hodgeman started showing up; at your games, in your driveway, and all those horrible old feelings from the past came roaring back. I don't know, Madison," he sighed, looking past her forlornly at the recollection. "I tried to push you out of my mind and refocus on football. But I didn't realize until today, when Edna came in and lambasted me about being a quitter and not fighting for you, that I was not only shortchanging myself, but also letting my guys down by not being able to really give them the focus and leadership that they deserve from me."

Sliding his chair up so that he was directly in front of her, he took both her hands in his, leaned forward and said, "I want you to stop seeing that guy. There's no way he can love you as much as I do. There is no way he can love both you and Rose the way I do…."

"Stop! Just stop right there," Madison said firmly, hushing him with an index finger to his lips as she stood and pulled him up from his chair and into her arms. "You had me at 'Is Rose in bed yet,'" she whispered in his ear before suddenly pulling back and saying, "I can't believe Edna chewed out both of us today! At first I was pissed that she would be butting into my personal business like that, but I didn't have to think about it very long to know that she was right in saying the only reason I went out with Vernon in the first place was that I was scared. I got cold feet because I was falling in love with you.

"Like you said, I was afraid to death of ever risking the pain of another failed relationship. I was even more scared to have Rose go through another disappointment like what happened with my split from her father. Especially the way Rose took to you almost immediately; I couldn't bear the thought of hurting Rose again if it didn't work out between us. Trust me, I never liked Vernon even a little bit, but Edna made me see it for what it was—a convenient way to hide behind the curtain of my true feelings for you."

They fell back into each other's arms for a moment until she leaned back and said, "Well for Christ's sake, are you going kiss me, or do I have to call Vernon in order to get a little action around here?"

Not wanting to leave Rose alone, they went back to Madison's and talked until well past midnight, finally falling asleep in each other's arms on the couch in the living room. Although both were usually early risers, they slept in and were awakened by a giddy Rose standing above them and asking in an excited and hopeful tone, "Does this mean no more Vernon and his bratty girls? Does this mean you guys like each other again?"

"I've never stopped liking your mother, Rose. You two are my favorite girls ever! Well, I guess Ethyl would be right up there with you guys, but only when she's delivering a freshly baked rhubarb pie. I don't know about Vernon... is he still going to be around, Madison?"

"No more Vernon, Rose. You're stuck with coach Carter hanging with us whether you like it or not."

Since Rose then squealed and jumped on top of them, Luke figured she was okay with the new arrangement.

HOLE IN THE WALL GANG CHATTER BEFORE ST. FRANCIS GAME

"Rumor has it our two young coaches are lovebirds again," Butch stated as Kip unlocked the door to the O.K. Corral on the Wednesday before the final regular season game at St. Francis, albeit at the unacceptable to the Hole in the Wall gang time of 7:11 a.m.

"That's news to me," deadpanned Harlan Horrall, bringing a hearty chuckle to the whole group when he added, "Last I knew she was still head over heels in love with me."

"The scorned lover is usually the last to know, Harlan," joked Kip.

"Bret tell you about that, Butch?" asked Duke Dickson.

"No, but Dee did. Said it was all the talk amongst the girls at practice last night. You know how high school girls are; hell, how women of all ages are when it comes to gabbing about their match-making results."

"According to Ernie, it's been the talk of the football locker room too," Wilbur Rimby chimed in. "Says the boys have been worried about coach ever since that Hodgeman guy started showing up."

"Well, hope the rumor's true, 'cause I for one will be glad to not have to look at Vernon Higgins sittin' behind our bench at every Goddamn game," stated Bones Bolstad to the unanimous head nodding approval of the entire group. "Never cared for that guy, although I sure did like his dad and grandpa."

"Since I'm pretty much heartbroken if them rumors of my Madison gettin' hooked up with Luke are true, let's move on and talk about the games coming up," interjected Harlan. "Big weekend for both the boys and girls with St. Francis and Wyngate, and both of them away games. So Kip, do you think we have a chance to pick up our first win against St. Francis since 1980, and for our girls to win at Wyngate for the first time since 1977?"

"I think our girls have a far better chance than the guys," Kip explained. "I think the wild card for the guys is how healthy Stefan is by game time Friday night. I hate to say this, but if he's anything less than 100%, I think we'll be screwed. But we gave Heberton everything they wanted without him, and don't forget that Tuf missed a couple of quarters too. I know for a fact I'm anxious to see what Luke comes up with for a game plan against them."

"All I know for sure is this," Art Fenner interjected, "You better get to the games early 'cause the house will be packed at both places."

Frank Cervenka quickly jumped into the mix to share his usual sour predictions. "Bulldogs are doomed either way, boys. Don't matter if Stefan, Tuf, or whoever is playin' or not. St. Francis simply has too much horsepower for us, and I don't care if it's Bill Walsh, George Seifert or Luke Carter coaching; we don't stand a chance. And let the record show that I am also predicting a Wyngate win in the girls' game. I sensed a little tension between the three older sisters and Sammi last weekend, so I'm thinkin' they're about to pull the famous Brewster sister blow up."

"Gee, don't think I've ever heard you be that upbeat and optimistic, Frank," said Harlan sarcastically. "Say Kip, would you lend me the 357 pistol you keep behind the bar so that I can go into the bathroom and blow my fucking brains out?"

REGULAR SEASON FINALE
VS. ST. FRANCIS

As they began the twenty-five minute jaunt to Fergus County Stadium in Centertown, the already geared-up occupants of the yellow school bus were eerily silent as Shanty Sweeney took a right turn out of town and drove down the Pacer Coulee hill and over the Warm Spring Creek bridge. There wasn't the hum of nervous energy and usual ribbing that normally accompanied the football team on an away game bus trip, nor any of the clever banter between Shanty and Bo Ramsay that Luke had come to expect and so immensely enjoyed.

Helluva week, Luke thought to himself. As if beginning preparation on Monday to take on the 8-time defending state champion in itself wasn't stressful enough, getting boxed between the ears by Edna for his personal life shortcomings was only the second strongest shock wave of the day. The top Richter scale tremor reading was saved for last: the dreaded news from Sheriff Couch that not only was the Tank/Dolph Holiday Village Mall incident being investigated, but that Tank was the primary suspect. Luke was actually relieved to know the status of the incident, as bearing the burden of the unknown was causing him to wake up in a cold sweat most every night.

Tuesday was even more stressful when Luke finally took Edna's more than pointed advice to stiffen his spine and approach Madison to claim his supremacy over the dastardly Vernon Higgins. He had never been more nervous or frightened when he picked up the phone to dial her number, but the result of his gut-wrenching plea to be her man couldn't have turned out better. And most importantly, it freed up his mind to truly focus in on his team and the preparation for the upcoming contest with St. Francis.

Luke had driven by Fergus County Stadium on his inaugural visit to Pacer Coulee, but the classic old structure that served as the home turf for both Fergus High and St. Francis was unique in a number of ways. To begin with, it was at least a mile away from either of Centertown's two schools, the main parking lot for the facility resting on a raised plateau on the town's southern edge. From there, the terrain's precipitous drop to a flat creek bed bottom below effectively bowled the main stadium field and the 10-lane all weather track that encircled it.

A vast expanse of practice fields and a well-maintained, rubberized court tennis facility occupied the balance of the area before abutting up to the wandering creek. The most interesting feature to the nearly Coliseum-looking amphitheater was the two-level parking rows that were carved out of the wall that dropped abruptly from the upper parking lot. It looked as if a super-sized grader had bulldozed an upper and lower parking platform that extended the full length of the west sideline, and the spaces were already filling up with cars and pickups. Luke guessed it was much the same as Pacer Coulee, where the Ethyl Groves of St. Francis were maneuvering to claim their long-reserved parking pews.

As Shanty navigated the yellow bus down the steep incline to the steel structure that served as the visiting team's locker room, T.O. said to Luke, "Who the hell that plays Class C football has their very own Stadium?" Failing to mention that Fergus High also played their home games there, he continued, "St. Francis, that's who. Fergus Freaking County Stadium? The rest of us 8-man peons don't have stadiums, we have fields; Smith Field, Jones Field, that's what we have. Usually named as memorials to dead guys that either built the field or were longtime school and community supporters. Shit, we play at boring ol' Pacer Coulee Field, and I'm guessing we'll rename it Shanty Sweeney or Edna Coffman Field, depending on who kicks the bucket first. Anyway, these St. Francis and Fergus guys spend their time worrying if they have enough replacement bulbs should one of these big stadium night lights blow up, while the rest of us worry about shit like covering up the gopher holes."

With a glance at Francis's huge Green Bay Packer green and gold striped converted tour bus that was beginning its descent from the parking lot plateau above them, T.O. launched into a renewed venomous rant, "And who in Class C has a fucking charter bus like that? Nobody, that's who... just them. Look at that. St. Francis Trojans plastered all over the Goddamn thing. Damn, I'd love to knock these assholes off."

For having never taped an ankle or wrapped a knee in his entire coaching career prior to his arrival in Pacer Coulee, Luke had surprised even himself at how efficient he had become at those tasks which had previously always been done by the Athletic Trainer. But as they settled in the visitors' field side locker room, he deferred the tape job on Stefan's ankle to T.O., who had 25 more years of experience in Trainer 101 on-the-job training than he did. While T.O. tended to Stefan and later to a knee tape job for Bret, Luke did the more mundane, preventative ankle wraps on the rest of the team.

Stefan had gamely spun the fib that the ankle was 100%, but in truth it was more like 50 or 60%. In Stefan's absence at practice, Luke had worked Ernie at running back, but Stefan wasn't the only casualty from the Heberton game the week before. Tuf Sturm would play, but he was slowed by a hip pointer and wasn't full speed either, so Ernie and Virgil Cottingham would get plenty of time at safety as well.

The October 19th evening was heavily overcast, the air rapidly cooling towards the predicted kickoff temperature of 39 degrees. It had rained off and on all day, and intermittent showers were projected throughout the night. The bowl effect from the stadium did lessen the impact of the cold northerly breeze that was swirling about the parking lot.

Once Luke got his players settled into the pregame warm up routine, as was his usual practice, he started to amble across the field to have a brief but friendly chat with the opposing coach. When coach Brunner spotted his approach and did a quick 180 retreat, he heard T.O. muttered from behind him, "Told ya he's a prick. He'll only talk to you after the game after he's kicked your ass."

"See all the college coaches here?" Luke asked, to change the subject.

"Cats, Griz, Wyoming, Wasu… all the Frontier schools and most of North and South Dakota, too. I hear Paul Pekovic and Will Bellini are getting a look from the Cats and Griz, although I think the Bellini brothers have already signed on with Carroll. Bertelson will likely follow his two older brothers to Dickinson State in North Dakota. Hell, if it's like most years, they'll have four or five guys playing college ball somewhere next year. Stronge will get a Division I offer, but it will be for basketball. Hey, you gonna do the usual and defer if we win the toss?" asked T.O.

"Nope, I just have a gut feeling that we should play defense first, even though wind doesn't look like it should be much of a factor."

Aaron's coin toss winning skills continued, and St. Francis got good field position on a nice return from Ricky Rae to the 37. They picked up a first down on three consecutive runs by the Bellini brothers to start the game. A play action pass completion to 6'7" Scott Stronge set the Trojans up with a first down on the Bulldog 11-yard line, but Tank stuffed two Will Bellini runs and sacked the quarterback Bertelson for a 4-yard loss to force a field goal try, which their excellent kicker Josh Judiman striped through the goal posts to give the Trojans a 3-0 start.

With Stefan less than healthy, Luke put Kimball alongside Aaron as the deep returners on the ensuing kickoff, and Kimball made a nice move and slipped up the sideline before being run out of bounds on the 31. Luke ran Stefan over Tank and Dolph on a simple fullback lead power on the first two plays, picking up a first down on the combined 14-yard gain. Then Luke called for Elvis to unveil his first true read on a speed option, where he made the right decision in keeping the ball and turned up field for a 12-yard gain to the 23.

Aaron picked up a couple of yards before Luke had Elvis roll out in a Twins formation, where he hit Bret at the 16 with a perfectly timed out route pass. An inside run by Aaron and an outside zone power run by Stefan gave the Bulldogs a 3rd and 3 from the 9. Luke split out Kimball to the side away from the towering Scott Stronge, and Elvis hit him on a quick slant down to the 3-yard line. Elvis scored on the next play on a keeper, but the 2-point conversion attempt failed, leaving the Bulldogs with a 6-3 lead with only a few minutes left in the first quarter.

Although Stefan gave a gallant and determined effort in the first quarter, it was obvious he was in pain and that his mobility was severely limited. Despite his objections, Luke made the decision early in the second quarter that he was done for the game. To make matters worse, Dolph's confusion of where to line up when Tank moved around on the defensive line required Luke and T.O. to scrap their plan to disrupt the Trojans' ability to audible away from a shifting Tank. It didn't take long for coach Brunner to take advantage of Tank being back at his usual location, and he had Bertelson change the play at the line of scrimmage so as to play away from the dominant force that was Tank Hollister.

While the Bulldogs did a decent job in containing the Bellini brothers in the run game, their zone coverage defense was decidedly over-matched in trying to defend the speed of Rae and the lengthy, sure-handed Stronge in the passing game. Without Stefan running the ball, Pacer Coulee had trouble generating a consistent offense and the Trojans scored two touchdowns in the second quarter to take a 17-6 lead into halftime.

There were only three possessions in the third quarter, all of which were lengthy, time consuming drives. Pacer Coulee mounted a nice drive after receiving the second half kickoff, moving the ball with option and passing plays. Unfortunately, their drive stalled on the Trojan 5-yard line when a 4th and goal pass to Bret Cassidy was tipped away by the long arm of Scott

Stronge. St. Francis then methodically marched the ball down the field, scoring on a 22-yard pass play to Rae, who had easily beaten the slower Bulldog defenders to the corner of the end zone. St. Francis drove down to the 9-yard line on their next possession, but a blitzing Aaron Coslet dropped Wyatt Bellini for a 4-yard loss and Tank sacked a scrambling Bertelson for another loss on the next play to force a 4th down. But the accurate leg of Josh Judiman guided a 37-yarder through the uprights on the final play of the third quarter to give the Trojans a commanding 27-6 lead.

Frank Cervenka's pronouncement to the Hole in the Wall gang on the sideline of, "Just like I told you boys, this game will be over by halftime," turned out to be a bit premature. Luke used the change of quarter time to huddle with his team. "These guys think we're gonna fold our tent in the fourth quarter. They don't know that we're not intimidated like everybody else, and that there's no quit in a cornered Bulldog. We're not out of this yet; not by a long shot.

"Okay, we're going to take this kickoff and go down and score. Aaron, we're going to keep banging you in there on inside dives to keep their inside backers at home, and then we'll keep running the speed option to the outside. With Stefan out, they'll probably force the pitch to Ernie, so Ernie, try to get to the edge and pick up what you can. Kimball? We're going to need you big-time now, so be ready to get the ball in space on flares and screens. We'll split you out some and try to hit some more slants and posts too. And Bret, getting the ball in Kimball's hands will result in some opportunities for you. Okay defense, they've scored their last points. As big and good as they are, the Pekovics can't handle you Tank, so raise havoc in their backfield. Bo and Bret? Make sure you contain; don't let the Bellini boys get outside of you on the sweep. Okay, let's get back in the game, one possession at a time."

And put up a fight the Bulldogs did. Kimball returned the kick to the 34-yard line and the Pacer Coulee offense ground out a 9-play drive, scoring on a 7-yard fade pass that Bret secured just before stepping out of the far corner of the end zone. With a big second effort, Aaron stretched the ball over the goal line to add on the 2-point conversion, and it was 27-14 with 8:02 remaining.

But the injury-plagued Bulldogs could get no closer. St. Francis was able to milk the clock with their powerful run game by double and triple teaming Tank, although the big man played off the blocks as he and the sure tackling Aaron Coslet made the Trojans runners earn every yard they got. But Bertelson was able to keep extending the drive by converting third and fourth downs with the pass, and they rammed in a final touchdown to take a 34-14 win.

"I'm proud as hell of you guys," an emotional Luke told his players in the locker room. "We were shorthanded without Stefan and Tuf, and you guys fought like hell. The score doesn't indicate how tough we played these guys. We played our guts out; so much heart, so much effort. This team doesn't have any quit in them, I can tell you that. So I don't want to see any more sagging chins and hanging heads—your coaches and all of Pacer Coulee are damn proud of you."

"I saw Edna talking with you on the field after the game," T.O. observed on the bus trip home. "What did she have to say?"

"She said this was the first Pacer Coulee team to show some old-fashioned Bulldog grit in a decade, and that she was Goddamn proud of the effort of each and every one of us."

"No shit? Didn't expect that from her in a loss to the Goddamn Catholics."

"Well, as usual, she did get the last word in. Said we needed to do a better job in coaching up our zone coverage in the secondary, and once again pointed out my deficiencies in third and long calls," said Luke with a grin.

"Thank God, wouldn't want her to go soft on us."

LADY BULLDOGS' SEASON FINALE VS. WYNGATE

"I don't know, Luke. I have a bad feeling about our final regular season game at Wyngate. To begin with, they're a damn good team, and we barely squeezed out a three point win at our place earlier in the year. And secondly, I think the Brewster sisters may have swallowed rather than smoked the peace pipe," Madison had explained to Luke on the Thursday night before the big season finale against the Red Raiders.

"Let me guess: Sonya, Sandra and Sabrina are a little bent out of shape with Sammi laying 33 on Stanton last week?"

"Yes, that and the fact that Sammi's scoring over the past six or eight games has given her the edge over Sonya in terms of points per game average," sighed Madison. "Plus, the older three sisters were pissed that I left Sammi and Clare in the Stanton game last Saturday after I pulled them out. What they don't seem to understand is that our second five is so bad that I have to have somebody in the game to get the damn ball up the court. And even after I explained to them that I told Sammi and Clare they couldn't shoot and were to just rebound and pass to the others for the shot, they still went into a pout. I sat the four of them down to discuss it and get the problems out in the open, but when Sonya gets in one of her funks… I'm starting to fully understand how poor Lester felt in trying to talk some sense into them. Especially Sonya—she's as stubborn as a damn mule."

With 6:48 left in the fourth quarter and the Lady Bulldogs down 48-43, Madison called on Sonya, who had been on the bench since the four minute mark of the third quarter with four fouls. "Okay, despite your four fouls, we have to get you back in. Barnhardt is killing us inside, and both your sisters have four fouls in trying to stop her. We'll go to a 2-3 zone so we have some help on her, but you guys can't foul. Barnhardt has three fouls herself, so Sonya, take it to the hoop and force her to defend you. But if they double you when you get it on the low post, look for Sammi and Clare on the perimeter."

And double team her they did, but Sonya ignored her wide-open sister on the 3-point line and fouled out on a charge as she recklessly tried to split two defenders. Sandra picked up her fifth soon after, fouling Bailey Barnhardt as she drove around her for a layup. Sammi and Clare did their best to whittle away at the nine point deficit in the final minutes, but the home crowd erupted in raucous celebration when the horn sounded and the Lady Red Raiders had handed the Pacer Coulee girls their first loss of the season by an eleven point margin.

HOLE IN THE WALL GANG DISCUSSES PLAYOFFS AND TOURNAMENTS

"How great is it to be back in the playoffs again?" inquired Butch Cassidy, grabbing one of Jeannie's freshly baked raspberry filled donuts that were rapidly disappearing from the plate of goodies being passed around the Hole in the Wall gang's table.

"How long has it been?" asked Duke. "Seems like about forever... maybe even longer than that."

"Damn near forever, for sure," replied Arthur Fenner. "'Twas '85, it was. We went on the road to Ennis for the first game and got our ass kicked 52-20. Remember the Willett brothers? One helluva Q.B. and receiver combo that went on to star at Tech."

In addition to the donuts, the second item that was passed around was the playoff bracket. "Well, at least we ain't on the same side of the bracket as St. Francis and wouldn't meet up with them until championship game," Bones Bolstad commented as he devoured the last of his usual helping of three donuts. "It's tough sledding in these playoffs when you go in as the third seed in your division. You don't get any home games and are on the road the whole way through unless a fourth seed pulls off an upset.

"First stop is Charlo, and then on to powerful Scobey for the quarterfinals, as I'm guessing they'll make quick work of their opener against Centerville," Arthur reasoned. Before anyone could respond, Harlan interjected, "You know Bones, if I sniff one of them there maple bars I gain ten pounds. If I eat the sum-bitch I gain twenty. It just pisses me off to sit here and watch you and your scrawny ass snarf three of those every damn morning and never gain an ounce. It just ain't right."

"Pretty damn good hike to Charlo," observed Butch, ignoring Harlan's complaints. "How far would that be?"

"Got it all right here," confirmed Arthur Fenner, always the historian of all matters concerning playoff travel. "Three hundred and thirty miles from here to Charlo, but we're only number four when it comes to the furthest distance traveled in the first round. Let's see, I have it all written down here somewhere... here it is. Farthest is 430 miles—Terry to Sunburst. Then Centerville to Scobey, which is 372; long way to go to get thumped. Third place belongs to the Belt to Wibaux trek at 357."

"Goddamn, Arthur," said Harlan Horrall, "you are a walking encyclopedia when it comes to this kind of shit. I suppose you already know how far it is to Scobey?"

Before Arthur could answer, Frank Cervenka butted in. "Jesus, didn't any o' you guys watch the St. Francis game last Friday night? I wouldn't be counting on this team to get out of Charlo with a win after that pounding."

"Goddamn it Frank, give the team some credit. We're missing Stefan and Tuf for most of the game, and it's a two-possession game with eight minutes left in the fourth. Everybody but you knows the game was a helluva lot closer than the score indicated. And I'm going to fricking shoot myself if you won the damn pool again this week."

"Then I'm thinking Kip better get out the 357 again," Wilbur Rimby surmised.

"Yup, I was just getting to that, Harlan," said Butch. "With picking Wyngate to upset our girls, and of course going with St. Francis, Frank won the pot... again."

"Jesus," moaned Harlan, the banter not quite as friendly this time around. "I hope you fall into your pile of money and frickin' suffocate."

WINSTON APPROACHES LUKE

Luke inwardly groaned when he saw Winston Blackburn exit his pickup and start ambling towards him after the Bulldogs had just finished the Monday afternoon practice in preparation for the opening round of the playoffs against Charlo. While Winston and his '81 red GMC pickup had been a frequent decoration of the northwest corner of the practice field for the entire season, this was the first time he had ever left the confines of his cab and approached Luke.

Luke had actually been expecting a visit from Pacer Coulee's only true British resident ever since he and son Alden had come to their secret agreement to let the frail kicker practice with the team, but not kick in a game. Although Alden had never said anything to him, Luke suspected that Winston was constantly badgering his son as to why he hadn't kicked since the third game of the season against Hodgeman.

"Hi there Winston," said Luke, reaching down deep to drag up even a moderately friendly greeting tone.

"Uh.. uh, hi there coach," stammered the tall and spindly fertilizer salesman. "So, you and the lads are off to Charlo, I understand?"

"Yes, heading for Charlo Friday morning. It'll be quite the bus trip for the kids."

"I see, I see," said Winston while gazing off into the sky as though searching for a yet to be discovered solar system. After what seemed to Luke as an uncomfortable period of silence, Winston finally got to the point of his visit.

"Uh, coach Carter... uh, I was wondering... especially after watching that soccer style kicker from St. Francis kick that ball into the goal... er, I guess you Yanks call them goal posts... yes, quite right, knock the ball into the goal posts, I was wondering if you might give my lad another shot at kicking, uh, whatchamacallit-uh, extra points and field goals?"

Before Luke could respond, Winston quickly continued in a more confident and flowing converse, as if he had regained his footing after a slippery start. "Reminds me of a story of my own youth, it does indeed. When I was a lad and on the Futbol team back in Cheshunt, England—11th grader I believe I was—we were playing our tournaments to determine the north London region champions. It was our World Cup, if you will. Anyway, we had a splendid team, but I wasn't seeing much field time until several of the blokes came down with a bloody nasty bout of bronchitis and couldn't play. Well, I finally got the chance to showcase my skills. Now I won't pretend that I scored any game winning goals or any such thing of the sort, but if I don't say so myself I shadowed the Hillingdon club's fine striker Lyman Lancaster, III for the entire match and pretty much single handedly limited the chap to only three goals and we Cheshunt lads advanced to the next match."

"That's amazing, Winston," replied Luke when Winston came up for a breath of air. "Good for you."

"Yes, well, thank you. But what I'm getting at, coach Carter, is that perhaps a similar opportunity could present for Alden in these playoffs. I know that he narrowly missed the one and only kick you let him attempt way back in the Hodgeman match, but I think it's high time you gave him another chance. I must say, your boys only seem to make about half of those, whatchamacallit—two pointer tries. So what do you say, coach? Might'nt you give him another go?"

"Winston, I'm going to be very upfront and forthright with you. Your son Alden is a really good young man. I like him a lot, as does everyone on the team. But Winston, he's been practicing hard every night for the entire season, and he's yet to make a kick from even the extra point distance, let alone an actual field goal. And the extra point attempt in the Hodgeman game was hardly a narrow miss, Winston. His kick hit Tank in the ass. Now, we actually have a season-to-date 2-point attempt conversion rate of 63%, so if you do the math it means we're scoring above the one point we would be getting even if we made 100% of our extra point kicking attempts."

Seeing Winston's hang-dog look at having to hear the reality of his son's kicking situation, Luke kindly put a hand on his shoulder and starting walking him back to his pickup. "Again Winston, Alden's a great kid, but he's simply not ready yet to contribute to the team as a kicker. Let's just encourage him to keep working at it, and if the day comes that it all clicks for him and circumstances change, I guarantee you he will get his chance. But until then, let's just let him enjoy being on the team and hanging out with the guys. Trust me, he gets it; he understands that his kicking is not yet at the level to help his team."

Winston's expression as he climbed into his cab clearly spelled his continued denial as to his son's true kicking capabilities, and Luke could only hope that Alden wasn't getting a steady dose of his father's late season Cheshunt defensive exploits every evening at the evening supper table.

TANK STOPS BO IN HIS TRACKS

"So Skin, what's it like living over at Miz C's?" Bo asked Elvis as the team was dressing into their street clothes after Wednesday's practice for the opening playoff game against Charlo. Before giving Elvis a chance to answer, he added, "Sorry ya gotta live with Tank. Man, that's gotta be tough. And even though that house of Miz C's has more stalls than a Hutterite dairy barn, I hear she stuck you and that big bastard in the same room. What's up with that? I'm telling you Skin, I wouldn't put up with that shit. I'd go on strike until I got my own room—or stall, as it were."

Everyone, including Tank and Elvis, laughed as Bo launched into one of his typical locker room soliloquies. "If'n I was you, Skin, I'd demand my own stall, I damn sure would. I mean, can you imagine being in the same room as Tank after he's devoured, like, two extra large, extra cheese 'Moos and Oinks' pizzas from the Calfe'? Good thing the Germans didn't have Tank at their disposal in World War two, or they would have gassed all of Europe with an army of one!

"And speaking of the Coffman residence," Bo continued, "how the hell does anybody get any sleep over there?"

"Why would they have problems getting to sleep?" inquired an innocent looking Ernie Rimby. "Ya mean 'cause of Tank's gas?"

"Jesus Ernie, you are such a derelict," replied Bo. "Do I have to spell everything out to you? Here's the deal at the Coffman household: one of the inhabitants has a bit of a problem because she makes a lot of noise all night long. Is the bulb starting to come on, Ernie, as to what the source of that noise would be?"

Several of the guys were starting to grin as they realized where Bo was heading, but Ernie, Earl and Brundage Spragg just stared at Bo with vacant eyes. "Fuck me running. Okay, little darlings, let Uncle Bo explain a couple of the facts of life to you dipshits. The reason nobody can sleep at night over there is because Clare lives there… is the bell ringing for any of you little honeys yet?"

"I still don't get it," said Ernie, as Earl and Brundage shook their heads in agreed puzzlement.

"Oh, for fucks sake. Let me spell it out for you," stated an exasperated Bo. "Clare's last name is Comes at Night… get it? Reason nobody can sleep over there is because she's loudly moaning when she's in the throes of all those orgasms she has all night long!"

Everyone's laughter was abruptly interrupted when Tank shot across the room and grabbed Bo by the throat, slamming him into the lockers. Gasping for air, Bo cried out. "What the fuck, Tank? What'd you do that for?"

"Don't you ever talk about Clare like that. Won't stand for it—won't tolerate it. You got that?"

"Got it. Fuck, let go of me, Tank. You're choking me, man!"

Tank momentarily released him before slamming him back into the lockers, and then stormed out of the locker room.

"Jesus Christ, what the fuck did I say to piss him off like that?" asked Bo, rubbing his throat as if to make sure it was still there.

"For a guy whom I consider to be fairly smart, you sure as hell can be a dumb shit," observed Aaron. "Everybody in the school knows there's something going on between Tank and Clare, but apparently you didn't get the memo."

"Yeah, no shit. Guess I didn't. Hey, could you guys help me to locate my Adam's Apple and and pop it back into place?"

THURSDAY NIGHT—DISTRICTS

"Can we swing by Dairy Queen for cones and shakes for the road?" Rose asked Luke as he swung out of the Fergus High Fieldhouse parking lot.

"What do you think, Abby?" Luke posed to Abby Herman, the other fifth grade passenger he was ferrying from the District 7C Tournament opening night.

"Well Mr. Carter, we did beat the stuffing out of Hodgeman, didn't we? I mean, that's cause to celebrate with a chocolate shake if you ask me."

"You got it, ladies. Onward to Dairy Queen it is."

Since it was a school night and the Lady Bulldogs had played the late game, Luke had offered to take Rose and her sidekick Abby home from the game. After securing the shakes and Blizzards from the D.Q. drive up window and beginning the twenty mile jaunt back to Pacer Coulee, Abby suddenly blurted out, "Mr. Carter, everybody in school and around town sure are glad that you and Ms. Danielsen are going out again."

"Abby!" cried Rose, slapping her arm hard enough to elicit an 'ouch' retort. "I told you not to talk about that around mom and Mr. Carter."

"Well, it's true. My mom and her friends talk about it all the time. Dad even said the old guys were talking about it down at the elevator, Osbournson's Implement, and Zenizek's Repair Shop. I mean, everybody knows, right?"

"It's okay, Abby," chuckled Luke, shaking his head in wonderment as to how, with all the important happenings going on elsewhere in the world, the status of the Luke/Madison saga could be possibly be the top item of discussion about school and town. Although he tried to steer the conversation in a different direction, it kept coming back to matters of romance. Thankfully for Luke, the talk centered on the high school age group. He again shook his head in amazement that a pair of 11-year-olds were privy to such information.

In addition to learning that the kids at school were perplexed as to why the once budding Elvis/Sonya relationship had suddenly cooled, he was informed that Aaron and Stefan had ended their relationships with their former long distance girlfriends and were now 'going out' with Bev Rood and Billi Jewel, although he never could quite figure out who was with whom.

After dropping off Abby and getting Rose into bed, Luke waited for Madison while watching TV in her far more decorated and comfortable living room. He laughed out loud as he remembered Madison's comment one night a few days after their reconciliation. "I don't mean to hurt your feelings Luke, but if we ever moved in together, which we could never do as long as we are in small town like this, but if we did I'm sorry to say that I'm not a real fan of your interior decorating skills. Not saying I don't like sparsely furbished rooms, but a card table and two folding chairs for a kitchen? Really? And a recliner that even Tank couldn't muscle into recline mode and a TV the size of a dollar bill in the living room? Sorry, just can't do 'er."

"Nice win honey," he said as he kissed her when she walked in.

"Well, I would hope that we could win handily over Hodgeman. But I'm telling you, if I can't get Sonya and the twins out of this pouty little funk they are in, we'll lose to Wyngate in the championship game on Saturday."

"Yeah, even as a spectator, albeit knowing there has been some trouble brewing, you could notice some tension there. And is it just me, or do the twins have some heartburn with both Sonya and Sammi?"

"Oh yeah, big time. They hate it that they are stuck in the middle of the more heralded older and younger sisters. I thought I had a handle on it, and I think I did for most of the season, but now I can see why Lester is gray beyond his years."

"I'm sure you'll figure it out. You look tired… I'll go home so you can hit the hay."

"What time does your bus leave for Charlo tomorrow?"

"Ten a.m. Lester has us booked to stay at the Campus Inn in Missoula, and I guess we'll get to practice at, what is it called? You know, the Catholic school that's in Missoula?"

"Loyola. Missoula Loyola."

"Yes, that's it. We'll practice on their field at 4:00, and head for Charlo the next morning. I guess it's about an hour from Missoula."

"We'll be at the sendoff tomorrow morning. The girls are pissed that you guys get Shanty for your bus driver, but I keep reminding them our trip to Centertown is 20 minutes while yours is six hours."

"But the girls have a legitimate argument, Madison. Twenty minutes with Howard the 'Ever Cheerful' janitor will seem like six hours."

"Good point… no, excellent point."

CHARLO/BREWSTER SISTERS

"Hi Rose," said Luke when his sad young neighbor answered the phone. After chatting for a few minutes and getting the 11-year-old's disappointed perspective about the District Championship loss to Wyngate that would force a Monday night challenge game with Range View, an obviously upset Madison got on the line.

"Congratulations on your big win, Luke! Where are you calling from?"

"Thanks. We're at the 4-Bs in Great Falls. Since it'll take a while to feed this group, I found a pay phone in the entrance."

"Tell me about your game. Butch called the bar and gave quarterly score updates. So 44-20? Wow, the boys must have played well."

"Yeah, they did. But frankly, our suspicions that the teams in the west were a little weak was true. I don't think Charlo would have finished any higher than fifth in our conference. Anyway, it was nice to be able to hold out both Stefan and Tuf so that they could be ready for next week up in Scobey. They had no answer for Tank, of course, and Aaron and little Ernie stepped up in the running game. Elvis was great too; heck, all the kids played well. I'm so sorry about your game. Want to talk about it? If not, we can wait until tomorrow."

"I think that would be best. I've delayed my meeting with the selfish brats, and I'm excluding Sammi from that description, until tomorrow morning at 10:00 for a reason. If I saw the older three right now, I'd strangle each and every one of them to within an inch of their lives."

MADISON LAYS DOWN THE LAW ON THE BREWSTER SISTERS

"Sit down," ordered Madison when the four Brewster sisters entered her living room to begin the meeting that she had tersely scheduled the night before. "Since we're not gathering here this morning for tea and crumpets, let's get right to it. When I first came to Pacer Coulee to interview for this job, do you know that I was told from the get-go that although you Brewster sisters were talented, you were also spoiled, selfish and downright uncoachable? Until about a week ago, I thought those characterizations of you girls were unfair and overblown. Oh, I saw plenty of evidence of the usual sisterly tensions and bickering that I've seen with other sibling combinations I have either played with or coached, but it was nothing so serious that it affected your ability to play together as a team when you were on floor. But boy, oh boy did that ever change last weekend."

Madison had directed the older three sisters to sit on the couch and had scooted a chair up adjacent to them for Sammi. As the tempo of her tone quickened, the obviously aggravated coach continued to deliver her message in a biting and hardened tone that the girls had never before witnessed from their usually calm and collected mentor. "Let me first say that when you add in Clare with you four, this is the most talented first five member team I have ever been around, either as a player or a coach. Note that I said the most talented and not the best—certainly not the best. The best teams I've been around were mature enough to put their petty jealousies and grudges aside when they hit the court. The best teams always find a way to put the team first. The best teams are able to overcome obstacles like deficiencies in talent by making up for it in heart, effort and a 'whatever it takes to help the team win' attitude.

"How sad it was to learn last weekend," bit Madison, her back and forth pacing in front of the girls hastening, "that not a single such trait was on display in arguably our biggest game to date in the season finale against Wyngate. Nope, not a glimpse of even one sign of what the best teams do to win. Instead, I saw a whole bunch of behavior that I don't even know if I have sufficient descriptive adjectives to describe, but how about if I throw out shallow, selfish, trifling, childish, disrespectful and contemptible for starters?

"And how foolish of me to think that the talk the four of us had after that disappointing performance over at Wyngate was going to erase such a sturdy stand of selfishness. What a fool I turned out to be. Little did I know that you were saving the height of your despicable and self-serving behavior for the District Tournament Title game!"

Then invading her space by taking the few steps to be standing directly above the oldest Brewster, Madison launched into Sonya. "Let's do a quick review of your situation, Sonya. You're a senior: last shot at the high school experience. Didn't make it out of districts your freshman and sophomore years. Beat like a drum by Range View, Marshall and Wyngate both years. Had a strong team last year, with most folks expecting a trip to State, but lost to Wyngate in the District final. Made it to Divisional but went two games and out. So at last, this should be your year.

"You're being recruited by Frontier schools. You've been blessed in this your senior year with the addition of two really good players in Sammi and Clare. Finally, you and your sisters have the last pieces of the 'how to beat Wyngate and get to State' puzzle. But no, you have instead chosen to let your true arrogant and self-serving colors shine through. God forbid that anyone else on the team, especially your sisters, have some success. If Sonya can't be the star, and I mean the only star, then Sonya is more than willing to let her team, school and community down by not doing what needs to be done to have a chance to beat the Wyngates, Chesters and Big Sandys of the world.

"And dry those tears up," Madison barked when the red-faced elder Brewster starting sniveling. "If there was ever a time to bawl in shame, then after the Wyngate games the last two Saturday nights was the time to do it.

"And you two aren't far behind your big sister in the petty and childish behavior department either," snapped Madison as she moved down the couch to stand in front of the twins. "Here's a news flash for you two; you're not nearly as talented as your older and younger sisters. Sorry, but them are the cold, hard facts. Does that mean you're not important contributors to this team? Of course it doesn't. You two have good size, are fundamentally sound and are a vitally important cog to the success of this team.

"I have been trying to hammer home the point all season the importance of everyone on the team having a role. I thought you two did a good job in understanding and fulfilling that role until two weeks ago. I'm not sure when you actually decided to go rogue and quit running the plays I called, or when your vision went so bad that you couldn't see when your sisters were open."

Still staying in front of the older sisters on the couch, Madison directed her next comments to Sammi. "I've got sisters of my own and have been around the block enough with this sibling thing as a player and a coach to know that you aren't totally innocent in this whole mess. I don't have any idea what happens within the confines of the Brewster household, but I do see what happens in practice and games. Unlike your older three sisters these past few weeks, what I do see from you is that you seem to manage to put any extraneous sisterly B.S. to the wayside when you take the court. Not once have I seen you not get the ball to an open sister; not once have I seen a sliver of an indication that you're not playing to the best interests of this team. I'm gosh darn proud of that. Even though you're the youngest by two years, you display the highest level of Brewster sister maturity by a wide margin.

"Now look at me, every one of you," Madison demanded to the now four sniffling girls. "Here's how this is going to go; I'll be damned if I'm going to put you four on the court for our Challenge game against Range View tomorrow night if you aren't willing to put any and all of this petty nonsense aside. I demand that the five girls I put out there to start the game be committed to putting the success of the team first. Read my lips: I will not tolerate anything less. Now, can I count on each and every one of you tomorrow night?"

"Yes!" they all confirmed in unison.

"Just so you understand: Sonya? Sandra? Sabrina? Make no mistake about it, because the first sign I see of even the most remote inkling of the crap I've witnessed the past two Saturdays, your selfish asses will be planted on the bench so fast your heads will spin. I mean it. I'd much rather lose to Range View with Dee, Betty Ann and Bev playing their hearts out to the very best of their limited abilities than to lose by watching you three throw away the best chance Pacer Coulee has ever had to advance to Divisional and on to State. So one final time, do we all understand each other?"

"We understand, coach. We won't let you down," answered Sonya as the other three nodded their heads affirmatively.

"Good. Practice is at 4:00, and don't forget to bring the all new you along with."

LESTER QUIZZES MADISON

"What the hell did you say to them, Madison? What the hell did you do to turn my girls around like that?" Lester shouted into Madison's ear while giving her an uncharacteristic bear hug after the Lady Bulldog's resounding 71-53 victory in the Monday night Challenge game against Range View. Madison couldn't have been happier with Sonya, Sandra and Sabrina's response to their Come-to-Jesus meeting the day before. Sonya and Sammi had played the inside out game to perfection and led the team with 24 and 23 points, respectively. The twins played with renewed energy and effort as well, rebounding well and playing solid defense while chipping in another 16 points between them.

"I just made a couple of suggestions, but they did the hard work and made it happen on their own. You should be very proud of them!"

"I'm proud of all of you! You keep playing like that and we'll make State."

"We'll have our work cut out for us to get out of Divisional having to negotiate through the likes of Chester and Big Sandy, not to mention Wyngate, who just got through beating us two weekends in a row. But if your girls play together like they did tonight, I like our chances," confirmed Madison.

Since the Challenge game had been on a school night, Luke had again brought Rose and Abby home from the game. Madison walked through the door just as the sports reporter on the 10:00 KFBB news program out of Great Falls was showing footage of the game. He went on to mention that Philipsburg had turned back Twin Bridges in their Western Division challenge to move on to the State Tournament.

"Not sure what magic wand you used on the Brewster girls,

but good Lord, whatever it was sure worked!" said Luke as he rose from the couch to greet her and give her a hug and a kiss.

"Well, I looked at it as a sort of life or death situation. To have this kind of talent and not even get out of Districts was simply not an option. If we had lost tonight, Edna would have tied me to the back end of one of the Central Montana Rail's locomotives and told the Engineer to not stop until he hit Chicago."

"Ha, you're probably right about that. So what did you say to the girls at yesterday's meeting to produce that kind of turn-around?"

"Let's just say that your girlfriend was like Billy Graham at one of his Revivals... I made them see the light."

SCOBEY QUARTERFINALS

"With the girls having a week break this weekend between Districts and Divisional, the whole damn town will be heading to Scobey for the quarterfinals!" Edna exclaimed to Luke, Madison and Lester. "With the feedback I've been getting from around town, I'm going to make some calls to Billings and Great Falls this morning and see what we'd be looking at cost-wise to charter a booster bus. And I'm also inspecting our transportation budget to see if we could swipe some funds to put towards chartering a nice big roomy bus to haul the team to Scobey as well. It's a long haul for the kids if we stuff them in Ol' Yeller. And I'm sure I can scrounge up the additional funding we need from the local businesses. I know Bill Koch would be more than willing, as usual, to give us a hand."

Luke just couldn't get over the amazing support and generosity that the little community had towards the school and its sporting activities. To think that enough people from a town of some 300 inhabitants could fill a booster bus to travel well over 300 miles to a football game was beyond him. But after watching the tape of Scobey's first round playoff 48-14 rout of a good Centerville team, Luke would take all the cheering Pacer Coulee fans that could be mustered up.

"Whatever bus we take, I've got the team booked at the Cottonwood Inn in Glasgow on Friday night," Lester explained. "It's a large motel and they'd probably be able to handle the booster bus as well, so let me know as soon as you can whether the boosters are a go. I can get that booked as soon as we get a head count."

As it turned out, Bill Koch and the rest of the local businesses funded the far more roomy and comfortable charter bus for the team, and the Hole in the Wall gang took over the details of putting the booster bus together. The Cottonwood Inn was more than efficient and gracious in accommodating the hundred-plus guests from the center of the state, and the bar and restaurant that was located within the heart of the motel benefited greatly from the enthusiastically hungry and thirsty crowd of Bulldog supporters.

As Luke, T.O. and the team were eating dinner in one of the motel's semi-private meeting rooms adjacent to the lounge, they all laughed uproariously upon hearing the deep and booming voice of Harlan Horrall jokingly quizzing Madison as to when she was going to dump Luke in favor of him. When the laughter quieted down, Bo got it started again when he jumped in with his most southern Texas drawl, "Well coach Carter, we'uns here at this here table shur are happier than a gol-dang 'ol pig in slop that you and that thar lady friend of yurs is gettin' all snuggly and smoochy again."

Luke could feel his face getting even redder when a dead serious Earl Wonderwald added, "We think you and Miz Danielsen are a perfect match, coach. We're plum happy that you're back together again."

The Scobey Spartans were the second ranked 8-man team in the state for a reason. T.O.'s explanation at Luke's initial interview that the eastern plains "grow 'em big out there" was an accurate one. Although they didn't have any players approaching the size of Tank, they were nonetheless huge across the front. Jed Rooz was a locomotive thick 285-pounder who, when paired with fellow 265-pound Peter Lee, made for a nearly unmovable force on either side of the line. Add in 220-pound battering ram fullback Levi Bowman and one could see why the Spartans had cruised through their conference schedule with nary a blip.

Aaron again won the coin toss and after a good return to the 27 by Stefan, the Bulldogs started their drive on the chilly, but snow-less November 3rd afternoon. Famous for its strong breezes that whip across the eastern plains, the winds were unusually subdued. Luke looked to the sky to give thanks to the calm conditions, as his only hope to beat the plow horse sized team was to throw the ball down field or otherwise get the ball to the perimeter where they could advantage the edge they held in team speed. Defensively, Luke and T.O. tightened up the interior, moving Tank to directly over center and placing Dolph and Tucker on the outside shade of the guards. They brought down the linebackers as well and hoped the stacking of the box could slow down their highly effective inside running game.

With a good mix of outside option and the pass, the Bulldogs advanced to the Spartan 14-yard line before giving the ball back on downs. A methodical drive highlighted by a heavy dose of Levi Bowman, this time on outside power plays designed to get the action further away from Tank, resulted in a touchdown and 2-point conversion to give Scobey the early lead. Elvis hit Kimball for pay dirt on a deep post as the quarter ended, and Pacer Coulee tied the game on Stefan's extra point run. Neither team could mount a scoring drive in the second quarter until the Spartans hit on a rare play-action pass to score just before halftime.

The slug fest continued in the third quarter with both teams moving the ball between the 20s, but neither was able to finish off a drive with a score. When the third quarter came to a close, the Spartans held the same 14-8 advantage that they enjoyed at halftime. With the veteran Spartan coach Bucky Harrison spreading his defense out to counteract the outside option and passing game, Luke started the fourth quarter by pounding Aaron on inside dives directly over the blocks of Tank and Dolph. Although the yards didn't come easily or in bunches, Aaron was able to pick up three consecutive first downs on the inside runs, causing the Scobey radio announcer to repeat several times, "That Aaron Coslet is a hard runner. He keeps those legs a pumpin' and he's tough to bring down." In order to shut down the newly found inside running game, Scobey was forced to add troops to the interior of the line. Luke took immediate advantage by calling a play-fake to another Aaron inside run, and Elvis hit a streaking Kimball Robbins on a go route for a score. The successful extra point attempt gave Pacer Coulee their first lead of the game at 16-14.

But the Spartans came roaring back, scoring after a time consuming drive to retake the lead, but Tank stuffed Bowman short of the goal line on the extra point attempt to keep the Bulldog deficit at 20-16.

"We've got 1:12 and two timeouts left, so no need to panic here boys," Luke calmly stated to his team as they gathered before receiving the kickoff. "I know we haven't done a lot of this Elvis, but when you see them spread it out to defend the pass and outside game, use either 12 or 22 to audible to Stefan on a draw. Otherwise, just go with the play I call in. Again, plenty of time, so everyone take a deep breath, clear your head and let's go get us a quarterfinal win."

Six seconds remained on the clock after Elvis threw an on-the-money 22-yard bullet to Bret Cassidy as he was making a precise out route cut at the 4-yard line, and the junior receiver secured it with his hands as he dragged a toe just inside the sideline marker stripe. With the clock stopped and one timeout remaining, Luke sent in his play call and a reminder to his captains to call an immediate timeout if the play was unsuccessful in the event there was still time remaining on the clock. The Pacer Coulee sideline and fans erupted in joy when Stefan made the final timeout and the second play call moot, taking a well-timed Elvis option pitch to the end zone as time expired, boosting the Bulldogs to a 22-20 last play win.

The seven hour chartered bus trip for the celebrating team and boosters seemed shorter than the 20 minute drive from Pacer Coulee to Centertown. When both busses stopped to eat in Glasgow, Madison, Lester, Edna and Bill Koch couldn't wait to tell Luke the highlight story of the booster bus as it was pulling out of Scobey. It happened that when the cheerful boosters had asked the bus driver to stop at the Town Pump on the edge of town to load up on snacks and refreshments, the only person that hadn't returned from the store was the Methodist Minister Samual Smythe. About the time they were going to send someone to look for him, he hollered to the bus that he needed Harlan Horrall to come help him. The already-in-good-spirits crowd aboard the bus cheered even louder when Harlan started hauling out the four cases of Budweiser that the tee-totaler Minister and Ethyl Grove had purchased for the 65 fellow occupants of the booster bus. It was a long but victorious ride back to the welcoming arms of Pacer Coulee.

SEMIFINAL WEEK SETBACK

Edna was so confident that her beloved Bulldog football and girls' basketball teams would be playing for State Championships on the Saturday following the upcoming weekend of the football semifinal and girls' Northern Divisional game that she had directed Bill to have his usually scheduled third Thursday of the month board meeting a week or so early.

"You need to do a little planning, Bill," she had informed him the week prior. "I'm telling you right now, you'll be here all by your lonesome if you hold the board meeting on the usual date. Shanty will be driving the bus that takes the girls to Billings for the first game of the State Tournament. I will be in Billings for the tournament, as will the rest of the town. The boys will be getting ready to play in the State Championship. So unless you want to be sitting in that old board room smoking and talking to yourself, you should either just cancel this month's meeting or schedule it for Monday the fifth. That's the Monday before the football semifinals and Divisional for the girls."

Bill relented and penciled in a reminder to have Bonnie call Shanty with the change of schedule. He wished he shared Edna's optimism that in two weeks both teams would be playing for State Titles, but Bill's nature was to take more of a 'don't count your chickens before they hatch' approach.

"Well where is the ornery old Irish coot?" asked Edna, as she, Otis and Bill took their usual positions around the ancient oak table in the bank board room. "I've got ten past nine on my watch. Are you sure you notified him of the meeting date change?"

"Yeah, I checked a minute ago with Bonnie, and she said she had called him on Friday and he confirmed that he'd be able to make it. I can't remember a time that he's missed a meeting or even been late. It's usually you that charges in here ten or 15 minutes late."

"Oh hush up. Well, I'm gonna go roust the old geezer. I've got a ton of School Board Chairman duties to get to with all the hoopla of the football and basketball activities going on this week, so I don't have the time to be waiting around all day for that damn old Irishman to show up. Okay if Otis stays here while I go get Shanty?"

"Yep, me and Otis will go over the monthly overdrafts and the past due loans list while you're gone," deadpanned Bill.

Ten minutes later Edna barged into the boardroom. With reddened eyes and tears streaming down her cheeks, she said softly, "Our Shanty is gone, Bill. I found him in his favorite rocker. Dear Lord, our Shanty is gone."

BILL AND EDNA HANDLE SHANTY'S AFFAIRS

There were two firsts that occurred for Bill that fateful morning that the Sweeney family heart curse came for its final visit with Shanty as he was resting in his favorite rocking chair. The first was the appearance of tears in Edna's eyes. The second was that of a distraught Edna striding across the boardroom and into Bill's arms for a long, sobbing embrace. In all the years that Bill had known Edna, from grade school through the current moment, he had never seen her cry. Nor had they ever hugged.

Although Shanty had never talked much about it, both Bill and Edna were well aware of the Sweeney heart curse. They never knew what the exact nature of the genetic defect was, but three of Shanty's brothers and two of his own sons had all died well before their time of heart attacks due to the condition. After the second of the sons had passed several years earlier, leaving only two overseas located children remaining in his family, Shanty had asked Bill to be his Personal Representative and Executor of his estate. Perhaps fortuitously, Shanty had informed him only a scant two weeks prior that he had just updated his Will and instructions and had been emphatic in reminding Bill that those documents were located in his Safety Deposit Box at the bank.

When Bill and Edna finally separated from their sad entwine, Bill quietly asked if Edna had thought to call the local volunteer ambulance service to have them attend to Shanty. "I'm sorry Bill; I was so shook up I didn't think to do anything."

"That's okay. You just sit down here and take a little rest. I'll make that call right now," said Bill. After attending to those details, he turned to Edna and said, "Shanty was just in here a week or so ago. He must have been experiencing some serious heart episodes, as he was very forceful in making sure that I knew he had updated his Will and instructions. I'm thinking the main reason he was so persistent in making sure I was aware of that was because he doesn't have any family in the country to make the necessary arrangements, and he's counting on us to handle such matters for him. Are you up to staying for a bit and reviewing the contents of that Safety Deposit Box with me?" After taking a moment to blow her nose and gather herself, Edna agreed to Bill's request.

"Holy shit," murmured Bill, after he had gone to the bank vault and retrieved the documents from the box. He began by reading out loud the cover page instructions that Shanty had clumsily pecked out on his old Smith Corona typewriter only a few weeks before.

JOSEPH PATRICK SWEENEY INSTRUCTIONS

I want my good and trusted friends Bill Koch and EdnaCoffman to see my wishes followed. I want Bill to handle all my financial affairs which ain't much. I'll just say now Edna that I really don't havemuch dollars as you think I do. The railroad pension not much at all. I do have a couple of Certificuts in the bank worth about$18,000 saved upand Bill will see from the Will I want it divvied up 5050 between Tank and Dolph. Bill you decide when how they should get it. My old house ain't worth much, but when you sell it buy new riding lawn mower down at Osbournson Implement for the football andbaseball fields, and divvy whats left 50 50 to St Anthony's and the Bulldog booster club. And I want Bill andEdna to handle all other requests and wishes I have. I only have one son and daughter left Both are missionaries and have lived and done there important work for God in countries across the world and not been back tothe states for years.

Neither have enough money to come back for my funeral so I ask only that you notify them of my demise after I've been done and buried. There last nown address in the Will.

As everybody nose, I'm Catholic and want to have a Catholic Mass funeral at St. Anthony's CatholicChurch here in Pacer Coulee Father Coughlin presiding. I want both Bill andEdna to say a few words after Father Coughlin gets down with his sermon. Edna don't say goddamn Catholics right there in church. then I want Bo to tell a Irish joke But not a dirty one. Tell him to use his best Irish brogue. I want my sweet young people friends Rose and Abby to bring up the Eucharistic Offering atMass. I want Emmy Laughlin to sing Danny Boy and When Irish Eyes areSmiling. I want 6 pallbearers. Bill, Edna, Kellie Cassidy, Tank, Dolph and Bo. I want all 97 of the Pacer Coulee school kids as honorary pallbearers. You don't have to list them all by name But make sure my flock of youngins is mentioned asthey are all my special kids and I believe the only reason the goodLord left me here this long is for them forsure.

My ticker been acting up lately so don't no how much time Igot before good Lord calls me home. Bill and Edna make sure the funeral dont be in middle of tournament or playoff game. So as little of distraction for the kids as possible. Ok guess thats about it See ya on the other side. Thanks BillThanks Edna. AS they say in Butte Never could of asked for better friends than the to of youz

Bill didn't get through the first paragraph before he choked up and just handed Edna the page to read for herself. After a second prolonged hug when both had finished reading the instructions, Bill and Edna quietly divided up the duties that needed to be attended to as a result of Shanty's passing. They jointly chose to risk the strike of a lightning bolt for going against one of Shanty's stated directives, but they quickly agreed that St. Anthony's Parish was way too small to accommodate the likely huge crowd of central Montana folks that would come to pay their respects to the treasured Pacer Coulee resident, and scheduled the funeral to be held at the gymnasium at the school. But they did follow the rest of his requests, to include setting the funeral for the coming Thursday at 11:00 a.m., leaving the girls plenty of time to get to Great Falls to play the late 9:00 p.m. game at the opening day of the Divisional Tournament.

"It'll be tough on the girls to climb on that bus and not see Shanty spring into the driver's seat. Dear Lord," sighed Edna, with a fresh tear making its way down her cheek. "You just couldn't wait a few more weeks until tournaments and playoffs were over, could you, you damned stubborn old Irish coot!"

SHANTY'S FUNERAL

"Good grief," muttered Edna to Bill, as she stood in the back corner of the gymnasium with the rest of the pall bearers and two of the staff members of Harrell's Funeral Home. "Here's another thing about the Goddamn Catholics… it takes their priests an hour and a half to say a regular Mass. A Catholic wedding or a funeral? You better plan on a good two hours. I'm glad we Methodists don't have to string everything out and ruin half a day to marry or bury someone."

The line waiting to enter the small gym foyer was a long one, the school parking lot already overflowing to the point that people were having to park a hundred yards away down at the football and baseball fields. The November 15 morning sky was overcast, and although the several inches of snow that had fallen a few days earlier had for the most part melted, the brisk easterly wind made the thirty-five degree air seem much colder. The church altar had been staged on the playing floor at the far end of the gym, and rows of folding chairs that had been set up on either side of the center aisle filled out the rest of the floor space. Along with the regular bleachers, the additional floor chairs created a seating capacity of over a thousand.

As Bill watched the legion of folks stream in, he wasn't surprised at the massive crowd that had gathered. Farmers, ranchers, businesspersons, school bus drivers, school officials and townsfolk in general had made the trek from all of central Montana, near and far. He recognized people from all the towns in Pacer Coulee's conference, as well as many from north central Montana communities that, despite in some cases being as far as one hundred and fifty miles away, were in the Class C Northern Division. It was just the way it was in small town, rural Montana. While certainly enjoying a competitive and hearty sports rivalry with their neighboring communities, there was a powerful bond that held all of central Montana together. And that bond was never more evident than on this day when all had gathered to honor and pay their respects to one of its most beloved characters.

The ushers filled the bleachers first, reserving the chairs on the floor for the Pacer Coulee student body that Shanty considered his immediate family. Lester and the elementary school teachers had made the joint decision that the K-3 kids would be released to their parents for individual family attendance preference. By the time the ushers began the orderly procession of seating grades four to 12, it was standing room only for the final folks who had shivered in the winter-like chill while waiting to enter the gym.

The twenty-seven combined members of the football and girls' basketball teams, all dressed in their blue game jerseys in tribute to their cherished bus driver and friend, were the last to be ushered up the aisle. They were seated in the reserve section nearest the altar, and Bill noticed there didn't appear to be a dry eye among them as they filed by the casket and pall bearers' position at the rear of the gymnasium. He whispered to Edna that they both needed to lighten the mood when they spoke, as the kids were having a difficult enough time without having to endure a couple of sad eulogies. Finally, the pall bearers, with Tank, Dolph and Bo dressed in their jerseys like their fellow teammates, followed the priest as they wheeled the casket to the front of the altar. Then true to Edna's prediction, Father Caughlan began the long and drawn-out traditional funeral Mass, closely adhering to the regimented Catholic protocol. Finally the time came for the sermon, and Edna, who had been grumbling under her breath about the ritual service since it started, leaned over to Bill and whispered that the service was now at the 'halftime' stage.

The lengthy sermon that most would have expected to be focused on Shanty's life was instead a fire and brimstone rant that had nothing to do with Shanty. Rather, the priest seemed to be chastising the weak and godless ways of the multitude of sinners that sat before him. The congregation breathed a collective sigh of relieve when Father Caughlan finally concluded his scolding and turned the podium over to Bill and Edna.

Both of their eulogies concentrated on the good life that Shanty had lived, and the positive impact he had long made on the community and all of central Montana, especially the students of Pacer Coulee. Their messages were upbeat and liberally sprinkled with stories that elicited laughter from everyone in the congregation except Father Caughlan, who sat as if frozen with his stone-faced head tilted back, eyes staring at the ceiling.

When Bill and Edna were finished, a none-too-pleased Father Caughlan stood and announced that one of Shanty's wishes was for Bo Ramsay to share some Irish jokes with the congregation. If it would have been anyone's funeral other than the beloved Joseph Patrick Sweeney's, he would have steadfastly refused to have his service soiled by such nonsense. But under the special circumstance that the request came directly from one of the parish's oldest and most revered disciples, he was forced to pretend he approved of the idea and summoned the lanky teenager to the podium.

"First of all," announced Bo in a clear, strong voice, "Shanty was the best. Like Mr. Koch and Miz Coffman said, he's been like an institution in our town and at our school for a long time. I don't ever remember nobody else driving the bus. As a kid, you just knew that he really cared about each and every one of us. It won't ever be the same around here without him, I can tell you that." Then with his familiar lopsided grin spreading across his face, he added, "And I'll miss him the most 'cause he's the only one that always laughed at my impressions and jokes. Anyways, he would cackle like crazy when I gave him the business in my Irish dialect, so I guess he wanted me to tell a few Irish jokes in his honor. Don't worry mom… I had to dig deep to find 'em, but I came up with a couple of clean ones." Transitioning immediately into his perfect Irish brogue, he began:

"Dermot McCann opened the paper and was dumbfounded to read in the obituaries that he had died. He quickly phoned his best friend O'Reilly and asked, 'Did ye see the paper? They said I died, they did!'

'I saw it,' said O'Reilly. 'So tell me, is it heaven or hell ye are callin' from?'"

Like a seasoned performer, Bo paused long enough for the crowd to react with laughter before continuing.

"Shamus walked into the bar and told the bartender to pour him a stiff one.

'Just had me a wee bit of a fight with the little woman,' he reported.

'Oh bejabbers, how did this one end up?' inquired the bartender.

'She came to me on her hands and knees, she did,' replied Shamus.

'Now that's a switch! What did she say?'

'She said, 'Come out from under the bed, Shamus, you little chicken.'"

Bo had to wait longer this time before moving on to the next joke, as local rancher Loyd Gilchrist was well into one of his famed boisterous fits of belly laughter. His was one of those laughs that was contagious, so it took significantly longer for the entire congregation to quiet enough for Bo to proceed.

"Paddy and Sean was chattin' on the street corner. 'What ye got in that there bag?' asked Paddy.

'Ain't goin to tell ye,' said Sean.

'You got to tell me,' pleaded Paddy.

'Ok then, I got ducks in the bag,' announced Sean.

'If I guess how many ducks are in the bag, will ye give me one then?'

'Okay Paddy, if you can guess the right number I will give you both of them.'

'Five! Ye got five of them!'"

Bo was on a roll, and quickly transitioned into his final joke.

"Kearney and O'Rordan are looking at the models in a mail order catalog, and Kearney says, 'Have ye ever seen such beautiful girls? And inexpensive too! I'm gonna order me one, I am.'

Three weeks later the two run into each other at the pub and O'Rordan asks Kearney, 'Did ye ever receive that beautiful girl you ordered from the catalog?'

'No,' replied Kearney, 'but it shouldn't be long now. She had all her clothes she was wearing in the catalog sent here yesterday.'"

With the laughter and cheers, especially those of Loyd Gilchrist, still reverberating off the gymnasium walls, Bo pointed to the heavens and in his vintage Irish speak hollered out. "Keep that ol' yeller school bus between the ditches Shanty, ye hear me now?"

SEMIFINAL GAME AT CHESTER

As Howard the 'Ever Cheerful' janitor pulled away from the gym side curb and pointed the yellow school bus towards Chester, Bo Ramsay's "Shanty my lad, will ya meet us at O'Malley's Pub on Kilkenny Street for one last pint to properly send ya off on your final journey?" was met with tears instead of the usual laughter that was elicited from a Bo/Shanty exchange. But somehow the Irish Brogue comment from the team impressionist seemed not only comforting, but an appropriate memorial or send-off of their friend into the heavens.

Luke forced himself to the matter at hand, the semifinal contest against the Chester-JI Coyotes. The 125 mile north-of-Pacer Coulee hi-line school came in as the number one seed out of the Northern Division, a ranking position that was not in the least unusual for them in both the near and distant past. The Coyotes were coached by a veteran Head/Assistant coach pair that had been at the school for over a decade. Billy Schapp and Jim Garrity were football teammates at nearby Northern Montana College in Havre at a time when the Lights were truly lighting up the sky with footballs. Upon graduation, Billy and Jim brought the wide open passing game of the Lights back to their Class C hometown of Chester, and were considered the innovators and masters in converting the principles of the Spread Offense from the 11 to the 8-man game.

Both coaches had talented sons on the team. Jeff Garrity was a gifted All-State senior quarterback, and speedy Wilson Schapp was his top receiver. Although the Coyotes didn't have a single player over 170 pounds, what they lacked in size they made up for in overall team speed. After watching several of Chester's games on film, Luke and T.O. were not at all happy in how the teams matched up.

"With our size advantage, I'm not too concerned about us being able to move the ball," Luke had explained to T.O., "but this spread offense is going to be a nightmare to defend. Garrity is extremely mobile and is used to throwing on the run, so getting to him is going to be a problem."

"No shit," confirmed T.O. "And how in the hell are we going to defend all these fleet little scat-backs that they flood the field with? We don't have one safety that can come even close to matching up speed-wise."

After much hair pulling and three pots of coffee, Luke and T.O. finally set their game plan. Not wanting to get in a scoring fest against this explosive and pass-happy team, limiting the Coyotes' time of possession was a major component of their strategy. Utilizing the Bulldog run game to milk the clock with long, time consuming drives would go a long way to minimizing the number of Coyote opportunities on offense.

"How good are you at dialing up a blizzard and a 50 mile an hour wind for about kickoff time?" questioned T.O. "That would damn sure be a major help in slowing that offense down."

As it turned out, Luke managed to call up exactly that. The usual two hour bus trip from Pacer Coulee to Chester took an extra 45 minutes due to blowing and drifting snow. Try as the Chester farmer volunteers did to keep the snow off the field with the tractor blades and snow blowers that they had brought to town, there was a good two inch covering by game time. And while the wind was not blowing at T.O.'s suggested 50 miles per hour, it was a strong and swirling northeasterly blast that made the 19 degree day bitter cold.

"So what would the wind chill temperature be?" Luke asked, assuming his livestock-raising assistant coach had plenty of experience in calculating wind chills in his head.

"Damned if I know. Somewhere between 'just plain fucking cold' and 'downright fucking miserably assed freezing cold' would be my best guess."

T.O. was on quite a roll, cracking Luke up again when the

boys were dressing out in the locker room before the game. Luke had instructed all the players to bring a pair of heavy white or black knee high socks as part of the armor of under/over garments to wear to combat the frigidly cold temperatures that were predicted for the game. When Brundage Spragg appeared in socks sporting a kaleidoscope of wild patterns and color, T.O. had barked out, "What the fuck, Spragg? Do you think we're here to go to one of Jane Fonda's aerobics classes? Are you here to join the other clowns at the fucking circus? You ain't setting foot on the field until you take that shit off!"

"While the spread offense is fun and exciting as hell for the fans to watch, you just saw why a team that can run the ball is going to have the advantage in the playoffs in a state like Montana. We lucked out weather-wise in Charlo and Scobey, 'cause most of the time the weather we just had is what you'll run into here in the north country. Especially when you get to the semis and finals and are midway into November," T.O. explained as Howard the 'Ever Cheerful' janitor was slowly maneuvering through the historic Missouri River town of Fort Benton on the way back to Pacer Coulee. Even when they had the swirling winds mostly at their backs, Chester couldn't get any semblance of their usual dynamic passing game going, and their backs spent a lot of time getting up close and personal with Tank when they were forced to go to their not-so-successful or unfamiliar run game. As a result, their only score of the game came in the second quarter when Tucker Greyson couldn't field the wind-altered path of Tuf's errant punt snap, and the Coyotes recovered the crazily bouncing ball in the end zone for a touchdown. And despite a good number of fumbles and muffed snap exchanges by both teams due to the inclement weather conditions, the Bulldogs were able to convert several long, time consuming drives before hitting the welcomed hot showers of the locker room with a 16-6 semifinal victory under their belts.

Just as Luke was about to shuffle his now frozen body

through the entrance to the welcoming warmth of the locker room, he heard Edna shout out his name. "We've got our rematch with the Goddamn Catholics," she reported. "They just whipped up on Wibaux 56-22." Grabbing Luke with both hands by his shoulders, she looked up at him with a stern and determined look on her face and said, "This is a lifelong dream come true for me—meeting St. Francis in the Title game. I have all the confidence in the world in you, son, to bring us home a State Championship trophy. And to take it from the hands of those arrogant Goddamn Catholics? Doesn't get any better than that!"

"No worries, Luke," Luke muttered to himself as went through the door to join his ice-numbed but celebrating team. "No pressure. No pressure at all. Hell, I break 70-game winning streaks all the time."

PEP RALLY BEFORE STATE TITLE
AND TOURNAMENTS

Luke shook his head in disbelief at the massive crowd that was spilling into the Bulldog gymnasium to attend the Wednesday morning joint pep rally and send-off of the girls and boys to the State Tournament and State Title game, respectively. "Trust me, we'll need to set up the folding chairs and the podium on the court floor for you and your teams, because the bleachers will be full," Lester had explained to Luke and Madison when they had been planning the event on Monday. "And we'll need to hook up the sound system, too."

"Do you really think there will be more townsfolk attending this pep rally than there was for the quarterfinals, semifinals and the Divisional tournament?" questioned Luke.

"Trust me, there will. The whole town and surrounding area will show up en masse. Geez guys, do you think little ol' Pacer Coulee has both their football and basketball teams going to State every year? This is a big deal! Grandmas, grandpas, aunts, uncles, cousins and friends are showing up out of the woodwork. It's gonna be full to the brim on Wednesday, you can count on it."

And full to the brim it was. Luke and Madison's team chairs were more than half empty as the crowd filed in, typical of small towns in that most all of the team members also played in the school band. With Leon Spraggins, the rotund, longtime Pacer Coulee music teacher robustly leading the way on his trumpet, the band belted out a number of tunes that kept the crowd standing and clapping. And the noise level rose to even higher decibels when Edna unleashed Otis Othello Coffman, VII, the most popular Bulldog of all, who raced up the aisle to join the teams with as much vim and vinegar as his seven-year-old arthritic legs would allow. When the band hammered out the school song before the speeches began, both Luke and Madison couldn't help but smile at the sight of their 86-year-old neighbor Ethyl Grove singing her heart out in the front row.

As if they needed an introduction to a most familiar audience, Luke and Madison introduced their entire squads of 17 and ten, respectively. Both coaches kept their speeches brief in thanking and recognizing the magnanimous support that they and their players had received from the townsfolk of Pacer Coulee all year long, as well as extolling the virtues of the work ethic and the team-first attitude of their players. Lester finished the program by reminding the parents and the fans to pick up a flyer as they exited, as they had all the information regarding tickets and team and pep bus schedules for both the football game and the girls' State Tournament.

"Can you believe the crowd that was at the sendoff?" Luke asked Madison after everybody had cleared out and they were on the way back to their classrooms. "I mean, we didn't have a crowd like that for the pep rally when we played for a State Championship when I was in high school at North Platte, nor when I coached at Lincoln High. And those were both huge schools in big towns."

"Yeah, these small towns are amazing," confirmed Madison. "It was pretty much like this when we went to the State Tournament when I played at Whitewater and coached at Fromberg, too. These little towns support their schools like none other, and I've even heard that the cities that bid for the State Tournaments prefer to land the Class B and C schools because they actually draw the better attendance and bring the most bodies to town. And obviously, the hotels and service industries love the business that they bring too."

"I know one thing for sure," said Luke, "we might as well just bag class the rest of the week. The kids are bouncing off the walls, and I'm not much better."

"I hear ya, I hear ya," laughed Madison. "Let the games begin!"

TITLE GAME VS ST.FRANCIS

Mid-November weather in Montana was as skittish and unpredictable as a green colt yet broken. You never knew from one year to the next whether Thanksgiving would dawn as a pleasant, sun-shining day with a temperature of 50, or a cloudy, snowy and breezy ten degrees. The weather Gods leaned more towards the latter on the November 17, 1990 day that the State Class C 8-man football Championship game came once again to Centertown, the widely recognized central-most location in the state. As Howard the 'Ever Cheerful' janitor began the yellow school bus's steep descent from the upper plateau to the floor of Fergus County Stadium, the overcast sky was intermittently spitting snow into a steady 20 mile per hour northwesterly wind, making the stated 19 degree current temperature reading feel much colder. Depending on which weatherman was being consulted, the projected 12:00 game time temperature was expected to be at or about 25 degrees. The four inches of snow that blanketed the field the Wednesday prior had been bladed or snow-blown off by the city's snow removal and street maintenance crews; so the field, albeit somewhat frozen, was expected to be in decent condition by kickoff.

Following the lengthy Montana High School Association State Championship protocol, both teams lined up all their athletes and coaches on their respective 30-yard lines. All 17 players and the two coaches of the visiting Pacer Coulee Bulldog team were introduced first, the process taking much less time than that required to announce the 37 players and five coaches for the home team St. Francis Trojans. Luke took the lengthy period of time it took to introduce the last 20 or so Trojans to review in his mind the two biggest developments that had occurred during the week leading up to the Championship game.

Both major events happened on Sunday; the first being when Kimball had approached Luke at open gym and announced that he was ready to play safety in the Title game. "It's time I step up for the team, coach," Kimball had told Luke. "I'm the only guy that has the speed to come anywhere close to covering Ricky Rae. So coach me up on coverage technique this week, and I'll give it a go." With that good news, Luke and T.O. spent the rest of Sunday making adjustments to their defensive alignment. Beginning on the line, they decided that the best way to utilize Tank was to move Dolph to nose guard and put Tank at the middle linebacker position. That solved the problem from the regular season contest where St. Francis was able to audible at the line in order to run away from Tank's side. The nose guard position lessened the confusion for Dolph, as his only job was to lock up with the center and hold his ground.

The next major change was going from zone coverage to strictly man, matching Kimball up with Rae at the one safety and moving Stefan to the other side to defend Stronge. Although undersized compared to the Pekovic boys, they put Tucker and Bret at tackles in the gap between the guards and ends. Bo and Aaron capped the offensive formation as hybrid defense ends/outside linebackers. After practicing it all week, both Luke and T.O. felt comfortable that the new alignment and the personnel playing it afforded them their best opportunity to control both the running and passing games of the powerhouse Trojans.

Although the steepness of the stadium bowl cut a west or northwesterly wind speed in more than half, it was enough of a factor that Luke opted to take the wind in the first quarter when Aaron won his fourth consecutive playoff coin toss. But going into the wind didn't affect the Trojans, nor did the new Bulldog 51 defensive alignment, as they methodically marched down the field on the first possession and scored on a 14-yard jump ball pass from Bertelson to the 6'7" Scott Stronge in the end zone.

But T.O.'s newly designed field goal defense strategy worked like a charm, as Bo swung behind the hard-charging Tank and timed his leap perfectly to block the extra point attempt.

Despite picking up two first downs on the ensuing drive, the Pacer Coulee drive stalled at midfield. Will Bellini fielded Tucker Greyson's punt at the 11-yard line, and only the punter's last gasp push that caused the returner to step out of bounds at midfield saved a touchdown. And while the Bulldog defense stiffened as Tank got more comfortable from his new linebacker position and started to make plays, St. Francis converted on two 4th downs en route to their second score on a 2-yard Will Bellini plunge. As expected, an irate coach Brunner had made the necessary adjustments to prevent a second Bo Ramsay extra point block, and the Trojans held a 13-0 lead as the first quarter wound down to the end.

"Settle down guys... we can move the ball on these guys, but we have to execute," Luke told his offense before taking the field to receive the kickoff. "They're going to be kicking away from Stefan, so let's go return right and give Kimball a shot at breaking one."

And break it Kimball did. He was able to field the ground ball at the left hash on the 14-yard line, and after taking several strides straight ahead he swung to the right and set up his blocks for a sideline return perfectly. Only the angle taken by the kicker Judiman kept the speedy returner from scoring, as he was able to get Kimball out of bounds at the Trojan 18-yard line. With only eight seconds remaining in the quarter, Luke split Bret out to the wide side of the field and Elvis hit him with a perfect over-the-outside shoulder pass as he crossed the goal line on a fade route. Elvis made it a 13-8 game when he scored the two-point conversion on a quarterback keeper.

Neither team could sustain a drive during the first six minutes of the second quarter, but when St. Francis intercepted a deflected Elvis pass and returned it to the Bulldog 32, they scored on the very next play when Bertelson delivered a just-over-the-reach of Kimball pass to Rae. Pacer Coulee responded with a nice drive and got back on the scoreboard on a pay-back play, as this time it was Kimball who beat the tight coverage of Ricky Rae to make the 26-yard touchdown catch. When Aaron was stopped just short on the 2-point conversion try, the Bulldogs had cut the lead to 20-14 with just 1:06 remaining in the first half.

But Will Bellini was able to break several tackles on the kickoff return, and worked his way to the Bulldog 38 before being brought down. When Bertelson hit Scott Stronge before stepping out of bounds on the 22, the clock was stopped at six seconds. "Goddamn kickers," spat T.O. as Josh Judiman's 39-yard field goal attempt slit the uprights for a 23-14 lead. "They oughta be outlawed in the 8-man game."

"Get some fluids, take your piss break and hustle back," Luke informed his team as they filed into the field locker room for halftime. Meanwhile, Luke and T.O. took their usual moment to huddle and share their thoughts on the half that had just transpired, and to discuss the strategy both offensively and defensively for the second half.

"Despite the touchdown receptions by Stronge and Rae, I think we actually did a pretty good job on them. Do you see any reason to go away from Kimball and Stefan continuing to go straight man on them?" Luke asked his assistant.

"No, hell no. It's our only chance of somewhat containing them," replied T.O. "We can't expect to totally shut those guys down; they're too damn good and Bertelson can really lay it in there. I'm good with doing what we're doing there."

"And I think our 51 defense is working fine," Luke commented. "With Bret and Tucker lining up in the B gaps, they're having a tough time getting off them and out to Tank, and I think he's about to raise even more havoc in the second half as he gets more comfortable in the new position."

"I agree. We had some breakdown by our outside backers that allowed the Bellini boys to get outside a few times, but that was mainly when Tuf and Danny were giving Bo and Aaron a blow. I'll go over it with them before we go back out, plus I won't run Tuf and Danny in there at the same time; we need to have either Aaron or Bo in there at all times."

"Agreed. And we need to get more pressure on Bertelson. What would you think if we blitz more when in obvious passing downs? Either loop to the A gaps with Tank and Dolph or bring one of the outside backers. Whatadya think?" asked Luke.

"I'm with ya. I'll remind the outside backers that the non-blitzer is responsible for any running back screens, draws and pass routes. As long as we don't give up any big plays, I'm feeling really good about limiting their scoring in this second half. What are you thinking as far as offense, Luke?"

"I think we'll be fine if we just execute what we've been doing. Can't turn it over like we did on the interception and give them the short field that resulted in their third touchdown. We'll keep running Stefan and Aaron on the inside stuff, and Elvis is doing a great job on his option reads. And despite how they match up against each other speed-wise, I think Kimball can get open against Rae, so we need to capitalize on that this second half."

"Alright guys, bring it in," Luke barked when the official's knock on the door indicated five minutes remaining until the second half kickoff. "We've got one half left in our season. ONE. FINAL. HALF. Everything we've done since the start of practice in August—all the practices, all the weightlifting, all the film study, all the games, all of the sweat, all of the blood and tears… it all boils down to this ONE. FINAL. HALF. Now is the time; this is the place. Because coach Barker and I believe in you guys, and I mean believe in you right down to our bare souls, and the fact that you guys believe in yourselves and even more in your brothers, here's how this thing is going to go: Unlike our game against these guys a short month ago, we're gonna outplay and outscore them in the second half. We're gonna do it for ourselves and our teammates. We're going to do it for our parents and our families. We're gonna do it for those incredible Pacer Coulee townsfolk out there that have been loyally following and supporting you guys for not only this season, but for your whole life. But here's what's going to be different about this final half: we're gonna finish it this time. We're gonna take down the mighty St. Francis Trojans and their 70-game winning streak right here, right now, right in their own backyard. And we're gonna take 'em down right in front of their mommies, their daddies, and their homely little girlfriends."

Luke held the chomping-at-the-bit boys at bay for the one final remark that sent the team roaring and bellowing out the door, ready to play the half of their lives. "One last thing before we take the field; to paraphrase the sage words of a wise and famous football player you all might happen to know: **LET'S GO KNOCK SOME DICKS IN THE DIRT!**"

Despite a decent return of the second half kickoff and picking up a couple of first downs, the Pacer Coulee drive stalled at the Trojan 33-yard line. But when St. Francis took over on downs, Big Tank stuffed the first three plays of their drive, forcing them to punt on 4th and 6 as coach Brunner screamed, "Goddamnit, would somebody block that big bastard!" Not wanting to give the deep back Stefan the chance to return, the punter rolled out and kicked a low-flying punt that skidded out of bounds on the Bulldog 22-yard line. Luke ran Stefan on a fullback lead power play over Dolph and Tank for seven yards on first down, and Elvis weaved his way for an 8-yard pickup on a speed option keep. A holding call against Dolph backed the Bulldogs up to their own 27, but Kimball got a step on Ricky Rae on a deep post route and Elvis hit him stride for a 53-yard touchdown strike. When Aaron powered into the end zone to add the two-point conversion, the Bulldogs had whittled the Trojan lead down to a single point.

"We got us a frickin' ballgame boys," growled Tank as he came to the sideline.

"Three and out guys, three and out," hollered T.O., looking up at the stadium's brand new digital scoreboard as if to prevent the scorekeepers from adding unearned points to pad the Trojan's 23-22 lead.

Luke could hear coach Brunner screaming at his offense to pull their heads out of their asses and take the ball down field and score. "Fuck you, Brunner," mumbled T.O. to Luke out of the side of his mouth when they clearly heard the enraged coach holler at his team, "No way this Goddamn outfit should still be in the game with us."

The rest of the third quarter was a standoff, with neither team able to venture past midfield. But a Kimball-muffed punt at the start of the fourth quarter was recovered by the Trojans, giving them excellent field position at the Bulldog 21. But Tank was a one-man wrecking crew, stopping Wyatt Bellini for a combined three yards of loss on consecutive inside run plays, and Bo kept contain to force Will Bellini into a pursuing Aaron and Tank for another 5-yard loss, bringing up 4th and 18 from the 29. "Who the hell kicks 46-yard field goals in 8-man football?" cried T.O. when Judiman split the uprights with room to spare to increase the St. Francis lead to 26-22.

The fourth quarter was another slug-fest, as neither team was able to string together more than a couple of first downs. At the 4:48 mark and St. Francis facing a 3rd and 6 from their own 32-yard line, Bertelson was able to toss a jump ball pass to a well-covered but fully extended Scott Stronge for a 16-yard gain. The Bulldogs stiffened and forced another 3rd and 8, but Bertelson again scrambled away from pressure and delivered a perfect sideline pass to Ricky Rae, who had abandoned his route and ran to the boundary upon seeing his quarterback escape from the pocket. The 8-yard gain gave the Trojans a 2nd and 2 on the 12, but on a hunch that Brunner would call another pass play, Luke and T.O. signaled in a call to blitz Aaron off the backside edge. Since the running back on his side had rolled with his quarterback to opposite side with the intention to give help to the monumental task of blocking a hard-charging Tank, the outside linebacker hit an unsuspecting Bertelson as he was attempting to deliver the ball to Scott Stronge at the goal line. Stefan was able to break off coverage and make a shoe top interception of the Aaron-caused errant throw and returned it out to the 23 before being pushed out of bounds by Bertelson and Will Bellini. Despite a momentary delay due to the vehement protest from coach Brunner that the ball had hit the ground before it was gathered in by Stefan, the Bulldogs had a first and 10 from their own 23 with 3:02 remaining in the contest.

"We have a God's plenty of time," Luke said calmly to Elvis, before sending him out on the field with the play. "No reason not to mix some run in with the pass, but when we run you have to get these guys lined up in a hurry. We do have all three of our timeouts left, but we need to use them judiciously. Okay, let's run counter to the short side, and then hustle everybody back and run triple option to the wide side. Then check with me for the next play."

Stefan picked up 3 on the counter, and Aaron 4 on the fullback give. Luke had Elvis run triple option again, this time keeping it himself and squirting forward for just enough yardage to pick up the first down. "Twins left, 56 roll," Luke called to Elvis, indicating the routes the receivers were to run and that the line protection and quarterback were going to roll out to the two receiver side. Kimball got a full step ahead of Rae on his cut, and Elvis threw a bullet to him just before he stepped out of bounds on the 40, stopping the clock at 2:06. Luke went right back to Twins to the wide side and had both receivers run short post routes, thereby taking their man coverage defenders with them and clearing the wide side of the field. Elvis did a nice job of looking off the inside routes and holding the linebackers while Stefan attempted to sell a block on the D end before quickly releasing and catching Elvis's well-timed flare pass. Stefan got to the sideline and was able to advance the ball to the 18 before Will Bellini and Ricky Rae were able to push him out of bounds.

The Trojans then sniffed out the quarterback draw play that Luke had dialed up and stopped it for no gain. Elvis got the team set up quickly for the next play, but Brunner sent Wyatt Bellini on a blitz on the next play and forced Elvis to throw it in the dirt ten yards short of Bret's comeback route. Facing a 3rd and 10 from the 18 with 1:29 remaining, Luke called timeout to give his boys a breather and to compose themselves. "Whatya gonna run?" T.O. asked Luke as he started towards the field.

"We're gonna see if a season's worth of practice has improved Bo's pass catching skills," answered Luke with a wry grin. "We're gonna run the ol' 'Bo Weak Side Guard Drag', that's what we're going to do."

"Fuck me running," replied T.O. with an eye roll. "God help us."

"Okay guys, focus up," said Luke, every anxious eye glued to his face awaiting the 3rd down call. "What do great teams do when its crunch time? They clear their minds—kick anything and everything that isn't a positive thought to the wayside. They zero in on the job at hand, and each and every teammate executes their assignment to perfection. Are you all with me?"

When all eight heads enthusiastically nodded in confirmation, Luke continued. "So here's what we're gonna do. You guys know the 'Bo Weak Side Guard Drag' play that we've been running every night at the end of practice all year, and just waiting for the perfect time to run it in a game? Nobody has ever seen it on film and these guys won't be expecting it. So now is the time; this is place.

"Okay, with a 3rd and 10, I can guarantee you they will blitz Will Bellini from his inside backer spot, so that will vacate the area you will be sliding into, Bo. Quick review: Kimball's split wide right and runs off Rae deep. Bret, you're in the slot and you run a clear out post. Elvis, play fake Stefan to the right and make it look like you're waiting for Bret to clear on the post. Stefan, you gotta be looking for the Bellini blitz and get a good block on him."

"Time's up—let's go," warned the official, but Luke held them back long enough to complete his instructions, "Bo, you gotta show block; make sure you block the D end for a count of two before releasing and running your underneath crossing route. And Bo? Listen to me… you ARE going to CATCH this sum-bitch, and when you do catch it, don't stop running until you hit the goal post."

"How many times out of five does he actually catch the ball in practice?" snarled a doubting coach Barker when Luke got back to the sideline.

"Sometimes once, most times none."

"Great fucking call, coach. And just who was it that accused you of being an offensive guru?"

The 'Bo Weak Side Guard Drag' went off exactly as predicted. Will Bellini did in fact blitz, but Stefan was waiting for him and was able to give Elvis enough time to complete his look off to the post pattern running Bret Cassidy. Bo was patient and held his block for the full two-count, dragging back just five yards across the line of scrimmage to enter the totally unoccupied territory of the middle and opposite side of the field. Luke, T.O. and the players on the sideline all collectively held their breath while the ball seemingly floated in slow motion through the space from the hand of Elvis His Own Horse to the outstretched hands of Bo Ramsay. Luke had worked many a long hour in trying to teach Bo to actually catch the ball in his hands before bringing it into his body, but it was as if the lanky senior couldn't master the timing of bringing his hands together in time to stop the ball from slithering through and bouncing off either his shoulder pads or face mask before falling to the ground.

But this time he did get a hand on the ball, albeit only one. Unable to bring in the second hand to secure the catch, the ball veered off his hand and into his face mask, where it careened into the air high above him. It seemed as though the slow motion button had been pressed, the breathless Bulldog sideline and crowd watching with agonizing helplessness as Bo bounced the ball up and down off his hands and body like a spastic juggler trying to keep three balls in the air. Thankfully there wasn't a Trojan close enough to him to either intercept or knock the ball to the ground, and just when it looked like the bobbling attempt to catch the ball was going to end badly, Bo somehow gathered it in and galloped untouched into the end zone.

"And you of no faith! Shame on you coach Barker," joked Luke as the two hugged in celebration of the lead-grabbing score. When Stefan followed a pulling Tank into the end zone on a sweep, the Pacer Coulee sideline and fans exploded in cheer, realizing that the 8-time defending State Champions couldn't tie or win the game with a field goal. Only a drive within the last 1:12 that culminated in a touchdown would do it for the Trojans.

"These guys have won the last eight of these for a reason," Luke told his team as they huddled before kicking it back to St. Francis. "There'll be no quit in that team, so we have to buckle down and defend like hell. Tucker, keep the kick on the ground. We don't need the Bellini boys or Rae getting a big return. We'll run our normal 5-1 unless they get past midfield, then be ready to go to our 2-3-3 zone when down, distance and clock favor it. Once we're in that zone, keep everything in front of you, and rally like hell to the ball. They only have one timeout left, so that's to our advantage. Alright Bulldogs, let's go win us a State Championship!"

Tucker picked a bad time to get a weak foot on the ball, and up-back Wyatt Bellini was able to field the resulting one hop looper in full stride and took it to midfield. Luke and T.O. jointly agreed to stay in the base defense for the first play from scrimmage, and the defense stopped a Will Bellini run for a 3-yard gain. Bertelson got his group to the line quickly and rifled a 6-yard quick out pass to Rae to stop the clock with 52 seconds showing. Bertelson picked up the first down on a quarterback sneak, but on the next play an obvious Paul Pekovik hold on a hard-charging Tank moved the Trojans back to the 40. When Tank flushed the heady St. Francis quarterback out of the pocket and brought him to the ground with a diving tackle for a 6-yard loss, it became a game of 46 for the 8-time defending State

Champions… 46 seconds to cover 46 yards to keep their streak alive.

Luke and T.O. only briefly conferred before deciding to go with the 2-3 prevent defense. As expected, coach Brunner split out Ricky Rae to the wide side of the field. Running his ends deep on fly routes, he hit Will Bellini on a delay flare for an 8-yard gain. Instead of going out of bounds to stop the clock, Bellini had cut back away from the sideline in hopes of breaking a longer run, but a picture perfect tackle by Aaron Coslet prevented any further gain.

"Wish the fuck I could scream that good," muttered T.O. as they could hear coach Brunner blistering Will Bellini for not getting out of bounds, yet somehow managing at the same time to instruct his quarterback to get everybody to the line and spike the ball to stop the clock. Twenty-six seconds remained when the Bertelson throw hit the ground.

"Thank you Lord, thank you," a grateful Wade Hoekstra shouted to the heavens from the sideline when Kimball knocked down an uncharacteristically under-thrown pass intended for Ricky Rae at the 25-yard line.

With 19 seconds on the clock, Luke called his last timeout and conferred with T.O. on the sideline before stepping into the defensive huddle. "I'm thinking they're going to split out Rae again and go to him on either a long post or fly route," Luke told T.O., "so let's put Kimball on him in tight man coverage and put Danny at single deep safety and double Rae over top."

"I'm guessing you're right. Just tell Danny to take the right angle so that he doesn't let Rae get ahead of him."

Since only Tank and Dolph were pass rushing, the Trojans were able to double team Tank with two of the Pekovics, plus keep one of the Bellinis in the backfield for additional support. But Tank broke off his bull rush with a quick spin move that forced Bertelson out of the pocket and moving towards the wide side of the field. "Goddamnit!" T.O. screamed when he and Luke saw that Ricky Rae had broken off his post route and was racing back to the side of the field that his quarterback was scrambling towards. Rae had a full two-step lead on Kimball when Bertelson released the pass, and it seemed like the slow motion button was pressed once again as the ball floated towards the angle of the goal line and the sideline. Kimball was unable to close the gap enough to bat down the perfectly thrown toss when it was caught on the 4-yard line, but was able to push him out of bounds on the 2.

Twelve seconds remaining. Twelve long, interminable seconds to determine if the 8-time defending State Champions would make it nine, or whether their conference foe upstarts would topple the apple cart.

With the clock stopped as a result of the prior play ending out of bounds, coach Brunner saved his last remaining timeout. He lined his team up in their traditional balanced formation with the Bellini brothers stacked in an I, and quick pitched to the deep back Will Bellini. As he followed his brother Wyatt into the space behind the blocks of two of the Pekovic linemen, there initially appeared to be enough of an opening for him to find his way into the end zone. But Dolph came out of his nose guard stance low and held his ground in occupying Irv Pekovik, which allowed Tank to flow from his linebacker spot to stand up the blockers and bring down the ball carrier for no gain.

Brunner quickly took his final timeout. Before stepping into huddle with his players, Luke said to T.O., "They've got time for two plays. I think they'll go to a jump ball with Stronge, and if they don't get it the first time, they'll go back to him again."

"Agreed," said T.O. quickly. "I say we move Aaron over to play him directly head up and jam the shit outa him coming off the ball."

"Yeah, and let's play Stefan a couple yards back and slightly inside so he can play the run but still react in time to go up and make a play on the ball."

With both coaches in agreement on the plan, Luke stepped into the huddle and calmly relayed the strategy, following with, "Clear minds, guys. This is no time to panic. Focus up. Read and react. They don't have any timeouts left, so they're calling two plays over there right now. If we stop them on this down, don't get caught napping; hustle back and get set up for the next play. Everybody good on what we're doing?"

"We got it coach," snarled Tank. "We got one or two plays left to knock some Trojan dicks in the dirt boys. Let's get 'er done and go hang a big-assed trophy from our goal post." As expected, Dolph immediately repeated Tank's words verbatim, and the Bulldogs charged back to defend the 2-yard line from a long 8-second onslaught from a team that hadn't come up shorthanded in their last 70 games.

As anticipated, coach Brunner positioned Scott Stronge to the wide side of the field, and split him three yards from the guard in order to give him more room to maneuver. Staying in a 2-point stance, Aaron squared him up and played as close to the lengthy receiver as he could without being offside. Stefan played slightly inside and three yards off the line of scrimmage, so he could play both a pass to Stronge or react to a run inside of him. Bertelson play faked a handoff to his back, causing Stefan to hold his position longer than he wanted. But with Aaron being able to delay the big receiver's release into his pattern in the end zone, Bertelson's hurried pass sailed just beyond the reach of Stronge and a leaping Stefan, and landed harmlessly out of the back of the end zone.

Three seconds remaining. The incomplete pass had stopped the clock, so Bertelson ran back towards their sideline to confirm what coach Brunner wanted to run on the last play.

"Whaddya think?" T.O. asked Luke out of the side of his mouth.

"I still think they go back to Stronge. I'd bet on it if they split him out wide to make it harder for us to jam him. If he goes wide, we need Stefan to go with him," Luke hollered back over his shoulder as he ran to the end of the coaching box to signal in their goal line defense and the coverage information to Stefan and Aaron.

It all comes down to one play, Luke thought to himself. All those practices—the wildly swinging ups and downs of eight regular season games—four playoff games; after all that, it comes down to ONE FINAL PLAY! ONE FINAL PLAY to pull off the biggest upset in the past decade in Montana's 8-man football league. ONE FINAL PLAY to bring home the first ever State Championship to the loyal residents of Pacer Coulee. ONE FINAL PLAY to bring home the first victory over St. Francis since 1980. ONE FINAL PLAY to give mascot Otis Othello Coffman, VII the first victory over St. Francis in his seven year life. ONE FINAL PLAY to bring home a State Championship trophy to Edna Coffman, made even more special by a rare and cherished win over the 'Goddamn Catholics'.

St. Francis lined up for the final play with Scott Stronge split out the same three yards as the previous play, but the formation was different in that Ricky Rae was also at a 3-yard split on the opposite side. The Bellini brothers were stacked in an 'I' directly behind the quarterback.

"What the fuck?" muttered T.O. "You ever seen that before?"

"Nope, they were never in that formation in the film we had on them."

As instructed, Aaron and Stefan moved into position to play Scott Stronge the same as they had on the prior play, and Luke waved in a signal to a confused Kimball to move up and crowd Rae on the line of scrimmage. Bertelson took the snap and stepped to the short side of the field, faking a dive to the fullback and continuing down the line with the tailback swinging five yards behind and outside of him in perfect position to receive a pitch.

"Reverse, reverse, reverse," screamed T.O. and Luke after simultaneously recognizing that Ricky Rae had reversed field and was about to catch Bertelson's pitch and turn on the jets to the now deserted opposite side of the field. When he realized what Rae was doing, Kimball quickly reacted to follow him, but Bertelson was able to knock him off course after he had pitched the ball. Most all of the rest of the team had been sucked into the short side of the field when the whole backfield was flowing to that side. Even Bo, who was playing the defensive end position on the wide side and was responsible to hold his position and contain anything that might come back his way, had moved farther to the inside than he should have.

Only one Bulldog sniffed out the reverse from almost the very beginning. As Tank took his first step in moving from his linebacker position to the direction of the play, his vision alerted him that the end was moving in the opposite direction than the rest of the backfield. He didn't need to hear the screams of 'reverse' coming from his sideline to know what was happening. Anticipating that Tank would quickly identify the play and reverse field, coach Brunner had instructed Scott Stronge, his end on the opposite side of the formation, to seal off the big man so that he'd be unable to recover and make a play. "All you gotta do is get in his way and slow him up," Brunner had told Stronge. "He can't run down Ricky anyway, especially if we get any kind of block on him."

And slow him down he did, but Tank tossed him aside and started on a dead run to the juncture of the goal line and the opposite sideline. Although Bo had crashed too far in to be able to backtrack and catch the speedy ball carrier, he was able to give the pursuing Tank a precious extra second by forcing Ricky Rae several steps deeper into the backfield, thereby lengthening the distance he had to cover to get to pay dirt.

The silence of the huge crowd was deafening, as all that either sideline or the legion of fans watching could do was await the outcome of whether the enormous Bulldog linebacker could chase down the fleet Trojan receiver before he squeezed inside the goal line flag and into the end zone.

LADY BULLDOGS FACE BIG SANDY FOR STATE TITLE

Facing the talented Big Sandy Pioneers on two consecutive Saturday nights was a daunting task, and while Madison was optimistic that the vastly improved Brewster sister relations and sense of unity would continue to be on display, there was still the season long challenge of the tendency of the older three siblings to get in foul trouble to contend with. Of particular concern was the Pioneers' 6'1" Myra Merkel, a senior All-State performer who was the most skilled of a solid starting five and the two promising young freshmen that came off the bench.

The Lady Bulldogs' downfall on the past Saturday night in the Northern Divisional Championship game came when Madison had to bench Sonya after she fouled Merkel to pick up her fourth infraction with two minutes to go in the third stanza. With the score knotted at 39 apiece at the time of the foul, it didn't take Big Sandy's grizzled veteran coach Roy Lattimore long to have his girls pound it in to Merkel, who scored two inside buckets and added a free throw on Sandra Brewster's fourth foul to give the Pioneers a 5-point advantage at quarter end.

Realizing that the game could rapidly get out of hand in their absence, Madison had put both Sonya and Sandra back in the game to start the fourth quarter and they were able to close the gap to two with six minutes remaining. But when Sonya and Sandra both picked up their fifth fouls shortly thereafter, Myra Merkel went on to score nine of her game-high 32 points over the final five minutes to lead the Lady Pioneers to a convincing 17-point win.

Pacer Coulee had drawn the Victor Lady Pirates for their

Thursday afternoon State Tournament opener, and with 21, 18 and 13 points coming from Sammi, Sonya and Clare, respectively, they had cruised to a 66-49 victory. Friday night proved to be a much tougher test, as they took on the run and gun Plenty Coups Warriors. What the Warriors lacked in size, they made up for in quickness and speed. Even the skilled ball handlers Clare and Sammi had trouble getting the ball up the floor against the relentless full court pressure, and the Indian girls forced 13 first half turnovers and led the rattled and depth-deprived Lady Bulldogs 34-27 at intermission.

Madison's third quarter decision to clear out the backcourt and let Clare bring the ball up the court by herself proved fruitful, as the change allowed the team to transition more smoothly into their half court offensive rhythm. Clare and Sammi were able to get the ball into Sonya, who had a 6-inch height advantage over the tallest Warrior. Her 16 second-half points led the girls to a strong second half comeback and a comfortable 11-point win.

"We played with these guys when we were able to keep our starting five on the floor," Madison reminded her team as they prepared to take the floor in the State Championship game against Big Sandy, a 56-47 winner in the other semifinal game against Wyngate the night before. Madison knew she was stating the obvious, as she was sure of how the scouting report on her team had read to the schools that participated in the State Tournament...

STRENGTHS: Strong starting five—6'1" Sonya Brewster, the best of the three Brewster starting post players, but twins 6'0" Sandra and 5'11" Sabrina solid contributors—despite the guards being only freshmen, 5'9" Sammi Brewster and lightning-quick 5'2" Clare Comes at Night are good ball handlers and shooters.

WEAKNESSES: Foul trouble tendencies for the three Brewster post players, especially Sonya and Sandra—most glaring weakness is lack of depth—first player off bench is huge drop down in talent.

"We're going to do a lot of mixing and switching defensively to try to keep Sonya and Sandra out of foul trouble. When we're in man, we're going to switch Sonya, Sandra and Sabrina in defending Merkel. Every time down we'll switch, so you girls have to remember whose turn it is on every possession. We'll also mix in an equal amount of our 2-3 zone to hopefully minimize our fouls. So let's defend Merkel tough, but we need to be smart; no stupid fouls and let's limit her free throw attempts. She was 12 for 14 at the line in last week's game, so we can't let her get to the charity stripe that many times again and expect to win.

"Sammi and Clare, work like hell to deny the entry pass from their guards into Merkel. They are one of the few teams that match up with us size-wise in the post, so on offense we need to look more for Sammi and Clare on the perimeter. Also look to run when we have the chance. They can't match Sammi and Clare's quickness, so let's get our rebounds out to them in a hurry and try to get some easy hoops in transition. Okay, everybody in… let's go bring Pacer Coulee their first girls' basketball State Title!"

Madison couldn't have scripted the first three quarters any better than it played out. The switching defenses seemed to throw Myra Merkel somewhat off her usual stellar game, and Sammi and Clare were deadly from the perimeter, helping the Lady Bulldogs to a 33-29 halftime lead. Even better than the lead was the foul count; only two each for Sonya and Sandra. Pacer Coulee increased the lead to seven by the end of the third quarter, but both Sonya and Sandra had picked up their third fouls in the stanza. Sandra picked up her fourth at the six-minute mark in the final quarter, but with Sammi and Sondra playing a perfect inside-out cat and mouse game, the lead had been increased to nine when Sonya was hit with her fourth at the 4:32 mark.

Madison called a timeout to give her girls a well-needed rest and to tell Sonya and Sandra that she was going to leave them in the game. "4:32 left girls. I'm not going to take you out, so you have to play smart. They're going to pound it into Merkel and she's going to try to draw your fifth foul, so let's go man with Sabrina playing Merkel with Sonya and Sandra giving help. But don't take any foolish chances. We'll give up a bucket here and there to keep you gals on the floor."

But coach Lattimore immediately went to Haley Howard, the post player that Sonya was now manned up on. Although she only had four points on the night, she drove against Sonya and put up a shot that Sonya appeared to block cleanly, but the official blew his whistle and indicated the senior Brewster sister had fouled with the body. There was 3:22 left when Howard went to the line and a tearful Sonya Brewster found a spot on the bench.

Although Haley Howard missed both free throws, the Lady Bulldogs' 9-point lead dissipated over the next three minutes and 15 seconds, much to the roaring approval of the large and boisterous Big Sandy crowd. When Myra Merkel drew Sandra's fifth foul with seven seconds left on the clock, she had just scored her tenth consecutive point since the 3:22 mark to put her team up 58-57. Madison called her last timeout just before Merkel was to step to the line to attempt to complete the 3-point play.

"Whether they make the free throw or miss, they'll come with full court pressure," Madison explained to the five girls that would go back out on floor, to include the white-faced, wide-eyed Dee Cassidy and Betty Ann Drury, the fouled out Brewster sister replacements. "If they make it, I want Sammi to take it out of bounds and Clare to come and get. Same thing if they miss; whoever gets the rebound, Clare's going to come get it. Either way, everybody clear out and get to our end with good spacing and let Clare bring it up herself. I want Sabrina on the right block, Betty Ann on the left. Dee goes to the left corner, Sammi to the right corner 3-point line. Clare, try to get to the middle of the court by the time you reach the top of the key. Use your quickness and take it to the hoop. Take the shot if you can get a layup or uncontested short shot for the win, but if Merkel makes the free throw we'll go for the 3 and the win. So drive down the right side and try to draw in whoever is defending the deep right corner. If you can dish it to Sammi for a good look at a 3, then we'll take that any day of the week. Okay, there's no need to panic here... seven seconds is plenty of time to do what I'm diagramming here. We can do this, girls," Madison said resolutely as they put their hands together and broke the huddle with a, "WIN!"

It wasn't lost on Madison that she was totally relying on her two freshmen to perform in crunch time to win the State Championship, but she felt comfortable that both of the youngsters were up to the task. As expected, Myra Merkel calmly drained the free throw, and Sammi quickly grabbed the ball, hopped behind the end line and handed it off to streaking Clare before the Pioneer defense had a chance to get set. But coach Lattimore had sent his three post players racing to the other end to get set up in the paint. Their two guards tried to trap Clare in the back court, but she was too quick for them, blowing by them with a sharp spin move and getting to the middle of the top of the key as the clock ticked down to three.

Damn, thought Madison when she saw that coach Lattimore had positioned Merkel at the midway point on the right side baseline, relying on his best player to step in and defend a drive down the key, or pop back out in the passing lane to disrupt a pass attempt to Sammi in the deep corner.

Clare started her drive to the left but darted back to right with a cross-over dribble. The move back to the right drew Merkel just enough towards the key to open a narrow passing lane to Sammi in the deep corner. When Clare rifled a behind the back pass through the sliver of space to a waiting Sammi, the time clock showed one second when the youngest Brewster released a high-arching shot from just beyond the 3-point line. The packed-to-the-rafters Billings Metra crowd fell silent, anxiously tracking the flight of the ball as it softly floated towards the rim...

FIVE YEARS LATER

"Let's go back the long way," Luke suggested to Madison as they pulled away from the O.K. Corral Bar and Grill. They had just attended the Sunday finale of the weekend celebration of the five-year anniversary of the 1990 Pacer Coulee Bulldogs football and girls' basketball State Championships. "Since we went by Marshall, St. Francis and Wyngate on the way here, I want to go through Deeden, Stanton and Hodgeman, just for old time's sake." Upon receiving a thumbs up, Luke completed the familiar small town illegal turn after backing out of his angle parking position and headed west. Both three-year-old Luke Jr. and 16-year-old Rose fell asleep by the time they passed the *"WELCOME TO PACER COULEE—HOME OF THE BULLDOGS AND THE 1990 STATE FOOTBALL AND GIRLS' BASKETBALL CHAMPIONS"* sign on the edge of town, and Luke and Madison shared a cup of silence while each mulled over the events of the enjoyable, late June weekend reunion with their former players and the wonderful townsfolk of Pacer Coulee.

When Luke crossed the Judith River bridge and climbed the hill that cast the traveler into the wide sweep of the great Judith Basin, it was as if his inaugural, five-years-prior blue sky and crystal clear mountain range view of the magnificent expanse had been captured in a snapshot and put on pause until this moment. He slowed and pulled over on the same pasture gate approach as he had in his initial journey. "Honestly Madison, I stopped in this very spot after my first interview. I just couldn't believe the beauty and the vastness when I came over the top of the hill, so I took a few minutes to enjoy the view and identify the mountain ranges from my road map. I think it was at this exact place that I decided Pacer Coulee and this Judith Basin would be a good place for me to start over. And to think that I had no idea of what was to come… I mean, no idea that I'd ever meet the love of my life here, or have the opportunity to coach a State championship team."

"Same thing here," Madison agreed. "I was looking for a fresh start, too. And who would have ever guessed that I'd meet Vernon Higgins, the love of my life? Just kidding honey, just kidding. Yes, who woulda thunk that our strictly by chance acceptance of the teaching and coaching positions in the little old town of Pacer Coulee back in 1990 would have resulted in us both having life changing experiences?"

As Madison grabbed a pillow and joined the kids by slipping off into slumber, Luke reflected back on the five years that had passed since the historic day of the dual State Championship in 1990. They still kept the clipping of the Pacer Coulee Chronicles article, along with several other Sylvia Graham column classics, on the bulletin board next to the fridge in their Bozeman home.

PACER COULEE CHRONICLES
SYLVIA GRAHAM, CORRESPONDENT

Holy cow, holy smokes and holy Toledo!! Saturday, November 17, 1990 will be forever inscribed in the heart and souls of all Pacer Couleans, for that was the day that coaches Carter and Danielsen led our football and girls' basketball teams to State Championships! Yessum and yessir, ya all heard that right! Those two achievements make for Pacer Coulee becoming the only school in state history to claim State Championships in two different sports on the same day!

So you better believe the buttons are bustin' out all over the place on Pacer Coulee Bulldog fans from near and far. I can tell you for sure that Yours Truly is prouder than a peacock of these fine young boys and girls that played their hearts out all season long. Coach Carter and his 17 squad member team took the field against the daunted St. Francis Trojans of Centertown, the 8-time defending

Class C 8-man Football State Champions that had won a remarkable 70 games in a row. The 4,500 sports fans that crowded the field at Fergus County Stadium in Centertown were loud and rambunctious from start to finish, as the contest went back and forth and wasn't decided until the last play of the game when Pacer Coulee's very own, very large and highly recruited Tank Hollister tackled the Trojan runner just short of the end zone on 4th down with only a few seconds remaining in the game, thereby securing a 30-26 win for the Bulldogs.

And our young ladies gave Yours Truly and all the Pacer Coulee fans another near heart attack some 6 hours later with another down to the last second finish in their State Championship game against those pesky Pioneers of Big Sandy. It's a good thing the tournament was held at the spacious arena at the Billings Metra, because there wasn't a spare seat to be had by the time the game began. When Sonya and Sandra Brewster fouled out with 3:52 remaining in the game, Big Sandy scored 10 unanswered points to take a 59-57 lead with only 7 seconds remaining. That's when our little whippersnapper of a freshman Clare Comes at Night dribbled through the Pioneer team and snapped a nifty behind the back pass to fellow freshman Sammi Brewster over in the deep right corner. Her 3-point shot rang true as the buzzer sounded, giving the Lady Bulldogs a 60-59 victory. At that point, as the famous Helena sportscaster Cato the Cat Butler would say, "The cat's in the bag and the bag's in the river, and it's time to saddle up and ride for home!"

And boy howdy did us Pacer Couleans have some kind of celebration to welcome our young champions back home! We celebrated all day Sunday, with blaring Fire Truck and Ambulance sirens leading the grand entrance of the teams into town on Bones Bolstad's big flat bed trailer that was pulled by both of Larry Coslet's teams of Percheron horses. We honored our youngsters with a big gathering and feast at the Community Center, where each of our fine young championship coaches gave a nice speech and thanked the entire Pacer Coulee community for

*all their support throughout the entire year. A
great time was had by all, and by the time the
celebration came to a close, Yours Truly was as
ready to hit the hay as Otis Othello Coffman VII,
the greatest Bulldog of all! In fact, Yours Truly
is too darn tuckered to report any other news from
this neck of the woods, so hope those that sent in
their news will understand. Until next time, Be
Careful Out There, ya hear?*

Luke had stayed busy during the winter following the
November victory over St. Francis by coaching the fifth and
sixth grade and Jr. High boys' basketball teams. Even though he
had no experience in coaching anything that wasn't played with
an oblong shaped ball, Lester had convinced him to give it a go.
Spring was just as hectic, in that despite again having no
coaching experience in the sport, Lester had badgered him into
being Mr. Mark's assistant track coach. Madison had also had a
harried few months following Sammi's last second winning shot
over Big Sandy by coaching volleyball and track.

Thanks to the height and skills of the Brewster sisters, her
volleyball team had enjoyed a very successful season. They
likely would have competed for a state title if she had been able
to talk Clare into playing, but still managed to bring home a
third place trophy. Madison did have prior experience coaching
track, so Lester appointed her as another of Mr. Mark's
assistants, working exclusively with the seven girls who had
gone out for the sport. Both the boys and girls brought home
third place trophies from the State Track Meet. Tank's Gold
Medal for his State record 63 foot shot put throw led the boys,
while Sonya and Sammi Brewster's second and fourth place
finishes in the high jump, along with Clare's third place medals
in the 1600 and 3200 meter runs, had led the girls.

Much had transpired over that winter on the Tank front as
well. The matter of the Great Falls shopping mall incident had
caused Luke to suffer in silence for weeks over the worry as to

whether Tank would be charged with the assault of the gang members, or whether Luke himself, as the adult in charge of the minor aged Tank and Dolph, would be charged with withholding evidence in a felony assault incident. He had received a call from Sheriff Couch only a few days before Christmas, asking him to meet that evening behind the very same abandoned granaries where they had rendezvoused several months before. By the time he reached the meeting location, Luke had worked himself into an anxiety-ridden frenzy, fearing that the worst of the possible news scenarios was about to be revealed. He knew he would never, ever forget the words that Sheriff Trent Couch spoke to him that night.

"I've got some news on the Detective Bessel front that I figured you needed to hear. Now mind you I haven't heard a word from him since I laid out your entire story, to include how those gangsters were in the process of raping that mentally compromised boy with a Goddamn beer bottle. Now Marv is a good man, and he didn't like the assault on that poor boy by those goons one bit, but I was worried that his hands were tied and he'd have to go after Tank for the assault so that the frickin' hospital lawyers could dive into the pockets of your school district, being that you had the boys up there in Great Falls on a school-sponsored function. Anyway, he called me this morning and told me that the gangster had slipped out of the hospital as soon as he was healthy enough to get out of bed, and that he hasn't been seen or heard from since. Nor has the other guy whose balls got knocked into his throat. So ol' Marv surprised me when he said that since the witness disappeared and will most likely never show his face again, he filed a final report stating that his investigation didn't uncover any evidence to substantiate any of the witness's claims from the interview conducted before he fled, and that he was recommending the case be closed. He told me on the sly, and make damn sure you don't repeat this, that he shredded all his interview notes that made reference to the giant in the blue bulldog cap, as well as everything that pointed to his suspicions that it was Tank who had whipped up on this guy. In Marv's own words he said, 'Fuck the hospital. I'm not going to be a part of putting a good kid in jail for defending his friend against a gang rape by a couple of Goddamn hoodlum druggies so that the hospital can recover some money.' So in a nutshell Luke, I feel confident in telling you that this case is buttoned up and closed."

But the Great Falls mall issue wasn't the only Tank matter that had taken up Luke's time and thought. After the State Championship game, the college recruitment onslaught cranked up to the point of being overwhelming. Luke had spent many long hours with Tank, analyzing his options and reviewing the pros and cons of going in-state versus out of state. Edna, Luke and Bill Koch had talked a reluctant Tank into taking his ACT College Entrance Exams a second time, which fortunately resulted in a high enough score to squeak by the required minimum for entrance into college. Despite the low score and his history of eligibility problems in high school, college coaches had swarmed the Pacer Coulee school doorstep whenever the recruiting rules allowed them to visit. Tank would only talk to the coaches if Luke was present in the room with him. Letters and post cards from colleges filled up the school mailbox daily. As the February 5th National Signing Day approached, the recruiting pressure intensified. Luke had sat down with Tank and Edna a few weeks prior and suggested they develop a list of criteria to begin a systematic process to whittle the colleges down to a workable number, which he suggested should be no more than four or five.

After several consecutive evenings of going through the newly created method of elimination, the school choices had been narrowed to Montana State, University of Montana, Washington State and Nebraska. But both Luke and Edna feared that any out of state school would be a poor choice for Tank, their concern being that he would be more susceptible to academic failure if he were that far from home and his comfort zone support group. When approached with their recommendation that he only consider the in-state schools, Tank seemed relieved and the choice was quickly narrowed to Montana State and the University of Montana.

On the Sunday afternoon before the upcoming Tuesday final signing date, Luke had received a summons from Edna to meet her and Tank at the Coffman residence, stating that Tank had reached a final decision and wanted to disclose it to the both of them. Luke shook his head and smiled at the remembrance of Tank's shocking announcement that day.

"I want to thank the both of ya's for helping me through this whole recruiting thing these last months. Coach, I know you've spent a lot of time going through all this college biddness, and I want ya to know I damn sure appreciate it. Anyways, I've plum thought and thought and thought about this. Haven't even been able to sleep normal at night 'cause I've thought about it so much. And well, I've finally come to a decision. Don't get me wrong, I like playin' football a lot, I really do. But I don't like school. Not really very good at it. As you guys know better than anybody, I had trouble stayin' eligible, even when everybody here was helpin' me. I know all those coaches said they have tutors and all that, but without you two… without Elvis, Clare, Dee and Aaron… I don't know. I just don't think I could keep my grades up, I really don't."

"All I really want to do is be a rancher. I'm gonna be 18 in June, so's I can take care of my ranch then, right? That's what I want to do. And I want to be with Clare. I'd really miss her if I went off to some school. Clare loves me and I love her. There, I said it—just so ya know. I can't leave her. I'm gonna marry her some day. And what about Dolph? What would Dolph do without me? We've already talked about it. He can just live at home and help his dad on the farm, and he can, like, he can be like a hired hand to me and help me during the time when his dad don't need him. I could maybe even pay him a few bucks; you know, maybe give him a calf or sumpthin' like that. So Miz E and coach, I ain't gonna go to no college. I know you guys was hopin' I'd go off and do good in college and play in the pros and stuff like that, but I'm gonna just stay here and be a rancher. I hope I ain't disappointing ya's or anything like that, but my mind's plum made up. Ain't nobody or nothin' gonna change it."

Luke smiled and laughed out loud when he looked back at the stunned look on Edna's face, and suspected that he had looked just as surprised. But he was impressed with her quick recovery and response to his decision to stay home. "That's fine, Terrance. You are the only one that should make that decision. You don't need to worry about doing what coach Carter and I might want you to do. You are not disappointing me, and I'm sure I can speak for coach Carter in that you aren't disappointing him either," she had said as Luke had nodded his head in agreement. "But young man, let me tell you one Goddamn thing that's not going happen. If you think that the day you turn 18 you are going to move Clare into your ranch house right along with you, then you've got another thing coming. Don't take this the wrong way, as I love Clare like I love you. Like a daughter and a son. But as long as I'm her guardian, you two aren't going to be shacking up and playing house until the clock strikes midnight on her 18th birthday. And you won't be getting married a moment before that either. You got that, you big lug?"

Luke laughed even louder thinking of Tank's reaction to the scolding, remembering that his face brightened into a slow grin as he said, "Read ya loud and clear, Miz E. We'll only get married and move to the ranch when the time is right and proper. And don't think I didn't hear ya all those times of you tellin' me to make proud the name Terrance. I mean, I'll always go by Tank, but Clare will have a man that loves her and treats her right. It won't be nothin' like the Terrance that hit me and my mom all the time, that's for sure. And we're plannin' on havin' a flock of youngins' too, and they'll know what it's like to have a mom and dad that really loves 'em and takes care of 'em. That much you can count on from me, Miz E, and you can take that to Mr. K's bank."

Luke had felt even better about Tank's choice to stay in

Pacer Coulee when Edna had informed him that she and Bill Koch had sat down and worked out a plan that would help ensure that Tank could succeed for the long term on the ranch. Bill had saved almost $30,000 for Tank in the cattle purchase arrangement that he and Edna had made for Tank's benefit back when he was in Jr. High. Bill authorized the release of most of that fund to be spent on the purchase of another 60 head of cows, and Edna leased the two sections of Hollister land that were purchased by her father at a foreclosure auction to Tank for a pittance, and wrote an addendum to her Will that transferred the ownership of the 1,280 acres to him upon her demise. He felt much comfort in knowing that Bill, Edna and all the good folks of Pacer Coulee would look after him.

As he glanced over at his still-sleeping wife and the other two loves of his life through the rear view mirror, Luke's mind drifted back to five years and a month ago. Luke and Madison had been married in the midst of a splash of purple and yellow wildflower blossoms in a meadow on Edna's ranch. The late afternoon sun had framed the North Moccasins in the backdrop, putting an exclamation mark on the calm and cloudless day. He had proposed to her unwittingly on April 1st, and deserved the "I will just shoot you if this is an April Fool's Day joke" response he got from Madison. Edna had graciously agreed to accommodate their request to have the early summer outdoor ceremony on her ranch. Since June weather in Montana was unpredictable at best, Edna assured them that the huge steel machinery storage building that would be set up for the reception and dance could be used to hold the ceremony should the weather turn uncooperative. Not surprisingly, Sylvia provided full blown media coverage of the gala event in her 'Pacer Coulee Chronicles' report that came out several weeks later. The column was still pinned in place on the kitchen bulletin board next to her six month prior State Championship report:

Wayne Edwards

PACER COULEE CHRONICLES
SYLVIA GRAHAM, CORRESPONDENT

Well boy-oh-boy was there ever a whopper of a shindig over on the Edna Coffman ranch this past June 1st! Lordy, Lordy, I swear the whole darn town of Pacer Coulee and half of central Montana attended the marriage celebration of our two fine young championship coaches, Luke Carter and Madison Danielsen. It turned out to be a glorious day to get hitched 'Under the Big Sky,' as the sunny, 70 degree temperature was just dandy for such an outdoor event.

Let's give a shout out to all who worked so hard to prepare for this joyful occasion. Kudos to the Pacer Coulee Booster and Lion's clubs for gathering up all the folding chairs at the Community Center and hauling them out to the Coffman Ranch. And thanks to all the Jr. High and High School students who showed up en masse to set up the seating in the freshly cut meadow behind the Coffman barns. And a big pat on the back to all these folks: Edna Coffman and Harlan Horrall for donating the beef and hogs, and to Kip Jordan and the crew at the Calfe' that catered the meal and provided the smokers to barbecue the wonderful steaks, hamburger and pulled pork. And a big hug to Ethyl Grove, Kellie Cassidy and Hazel Koutensky for baking all the wonderful pies that were devoured by the young and old alike.

Once everyone was seated, Tank Hollister, Tuf Sturm and Clare Comes at Night escorted on horseback the about to be married couple that were riding in fine style on a fancy old covered wagon drawn by Larry Coslet's handsome team of draft horses. Emma Laughlin and the Pacer Coulee Crooners provided the music to highlight the grand entrance, as well as the two beautiful songs (Yours Truly's Dolly Parton favorite "I Will Always Love You" included!) during the ceremony. Their vocal chords must have been tuckered out the next day, because they sang all through the reception, and of course they played till all hours at the dance.

Our Superintendent Lester Brewster must have

sneaked out and got himself ordained, as he was the Officiant for the proceedings. Coach Carter's assistant coach T.O. Barker was the Best Man, while all the members of the State Champion football team stood as his groomsmen. Madison's very grown up about to be 6th grader Rose stood up next to her mom, and my gosh did the two of them look as pretty as a Wally Akers photograph of a setting sun over Square Butte. Madison's two sisters and all the gals from the State Champion girls' basketball team filled out the parade of bridesmaids. Both teams were resplendently decked out in their game jerseys. And don't forget Otis Othello Coffman, VII! I guess our very special Pacer Coulee mascot sort of acted as a combination of Ring Bearer and Flower Girl, as he strutted up the center aisle along with the teams. And during the ceremony he kept going back and forth between Tank Hollister on the groomsmen side, and Clare Comes at Night on the bridesmaids' end. Yours Truly has no idea how that little mite of a Clare has the strength to lift that big lug of a bulldog up and onto her lap, but by golly she does! On a more somber note, Pacer Coulee's own Shanty Sweeney was looking down at the doins' from above. An empty chair up front was draped with a jersey that had 'Shanty' printed above the number '1' reminded everyone that the dear friend our community lost last fall was there in spirit.

And you better believe a good time was had by all at the reception and dance! Folks from age 2 to 90 enjoyed the wonderful meal and fellowship. And then everyone hooted, hollered and danced up a storm till the wee hours of the morning. Even Yours Truly kicked up her heels until her darned old bunion started acting up again. Please join me in giving the newlyweds a great big smooch and hug, and best wishes for a long and happy life together! As always, Be Careful Out There, ya hear?

Luke's thoughts drifted back to when he and Madison had last visited Pacer Coulee, almost exactly two years before. The event they returned for was held on June 11th, the very day that Clare Comes at Night turned 18 years of age. But the occasion was held to not just to commemorate her birthday, but to also celebrate Clare's marriage to one Terrance 'Tank' Hollister. The ceremony took place in the very same Edna Coffman flowering meadow where Luke and Madison were wed. Lester had to renew his Ministry endorsement, as he officiated the affair. Dolph was the best man, and Luke joined Elvis, Bo Ramsay and Tuf Sturm as a groomsman. Madison, Sammi Brewster, Anna Rimby and Dee Cassidy stood as Clare's bridesmaids. Edna, sharply dressed in a style similar to Clare's colorful Native American ankle length gown, escorted Clare up the aisle. Luke learned that Edna had dispatched Greg Bolstad to shore up and remodel the dilapidated A-frame shack that had once served as the Hollister abode, and Tank and Clare proudly showed him and Madison their newly renovated digs, to include the recently constructed and freshly stained front porch and deck that Tank had recently added on.

And finally, Luke reflected on the just-completed reunion weekend. In addition to he and Madison getting reconnected and caught up with all the members of their State Championship teams, the highlight of the occasion was getting to meet the recently turned one-year-old Clarabelle Edna 'Belle' Comes at Night Hollister. Watching big Tank, who had ballooned to over 370 pounds since his playing days, fuss and cater to his tiny daughter was nothing short of endearing. But that relationship might well have been overshadowed by the obvious connection between Edna and Belle. Edna's rough and weathered exterior warmed and softened like an ice fisherman's frozen beard in a warming hut at the sight and sound of the little girl. "Come to grandma, Belle. Come to grandma," she would say, in a welcoming and inviting tone that seemed foreign coming from the lips of the intimidating woman. When Belle responded by toddling towards her in a sing-song "Nana... Nana," tears welled in both Luke and Madison's eyes. And then there was

Clare. She couldn't have looked more beautiful, and outwardly exuded a countenance of contentment and happiness. The young Indian girl couldn't stop smiling when Madison had inquired, "My goodness, when did my shy little point guard that never uttered a word become such a chatter box?"

Second only to the arrival of little Belle was the introduction of Otis Othello Coffman, VIII. Like a Law Professor Emeritus, Otis the seventh was still the first name on the office door, but at 12 years old he was well past his prime. Prior to the appearance of Otis the eighth, he spent most of his hours napping on his comfortable dog bed at the foot of Edna's rocking chair. But he had such scant little tolerance for the rambunctious pup that Edna thought it best that he reside full time at the Hollister residence. Thankfully, the senior Otis seemed to hold young Belle in much higher regard than his unruly pup successor.

Luke and Madison enjoyed catching up with all activities and accomplishments of their former students and players during the past five years. Dolph was still living with his parents, but spent a lot of time working for and being with Tank and Clare. He was enamored with young Belle and doted over her incessantly. When the toddler was baptized, Dolph was appointed as a proud as punch Godparent. Tuf Sturm, Bo Ramsay, Virgil Cottingham, Travis Cederholm, Brundage Spragg, and Ernie Rimby had all returned to the family farm or ranch. Bret Cassidy had become the new Shop and Vo-ag teacher the year before, replacing the retiring Mr. Marks. Bret was also the new Bulldog football coach, with Virgil and Ernie serving as his assistants. The three young coaches all bemoaned over the fact that the last victory over St. Francis was in the 1990 Title game.

Aaron Coslet was in his first year of Law School. Stefan Tillerman had received a scholarship to Western Montana College in Dillon to play football, where he was one of the top rushers in the Frontier Conference the past fall. Kimball Robbins was in his second year at Montana State University in Bozeman, where he was a promising sprinter for the Bobcat track team.

Dee Cassidy was about to enter the Veterinarian Program at Colorado State. Sonya Brewster had accepted a scholarship at Rocky Mountain College in Billings, where she enjoyed a stellar career playing for coach Marcella Connor. Sammi Brewster had just finished her first year at the University of Montana, where she was seeing meaningful minutes as a freshman playing for the legendary coach Robert Dervig. Elvis's high level of play and 4.0 GPA garnered offers from Montana State and the University of Montana, among other Division I schools. He chose, however, to stay close to home and go to a smaller college, and had just finished his second year with the Yellowjackets of Eastern Montana College in Billings. In addition to being among the leading scorers in the nation at the Division II school, Elvis was continuing with his 4.0 tradition and was majoring in Education Administration, planning to return to Fort Belnap someday and make a positive impact on the Reservation as the school Superintendent.

The weekend had also been fun in that they were able to renew old friendships and get updated on the happenings of the community. Although he had hired a Vice President, 75-year-old Bill Koch still spent a half day at the bank and reportedly continued to call the shots in the management of the bank. Kellie Cassidy was still a whirlwind about town, delivering her mail and serving as the town's unofficial veterinarian. Kip Jordan still opened the O.K. Corral Bar and Grill at roughly 7:00 for the benefit of Butch Cassidy and the Hole in the Wall gang. Luke was saddened to hear that Duke Dickson, one of the coffee club's most prominent members, had died of pneumonia, but the rest of the Hole in the Wall gang had remained intact. Frank Cervenka was still irritating everyone with his depressing negativity, and Harlan Horrall had everybody laughing when he kept reminding Madison at the reunion that he was still an available bachelor. Lester and Sharon were in their same positions at the school and had enjoyed watching Sonya play at Rocky Mountain. They remained ready and willing to take the much longer trek to Missoula to watch Sammi's home games.

But it was Edna that Luke's thoughts kept returning to. What an impact the now 77-year-old woman had had on his and Madison's lives. At one time or another over the year they had spent in Pacer Coulee, the hardnosed school and community icon had carefully guided them through the tortuous tunnels of life's complexities. It was her that had hired them; her that had molded them; her that had scolded them; her that had challenged them, and her that had brought them together in a way that not only benefited them, but their students and players as well. Edna had an uncanny way of always seeing the big picture, and Luke greatly admired her unrelenting efforts to do what was in the best interests of the students and the community of Pacer Coulee as a whole. And while the arrival of Belle had clearly shifted her focus to grandmotherly duties, when Luke had inquired whether she was still chairing the School Board she had replied, "Hell yes, I can't leave now. We haven't beat the Goddamn Catholics since you were here in 1990, so somebody has to ride herd over these kids and young coaches. God only knows they need a swift kick in the pants every now and then, just as you and Madison did when you here."

As Luke slowed and turned south at Eddie's corner, he took a 360 degree look at the Judiths, Big Snowies, Little Belts, Highwoods, and Square Butte, all glistening in the just-beginning-to-fade late afternoon sky. He shook his head again in amazement as he thought about the great experience he and Madison had enjoyed in the tiny little community of Pacer Coulee. They had commented many times since leaving that the rest of the world should know what it's like to have the commitment to family, friends and neighbors like they had grown to admire in the great Judith Basin of central Montana. Everyone should be so lucky to experience rural, small town America living, even if only for a short period of time.

Madison stirred as Rose called out from the back seat, "Are we home yet?"

"Not yet honey, we've got a ways to go to even get to Heberton."

With that, Madison and Rose both changed positions and drifted back to sleep, and Luke's mind meandered to the trail of life events that had occurred since they were married five years prior. Madison's former Athletic Director from Laurel had taken the same position at Bozeman High School a few years before he and Madison had come to Pacer Coulee. He had surprised them with a phone call in early April of 1991 with a request that they meet midway for dinner at the Sportsman in Heberton to discuss a career opportunity for them both. Despite the wonderful experience they had had at Pacer Coulee, Luke and Madison jumped at the offer to become the head football and girls' basketball coaches, respectively, at Bozeman High School. The job was further enticing in that Madison was able to fill an open position in the Math department, and Luke had accepted a newly created appointment to develop sport specific weight and agility conditioning programs for both the High School and the Jr. High. Luke smiled in remembrance of the special send off they received from the kids and community of Pacer Coulee.

Luke had stayed in the Bozeman High position for four years, building up a football program that had languished for the four or five years prior to his arrival. He coached his team to the Class AA semifinal game in years three and four, losing both years to the juggernaut that was CMR high school in Great Falls. His good fortune in career advancement took another positive turn just this past spring when he was asked to join the Montana State University staff as the quarterbacks' coach and passing game coordinator. His dream of becoming a Division I college level offensive coordinator had come to fruition just a few months before when he was promoted to the lofty position right before spring ball was to commence.

Madison was still at the high school, and her teams had reached the finals at the State Tournament twice, winning one of them in her second year. Rose was an upcoming sophomore, and after already stretching to a height of 5'10", was expected to be a starter and major contributor to her mom's team in the fall. In addition, she was a delight to be around, and her and Luke's bond had only grown stronger over the past five years. And then Luke and Madison were overjoyed in the arrival of Luke Jr., who now as a typical three-year-old had made everybody's life not only more hectic, but infinitely more interesting. He followed Rose around like a puppy, and she and all her friends spoiled him to no end.

What a five years, thought Luke, as he drove west past Heberton and on through the tiny dots on the map that were Two Dot, Martinsdale and Lennep. Turning south towards Wilsall, he marveled at the stark beauty of the majestic Crazy mountains to his east, Absarokees to the south, and the Bridgers guarding Bozeman to the west. Once they skirted the Bridger mountains and dropped into the Gallatin valley, Luke would take his family to their nestled-amongst-the-cottonwood-trees home that bordered the famous trout stream that was the Gallatin River. From there, it was not far to the little cabin where Luke and his family had stayed on their vacation to Yellowstone Park and Montana so many years before. Little did he know at his then 11 years of age that he, his wife and two children would be living in a home a stone's throw away from that summer guest cabin some 29 years later.

Yes, the wondrous places the whirlwind of life had taken him over the last five years. He smiled broadly thinking of how Sylvia Graham of the Pacer Coulee Chronicles might sum it up in her own unique way:

"Boy howdy and Lordy, Lordy! Let's give a shout-out to ol' Luke Carter, as he's had quite the ride since he rode the ripples of Warm Spring Creek into the town of Pacer Coulee! Yessum and Yessir, it was a ride to remember. I gotta go now, but don't you forget-Be careful out there, ya hear?"

ABOUT THE AUTHOR

Pacer Coulee Chronicles is Wayne Edwards's first novel.

Born and raised in Denton, a small hamlet of 300 residents located in the heart of the expansive wheat and cattle country of rural, central Montana, Wayne returned to his hometown as the 3rd generation banker of the independent, family owned agricultural bank that was started by his grandfather in 1929. Typical to the small town way, when the local high school football coach left shortly before the start of the 1991 season, Edwards agreed to serve as the interim head coach at the 8-man football school. The interim designation turned into a highly enjoyable and satisfying six year stint.

Edwards, a Montana High School Association Athletes Hall of Fame inductee, was a three sport standout at Denton High and an All Conference tailback at Montana State University. It was this playing and coaching experience that served as inspiration in his creation of the entertaining fictional story that is *Pacer Coulee Chronicles.*

Wayne and his wife of 45 years, Lorinda, are now retired from their thirty year banking career. The couple enjoys spending time with their three grown daughters, son-in-laws and eight grandchildren. They split their time between their Bozeman, Montana and Cave Creek, Arizona homes. Wayne has written a Children's Book (*Buster the Bridger Mountain Bear*) which is scheduled for a January 2021 release.

He is currently working on a Middle Grade/Young Adult fiction novel (*A Stone's Throw*) with an anticipated launch date in the fall of 2021.

CPSIA information can be obtained
at www.ICGtesting.com
Printed in the USA
LVHW031449290121
677804LV00003B/28